The Fortress of Glass

The Fortress of Glass

THE FIRST VOLUME OF
The Crown of the Isles

DAVID DRAKE

A TOM DOHERTY ASSOCIATES BOOK

NEW YORK

THE FORTRESS OF GLASS: THE FIRST VOLUME OF THE CROWN OF THE ISLES

This book is printed on acid-free paper.

Edited by David G. Hartwell

A Tor Book
Published by Tom Doherty Associates, LLC
175 Fifth Avenue
New York, NY 10010

www.tor.com

Tor® is a registered trademark of Tom Doherty Associates, LLC.

First Edition: April 2006

Library of Congress Cataloging-in-Publication Data

Drake, David.
    The fortress of glass / David Drake.
        p. cm. — (The crown of the isles ; bk. 1)
    "A Tom Doherty Associates book."
    ISBN 0-765-31259-X
    EAN 978-0-765-31259-4
    I. Title.
    PS3554.R196F673 2006
    813'.54—dc22

                                    2005016727

First Edition: April 2006

Printed in the United States of America

0   9   8   7   6   5   4   3   2   1

TO MARK L. VAN NAME.

Again, sort of.

Acknowledgments

Dan Breen continues as my first reader, just as careful and crotchety as ever. He tends toward proper grammar (some might say pleonasm), and I tend toward the striking ellipsis (sometimes more striking than intelligible), so we make a good team.

Dorothy Day has been doing continuity checking for me on this and several previous books. That is, I'll need to know the name of (to pick a real example) Katchin the Miller's wife, and she'll tell me that it depends on which book I choose. (I've needed a continuity checker longer than I've had one.)

My Webmaster, Karen Zimmerman, has a skill at finding data that goes beyond craftsmanship. When I need a reference, it appears magically in my in-box within a couple hours.

Mark Van Name has been my friend for more than twenty years, and for that reason I dedicated a book to him back in 1990. Mark is a variety of things besides being my friend, however. Among them, he's a management and marketing consultant, in which capacity he advised me on the structure of The Crown of the Isles, the trilogy of which this novel is part.

Computers (two of them) Died in Making This Book. (Yes, I'm used to it by now.) Mark, my son Jonathan, and Jennie Faries got me out of holes.

My wife, Jo, bore with me, fed me superbly, and kept the house as clean as possible under the circumstances. (I'm really going to clean up my mess of paper now.)

My thanks to all those above, and to others who just by being nice people made my world brighter than it would've been otherwise.

Author's Note

As before in the Isles series, I've based the magic on that of the Mediterranean Basin in Classical times. The *voces mysticae* (which I've called words of power) are taken from real spell tablets. Their purpose was to call the attention of demiurges (entities between men and Gods) to the wishes of the person casting the spell. I do not personally believe in Classical magic or any magic, but neither do I choose to pronounce the *voces mysticae* aloud: I've been wrong before.

In my writing I always use bits and pieces not only of history but of other fiction, scenes and phrases that made a strong impression on me. This time the plot was shaped in part by my study of *Spawn*, a story by P. Schuyler Miller. Those of you who haven't read *Spawn* can find it reprinted in the fat anthology *The World Turned Upside Down*, along with many other stories which the three editors found particularly memorable.

Another direct influence was Ovid, who can be amazingly evocative with a mere line or two. For an example of what I mean, compare (on my Web site, david-drake.com) my translation of the Perseus section of the *Metamorphoses* with the portion of *Fortress* involving Cashel and the Daughter of Phorcys.

Again as usual, I've translated scraps from real Latin poets into the fabric of this novel. While it's rarely a good idea to assume that a fictional character is expressing the author's real beliefs, I will note here that Garric's observations on *O fons Bandusiae* summarize the reasons I carried the OCT edition of Horace with me through my time in the army in 1969–71. There are times and places in which it's very important to have proof that civilization exists, or at least that it once existed.

The Fortress of Glass

Chapter

1

TENOCTRIS THE WIZARD stood in the prow of the royal flagship, staring intently at the sky. "Sharina," she said, "we're suddenly in a focus of enormous power. There's something here. There's something *coming* here."

Sharina glanced upward also. "Is it good or bad?" she asked, but the wizard was lost in contemplation.

Cumulus clouds were piled over the island of First Atara on the northern horizon, but here above the *Shepherd of the Isles* there was only a high chalky haze. Whatever Tenoctris was looking at couldn't be seen by an ordinary person like Sharina os-Reise.

Sharina grinned: or, for that matter, seen by Princess Sharina of Haft. In preparation for meeting the ruler of First Atara, she was this afternoon wearing court robes—garments of silk brocade stiffened with embroidery in gold thread. They were hot and uncomfortable in most circumstances; here on shipboard they were awkward beyond words. The *Shepherd* had five oarbanks and was as big as a warship got, but the deck of her streamlined hull was no wider than necessary to allow sailors to trim the yards when the vessel was under sail.

Sometimes Sharina wondered whether she'd feel more at ease in formal garments if she'd been raised wearing them. Liane bos-Benliman, her brother Garric's noble fiancée, certainly wore hers with calm style. On the other hand, Liane did everything with style. If Liane hadn't been such a *good* person and so obviously in love with Garric, even Sharina might've felt twinges of envy in thinking about her.

Sharina and Garric had been raised by their father, the innkeeper in the tiny community of Barca's Hamlet on Haft. No school for the wealthy could've educated them better in the literature of the Old Kingdom than Reise himself had, but they'd grown up in simple woolen tunics and had gone barefoot half the year.

Sharina grinned. She guessed she could learn to wear court robes more easily than even Liane could learn to wait tables in a common room packed with sheep drovers and their servants, many of them drunk.

Horns and trumpets were calling, slowing the hundred and more ships of the royal fleet to a crawl. A little vessel draped with gaudy bunting was coming out to meet them with a wriggle of oars.

One of the royal triremes, the swift and handy three-banked vessels which were the backbone of the fighting fleet, had already come alongside the stranger and passed it as harmless, though that didn't explain why the island's authorities felt a need to approach Garric—Prince Garric—at sea. No reasonable official would choose to negotiate on the wobbling deck of a warship, since even people who weren't seasick would find a conference table in the palace a better location for spreading documents and consulting ledgers.

"There seem to be five—no, six passengers," Sharina said, peering down at the deck of the twenty-oared barge bringing the Ataran delegation. She frowned and added, "And one of them's just a boy."

The island's present ruler called himself King Cervoran, and his ancestors for hundreds of years had claimed the title "king" also. They'd gotten away with it because First Atara kept to itself, never making trouble for its neighbors or for the King of the Isles in Valles . . . and because for generations the King of the Isles had ruled little more than the island of Ornifal and eventually had ruled nothing outside the walls of the royal palace.

That'd changed when the present King of the Isles, Valence III, adopted a youth named Garric, a descendant of the ancient line of Old Kingdom monarchs, as his son and heir apparent. It *had* to change. Unless there was a strong hand on the kingdom's rudder, the same forces that swept up Garric and his sister would smash the new kingdom. The second catastrophe would leave nothing, not even savage tribes that might climb back to civilization in a thousand years.

It was all well to say that every man should live his life without being pestered by distant officials. That's the way things had been in Barca's Hamlet, pretty much, simply because the community was a tiny backwater on an island which had ceased to be important a thousand years before.

Most of those who said that *now,* however, were local nobles. What they meant by freedom was that nobody from Valles should tell them how they should treat their own peasants. A peasant given the opportunity generally prefers a bully on a distant island to a bully in the castle overlooking his farm. Even better: Garric's government *didn't* bully and it tried to protect its citizens.

Garric hadn't set out to conquer the other islands of the kingdom; rather, he was visiting them one by one in a Royal Progress— accompanied by a fleet and army that obviously could crush any would-be secessionist. As a result, the reunification of the Isles was taking place in conference rooms, not on battlefields.

Tenoctris clasped her hands and muttered in reaction to the pageant she alone saw in the sky. If there was proof that the Gods rather than blind chance ruled the world, it was in the fact that the same cataclysm that brought down the Old Kingdom threw Tenoctris forward from that time to this one.   ·

Wizards used the powers on which the cosmos balanced. These waxed and waned in thousand-year cycles and were at a peak now. Because wizards remained for the most part as blind, clumsy, and foolish as they'd been when they'd conjured music and baubles from the air to amaze guests at a feast, disaster loomed over the New Kingdom as surely as it had wrecked the Old.

Even in these days Tenoctris could affect very little through wizardry, but she saw and understood the powers which greater wizards used in ignorance. Her knowledge and the strong hand of Prince Garric of Haft had so far been enough to reunify the kingdom, and the Isles had to be unified if they were to face the threats, human and demonic, which had swollen as the underlying powers increased.

No one could look at the present world and doubt that Good and Evil existed. Those who thought they could remain neutral in the struggle had chosen Evil, even though they wouldn't admit it.

Sharina put her arm around Tenoctris for companionship. The old wizard had lived seventy years or more, and something of the weight of the ten centuries she'd been thrown forward seemed to lie on her shoulders also. Tenoctris didn't believe in the Great Gods and all she'd ever wanted from life was peace for her studies, but she was spending her life in the service of Good.

As were Garric and Sharina and their friends; as were all the members of the royal army and the royal administration. Individually they included better folk and worse, but all were on the right side in the greater struggle . . . or so Sharina believed.

She smiled again, broadly this time. She *did* believe that.

Sharina turned to watch the barge nuzzle the *Shepherd*'s high, curving stern where Garric stood with Liane, a pair of aides, and a squad of black-armored members of the Blood Eagles, the bodyguard regiment. Garric's silvered breastplate made him look both regal and heroic—which was the purpose, of course; nobody expected fighting here on First Atara.

Sharina noticed he hadn't donned the helmet with the flaring gilt wings that completed the outfit, though he probably would before they landed. By the time her brother was fifteen he was already the tallest man in Barca's Hamlet, and the helmet added a full hand's breadth to that height.

Garric was strong as well as tall, but there was a stronger man yet in the community: Cashel or-Kenset, an orphan raised by his twin sister, Ilna, after their grandmother died; a quiet fellow, gentle as a lamb and without a lamb's querulous self-importance. A man taller than most, broader than almost any, and stronger than anyone he'd ever met or was likely to meet.

He stood now behind the two women like a wall of muscle, his hickory quarterstaff an upright pillar in his right hand. Sharina, still touching Tenoctris with her left hand, put her right in the crook of his elbow. Cashel smiled because he usually smiled, and he smiled wider because Sharina touched him. It would've embarrassed him to take her hand in public, but nobody seeing the two of them together could doubt that they loved each other.

Sailors from the barge had thrown lines from bow and stern aboard the *Shepherd;* crewmen snubbed them to the outrigger that carried three of the flagship's five oarbanks. The sailing master was blasting the barge captain with remarkable curses, though, at the notion that the smaller vessel would be allowed to lie hull to hull, where it'd scrape the flagship's paint. The barge captain swore back.

"We've been three months since the ships were overhauled in Carcosa," Sharina said, frowning. "I don't see that a few more scrapes are going to be noticed."

Sailors tended to carry out their business as though the officials traveling as passengers didn't exist. She and Garric had been taught to keep their affairs—the inn's affairs—secret from the guests. This slanging match between the officers of the two ships offended Sharina's sense of propriety, though the curses themselves did not.

"I think what he's saying is that we're fine people from the palace in Valles," said Cashel, quietly but with something solid in his tone that wouldn't have been there if he were better satisfied with the situation. "And they're just nobodies from the sticks. Only we're not, not all of us; and I guess that fellow'd have been as quick to call *me* a nobody back before Garric got to be prince and it all changed."

"Not to your face, Cashel," Sharina said—and kissed him, surprising herself almost as much as she did her fiancé. It was the perfect way to break his mood; Cashel's face went the color of mahogany as he blushed under the deep tan. They were in the shelter of the jib boom, though, and everybody else was looking toward the stern, where the delegation was swaying aboard on a rope ladder. Nobody was likely to have noticed.

"Do we know why these people are meeting us at sea?" Tenoctris said.

Sharina jumped. The older woman had been so thoroughly lost in her own thoughts that Sharina'd forgotten her presence.

"Ah, no," she said. "We could join them in the stern if you'd like, though. They're certainly an official delegation, so I guess it's our duty to be there."

"Right," said Cashel, turning and starting down the walkway stretching the length of the ship between the gratings over the rowers. There wasn't much room, but the sailors on deck would get out of his way, though they might be so busy they'd ignore the women.

Sharina motioned Tenoctris ahead of her and brought up the rear. She didn't have Cashel's bulk, but her tall, slender body was muscular and she had reflexes gained from waiting tables in rooms crowded with men.

"They may have nothing to do with what I feel building around us," Tenoctris said quietly, perhaps speaking to herself as much as to her younger companions. "But their meeting us at sea is unusual, and the way the forces are building is *very* unusual; almost unique in my experience."

"'*Almost* unique,'" Sharina said, delicately emphasizing the qualifier.

"Yes," said the wizard. "I felt something like this in the moments before I was ripped out of my time and the island of Yole sank into the depths of the sea."

O NE OF GARRIC's guards gave his spear to a comrade so that he had a hand free to reach over the railing to the twelve-year-old climbing the swaying ladder ahead of five adults. "Here you go, lad," he said.

"Have a care, my man!" cried the puffy-looking bald fellow immediately behind the boy. "This is Prince Protas, the ruler of our island!"

"All the more reason not to let him fall into the water, then," said Garric, stepping forward. "Since I'm told that right around here it's as deep as the Inner Sea gets."

He took the boy's right hand while the soldier gripped him under the left shoulder, and together they lifted him aboard. Protas tucked his legs under him so that his toes didn't touch the rail. Though he didn't speak, he bowed politely to Garric and dipped his head to the soldier as well, then slipped forward to get as much out of the way as was possible on the warship's deck.

The plump official reached the railing. Garric nodded a guard forward to help him but pointedly didn't offer a hand himself.

"That would be Lord Martous," Liane whispered in his left ear. "Protas is King Cervoran's son, but Cervoran was ruler as of my latest information."

Among Liane's other duties, she was Garric's spymaster; or rather she was a spymaster who kept Garric informed of events from all over the Isles, whether or not they took place on islands which had returned to royal control. Her father had been a far-traveled merchant. Liane of her own volition—Garric wouldn't have known what to ask her to do—had turned his network of business connections into a full-fledged intelligence service. It'd benefited the kingdom more than another ten regiments for the army could've done.

Lord Martous had an unhappy expression as he struggled aboard in the soldier's grasp. Garric shared his mind with the spirit of King Carus, his ancient ancestor and the last ruler of the Old Kingdom. Now the image of Carus grinned and said, *"If I know the type, he looks unhappy most of the time he's awake. Being manhandled over the railing just gives him a better reason than usual."*

Martous straightened his clothing with quick pats of his hands while he waited for the remainder of the delegation to climb onto the deck, aides or servants from their simpler dress. One of them carried a bundle wrapped in red velvet.

The delegates wore baggy woolen trousers and blouses, felt caps, and slippers whose toes turned up in points. Martous and Protas had long triangular gores of cloth of gold appliquéd vertically on their sleeves and trouser legs; those of the other men were plain. The wool was bleached white, but it was clear that First Atara's society didn't set great store on flamboyant personal decoration.

Garric preferred simplicity to the styles of the great cities of the kingdom, Valles and Erdin on Sandrakkan, or even Carcosa, which now was merely the capital of the unimportant island of Haft. It'd been the royal capital during the Old Kingdom, and it remained a pretentious place despite its glory being a thousand years in the past.

Garric grinned at Lord Martous: a balding little fellow, a homely man from a rustic place who was incensed that he and the boy on whom his status depended weren't being treated with greater deference. That implied that pretentiousness was one of the strongest human impulses.

"Come along, Basto, come along," called Lord Martous to the aide struggling with the bundle. Then on a rising note, "No, don't you—"

The latter comment was to Lord Attaper, the commander of the Blood Eagles and a man to whom Garric's safety was more important than it was to Garric himself. Attaper, a stocky, powerful man in his forties, ignored the protest just as he ignored all other attempts to tell him how to do his job. He plucked the package from the aide's hands and unwrapped it while the aide came aboard and Martous spluttered in frustration.

"I'm sorry you had to scramble up like a monkey, Prince Protas," Garric said, smiling at the boy to put him at his ease. Protas was obviously nervous and uncertain, afraid to say or do the wrong thing in what he knew were important circumstances. "I'd expected to meet you—and your father, of course—on land in a few hours."

"King Cervoran is dead, sir," Protas said with careful formality. He forced himself to look straight at Garric as he spoke, but then he swallowed hard.

"Yes, yes, that's why we had to come out to meet you," Martous said, pursing his lips as though he were sucking on something sour. "His Highness died most unexpectedly as he was going in to dinner last evening. Quite distressing, quite. He fell right down in his tracks. I was afraid the stewards had dropped something on the floor and he'd slipped, but he just—died."

"I probably *could* give you advice on housekeeping in a large establishment," Garric said, smiling instead of snarling at the courtier's inability to come to the point, "but I really doubt that's why you've met us here at the cost of discomfort and a degree of danger. Is it, milord?"

Martous looked surprised. "Oh," he said. "Well, of course not. But I thought—that is, the council did—that since you were arriving just in time, you could preside over the apotheosis ceremony for King Cervoran and add, well, luster to the affair. And of course we needed to explain that to you before you come ashore because the ceremony will have to be carried out first thing tomorrow morning. The cremation can't, you see, be delayed very long in this weather."

"Apotheosis?" said Liane. She didn't ordinarily interject herself openly into matters of state, but Lord Martous was obviously a palace flunky, and not from a very big palace if it came to that. "You believe your late ruler becomes a God?"

"Well, I don't, of course *I* don't," said Martous in embarrassment. "But the common people, you know; and they like a spectacle. And, well, it's traditional here on First Atara. And it can't hurt, after all."

"This doesn't appear to be a weapon, milord," said Attaper dryly. "Shall I return it to your servant, or would you like to take it yourself?"

The velvet wrappings covered a foiled wooden box decorated with cutwork astrological symbols. Inside was a diadem set with a topaz the size of Garric's clenched fist. The stone wasn't particularly clear or brilliant, even for a topaz, but Garric didn't recall ever seeing a larger gem.

Protas, forgotten during the adults' byplay, said in a clear voice, "We brought it to your master the prince, my man. *He* will decide where to bestow it."

Garric nodded politely to the young prince. "Your pardon, milord," he said in real apology. "We've had a long voyage and it appears to have made us less courteous than we ought to be."

He took the diadem. The gold circlet was thicker and broader at the back to help balance the weight of the huge stone, but even so it had a tendency to slip forward in his fingers.

Cashel had led Sharina and Tenoctris to the stern, but now he stepped aside and let the women join the group of officials. When he caught Garric's glance over Tenoctris' head, he smiled broadly. Cashel stayed close to Sharina, but he wasn't interested in what the locals had come to discuss and didn't pretend otherwise.

Cashel wasn't interested in power. He was an extraordinarily strong man, and he had other abilities besides. If he wasn't exactly a wizard himself, then he'd more than once faced hostile wizards and crushed them. That alone would've gained him considerable authority if he'd wanted it. Add to that his being Prince Garric's friend from childhood and Princess Sharina's fiancé, and a great part of the kingdom was Cashel's for the asking.

But he didn't ask. Cashel wouldn't have known what to do with a kingdom if he'd had it, and anyway it wasn't something he wanted. Which of course was much of the reason he *was* Garric's closest friend: Garric didn't want power either.

"*That may be,*" said Carus. "*But the kingdom wants you; needs you anyway, which is better. Otherwise the best the citizens could hope for is a hardhanded warrior who knows nothing but smashing trouble down with his sword until trouble smashes him in turn. Somebody like me—and we know the bad result that leads to.*"

The ghost in Garric's mind was smiling, but there was no doubt of the solid truth under its lilt of self-mockery. Garric grinned in response; the delegates saw the expression and misread it.

Lord Martous stiffened and said, "The crown may seem a poor thing to you, milord, a mere topaz. But it's an ancient stone, very ancient, and it suits us on First Atara. We were hoping that you would invest Prince Protas with it following the ceremony deifying his father."

Garric glanced at the boy and found him chatting with Cashel. That probably made both of them more comfortable than they'd be in the discussion Garric and Martous were having.

Both the thought and the fact behind it pleased Garric, but he politely wiped all traces of misunderstood good humor from his face before he said, "I'll confer with my advisors before I give you a final decision, milord, particularly Lords Tadai and Waldron, my civil affairs and military commanders. That won't happen until we're on land."

"But you're the prince—" the envoy protested.

"That's correct," said Garric, aware of Carus' ghost chuckling at the way he handled this bit of niggling foolishness. "I'm the prince and make the final decisions under the authority granted by my father King Valence III."

Valence was so sunk within himself in his apartments in a back corner of the palace that servants chose his meals for him. He wasn't exceptionally old, but life and a series of bad choices had made a sad ruin of a mind which on its best day hadn't been very impressive.

"But I have a staff to keep track of matters on which I lack personal knowledge," Garric continued. "The political and cultural circumstances of First Atara are in that category, I'm afraid. I have no intention of slighting you and your citizens by acting in needless ignorance. We weren't expecting King Cervoran's death, and it'll take the kingdom a moment to decide how to respond."

"Well, I see that," said Martous, "but—"

"I'd have tossed him over the railing by now, lad," Carus said. *"By the Lady! It's a good thing for the kingdom that you're ruling instead of me."*

Garric looked into the big topaz. There were cloudy blotches in its yellow depths. The stone had been shaped and polished instead of being faceted, and even then it wasn't regular: it was roughly egg-shaped, but the small end was too blunt.

It was a huge gem, though; and there was something more which Garric couldn't quite grasp. The shadows in its heart seemed to move, though perhaps that was an illusion caused by the quinquereme's sideways wobble. Only a few oars on the uppermost bank were working, so the ship didn't have enough way on to make its long hull fully stable.

Liane touched his wrist. Garric blinked awake; the eyes of those nearby watched him with concern. He must've been in a reverie. . . .

"I'm very sorry," he said aloud. "It was a long voyage, as I said. Lord Martous, while I won't swear what my decision will be until I've consulted my council, I can tell you that I intended to grant the rank of marquess within the Kingdom of the Isles to the ruler of First Atara— whom of course we believed to be Lord Cervoran."

"King Cervoran," Martous protested quickly.

"King is a title reserved for Valence III and his successors as rulers of the Isles, milord," Garric said. He didn't raise his voice much, but his tone made his meaning clear. "That is not a matter King Valence or I will compromise on."

"Well, of course you can do as you please, since you have the power," Martous said unhappily to the deck plank which his gilt slipper was rubbing. In a tiny voice he added, "But it isn't fair."

Garric opened his mouth to snap out a retort. The grim-faced ghost in his mind would've backhanded the courtier for his presumption or possibly done something more brutally final. Perhaps it was that awareness that allowed Garric to catch himself and laugh instead of snarling.

"Lord Martous," he said mildly. "The kingdom is under threat from the forces of evil. The *people,* all those who live on all the scores of islands large and small within the circuit of the kingdom, are threatened. We and those whom we rule won't survive if we aren't united against that evil. I hope that in a few years or even sooner you'll be able to see that First Atara is better off as a full part of the kingdom than it would've been had it remained independent; but regardless of that—"

Garric made a broad gesture with his right arm, his sword arm, sweeping it across the long line of warships to starboard. As many more vessels were arrayed to port.

"—I'm very glad you understand that the kingdom has the power to enforce its will. Because we do, and for the sake of the people of the Isles, we'd use that power."

"We're not fools here," Martous said quietly, proving that he after all *wasn't* a fool. "We cast ourselves on your mercy. But—"

His tone grew a trifle brighter, almost enthusiastic.

"—I do hope you'll see fit to crown Prince Protas in a public ceremony. That will be quite the biggest thing that's happened here since the fall of the Old Kingdom!"

Garric laughed, feeling the ghost in his mind laugh with him. "I trust we'll be able to come to an accommodation, milord," he said, glancing toward the prince and Cashel. "I'm sure we will!"

CASHEL OR-KENSET PRICKLED all over, as if he'd gotten too much sun while plowing. That could happen, even for a fellow like him who'd been outside pretty much every day he could remember, but it wasn't what he was feeling this afternoon.

This was wizardry. He'd known his share of that too, in the past couple years since everything changed and he'd left Barca's Hamlet.

Cashel held his quarterstaff upright in his right hand; one ferrule rested on the deck beside him. He crossed his left arm over his chest, letting his fingertips caress the smooth hickory.

In his tenth year Cashel had felled a tree for a neighbor in the borough and taken one long, straight branch as his price for the work. He'd cut the staff from that branch and had carried it from that day to this.

A blacksmith traveling through Barca's Hamlet on his circuit had fitted the first set of iron butt caps, but there'd been others over the years. The staff, though, was the same: thick, hard, and polished like glass by the touch of Cashel's callused palms and the wads of raw wool he carried to dress the wood. It'd been a good friend to Cashel; and with the staff in his hands, Cashel had been a very good friend to weaker folk facing terrors.

Just about everybody was weaker than Cashel. He smiled a little wider. Everybody he'd met so far, anyway.

The little boy who'd come aboard with the puffed-up fellow and the servants looked uncomfortable as he edged back from the adults talking politics. Getting up on their hind legs, really. The fellow from First Atara was trying to make himself big and Garric was pushing him back, showing him he wasn't much at all. With luck the fellow'd stop making trouble before he wound up with a headache or worse.

A shepherd didn't have a lot to learn about how people behaved in a palace. It was all the same, sheep or courtiers.

Being uncomfortable while folks talked about things he didn't know about or care about wasn't new to Cashel either, so he grinned at the boy in a friendly way. It was like he'd tossed him a rope as he splashed in the sea: the boy stepped straight over to Cashel and said, "Good day, milord. I'm Prince Protas. Are you Lord Cashel? I thought you must be because you're, well . . . you're very big. I've heard of you."

Protas spoke very carefully. He was trying to be formal, but every once in a while his voice squeaked and made him blush. Cashel remembered that too.

"I'm Cashel," he said, letting the smile fade so Protas wouldn't mistake it as mocking his trouble with his voice. "Not 'lord' though. And I've met bigger folk than me; though not a lot of them, I'll grant."

Protas nodded solemnly. He looked away from Cashel, facing in the general direction of First Atara. "My father King Cervoran died just yesterday," he said. "Lord Martous tells me that I'm going to be king now in his place, or whatever Prince Garric lets me be called."

"I'm sorry about your father, Protas," Cashel said, meaning it.

Kenset, his father and Ilna's, had gone away from Barca's Hamlet and come back with the two children a year later. Kenset had never said where he'd been or who the twins' mother was. He hadn't said much of anything by all accounts, and he hadn't worked at anything except drinking himself to death. He'd managed that one frosty night a few years later.

The children's grandmother had raised Cashel and Ilna while she lived. After she died, leaving a pair of nine-year-olds, they'd raised themselves. Ilna always had a mind for things, and Cashel as a boy had a man's strength. When he got his growth, well, his strength grew too. They'd made out with Ilna's weaving and Cashel doing whatever needed muscle and care. Mostly he'd tended sheep.

"I didn't know my father very well," Protas said, continuing to look out to sea. Cashel guessed the boy really didn't want to meet Cashel's eyes, which meant either he was embarrassed or he figured Cashel'd be embarrassed by what he had to say. "He was very busy with his studies. He was a great scholar, you know."

"That's a fine thing to be," Cashel said. He meant it, but mostly he spoke to help the boy get to whatever it was that he *really* wanted to say.

Cashel'd learned to spell his name out or even write it if somebody gave him time and didn't complain that the letters looked shaky. He was proud of knowing Garric and Sharina because they read and wrote as well as anybody even though they'd come from Barca's Hamlet instead of a big city. Those weren't skills Cashel felt the lack of himself, though.

"My father King Cervoran was a wizard, L-Lor . . . Master Cashel," Protas said, his voice squeaking three times in the short sentence. He glanced sideways, then jerked his eyes away like Cashel had slapped him. He kept talking, though. "You're a wizard too, aren't you? That is, I've heard you are?"

"I don't know where you'd have heard that . . . ," Cashel said, speaking even more slowly and carefully than he usually did. He cleared his throat, wishing there was room so he could spin his quarterstaff. That always settled him when he was feeling uncomfortable, which he surely was right now. "Anyway, I'd as soon you just called me Cashel with no masters or lords or who knows what elses. It's what I'm used to being called, you see."

"I'm sorry, M-Mas . . . *Cashel*," the boy said. He sounded like he was ready to start blubbering. "I didn't mean to say the wrong thing. I'm just so, so—oh, Cashel, I just feel so alone!"

Cashel squatted down so that his face was a bit lower than the boy's instead of staring down at him. He didn't look straight at Protas either, because that might be enough to push the boy into tears.

"I'm not a wizard like most people think of wizard," Cashel said quietly. He didn't guess anybody but Protas could hear him over the sigh of the light easterly breeze; and if they could, well, he wasn't telling any more than the truth. "I don't know anything about spells or the like. Only my mother. . . ."

He paused again to figure just how to say the next part. Protas was looking at him straight-on now. He seemed interested and no longer on the verge of crying.

"I didn't know my mother till I met her just a little bit ago when we were on Sandrakkan," Cashel went on. He gripped the upright staff with both hands, taking strength from the smooth hickory. "She was a queen in her own land, and she was a wizard. Not the way Tenoctris is by studying and memorizing old books, but sort of born to it. Tenoctris says my mother is really powerful; and I guess she must be, from the things I saw her do."

He cleared his throat again, then made himself look up and meet the boy's eyes squarely. "I guess I picked up some of that from her," Cashel said. "I did and Ilna did too, only not the same way. Ilna can do things with cloth, weave anything and make a net that catches somebody's mind when they look at it. And Ilna's smart, too, like our mother."

He grinned broadly. "Not like me," he added. "I'm about smart enough to watch sheep, but that's all."

"King Cervoran wasn't a wizard in a bad way," Protas said. He was still facing Cashel but his eyes were fuzzy; looking back into the past, most likely. "He just used his art to learn things. That was the only thing that was important to him, learning things."

Cashel nodded. "There's people like that," he said carefully. It struck him as strange to hear Protas talking about his father so formally, but he wasn't the one to judge. He didn't talk about Kenset much at all.

But then, maybe Cervoran hadn't had any more to do with Protas than Kenset had with his children while they were growing up. The things Cervoran wanted to learn about didn't seem to have included his own son.

"I thought . . . ," Protas said, then looked away again. "I thought when I heard about you that you were like my father. With your art, I mean. That you didn't use wizardry to hurt people. That's so, isn't it?"

"Well, I try not to hurt good people," Cashel said. "I've met my share of the other kind, though, and some of them got hurt. By me."

He understood what the boy was getting at now. Though he didn't want to be unkind to Protas, he didn't intend to let him think Cashel was going to be some kind of father to him.

He grinned broadly. "Look, Protas," he said, "being a, well, a wizard the way I am isn't anything to be proud of. It's like Sharina having blond hair: it's the way she was born and I was born. The way she reads things, though—that she worked to do. Sharina's a scholar and Garric too; that's something they did all by themselves. And I'll show you what I did and I *am* proud of."

Cashel looked both ways to make sure not only that there was room but also that nobody was about to step where he was going in the next instant; then he hopped to the railing. The ship heeled a trifle; Cashel was a solid weight, and the *Shepherd of the Isles* was both slender and perfectly balanced.

Master Lobon, the sailing master, turned and snarled, "Hey, you moron!" When he saw he'd shouted at Cashel, *Lord* Cashel the prince's friend, he swallowed the rest of what he was going to say with a look of horror. Lobon's opinion of what Cashel was doing hadn't changed, but he wished he hadn't been quite so open with it.

Cashel was facing seaward on the stern rail. He crossed one bare foot over the other and turned so he could meet the eyes of everybody on the *Shepherd*'s deck, then started his staff spinning slowly in a sunwise pattern.

He grinned. The sailing master was right about the foolishness, but it was in the good cause of lifting Protas' mind out of whatever bad place his father's death had put him in. Besides, Cashel needed the exercise after a day at sea.

The staff spun faster. The gentle sway and pitch of the ship wasn't a problem; Cashel was used to crossing creeks on rain-slicked logs, carrying sheep which were still muddy and kicking in terror from the bog he'd dragged them out of.

Everybody was looking at him now. Garric grinned with his hands on his hips; Sharina's expression was a mixture of pride and love. How amazing it was that she loved him! The ferrules blurred into a gleaming circle.

Cashel lifted the whirling staff overhead, feeling the tug of its rotation fighting the strength of his powerful wrists. He gave a shout and jumped from the railing, letting the hickory carry him around so that he faced seaward again; shouted, jumped, and faced the ship, the staff still in his hands.

Cashel jumped down to the deck, flushed and triumphant. The pine planking creaked dangerously at the shock; he'd hit harder than he'd meant to. He was making it look easy—that was half the trick, after all—but it'd taken a lot out of even his great muscles. After the strain, his judgment wasn't as good as maybe it ought to've been.

"There!" Cashel said to Protas, fighting the urge to suck in air through his mouth. "That's not something I was born to or given. That I can do because I worked till I could. *That's* something I'm proud of!"

But as he spoke, his skin itched like hot coals. Wizardry was building to the breaking point in the world about him.

ILNA OS-KENSET SQUATTED on the foredeck of the cutter *Heron,* a hand loom in her lap and her eyes on the sky. She was weaving a pattern that'd be abstract to the eyes of those who viewed it: blurred, gentle curves of grays and blacks and browns, the colors of a coast soon after sunset. All the hues were natural; Ilna didn't trust dyes.

She smiled faintly. She didn't trust most things. In particular she didn't trust herself when she was angry, and she'd spent far too much time being angry.

Though the plaque Ilna wove looked to be only an exercise in muted good taste, the pattern would work deep in the minds of those who glanced at it. They wouldn't be aware of the effect, not consciously at least, but they'd go away soothed and a little more at peace with the world and themselves.

Ilna smiled again. It even worked on her, and her disposition was a very stiff test.

"Give us a song, Captain!" called the stroke oar, a squat fellow with his wrists tattooed to look like he was wearing bracers.

"Aye, give us 'The Ladies o' Shengy,' Cap'n Chalcus!" agreed one of the rowers from the lower tier, sitting on deck now that the ship idled along with only the slow strokes of four oarsmen to keep her steady in the swell.

The *Heron* had a crew of fifty rowers in two tiers, with a dozen officers and deckhands for the rigging when her mast was raised. She was a stubby vessel, neither as fast nor as powerful as the triremes that made up the bulk of the royal fleet let alone the quinqueremes which acted as flagships for the squadrons and fleet itself.

For all that, the cutter was a warship. Her ram and the handiness of her short hull made her a dangerous opponent even to much larger vessels.

Ilna's smile, never broad, took on a hint of warmth. A fishing skiff would be a dangerous opponent if Chalcus commanded it.

"I will not sing such a thing and scandalize the fine ladies here with us," said Chalcus, but there was a cheery lilt in his voice. He bowed to the ten-year-old Lady Merota, seated on the stern rail like an urchin and not the heiress to the bos-Roriman fortune, then bowed lower yet to Ilna in the bow. "But I'll pass the time for you with 'The Brown Girl' if there's a swig of wine—"

The helmsman lifted the skin of wine hanging from the railing by him where the spray kissed it. He slapped it into Chalcus' hand, though neither man looked at the other as they made the exchange.

"—to wet my pipes," Chalcus concluded as he thumbed the carved wooden plug from the goatskin and drank deeply.

He was a close-coupled man, not much taller than Ilna herself. Chalcus looked trim when dressed in court clothing; he was hard as a mahogany statue when he stripped to a sailor's breechclout, as he did often enough even now that Garric had made him the *Heron*'s captain.

In a breechclout you saw the scars also. Several of the long-healed wounds should've been fatal. If one had been, Ilna would never have met him. It was hard to imagine what value she'd find in life at this moment were it not for Chalcus.

" 'The Brown Girl she has houses and lands . . . ,' " Chalcus sang in his clear tenor. His eyes continued to smile at Ilna till she leaned around to look at the sky again while her fingers wove. " 'Fair Tresian has none. . . .' "

Chalcus had sailed with the Lataaene pirates in southern waters. He didn't talk about those days or other days of the same sort he'd lived in the course of collecting the scars on his body. Ilna supposed Chalcus had as much on his conscience as she did on hers, though he carried the burden lightly as he did all things.

" 'The best advice I can give you, my son . . . ,' " Chalcus sang, his voice shining like a sunlit brook, " 'is to bring the Brown Girl home.' "

Ilna didn't ask whether Chalcus was a good man or a bad one. He was her man, and that was enough.

Something rippled and seethed behind the sky's curtain of thin clouds. Ilna's fingers worked, weaving contentment for people she didn't know through ages she couldn't guess. Her patterns would last for the life of the wool, and that could be very long indeed.

Ilna'd always had a talent for yarns and fabric that went beyond mere skill. She could touch a swatch of cloth and know where the flax had grown or the sheep had gamboled; and she knew also what'd been in the heart of the one who wove it.

By the time she was twelve everyone in the borough knew that Ilna os-Kenset wove fabrics softer and finer than anyone else around. Before she left Barca's Hamlet at eighteen, two years past, merchants came from Sandrakkan and even Ornifal to buy her subtly woven cloth.

" 'He dressed himself in scarlet red . . . ,' " Chalcus sang. The *Heron*'s crew, sailors as coarse as the hemp of the ship's rigging, listened to the lovely, lilting voice. Other men lined the near rail of the *Shepherd of the Isles*. " 'He rode all o'er the town. . . .' "

Ilna's road had led from Barca's Hamlet to Carcosa, the ancient capital on the other coast of Haft; and from Carcosa she'd gone to Hell, where at the cost of her soul she'd learned to weave as no human could. She'd used her new skills in the service of Evil and in her own service, because she'd returned from Hell as surely an agent of Evil as any demon was.

Garric had freed Ilna from the darkness she'd sold herself to for love of him, but nothing—no deed, no apology, no remorse—could undo the things she'd done while she rejoiced in the power to make others act as she and Evil chose. So be it. She'd live the best way she could, helping the friends who'd been wiser and stronger and knew Evil only as an enemy. And whenever she could, she'd weave patterns that would make life a little less bleak for those who saw them.

The patterns helped even Ilna os-Kenset, who'd never forgive herself for the harm she'd done through anger and pride in her own skill. Her fingers worked, and her lips quirked wryly. She wasn't good at forgiving others either, if it came to that.

" '. . . they thought that he was the king,' " Chalcus sang, and Merota joined in on the harmony. Ilna glanced back. The child was clasping the sailor's left hand in both of hers, her face bright with delight.

It was remarkable the way the noble Lady Merota had taken to them, the peasant girl and the sailor who'd once been worse things.

Merota had tutors, of course, and advisors to manage the properties and investments to which she'd fallen heir; but her parents were dead, and she'd never had anything like real friendship until she met Ilna.

Ilna knew how people treated an orphan girl without anyone to protect her. She couldn't change the whole world; but while she lived no one was going to use Merota as a stepping-stone on their route to wealth and power.

The clouds on the eastern horizon had grown into an overcast smearing the heavens like lime wash over gray stone. The sun, barely past zenith, was a bright patch to the south. The sky wasn't stormy, and the sea moved as gently as ripe barley ruffled by a breeze. The threat, the lurking power, was no part of the natural world.

But it was present nonetheless.

" " "What news, what news, Lord Thoma?" she said,' " sang Merota, taking the women's parts alone now. " " "What news have you for me?" ' "

Sailors were hard men, and sailors willing to serve under Captain Chalcus were often harder still; some of the *Heron*'s crew were little more than brutes. They listened to the girl with pleasure as innocent as her own.

It should come very shortly, Ilna thought, trying to read the pattern above the heavens.

" " "I've come to ask you to my weddin',"' " Chalcus sang, and the heavens split with a continuing roar.

A blue-white glare hammered down, brighter than the sun in the first instants and growing brighter still. Ilna jerked her eyes away, but even the reflections from the wave tops were so painfully vivid that she found herself squinting.

The clouds bubbled back like mud shocked by a thrown stone. Something was coming, and it was coming fast.

"Man your bloody benches!" Chalcus said. He was shouting, but even so the words were little more than a whisper over the sound of the sky tearing apart. *"Get a way on, ye beggars, or the Sister'll swallow us down to Hell where we belong!"*

As Chalcus spoke, he grabbed Merota by the back of her tunics and tossed her aft, under the rising curve of the stern piece where the helmsman stood. It wasn't a safe place, but there was no real safety on a cutter; and as for gentle, that could wait for when there was time.

Ilna unpinned her hand loom, folding it with the warp and weft still in place and returning it to its canvas bag. She worked methodically, making the same motions at the same speed as she would if the *Heron* had landed in Mona Harbor and she were preparing to go ashore. She always moved as quickly as she could without error; and if putting away her weaving was the last thing Ilna os-Kenset did, then it too would be done properly.

The roar pounded the sea and the ships, a weight like a storm wind that made men flinch from its force. Not all the oars were manned but most were, and rowers were hauling back on their looms. Chalcus' orders were driving them, but reflex drove them also. Men try to do the thing they know in the midst of a chaos they don't understand.

Ilna slung the strap of the loom bag and rose to her feet. The blaze in the sky threw her shadow as a black pool at her feet. She didn't know why Chalcus had ordered the rowers to their posts; perhaps it was merely to give them a task and prevent panic. Another man might've been trying to get away, but the thunder raced too fast for the *Heron* or any other human device to escape.

Besides, Chalcus wasn't the sort to think first of running.

The object struck the sea with a cataclysmic flash, as far to the south of the royal fleet as the island was to the north. Steam and water spouted skyward. There was a moment of silence, broken only by ringing in Ilna's ears from the punishment they'd taken during the thing's passage.

"Port oars stroke!" Chalcus shouted. "Starboard back water! Bring us bow-on, you dogs, or the fish'll kiss our bones!"

The *Heron* jumped as the sea slapped its keel, knocking Ilna and every standing man save Chalcus to the deck. The blast of sound through the air followed, noticeably later and less violent.

Water lifted in a mountain-high ring about the column of steam, racing outward at a pace beyond that of a galloping horse. The wave's height lessened as its circle expanded, but it'd still be of immense size and power when it reached them.

"It's the Shepherd's slingstone!" cried a sailor, weeping over his oar-loom. "Ah, mercy on a poor sinner!"

"It's a meteor!" piped Merota, hugging the sternpost with both arms. "It's a stone from the sky and we've seen it! We've seen it!"

"All oars stop!" shouted Chalcus. "Now together boys, forward and put your backs in it. Stroke! Stroke! Stro—"

The squadrons to starboard, south of the *Heron* and the flagship, were in confusion, dancing like straws in a millrace. Ships lifted on the rising wave, then slid or tumbled off the back. Some capsized and one trireme, older or harder used than most, broke in the middle like a snake under a spade.

"Ship oars!" Chalcus cried. "Wait for it my buckos, my heroes, for—"

A wave washed the cutter's deck bow to stern. Ilna, caught unaware, grabbed a jib stay. She hadn't been consciously aware of it, but in the crisis her instinct went to a rope and saved her. The sea rushed past, bubbling and powerful, but a lifetime of working looms had given Ilna a grip and muscles equal to this test and worse ones.

The *Heron* lifted from the back of the wave and bucked onto an even keel. Here the cutter's short hull glided over what meant danger to a longer vessel.

Chalcus stood silent, surveying the whole situation while the officers under him sorted out their divisions. The crisis was over for the *Heron*. The wave-crest moved on, shaking ships like rats in a dog's jaws and leaving flotsam in its wake.

"Ahead slow!" Chalcus called. "Holpa, Rennon, Kirweke, and Lonn—fetch yourselves lines and stand in the bow. There's men in the water as'll drown if we don't get them out!"

Ilna joined him. Merota, cautiously holding the rail, got up also and took the sailor's hand when he reached back for her.

"There's many that'll drown despite us, too," Chalcus said in a voice pitched for the pair of them. "We're one small ship and there's a dozen foundered or I miss my bet. But we'll do what we can."

"Chalcus?" said Merota. "That was a meteor, a really big one. Can we go see where it landed?"

"Where it landed, child . . . ," Chalcus said, looking toward the pillar of steam now piercing the roiling overcast, "is a trench deeper than any man's plumbed. There'd be nothing to see, whether it's your scholar's meteor or the Shepherd's slingstone as simple folk like me were raised to think."

"You don't believe in the Shepherd *or* the Lady, Chalcus," Merota said sternly.

"Aye, there you have me, dear one," said the sailor, but the banter was only in his tone and not his eyes. "Nor perhaps in the Sister who rules the Underworld. But if there was a Sister and a Hell for her to rule, I think we might find them in a place that looks much—"

Chalcus nodded toward the column of steam, still rising and now seeming to sparkle at the core.

"—as that one does."

"Yes," said Ilna, her eyes on the horizon. "And I've never found such a lack of trouble in this world that I needed to borrow it from the heavens."

Chapter

2

"THIS IS THE palace," Protas said, standing in the stern of the barge that was carrying Cashel with the delegation returning to Mona, the island's capital. He cleared his throat. "I suppose you've seen much better ones, though? Haven't you, Cashel?"

Mona had a good harbor unless the wind came from the southwest, but it wasn't big enough by half to hold the battered royal fleet. That wasn't a surprise: Cashel didn't guess there was a handful of places in all the kingdom that could. There'd be ships dragged up on every bit of bare shore for miles around the city tonight, trying to repair damage from the meteor.

At least the beaches of First Atara seemed to be sand, not the fist-sized basalt shingle that lay beyond the ancient seawall of Barca's Hamlet. That was hard on keels, and for all their size warships were built lighter than the fishing dories that were the only ships Cashel'd known while he was growing up.

"I've seen bigger places, palaces and temples and even the main market building in Valles," he said. "I don't know I've ever seen a nicer one. Still, I'm not one to talk. I spend most of my time outdoors when people let me."

Cashel had thought about the question instead of just saying something. Sheep were better than people about waiting for you to think before you said something; people were likely to push you to answer *right now*. Cashel's mind didn't work that way, that quick, unless there was danger. Besides, it seemed to him that the folks who were quickest with words were likely to be the last folks you wanted beside you when danger came at you—out of the woods, up from the sea, or maybe roaring down through the heavens like just now.

Lord Martous stood nearby. The barge wasn't so big that you could be on it and not be close to everybody else who was, but he was kind of pretending that he wasn't anywhere in shouting distance of Cashel and the prince. Martous hadn't been best pleased when Protas asked Cashel to come ashore with him, but whatever he'd started to say dried up when Protas gave him a look.

Chances were Martous had done pretty much as he pleased in the past, with Cervoran off in his own world of studies and Protas a boy whose father didn't pay him a lot of attention. Things were different now, and Martous was smart enough to see that. Maybe Cashel standing behind the prince like a solid wall had helped the fellow understand.

Cashel didn't like bullies. Cashel particularly didn't like folks bullying children, even if they weren't being especially mean about it.

Sharina had said for Cashel to go along with Protas on the barge. He guessed it had something to do with the politics she and Garric and the others had been talking about to Martous, but Cashel couldn't be sure. She might've just been being nice to the boy.

Sharina *was* a really nice person—and smart too, smarter than a lot of people thought so pretty a woman could be. He'd seen it happen with fellows, treating Sharina like she didn't have anything behind her blue eyes except fluff and then bam! learning she'd been two steps ahead of them the whole way.

The palace sat on a platform built up from the edge of the harbor. Most of the frontage was a limestone seawall with statues—Cashel counted them out on his fingers: six statues—set up along it. The bronze was old enough to be green, but that didn't take long in salt air.

The barge was pulling up to where a ladder with broad wooden rungs was set into the wall. The big wave had swept off the bunting and almost swamped the boat.

Cashel grinned, thinking about Martous huffing and puffing up the ladder to reach dry land. It wasn't a bad climb, not as much as a man's height, but chances were it wasn't a kind of exercise the courtier got very often.

The palace itself was a series of long buildings with colonnades facing the sea across a strip of lawn. Behind the ones on the seafront were other buildings with two or three stories; all the roofs were red tile. The lawn must've taken a lot of work to keep so smooth.

In the cities Cashel'd visited before, swatches of green were planted with flowers and fruit trees. Back in the borough, of course, anything that wasn't fenced off for a kitchen garden had been pecked and trampled to bare clay. It was all a matter of taste, Cashel knew, but so far as *his* taste went grass ought to be in a meadow with sheep grazing.

Lord Martous yipped little orders to the barge crew, which they seemed to be ignoring. Two of them tossed lines ashore to servants who snubbed them on bollards, then leaned into the ropes. That took the shock of stopping the barge in a few hand's breadths and sucked it against the seawall.

Cashel'd known what was coming. He spread his feet, butted his staff down on the deck, and put his free hand on Protas' shoulder. The boy swayed. Martous yelped as he fell forward and had to grab the ladder; the servant stumbling into his back didn't help his temper any either.

Protas turned and looked up at Cashel with wide eyes. "Could you lift me up to the ground, Cashel?" he said.

Cashel chuckled. He turned his staff crossways and said, "Sit on it, then, between my hands. No, face away from me."

"What are you doing?" said Lord Martous. "Oh my goodness, you mustn't—"

Lifting wouldn't have been enough unless the prince crawled onto the stonework. Instead Cashel launched him, lobbed him like a bale being offloaded. The boy cried in delight, but when he landed he overbalanced and went down on all fours. There was no harm done, though.

Protas hopped to his feet again and turned, dusting his palms and grinning wider than he had since Cashel met him.

"Oh, Cashel!" he cried. "I wish I could be as strong as you!"

"You don't have your growth yet, Protas," Cashel said. "Anyhow, it was no great thing."

Nor was it; the boy was small for his age. Half the men in Barca's Hamlet could've done what Cashel just had, if not quite so easily.

He had to admit the praise from a nobleman pleased him, though. Granted, a young nobleman; but one born to the rank, not like he'd have been if he let people call him "Lord Cashel." It was funny that something he didn't want for himself looked like a big thing in another fellow.

"Let me show you around the palace, Cashel!" Protas said cheerfully. In a colder tone he added, "Lord Martous, kindly take yourself out of Cashel's way so he can join me."

Martous, still holding on to the ladder with a dumbfounded expression, opened his eyes wide in dismay and irritation. "I—" he said. "I don't—"

A servant touched him on the arm and eased him back from the ladder. Martous didn't fight the contact, but he didn't seem to know what was going on. This'd been a hard afternoon for the poor fellow.

Cashel climbed carefully, placing his feet near the ladder's uprights. Salt and sunlight ate the strength out of wood, and if he bounced his weight down in the middle of the rungs chances were he'd break them to kindling.

He could've set his staff on top of the seawall to wait for him, but instead he held it between his right thumb and little finger and used the other three to climb with. Nothing was likely to happen that he'd need the staff for; it was just a habit. Besides, "not likely to happen" wasn't the same as "couldn't happen."

A dozen royal vessels were already hauled up on shore within the harbor. The crews had made room by tossing out of the way cargo waiting to be loaded on merchant ships and pushing down sheds.

That was inconvenient for the folks who lived in Mona, but traveling around with Garric had taught Cashel that it *always* was inconvenient to have an army come calling. It was just one of those things, like winter storms or your sheep getting scrapie. He figured the locals understood that, or anyway they knew better than to make too big a fuss about it.

Four wooden wharfs reached out a little way into the harbor. They were big enough for small merchant ships, tubs with one mast and a crew of half a dozen, but they were no good for warships that had to be brought up out of the water every night. Otherwise their thin hulls'd get waterlogged and rot before you knew it.

Mona didn't seem to be a very busy place; that fit in with Sharina saying that First Atara pretty much kept to itself. The goods Cashel saw were mostly salt fish in barrels and barley packed in burlap sacks instead of big terra-cotta jars like grain came into Valles down canals from northern Ornifal.

The pottery packed in wicker baskets had likely been landed from other islands but not moved out of the way before the fleet arrived. The owners were probably moaning about it now, but they'd soon learn that Prince Garric paid for the damages he knew there'd be just as sure as the sun rose.

"Oh . . . ," said Protas, looking about the harbor, his eyes wide. "Oh. . . . I don't think I've *ever* seen so many people. At one time."

Cashel grinned, following the line of the boy's eyes. Soldiers swarmed over the foreshore and more were packed aboard ships waiting to unload.

"I never saw a place with more houses together than you could count on your fingers and toes till I went the first time to Carcosa," he said. "That was like seeing the sea, only all the little wave tops were people. I didn't know there could be that many people."

The ships that had landed first were starting to slide back into the water, making room for new arrivals. Protas frowned and said, "What's happening, Cashel? Why did these warships come in if they're just going to leave again?"

"Well, they're not warships exactly," Cashel said. "They're triremes, all right, but they're only rowed from one set of benches. The other two have soldiers on them—or they carry cargo, of course, but all of these have soldiers. They're putting them ashore to, well, in case there's something that'd be dangerous to G—to Prince Garric. The rowers will haul them out again a little ways off so there's room for others to unload."

Two years ago Cashel hadn't seen a trireme or heard the word, but here he was talking about them like he was a sailor himself. Well, he wasn't; but he'd learned enough by being around Garric to answer the boy's question. He wasn't a weaver either, but Ilna's brother knew something about cloth.

"What danger could there be in Mona?" Protas said in puzzlement.

"Well, not from you folks," Cashel said. "But things do happen, that's so. It isn't that Garric worries; but you know, the people around him have their own ways of doing things and he's too polite to make a big fuss about it."

Lord Martous had gotten to the top of the ladder, helped by two of the servants who'd climbed up ahead of him. Protas glanced at the fellow and said, "Yes, I see that." He cleared his throat and added, "Well, come along, Cashel, and I'll show you the inside."

Protas set off for the nearest portico. Cashel paused just long enough to wave his left hand toward Sharina and his other friends on the *Shepherd of the Isles,* easing toward a wharf with a lot of angry shouting from the sailing master. Two sailors in the ship's bow held a long board covered with red cloth.

The aides and stewards with Garric didn't think it was right that the prince should climb over the side and splash to shore in the shallows. They'd made a gangplank, probably a hatch cover that they'd nailed a cloak onto or something of the sort. Like Cashel'd said, the folks around Garric had their own ways of doing things.

Soldiers milled around everywhere, but they were all part of the royal army who'd just landed. All the local people standing in the colonnades gaping at the fleet or hanging from the upper-story windows that overlooked the harbor were civilians. The women wore blouses and trousers same as the men did but they also had bonnets, some of them dangling with ribbons.

Nobody seemed to stand much on ceremony, even here in the palace. Cashel didn't feel at home, exactly—he never would with this many people around. But he didn't feel near so out of place as he did back in Valles.

Protas led Cashel through the portico and into the tall building on the other side. They were connected with a little covered walk; a dogtrot, Cashel would've called it back at home, but he supposed it had a fancier name if it was made of stone and the ceiling was painted with girls and bearded men with fish tails who swam with a sea serpent.

"King Cervoran's apartments are up on the top of this building," Protas said. A servant curtsied to him as they walked through the central hall; there were stairs up on either side of the room. "My rooms are in the east wing. Where will they put you, Cashel?"

"Protas, I couldn't say," Cashel said. He thought about adding, "Close to Sharina is all that matters," but he decided he wouldn't. There wasn't much privacy either in a palace or a village like Barca's Hamlet, but Cashel wasn't one to talk about things that weren't anybody else's business.

They went right on through to the other side of the building. There was a big plaza here, bare dirt but with occasional clumps of tough grass managing to survive.

"This is where we hold the first-day markets every week," Protas explained. "The farmers come in from the fields with produce, and people in Mona sell what they've made too."

There were new-made bleachers along the south edge; the wood was still raw and some planks oozed sap. That was nothing compared to the three-layer pyramid in the middle of the plaza, though. It'd been built from brushwood hurdles covered with boards and bunting. On the very top was a chest or cabinet that'd been draped with cloth of gold. Something lay on it, but Cashel couldn't tell what from down below.

The boy stopped and looked at Cashel, apparently expecting him to say something. He didn't know what that should be, so he asked, "What's that, Protas?"

"That's the pyre," Protas said. "Tomorrow it'll be lighted and King Cervoran will rise to the heavens. He'll be a god, then."

The boy looked desperately unhappy. Cashel put an arm on his shoulder and turned them both back toward the building they'd walked through.

"Let's see if we can find Princess Sharina," he said quietly. It was the first thing he could think of that didn't involve looking at a wizard's corpse.

"THIS IS THE queen's suite, ah, Princess," said Lord Martous. He pulled open the door to the left at the head of the stairs. "It hasn't been used in, well, twelve years since the late queen passed over in childbirth, but I directed that it be aired out and put in order as soon as we learned that . . . I hope you find it . . ."

Sharina stepped into the suite. Tenoctris and Cashel, the latter carrying the satchel with the paraphernalia of the old wizard's art, followed her and Martous at a polite distance. Cashel was his usual calm, solid self, but Tenoctris was as silently tense as a cat sure there's a mouse hiding somewhere nearby.

The suite had a short entrance passage, three main rooms, and a curtained alcove for a servant; she and Cashel wouldn't be needing that last.

There was a hint of mildew in the air, but the walls were freshly washed. They were age-darkened oak wainscoting below a waist-high molding with frescoes of fanciful landscapes from there to the ceiling. The damp had lifted out patches of plaster, leaving white blotches.

Cashel smiled. "I like wall paintings," he said.

"I'm sorry about the water damage," Martous said in a tight voice, "but there wasn't time to order repairs. The funeral and coronation had to be the first priority, I'm sure you see."

"I like where the plaster's gone, too," Cashel said. "It looks kind of like clouds are drifting over the hills."

Sharina didn't let her smile reach her lips. Lord Martous almost certainly thought Cashel was being sarcastic. Cashel was never sarcastic. Moreover, he had the perfect innocence that protected him from other people's sarcasm. What somebody else would recognize as a cutting remark struck Cashel as praise, often from an unexpected quarter.

"Yes, this will be satisfactory," Sharina said in a coolly neutral voice. She knew the chamberlain's type well enough to be sure that he'd want to talk—and argue—longer than she'd want to be in his company. That meant the less said, the better.

Sharina'd been raised in a garret of her father's inn, and during her travels since leaving Barca's Hamlet she'd slept rough in hedges and on the bare stone floors of dungeons. She'd been in bigger, better-appointed palaces than this one, but it was nonetheless a palace.

The central room was lighted by a glazed dome in the ceiling; the two smaller rooms on the north wall had beds, the only furniture in the suite. Martous probably assumed that the royal party traveled with complete furnishings. That wasn't correct: Prince Garric's expedition from Ornifal to the islands of the west and north was diplomatic, a Royal Progress rather than a military campaign—but it could become a military campaign in a heartbeat. Garric traveled as light as his ancestor King Carus had. While his aides and servants might complain about the simplicity, his sister didn't mind in the least.

"Where does that go?" Tenoctris asked, looking at the door in the west wall. With her fingers tented before her, she looked more than ever like a cat hunting.

"That leads to King Cervoran's apartments," Martous said heavily. "I've assigned them to Prince Garric, though I really wish he'd found time to approve the choice. Now, Princess, I hope you'll come with me and—"

"In a moment, Lord Martous," Sharina said. She walked to the door and opened it, finding another door behind it. That wasn't locked either; she pushed it open. Beyond were royal servants arranging chests they'd brought up from the harbor. Trousered local people looked on and tried to help.

Sharina moved aside as Tenoctris stepped briskly past with Cashel at her elbow. He grinned at Sharina as he went by, as placid and unobtrusive as a well-trained pack pony. Of course, if trouble arose, Cashel was more like a lion.

Ignoring Lord Martous' chatter, Sharina surveyed Garric's suite. She found herself frowning. There was nothing she could point to, but—

"I won't speak for my brother," Sharina said, "but personally I don't think that I'd be comfortable in these quarters. What other rooms can he use?"

At the moment Garric was with Liane and his chief military and civil advisors in what'd been a courtroom in an adjacent building; they were consulting with Ataran finance officials. Part of the reason Martous was peevish was that he had nothing useful to add to such an assembly. Lord Tadai had told him so in a tone of polished disdain that'd crushed his protests more effectively than the snarling ill temper Lord Waldron had been on the verge of unleashing.

Sharina could've been present if she'd wanted to be. She hadn't, and seeing to living arrangements and plans for Lord Protas' coronation the next morning was a better use of her time from the kingdom's standpoint besides. Tenoctris had asked to accompany her, and Cashel had joined them after he handed Lord Protas off to his tutors. Cashel's own lack of education had made him more, not less, convinced of its value.

"I don't understand what you mean!" the chamberlain said. His horrified reaction was the first time Sharina recalled hearing something that could be described as high dudgeon. "Why, these are the finest rooms in the palace, the finest rooms in the kingdom! They were the king's rooms!"

"They were a wizard's rooms," said Tenoctris, seating herself cross-legged on the floor. Cashel set her satchel beside her, open; she took from it a bundle of yarrow stalks wrapped in a swatch of chamois leather. "The work Cervoran did here leaves traces behind which can be felt by people who aren't themselves wizards. It affects Princess Sharina, and it might very well affect Prince Garric."

The queen's suite had a floor of boards laid edgewise and planed smooth, solid and warm to the feet even without a layer of carpets over it. The king's side of the building had probably started out the same, but at some point a layer of slates had raised it an inch. Words and figures had been drawn on the floor in a variety of media: chalks, paints, and colored powders. The fine-grained stone retained them as ghostly images.

"Really!" said Martous. "It wouldn't be proper to place Prince Garric anywhere else. These are the royal apartments!"

"Protas said his father didn't use spells to hurt other people, Tenoctris," Cashel said. "Was the boy wrong, then?"

Tenoctris held the yarrow stalks in the circuit of her right thumb and forefinger. She cocked her head quizzically toward Cashel with a expression.

"No," she said, "I think Cervoran was interested in knowledge for its own sake rather than for any wealth or power it could bring him. I'm of a similar mind myself, so I can sympathize. Only . . . only I've gained most of my knowledge by reading the accounts written by greater wizards than I. Cervoran searched very deeply into the fabric of things himself. He gathered artifacts as well as knowledge—"

She nodded toward a rank of drawer-fronted cabinets against the west wall. Above them hung a tapestry worked mostly in green. It showed a garden in which mythical animals strutted among the hedgerows.

"—and stored them here. To me these rooms are a clutching tangle, like being thrown into briars. Even to laymen, at least to a sensitive layman like Sharina, I expect this would be evident and uncomfortable."

"It's like shelling peas in bed," Sharina said, speaking precisely to emphasize her point, "and then lying down on the husks. Milord, I've become *quite* sure that my brother will require other accommodations."

"This is very unfortunate," the chamberlain said, hugging himself in obvious discomfort. Sharina couldn't tell whether he was complaining about her decision or if he felt the whirling sharpness of ancient spells also. Martous might not know himself. "Very. Well. I'll give orders. There are rooms in the west wing, though that'll mean . . ."

He caught himself and straightened. "Be that as it may," he resumed in a businesslike tone. "Are you ready to go over the arrangements for the apotheosis and coronation, in lieu of the prince?"

"Tenoctris?" Sharina asked. The old wizard was looking into a drawer she'd just opened, holding her hands crossed behind her back as if to prove that she had no intention of touching the contents. The yarrow stalks lay on the floor where she'd been sitting. So far as Sharina could see, they'd fallen in a meaningless jumble.

Tenoctris pushed the drawer shut. She looked up and said, "I'm done for the moment. There's nothing acute to be dealt with, though—"

She turned her head toward the chamberlain with her usual birdlike quickness.

"—Lord Martous, I suggest you have these rooms closed until I've had time to go over the collection. There's nothing that I'd consider dangerous in itself, but there are a number of items which could be harmful if misused. Also there's a chance they could draw *actively* dangerous things to them."

The servants had stopped working and moved to the south wall when Cashel and Sharina entered. Sharina made a quick decision and said to the steward in charge, "Master Tinue, please move Prince Garric's impedimenta back out of here and carry it to the west wing. Lord Martous will give you specific directions. I'm ordering this on my authority."

"I'll take them!" one of the locals said eagerly. She looked at Martous and said, "You want them in the rooms over the old banquet hall, that's right, isn't it?"

"Yes, yes," said the chamberlain unhappily. The locals were already grabbing chests with far more enthusiasm than they'd showed previously. "If the princess insists, we have no choice."

He shook his head as the servants bustled out. "It won't be hard to keep them away from this suite if that's what you want," he said in a low, bitter tone, the first hint that Sharina'd heard that he had normal human emotions. "The problem was getting them to go in and clean the suite decently. And King Cervoran was no help, no help at all! He didn't seem to care if cobwebs and dust covered everything!"

"I can imagine that would be frustrating," Sharina said with honest sympathy. "Regardless, the real uncleanness was a result of your master's art rather than mere dirt, so the lack of ordinary cleaning didn't make much difference. There'll be time to correct the problem after Lord Protas becomes marquess."

Sharina'd been chambermaid in her father's inn while she was growing up. It was a job you could only do well if you convinced yourself that it mattered, that you were really making the world better instead of performing a meaningless ritual which the events of the coming night would completely undo. Martous didn't have her personal experience with the work of cleaning, but they could agree that it was a worthy end in itself.

"Yes, of course," the chamberlain said. He opened both hands in a gesture that was just short of shooing the visitors to the connecting door. "We'll do that now."

Tenoctris bent to retrieve her yarrow stalks; age asserted itself and the motion caught halfway through. Cashel touched her shoulder to indicate he was taking over, then swept up the spill with his left hand. He handed the stalks to Tenoctris, then lifted the satchel while she wrapped them again.

Martous opened and closed his mouth. He was obviously fuming, but he had enough control not to say something which, when ignored, would underscore his complete lack of importance.

"I thought a divination might direct me to the source of the power that surrounds us here," Tenoctris said, shaking her head wryly as she put the stalks away. "It completely overwhelms me. I can't determine a direction."

"You mean which object in Cervoran's collection is causing it?" Sharina said as they returned to the queen's suite. Her servants were opening the sole chest of clothing that accompanied her.

"Cervoran didn't have any talisman of such weight as this," Tenoctris said. Her voice was carefully emotionless, which probably meant that she was worried. "This is . . . a very serious business. I don't call it a threat, but the thing around us is so enormously powerful that we're in danger even if it isn't hostile."

She smiled cheerfully, breaking her own mood. "A hailstorm isn't hostile to the flowers in a garden," she added. "But it will flatten them anyway."

"You'll find a way out, Tenoctris," Cashel said calmly. It wasn't bravado when he spoke: it was the belief of a mind so pure and simple that no one listening could doubt the truth of the words. "And we'll help you, like we have other times."

Sharina gripped Cashel's left biceps and hugged herself to him. It wasn't the conduct expected of a princess in public, but it was what she needed just now.

"Not that way please," said Martous as Sharina and her companions moved toward the door to the stairs. He gestured toward the north facing room with the bed. "I can explain better from the balcony."

Sharina led. The chamberlain seemed to expect it, and Cashel as a matter of course brought up the rear—unless he thought there might be trouble ahead. It was the position from which he'd badgered flocks along the road. Sharina suspected Cashel felt much the same way about her and Tenoctris as he had for the sheep for which he'd been responsible back in the borough.

The balcony ran the full breadth of the room, but it was narrow front to back. It was plaster-covered, but the way it creaked under even Sharina's slight weight suggested that it was built from wattle and daub; the hollow clack she got from a rap of her knuckles confirmed the suspicion. An outside staircase led down to a plaza.

"Cashel?" she said doubtfully, looking over her shoulder as Tenoctris and the chamberlain joined her on the balcony.

Still standing in the solid-floored bedroom, he grinned. "I guess it'd hold me," he said. "But I don't see that it needs to now."

"I had a stand built for the gentlemen and ladies of the kingdom," Martous explained, gesturing toward the plaza. "Now that you're here, I suppose some of you Ornifal nobles will share it. And of course the two princes will be in the center of the lowest tier. I'm having another throne built for Prince Garric."

By "gentlemen and ladies of the kingdom," he means the gentry of First Atara, Sharina translated mentally. She kept her lips neutrally together. It wouldn't be proper to snarl at the chamberlain's pretensions, but that might be less offensive than laughing at him as she'd come close to doing.

The plaza spread broadly, covering perhaps ten acres without permanent buildings. On three sides of it were tents and kiosks, and to the south were bleachers—the stand Martous referred to.

In the center of the plaza was a pile of brushwood nearly as big as the palace. On top of it, just lower than the eyes of those on the balcony, lay a corpse on a bier of gold cloth.

Despite the distance, Sharina could see that the dead man had been middle-aged; he was balding though not bald, and plump without being really fat. His cheeks were rouged, but the flesh was already beginning to slump from them. Silver coins covered both eyes.

"When Lady Liane has a moment, she'll give you direction as to the seating arrangements," Sharina said firmly. "She has an excellent grasp of protocol, and I do not. She'll consult with Lord Attaper, the commander of the royal guard, and I advise you not to argue with the decisions they make."

She cleared her throat. "There will be provision for guards," she added. "Probably more guards than you think—" *Or anybody not himself a bodyguard thinks,* Sharina added in her heart. "—is necessary or even conceivable."

"If you say so," the chamberlain said. He added fretfully, "Time is very short, you realize."

Sharina realized that perfectly well, so she didn't comment. It was proper that the chamberlain should have his own priorities, but those weren't the priorities of the Kingdom of the Isles as personified in Prince Garric and his closest advisors.

Tenoctris glanced at the corpse, then turned her attention to the shacks and tents around the edges of the plaza. Country folk had raised them for shelter, in some cases forming little hamlets of half a dozen families around a single cook fire. Peddlers and wine sellers moved through the crowd, either carrying their stores on their backs or accompanied by a porter or a donkey. The gathering had more the atmosphere of a fair than a funeral.

A fence of palings and rope picked out with tufts of scarlet wool marked off an area the width of a bowshot around the pyre. There were no guards to enforce the boundary. Either the peasants of First Atara were unusually obedient folk, or they understood just how big the blaze would be and had better sense than to come too close.

Tenoctris fixed the chamberlain with her quick eyes. "Do the ceremonies you've mentioned involve wizardry?" she asked.

"Oh, good heavens, no!" Martous said. "We're not that sort of people here on First Atara."

He paused, connecting what he'd just said with what he and the visitors knew of the late king. "Ah," he said. "Well, King Cervoran was, of course, but that was him. His father raised show rabbits, you know. My first job in the palace was as page of the rabbits. Ah. Really, there was no harm in the king, just, well, interest. And there's nothing of the sort in the apotheosis ceremony, not at all."

Patting his hands together to close the discussion in his mind, Martous continued, "The ceremony actually started before you arrived in Mona. A delegation of nobles carried the late king from the palace while choruses of boys and girls lined the path to the pyre, singing hymns to the Lady."

He frowned. "The boys' chorus might've been better rehearsed," he admitted, "and there was some difficulty with the staircase up the front of the pyre, but I think things went well enough given how short my time was. Quite well!"

Sharina smiled. The staircase Martous mentioned was a steep contrivance with notched logs for stringers and treads also fashioned from logs with an adze rather than a saw. Cloth runners—muslin dyed shades of red ranging from russet to pale pink—made the stairs presentable from a distance but also made them harder to climb.

Sharina supposed it hadn't seemed reasonable to waste effort on the details of something meant to burn in a day or two. The person making the decision—probably the chamberlain himself—might've considered the problem a group of out-of-condition country squires would have climbing the structure while carrying a laden bier, however.

"Tomorrow morning at the ceremony," Martous continued, "Prince Protas will light the pyre. I do hope it goes well. The brush had to be bundled while it was still green, I'm afraid. If only we'd had more notice about the king's health so that we could've started preparations sooner!"

"King Cervoran appears to have been very remiss," Sharina said. She was making a pointed joke to remind the chamberlain to *think* about what he was saying. He merely nodded agreement, too lost in his own concerns to have any awareness of the wider world.

"After the fire's been lighted," Martous said, "Protas will throw on a lock of his hair. I've already had one prepared by the palace hairdresser so that there'll be no problem there. The chief nobles will file across the front of the pyre and sprinkle incense."

He looked sharply at Sharina as though she'd suddenly become interesting. "How many of you Ornifal nobles will be joining the procession? A rough number, if you please?"

"None," said Sharina. "And I must remind you that we're the delegation of the kingdom, not of the island of Ornifal alone. I, for example, am Princess Sharina of *Haft*."

"Ah," said Martous. "Ah, yes."

He turned his face toward the plaza, pressing his lips out and in several times. At last he continued, "The choruses will perform during the ceremony. I *do* hope we won't have a repetition of the regrettable business with the boys singing that they're 'impure with vices' as they did during the presentation. Anyway, when nobles have finished casting incense and the pyre is burning properly, a dove symbolizing the late king's soul will be released from beside Prince Protas' throne—"

"From the throne rather than from the pyre itself?" Tenoctris asked. "When I've seen this sort of ceremony in the past . . . ?"

"Well, there was a problem with the cage opening during the rites of the late king's father," the chamberlain admitted. "In fact, some of the . . . the more superstitious members of the populace ascribed King Cervoran's devotion to wizardry to, well, that problem. This is foolishness, of course, but I decided not to take a chance on having it happen again."

Tenoctris nodded. "My parents would've been glad of an excuse on which to blame my interests," she said. "In their hearts, I'm sure they were afraid it was their fault. Though so far as I've ever been able to tell, there's nothing more mystical about skill at wizardry than there is in preferring fish over mutton."

"As soon as the dove has flown . . . ," Martous said. He was looking at Tenoctris as he spoke, his eyes wide, but he suddenly flushed and jerked them back to the pyre. "As soon as that's happened, I say, Prince Garric will stand and crown Prince Protas with the ancient topaz diadem—he'll be holding that through the rites. There'll be a general acclamation. I hope—"

He looked coldly at Sharina.

"—that we may expect the *royal* party to join in the acclamation?"

"You may," Sharina said in a neutral voice.

Lord Martous took a deep breath. "Then," he said, clasping his hands, "I believe we're ready for the ceremony. Except for the seating arrangements. If you don't mind, I'll take my leave now. I need to talk with the master of the boys' choir."

"I hope your discussions go well, milord," Sharina said, but the chamberlain was already halfway to the door.

She knew she should feel more charitable toward him. Only a fussy little fellow concerned with trivia could've made a good chamberlain. Given that, Martous was more than competent.

Tenoctris faced the pyre, but Sharina couldn't tell where the old wizard's mind was. "How do the arrangements strike you, Tenoctris?" she asked.

"What?" the wizard said, falling back into the present. "Oh. The arrangements seem perfectly regular. A little ornate for so—"

She smiled.

"—rural a place, but one finds that sort of thing in backwaters . . . if you'll forgive my prejudices. I've always been more comfortable in communities that value books over turnips."

"I'm glad to hear it's all right," Sharina said. "I was worried that something might happen."

"So am I, my dear," Tenoctris said. "The human arrangements are regular, as I said; but I'm by no means sure that we humans will have the final say in what happens tomorrow."

*T*HE COMBINED SIGNALERS of the royal army, some fifty men with either straight trumpets or horns coiled about their bodies, stopped playing at a signal from Liane. It seemed to Garric that the plaza still trembled. Even so there was only an instant's pause before the combined signalers of the fleet, fifty more men determined to outdo their army counterparts, took up the challenge.

Garric groaned, looking down at the topaz crown resting on a pillow in his lap. The images in the heart of the yellow stone danced in the play of the sun. He hid a grimace and leaned to his left, bringing his lips close to Sharina's ear. He had to be careful because he was wearing his dress helmet, a silvered casque from which flared gilt wings.

"I should never have allowed them to do this," Garric said. "It was Lord Tadai's idea, a way that we could contribute something unique to the funeral ceremonies, but it's *awful*."

"The locals seem to like it," said Sharina. He more read the words on her smiling lips than heard them. "I'm sure they've never heard anything like it before."

Neither had Garric, though some really severe winter storms had been almost as deafeningly bad. The signalers were skilled beyond question, but they and their instruments were intended to blare commands through the chaos of battle. It was remarkable what they could do when grouped together and filled with a spirit of rivalry.

But as Sharina'd said, the islanders filling the plaza seemed to love it. That went for both country folk and the residents of Mona itself. City dwellers on First Atara tended to sew bright-colored ribbons on their dress garments, but there wasn't as much distinction between urban and rural as there would've been on Ornifal or even Haft.

Sharina wore court robes of silk brocade with embroidery and a cloth-of-gold appliqué to make them even stiffer and heavier. Garric's molded and silvered breastplate wasn't comfortable, but at least it wouldn't prevent him from swinging a sword. The court robes were far more restrictive.

Normally Liane would be seated slightly back of his left side, formally his aide because she wasn't legally his consort. They'd planned the wedding over a year before—but events had prevented the ceremony, and further events had pushed it back again. The royal wedding would be an important symbol that the Kingdom of the Isles was truly united for the first time in a thousand years. . . .

But before he claimed the symbol, Garric had to create the reality. He grinned. Kingship was much more complicated that it'd seemed when he read Rigal's epic *Cariad*. The hero Car had fought many enemies, both human and supernatural, in founding his kingdom, but he'd never had to settle a wrangle between the Duke of Blaise and the Earl of Sandrakkan as to the order of precedence of their regiments when the royal army was in full array.

"I could handle that for you, lad," said the image of King Carus, shaking his head in rueful memory. *"Nobody argued with me about anything to do with the battle line because they knew I'd take their head off if they did. Unfortunately I dealt with tax commissioners pretty much the same way, and I can't tell you how much trouble that caused."*

Today Liane was in charge of the royal involvement in the funeral and apotheosis rites. She had an instinctive feel for protocol and precedence, what should or shouldn't be done in a formal setting. That was a better use of her talents than sitting beside Garric and calming him by her presence; but he half-wished now that he'd left the arrangements to one of Lord Tadai's stewards.

The shrieking of horns and trumpets halted. Choruses of boys and girls came forward from behind the bleachers. The youngest singers were only six or so, and the choir masters and assistants trying to keep the lines in order looked more harassed than the children did. It was almost time to light the pyre.

Lord Protas was to Garric's right; Lord Martous was whispering to him. The boy looked stiff and uncomfortable, but that's how he'd looked ever since Garric met him on the *Shepherd*. Garric realized with a touch of sadness that a twelve-year-old boy whose father had just died was an obvious subject for sympathy, but he—Prince Garric of Haft—had none to spare.

Protas seemed biddable. He could take over the government of First

Atara with the "advice" of a commissioner from Valles, leaving one fewer problem for Prince Garric to concern himself with.

"There's nothing wrong with sympathy," said King Carus, standing on the balcony of a tower that might never have existed. *"And don't pretend that you lack it. The trouble comes from letting sympathy keep you from doing what has to be done. Anger does less harm than false kindness; and I've got plenty of experience of how much harm anger does."*

Martous handed Protas a glass bowl in a filigreed framework; it held a pine torch lying on a bed of sand which'd been soaked with oil. Sluggish flames wobbled from the sand as well as the pine.

"Go, Your Highness!" the chamberlain snapped. "Don't delay the ceremonies!"

Garric put his right hand on the boy's shoulder and squeezed it, smiling at him. He didn't speak. Protas nodded appreciatively, then got up and started across the broad cleared space toward the pyre. His back was straight and his stride firm except for one little stumble.

"No sympathy!" repeated King Carus with a gust of laughter.

Tenoctris sat cross-legged on the ground beside the bleachers where she'd asked to be. A lifetime of studies with no servants and little money had made her adept at making do with what was available. There was almost always a floor, but chairs and stools were harder to come by; she'd gotten into the habit of drawing her words and symbols of art on the surface she sat on.

Garric glanced at the old wizard. She was muttering an incantation over a figure drawn on ground packed hard by the feet of generations of buyers, sellers, and spectators. The bundle of yarrow stalks lay by her left knee and a vellum scroll was partly unrolled to her right, but she didn't appear to be using either one.

The four Blood Eagles detailed to guard Tenoctris formed an armored U shape on all sides of her but in front. They kept their eyes on the crowd and possible threats rather than looking at what Tenoctris was doing, but her wizardry didn't seem to worry them the way it would most laymen. Lord Attaper had learned to pick the wizard's guards from those who knew something about the art: men who'd had a nanny who worked spells or whose father's cousin was a cunning man back in their home village, that sort of thing.

Cashel stood behind Sharina's throne, as placid as a resting ox and as impressively big at a quick glance. When Garric's eye caught him, he smiled softly. He was unique among folk dressed in splashy finery: his tunics were plain except for a curling pattern in subtle browns that Ilna had woven into the hems.

Spectators who'd seen Cashel brought their eyes back to him, though. That was partly because of the simple elegance of the man and his costume, but also because of that woven pattern. No fabric that Ilna wove was *only* a piece of cloth.

Protas had covered most of the distance between his throne and the base of the pyre. Liane signaled the commanders of the ad hoc military bands; they in turn snapped commands to their units and raised the tools they used for directing. The fleet's music master had a slim silver baton, but his army counterpart used the long straight sword he carried as a cavalry officer. The musicians lifted horns and trumpets to their lips.

Light trembled over the instruments of brass and silver and even gold. Tenoctris glanced up; Garric followed her eyes. The sound of the second meteor, for now only a rasping undertone, reached his ears as he saw the fluctuating light and looked quickly away.

"May the Shepherd guard me!" a man called in a high-pitched voice.

The signalers blew together. For a moment, the shriek of their instruments filled the air, but the thunder of the oncoming meteor overwhelmed even that raucous blast. People throughout the crowd were shouting though their voices went unheard, and the ancient king in Garric's mind said, *"Sister swallow me if it isn't coming straight at us!"*

Protas didn't stop or look up. Lifting the torch from the bowl in which it rested, he touched it to the fagots. Yellow flames spread too swiftly for green wood: the bundled brush had been soaked with oil. Protas backed a step and paused, then hurled the burning bowl onto the pyre also. It shattered on the steps, igniting the red muslin.

The meteor exploded unthinkably high in the heavens. For a moment there was only the flash; then the sound reached the crowd, throwing everyone to the ground. Garric felt himself lifted, then slammed down hard. The crudely built throne cracked under his weight, and the casque bashed his forehead.

He stood up. His ears rang and he felt each heartbeat throb in his skull. There was a stunned silence over the plaza, relieved by the sounds of prayers and sobbing. The fire was beginning to bite on the funeral pyre. A crackling indicated that the olive oil and beeswax had ignited the wood.

Garric looked at the topaz crown in his left hand. His grip had twisted the soft gold circlet, but the big stone was more vividly a diamond. The things moving in the brightness were no longer ows but streaks of flame spinning sunwise around the white-hot hea the stone.

Garric was spinning: not his body but his mind. He felt the suction and tried to throw down the topaz, but he couldn't open his grip. Voices cried wordlessly like a winter storm.

"Hold me!" Garric tried to say, but he couldn't make his lips move nor even form the words in his mind. The circles of light boring through his eyes wrenched his consciousness out of the waking world. He hovered for a moment above the plaza, watching his garments flatten on the ground where he'd been standing. His helmet bounced once and came to rest on its rim, the gilded wings shivering.

The plaza and the pyre were gone. Garric stood on a gray road, naked and alone, and fog swaddled his brain.

Ilna put her right arm over Merota's shoulders as what the girl called a meteor snarled like a landslide toward them through the bare sky. If it hit the plaza—and it certainly appeared that it was going to—there was nothing anyone could do that'd make a difference.

If Ilna'd been alone, she'd have taken lengths of yarn out of her left sleeve and begun knotting a pattern. She smiled wryly. Her powers were considerable but they didn't rise to ripping large rocks out of the sky, so that wouldn't have helped either. The work made her feel more content, though.

She wasn't alone. She was responsible for Merota, and though the girl was putting a brave face on it she was understandably terrified. Ilna wasn't going to fill her last moments of life with the knowledge that she'd just abandoned a frightened child.

She, Merota, and Chalcus had been seated on a middle row of the bleachers, down at the right end. The rows beneath them—three; she'd counted them off on her fingers as she stepped up—were the seats of the island nobility who were going to march up to the pyre and throw on incense. The rows above—two more—were nobles as well, but seated higher because they were less important and didn't have any duties during the funeral except to be part of the spectacle. They were rich farmers for the most part, judging by their talk and gaudy tastelessness.

Those folk were the problem now. They were trying to get to the

ic they probably wouldn't have cared if that
ʾoman and the ten-year-old girl in her charge.
ιalcus jumped onto his seat and faced them,
drawn. One fellow tried to push through any-
ιoved too quickly to see. The panicked local
ʾace and sprang back, three long gold chains
eachers. Blood from his slit nostril flickered in

Ilna's smile grew minusculely wider: Chalcus understood duty also.
If she was about to die, and it certainly seemed that she was, she was fortunate to do it at the side of a man in the best sense of the word.

The slingstone—the meteor, since Merota was educated and doubtless knew the right word—exploded high in the sky. Ilna's face was bent
down but she felt the flash on the backs of her hands. She braced herself
because she remembered what'd happened when the earlier meteor hit
the sea, but the shock wave this time was beyond anything she'd imagined.

Clutching Merota with one hand, Ilna turned an unintended cart-
wheel. The bleachers, raw wood beneath a drape of red muslin like the
steps up the pyre—had flexed down and then sprung back again. She
tried to grab Chalcus—for the contact rather than because it'd help in
any material way—but he was spinning off in a different direction.

Ilna, Merota, and several handfuls of other spectators crashed down
onto the bleachers together; boards broke. The whole structure collapsed
in a tangle of splinters and torn cloth.

Ilna jumped to her feet. The back of her right wrist was skinned, but
she wasn't really injured.

"Merota, are you hurt?" she said. The girl wrapped her arms around
Ilna's torso and sobbed into the bosom of her tunic.

People were shouting and crying, but only a few of them had real
injuries. A splinter as long as a sword blade had run through a middle-
aged woman's right calf. She stared at it in shocked amazement; Chalcus,
glancing first to see that Ilna and Merota were all right, knelt at the victim's side. He sheathed the sword he hadn't lost in the tumult, then used
the dagger to cut a length off his sash for a bandage or tourniquet.

Ilna looked around plaza. The troops who'd been formed by battal-
ions in a semicircle around the bleachers had fallen like tenpins, their armor and weapons clattering. Now they were picking themselves up and
dressing their ranks. Some soldiers were gray-faced with fear, but instead

of running they trusted their safety to discipline and their fellows just as they'd been trained to do.

Ilna supposed that sort of training was useful—for people who couldn't simply overcome their fears by willpower. She was afraid of many things: afraid of failure; afraid of making a fool of herself; afraid of her own anger. She wasn't in the least afraid of death.

The locals weren't as fast to get to their feet as the soldiers were, and when they did they often stumbled away from the plaza. Ilna didn't blame them: the air had a metallic taste, unpleasant and rough on the back of her throat.

Her ears rang from the blast, but she could hear sounds again. A local screamed and pointed toward the pyre. Other islanders turned to follow the line of his arm, then screamed in turn. Their drift became a panicked stampede.

Ilna looked at the pyre also. The lowest level was burning, though the green brushwood made smoky flames. They crackled like sea ice breaking on the coast in an inshore gale.

The bier at the top of the third stage was disarranged. The corpse got to its feet, dragging away the cloth-of-gold drapery. It swayed, wax-pale except where it was rouged, and took a step by pivoting its whole leg at the hip. Its mouth moved, but any words it spoke were lost in screams and the sound of the fire. The corpse took another step to the muslin-covered staircase, then a third.

"Help . . . ," it cried in a piping voice. It stumbled to its knees. "Me. . . ."

The flames were rising higher. The fire had taken hold slowly, but before long the brush would dry and turn the structure into a dancing, orange-red incandescence.

"I'm coming, Your Highness," called a plump man whose tunic and trousers were decorated with silver gores. It was Martous, the chamberlain; the man who'd sent the boy prince to ignite the pyre. He tried to go forward but stopped, paralyzed by fear and indecision.

Ilna weighed the situation coldly, as she did all things. She patted Merota's shoulder reassuringly, then gave the girl a little push in the direction of Chalcus. "Go to Chalcus, milady," she said. "Quickly now!"

The corpse got up again. It tried to walk and fell immediately, rolling down the stairs to the broader second stage. Flames were already licking up the wood on the adjacent side.

Ilna gathered her tunics above her knees and ran toward the pyre.

Cashel was watching over Sharina whose court dress hobbled her as effectively as leg-irons would. Chalcus was saving a woman who'd bleed to death without his help. That was slight recompense for the many lives he'd let out with his sword and less merciful means, but it was something—and besides, somebody had to watch Merota.

Garric was . . . Ilna didn't know where Garric was. All she could see as she ran was his unique winged helmet lying on the ground near his broken throne, and beside it a tunic reeved through his ornate cuirass.

Where is Garric? But the question could wait for now. Ilna reached the side staircase and started up.

The steps were uneven, forcing Ilna to look down at her feet instead of keeping her eyes on the man she was rescuing. The corpse. She supposed she shouldn't complain. Only a desire for symmetry had caused the islanders to put steps on all four sides to begin with. The flight up the front had been sufficient for the procession placing the bier.

Ilna'd never seen the point of funerals in the first place. All that remained when a person died was meat, and human flesh was as useless as fallen leaves in autumn. For sanitary purposes it had to be disposed of— in a hole, in a fire, or simply by throwing it into the sea.

She glanced up as she reached the top of the first tier: the late King Cervoran had gotten to his feet again and was wallowing down the middle flight of steps. "Help . . . ," he squeaked.

Ilna continued toward him. Apparently she'd been wrong about funerals. That wasn't her first mistake, but each one made her angry with herself.

She began breathing through her mouth. The wind shifted slightly and wreathed her in smoke; she felt the hair on the back of her neck shrivel.

"Me . . . ," the corpse said.

Close up King Cervoran still looked like a corpse of several days, but he was quite obviously alive. The coins that'd covered his eyes were gone. The whites and irises both had a yellowish hue, but the pupils were feverish and bright; they focused on Ilna.

Cervoran's lips were violet under the smear of the undertaker's rouge; the tongue between them was black. He repeated, "Help . . . me. . . ."

Peasants aren't squeamish. Ilna took Cervoran's left wrist in her hand and wrapped his arm over her shoulders. It was like handling warm wax which smelled of decay. She wondered if the arm would pull out at the shoulder; it didn't, at least not just now.

Heat hammered her as the fire roared to full life. A ball of flame flared at Ilna's side and vanished, an outrider of the main blaze. Before she started down, she pulled Cervoran along the tier to put the bulk of the pyramid between them and the fire. She could feel the back of her tunics searing and shrinking. The cloth would be brown and brittle after this, no use even for wiping rags.

Of course, that assumed there *was* an after. . . .

Cervoran didn't fight her, but he was barely able to keep his feet under him. She dragged him along. "Yes . . . ," he said. His voice wasn't loud, but it pierced like a bradawl.

They reached the staircase down the north side, opposite where the boy'd lighted the fire which was now waving like a banner over the bier. Ilna was beginning to feel Cervoran's weight in her knees.

Because this was a formal event she wore sandals, which she wouldn't normally do in weather so warm. She caught her left heel stepping down and had to throw her right leg out to keep from pitching onto her face with the former corpse on top of her. Cervoran twisted, trying to help but unable to move his legs quickly enough. It was like carrying a desperately sick man.

They were midway down the middle tier, some twenty feet above the ground, when Ilna felt the pyre collapse with a roar behind them. A column of sparks shot skyward, then mushroomed and rained back.

The pyramid was a stack of hurdles with no internal structure. When the flames ate away the bundled brushwood on the south, the whole thing fell toward the bleachers.

Ilna felt the staircase tilting backward. The stringers were lifting from the ground, threatening to catapult her and Cervoran back into the flames.

Ilna leaped off at an angle, pulling Cervoran along with a strength that'd have surprised anyone who hadn't seen her work a heavy double loom with the regularity of a windmill turning. Her right shoulder brushed the top of the lowest stage. The impact rolled her and her burden so that the late king hit the ground sideways an instant before she did.

There was a shock and a *smack* like a bundle of wet cloth thrown onto stone. Ilna rolled reflexively and was up again before she knew whether she'd been hurt by the fall.

She hadn't. The pyre was still tumbling into a state of repose, bales of brushwood rolling onto the blazing coals of those that'd ignited earlier. Men were shouting. A soldier tried to grab Ilna, but she slapped his hand away.

The chamberlain and another palace official caught King Cervoran under the arms and began carrying him away from the fire. The fall didn't seem to have hurt him, but that was hard to tell. Cervoran's legs moved as well as they had before. Ilna walked along through eddies of soldiers and a scattering of local civilians, looking for someone she recognized.

"I am . . . ," the late king said shrilly. "I am . . ."

"Your Highness?" said the chamberlain, his own voice rising. "You're King Cervoran."

"I am Cervoran!" the corpse cried. "I am Cervoran!"

"Ilna!" Liane said, catching Ilna's wrists in her hands. Garric's fiancée was usually composed, but her features had a set, frightened look now. "Have you seen Garric? What's happened to Garric?"

G ARRIC WALKED ONWARD, certain only that he had to keep moving. He didn't feel his bare feet touch the gravel, but he supposed they must be doing so.

He was walking toward a goal. He didn't know what it was or how far away it was, but he *knew* he had to go on. His head buzzed and his vision was blurry, and he kept putting one foot in front of the other.

There was a figure beside him. He wasn't sure how long it had accompanied him. He turned to it and tried to speak; his tongue seemed swollen.

"Who are you?" the figure asked. It was a man, but Garric couldn't make out his features or clothing because of the spiderweb clogging his eyes.

"I'm Garric," he said, forcing the words past his dry lips. "I'm Prince Garric of Haft, Lord of the Isles."

"Prince Garric?" said the other figure. It was leaving him, fading into the hazy shadows the same way it had appeared. "Prince Garric was the last King of the Isles. He and his kingdom have been gone for a thousand years. . . ."

Garric walked. There was light in the distance, but the foggy darkness was close beside and behind him.

Chapter

3

GARRIC TOOK ANOTHER step forward. The air was chill and humid, suddenly filled with the odors of life and decay. His foot splashed ankle-deep in muck, throwing him forward. His brain was too numb to keep him upright, but at least he managed to get his arms out. He landed on all fours instead of flopping onto his face.

Endless grayness had become fog-shrouded sunlight.

Something hooted mournfully beyond the mist. He couldn't tell how far away it was or even be sure of the direction. The sun was a bright patch in the thick clouds almost directly overhead.

Garric stood carefully. He was stark naked, but so far as he could tell he hadn't been hurt by whatever'd happened. He had a memory of falling into the cloudy heart of the topaz, but he also recalled seeing the diadem bouncing on the ground beside his helmet and tunics. Both those things couldn't be true.

"And maybe neither is, lad," said King Carus. *"But we're not on First Atara now, nor anyplace I've been before."*

The animal hooted again. It didn't sound especially dangerous, but it was certainly big. Even if it were vegetarian, whatever hunted it would be large enough to be dangerous to an unarmed man. . . .

Garric made a more focused assessment of his surroundings, looking for a weapon. A branch stuck out from a fallen tree. He gripped it with both hands, but it crumbled instead of providing a club.

Trees three or four times Garric's height were scattered over open marsh. The trunks all tapered upward from thick bases, but their foliage varied from needles and fronds to long serpentine whips.

He generally couldn't see more than ten feet in any direction, but swirls and eddies in the mist gave him occasional glimpses out as far as a bowshot. The distant terrain was low-lying and muddy with patches of standing water, more or less identical to the patch on which Garric stood.

It was raining, though it'd taken him a moment to realize that because the air was already so sopping wet. He started to laugh. Aloud, though there was nobody around save the king in his mind, he said, "Well, I've been in worse places, but I won't pretend this is a good one."

"Keep your eyes open, because this is the sort of place that can get worse fast," said Carus. His image grinned in amusement. He and the blue sky above the rose-twined battlements where he stood were all created by Garric's imagination. *"There's times I don't mind not having a body anymore."*

The breeze was from the south. Garric thought he smelled smoke, so he started walking in that direction for lack of a better one. It could've been a fire lighted by lightning, of course; or a meteor.

Or nothing at all; the air was thick with rot and unfamiliar plant odors, so he might be imagining the smell. But smoke *would* linger in a thick atmosphere like this.

A dozen pairs of small eyes watched him from the edge of the pond he was skirting. When he turned to face them, they disappeared in a swirl and a series of faint plops.

"I never cared for raw fish," said Carus, watching as always through Garric's eyes, *"but it's better than starving. Unless peasants—"*

He grinned again.

"—know how to build cook fires in a swamp?"

Garric smiled also. "This peasant doesn't," he said.

Thinking about raw fish, he stepped into a grove of a dozen or so stems sprouting from a common base. The trunks ranged from thumb thick to three fingers in breadth. He twisted one in both hands. It was springy and so tough that even his full strength couldn't bend it far out of line.

One of these saplings would make a good spear shaft or fire-hardened spear if he could cut it free. He hadn't seen any exposed rock, even a slab of shale or limestone he could use to bruise through the wood. Maybe there were clams whose shells he could—

A man in a cloth tunic, a cape, and a plaited hat stepped out of the mist on the other side of the grove. He was bearded; a scar ran down the left side of his face from temple to jaw hinge. He carried a spear with a barbed bone tip, and a fine-meshed net was looped around his waist.

"Wah!" the stranger cried. Other men were following him. The nearest carried a club. He stopped, but two spearmen spread out to either side.

Garric felt the king in his mind tense for action. Carus was judging weaknesses and assessing possibilities: *Grab the spear from Scarface and kick him in the crotch to make him let go of it; stab the man to the left with the spear point, then slam the butt into the face of the man on the right; back away and use the point again on the fellow with the club. Most people don't react quickly enough to instant, murderous violence. . . .*

Garric raised his empty right hand, palm forward, and said, "Good day, sirs. I'm glad to meet you."

"If only you had a sword!" King Carus muttered.

If only I had a breechclout, Garric thought.

The strangers halted where they were; the pair on the sides edged closer to their fellows. They began to jabber to one another, punctuating the words by clicking their tongues against the roofs of their mouths. The language was nothing Garric had ever heard before; nor had Carus, judging by his look of stern discomfort.

Garric lowered his right arm and laced his fingers before him, resisting the urge to cover his genitals. Maybe one of the strangers would loan him the short cape they all wore? Though for him to tie it around his waist might be seen as an insult. . . .

Scarface kept his eyes on Garric while he talked to his fellows. He seemed to be the leader, though he was only in his mid-twenties and one of his fellows was easily a decade older.

The discussion ended. Scarface clapped his left palm on the knuckles of the hand holding his spear, then spoke slowly and distinctly to Garric. The other three men watched intently. The words were as meaningless as the rhythmic glunking of a frog.

Garric opened both hands at shoulder height. "I don't understand you," he said, smiling pleasantly, "but I'd like to go with you to your village. Perhaps we can—"

The strangers to either side dropped their spears, then walked forward and grabbed his wrists. One tried to twist Garric's arm behind his back while freeing the length of rope looped over his shoulder.

"Please don't do this!" Garric said, stepping backward to keep the strangers from surrounding him. He continued to smile, but he didn't need his ancestor's instincts to make him tense. He was half a head taller than the biggest of the four; but there *were* four of them.

The man gripping Garric's right arm snarled something and twisted harder. Garric had fought—and won—his share of wrestling matches in Barca's Hamlet. He let the stranger pull him to the right, then pivoted and lifted the fellow off the ground in a swift arc, using the man on his left as an anchor.

The stranger gave a bleat of fear. Garric let him go at the top of the arc and turned to watch him splash headfirst in the nearby pond. A pair of fingerlings squirted out of the water and danced across the surface for a yard or more on their tails before diving back in. The man who'd been struggling with Garric's left arm backed away showing his teeth.

Garric smiled and raised his hands again. He was breathing hard and he was afraid his expression looked like a wolf's slavering grin, but he was *trying* to be friendly.

"I'd be pleased to go with you," he said. Obviously the strangers couldn't understand him any better than he could them, but he hoped his quiet tone would make an impression. "But I won't allow you to tie me up. You don't need to do that."

Scarface grimaced and called something to his companions. The older man at his side, standing with his club raised, looked at him in surprise and protested. Scarface repeated the command, this time in a growl.

The man Garric'd thrown into the water stood up, wiping the muck from his forehead with the back of his hand. He glared at Garric, but when Garric looked squarely at him he paused where he was with one foot raised instead of getting out of the pond.

Garric bowed to Scarface, then gestured back in the direction the strangers had appeared from. "Shall we go?" he said.

Scarface guffawed loudly, then broke into a broad grin. He called something to the man standing in the pond. That fellow scowled, but he undid the fishbone pin at his throat and tossed his cape to Garric. The others laughed.

Scarface made a fist with his left hand, then touched the knuckles to Garric's. He gestured southward and turned. Garric clasped the cape around his midriff and walked alongside Scarface, matching his strides to the other's shorter legs.

"Now for a sword," murmured King Carus; but his image was smiling.

Ilna wasn't impressed by the quality of the tapestries covering the council chamber's walls. Still, they *were* tapestries instead of wall paintings like she'd found in most of the cities she'd been to. She wondered vaguely who or what the council on First Atara might be, but that didn't matter much.

Ilna stood at the back, moving slowly sideways as she followed the woven patterns more with her soul than with her eyes. At the table in the center of the room, members of Garric's court argued about what to do now that the prince had vanished. Everybody had an opinion and every opinion was different, which struck Ilna as absurd. There was only one possible answer to fit the present pattern.

Her face was hard. By virtue of the fact that Ilna os-Kenset was one of Prince Garric's oldest and closest friends, she could state her opinion; which everyone else would listen to politely and as politely ignore. None of these nobles, whether soldiers or civilians, cared what an illiterate peasant thought. Therefore Ilna looked at a marginally competent tapestry while her social superiors nattered pointlessly.

"It's not just food for the personnel," Admiral Zettin was saying forcefully. "If there's a serious storm—and in this season, we could get one at any moment—the ships aren't safe just drawn up on shore like they are. I won't answer for the losses if we don't return to Valles immediately."

Sharina was at one end of the table; Cashel sat at the corner to her left, the quarterstaff upright beside him and an expression of placid interest on his face. At this sort of event, Cashel looked like a well-trained guard dog, quiet and calm and not at all threatening unless someone did the wrong thing.

Ilna grinned faintly. Cashel *was* a well-trained guard dog. His silent bulk was the reason the others nattered instead of snarling, even the two military rivals seated across from one another at the opposite end of the table: Lord Waldron, the army commander; and Lord Attaper, who commanded the bodyguards, the Blood Eagles. Without Cashel's presence, they'd have been bellowing at each other, ignoring the presence of Princess Sharina.

Several people began talking all together, disagreeing with Zettin in as many different fashions as there were voices. None of the questions really mattered, and they were dancing around the question that *did* matter: who would rule until Garric returned?

Who would rule if Garric never returned?

Ilna looked at the tapestry on which a peasant plowed behind a span of oxen. On a hill in the background rose a castle whose corner turrets had red conical roofs. It didn't look anything like this palace or any building Ilna would expect to find on First Atara.

She touched the fabric—wool on a warp of linen—and felt a warm impression of the hills of central Haft. She might well have passed close to where the tapestry'd been woven when she walked from Barca's Hamlet to Carcosa on the opposite coast a few years before.

She might've been physically close, but the tapestry'd been woven unthinkable ages before she'd been born. It was ancient, a relic of the Old Kingdom like some of the books Garric and Lady Liane read; Garric's fiancée, Lady Liane. . . .

Ancient or not, the weaver hadn't been very skilled. First Atara must always have been the sort of backwater it was today, a quiet place where folk grew grain and minded their own business. Barca's Hamlet had been that sort of place, but then it all changed. That would happen on First Atara too, whether the folk here liked it or not.

Ilna smiled, this time without humor. It didn't matter what people or what threads, either one, thought of the pattern they were woven into.

"With all due respect—" said Lord Tadai. From the tone of his voice, that meant no respect at all. He stopped because he heard loud voices outside the door.

The soldiers at the table rose. So did Cashel, still placid but holding his staff in both hands.

It was Chalcus, though, standing at Ilna's side, who murmured, "Stay, child," to Merota. He swaggered to the door and pulled it open with his right hand. Only someone who knew the man Chalcus was would have noticed that the movement put his hand very close to the hilt of his in-curved sword.

The six guards outside were Blood Eagles. They'd backed to keep as far as they could from the pair of men coming toward them across the courtyard. Now there was no farther to retreat, so they'd lowered their spears. The men approaching would run themselves onto the points un-less they stopped.

Ilna didn't care for soldiers as a class: a life spent in killing other men seemed to her at best unworthy. The Blood Eagles were the best of their sort, however, and she appreciated good craftsmanship in any line of work.

"Please, Your Highness," begged the chamberlain, Lord Martous, as he stood wringing his hands behind Cervoran. "Please, another time?"

Cervoran—King Cervoran—looked much as he had that morning when Ilna dragged him from the pyre. His garments'd been changed; the trousers and tunic he wore now weren't singed and smoke-stained. Nonetheless the same bluish cast underlay Cervoran's pallor, and his fin-gers looked like suet-stuffed sausages. He walked normally now, except for a slight hitch in his step of a sort common in old people and not un-known in younger ones.

"Sir!" the under-captain commanding the guards said to Attaper. "We told him to stop, but he just keeps coming!"

The Blood Eagles were brave men by definition: they'd volunteered to protect a warrior prince who regularly put himself in the hottest part of the fight. This officer and his men had watched Cervoran get up from his bier, though.

Wizardry was the only cause Ilna could imagine that would've allowed a dead man to rise. The guards were clearly of the same opinion, and the courage to face death didn't necessarily mean the courage to face wizardry.

Cervoran stopped just short of the spear points. Those in the coun-cil chamber watched him; some calmly, some not. The smile on Chalcus' face was probably genuine, but there was sweat on Lord Waldron's brow. The old warrior wouldn't run from what he feared, but his fear was no less real for his ability to master it.

Sharina looked past Cashel's left shoulder; the quarterstaff was a di-agonal bar protecting her from anything that might come through the doorway. Cashel's expression was as placid as that of an ox in his stall, but Ilna could see the way the muscles tensed in her brother's throat and bare forearms.

Cervoran raised his right arm and pointed a doughy finger at Cashel. "You," he said, piping like a frog in springtime. "Who are you?"

"I'm Cashel or-Kenset," Cashel replied. His face didn't change. He didn't add a question of his own or put a challenge in his voice, the way a less self-assured man might have done.

"Come with me, Cashel," Cervoran said. "It is necessary."

Attaper stepped forward, his hand on his sword hilt. "Lord Cervoran," he said in too loud a voice, "you have no business here. This is a *royal* council!"

"Come with me, Cashel," the former corpse repeated.

"Sharina?" said Cashel. "Do you need me? Because I wouldn't mind going along with him, Lord Cervoran I mean. Since he says it's necessary."

"Yes, all right, Cashel," Sharina said. She put her right hand on his shoulder, squeezed, and released him. "I trust your judgment . . . and your ability to deal with any problems that arise."

Cashel grinned. "Let me by, please," he said to the guards, but they were already stepping sideways to let him past.

"It is necessary," Cervoran squeaked. He turned and started back toward the opposite wing of the palace—the servants' quarters and storage rooms. Cashel walked at his side, the quarterstaff slanted across his body; the chamberlain followed nervously behind them.

Ilna looked at the pattern her fingers had knotted during the tableau that'd just ended. "Close the door if you would, Chalcus," she said in a clear voice.

She turned and eyed the room, the gathering of the most powerful folk in the Kingdom of the Isles. "Now," said Ilna. "I think it's time to acknowledge Princess Sharina as regent until her brother the prince comes back."

Sharina was startled at Ilna's words, but it was very like her friend to speak her mind. Admiral Zettin—a good man, but one who didn't know Ilna as well as Waldron and Attaper had come to do—looked at her with an irritated expression and said, "I don't think—"

"That's nothing to brag about, milord," Liane broke in, emphasizing by her nasal, upper-class Sandrakkan accent that she was *Lady* Liane bos-Benliman. "If you *did* think, you'd realize—as we all do, I'm sure, in our hearts—that the kingdom needs someone in Prince Garric's place as regent if it's to function, and that the princess is the proper choice. If Garric could've done so, he'd have appointed his sister, as he's done when necessary in the past."

Sharina grinned, but only in her mind. She didn't want the job, but she knew Garric didn't want it either. He was the correct person to hold the mutually antagonistic nobles together—nobody's man, and therefore the man for everyone. While Garric was gone, Sharina was almost the only one who could take his place.

Almost the only one: Liane too had the knowledge and intelligence to rule. But Liane was from Sandrakkan, while the strength of the royal army and fleet came from Ornifal. Haft, where Garric and Sharina'd been born, had been unimportant since the fall of the Old Kingdom. The haughty rulers of Ornifal and Sandrakkan and Blaise could bow to someone from Haft as representating the kingdom without losing face to a rival island.

Besides, Liane preferred to work behind the scenes. She sat quietly at Garric's elbow, ready to hand him necessary documents or whisper information; and she worked more quietly still in managing the kingdom's spies. When Liane spoke it was to the point—and occasionally very pointedly, as to Zettin just now—but that wasn't her usual style.

"I have the greatest respect for the princess," said Lord Waldron, making a half-bow toward Sharina, "but Prince Garric's disappearance may mean there's a military threat looming. While the army will be loyal to whoever stands in the prince's place—"

"I'm sure Princess Sharina will be able to delegate military affairs," said Liane tartly, "as she and indeed her brother have done in the past. I consider it very unlikely that Prince Garric was snatched away by a hostile army, though, milord—if that was really what you were implying?"

"Well, I didn't mean that, of course . . . ," Waldron muttered. He scowled, looking around the room angrily as if searching for a way out of his misstatement.

Lord Attaper opened his mouth, probably to gibe at his rival Waldron. Before he got a word out, Liane said, "I believe we're in agreement, then. Lord Attaper, are you ready to serve Princess Sharina loyally?"

Attaper stiffened as though slapped, then grinned at the way Liane had outmaneuvered him. "Yes," he said. "Princess Sharina is clearly the best choice to fill what we hope will be a short-term appointment. Ah, are we any closer to knowing just what did happen to the prince?"

Liane could've answered that, but it was properly a question for Sharina herself. She nodded to Attaper and said, "Tenoctris is searching the, ah, former king's library, which I gather is rather extensive."

She cleared her throat. She'd started to say, "the late king's library," and part of her still thought that might be the correct term.

"At any rate," Sharina continued, "Tenoctris will tell us if she learns anything useful. *When* she learns, as I hope and expect."

Cashel's presence had kept the previous discussions quiet but not calm. Much as Sharina appreciated having Cashel close to her, it was a good thing now that he'd left. The dynamic of the meeting had changed abruptly when Ilna spoke. Power had shifted from the males in the room to her, Ilna, and Liane. If Cashel were still here, the tension between him and the three military men would've prevented that from happening.

"Ah, Your Highness?" said Zettin, glancing warily toward Liane. "The matter of the ships still remains. If we return to Valles in the next few—"

"We'll remain here until further notice," said Sharina with crisp certainty. "Garric, ah, departed from here. Unless Tenoctris says otherwise, I believe this is the place he's most likely to return to. I regret the risk to the ships, but Prince Garric is our first concern."

Lord Waldron glanced sidelong at Lord Attaper. He smiled slightly when their eyes met.

Lord Tadai touched together the tips of his well manicured fingers before him and coughed for attention. Tadai didn't have a formal title, but he carried out the duties of chancellor and chief of staff for Garric while the prince was traveling.

"Milords Waldron and Zettin?" he said in his butter-smooth voice. "I'd appreciate it if you'd direct your provisioning officers to meet with me as soon as we're done here. My staff has made preliminary contacts with local officials regarding our initial requirements, but I'll need more detailed information if we're going to remain on First Atara."

He bobbed his chin to Sharina.

"I believe we're done for now," Sharina said, glancing toward Liane and receiving a minuscule nod of agreement. "If each of you will leave a runner with me, I'll let you know as soon as I hear what Tenoctris has to say. I'm going up to see her now."

As the others present started to rise, a scream sounded outside. Heavy wood cracked, then masonry fell with a rumbling crash. A beam had broken—had *been* broken—and the pediment it supported had come down with a roar.

Chalcus threw open the door and slipped into the courtyard, his sword and dagger in his hands. The council's military officials followed, drawing their weapons also. Lord Tadai and the other civilians got up and eased toward the back wall.

Sharina's eyes met Ilna's. Ilna patted Merota's head and said something; the girl ran to Liane and took her hand. Together Ilna and Sharina, friends from earliest childhood, stepped into the courtyard behind the armed men to see what was going on.

The palace was built around three sides of the courtyard. Besides the portico where the palace clerks and laundrymen worked in good weather, there was an herb garden for the kitchen and benches shaded by nut trees for nobles. The eight-foot-high back wall had double doors opening onto an alley leading to the nearby harbor. Sharina supposed furniture and bulk foodstuffs normally came in that way. An innkeeper's daughter noticed things like that.

The thing coming through the wall now, having torn out the transom and burst the gate leaves, was green, barrel-shaped, and taller than the wall. It held a soldier in one of its feathery tentacles and folded another over his face. A twist tore the man apart in a gush of blood.

There were troops in the alley and others pouring into the courtyard from the palace. Everyone was shouting.

The under-captain at the door to the council chamber turned and saw Sharina. "By the Lady!" he cried. "Princess, you've got to get out of here!"

Because this had been a working meeting of Garric's closest advisors, Sharina'd been able to change out of court robes into double tunics not terribly different from what she'd have worn on very formal occasions back in Barca's Hamlet. The fabric was bleached instead of being the natural cream color of "white" wool, and the sleeves had black appliqués of Ilna's weaving.

Ilna said the patterns were unconsciously soothing to anyone who looked at them. Sharina believed her friend, but given the rancor of some council meetings it was hard to imagine how they could've been much worse.

Between her outer and inner tunics Sharina wore a heavy Pewle knife, her legacy from the hermit Nonnus. He'd used it to save her life at the cost of his own. She didn't carry the knife as a weapon—though she'd used it for one—but rather because touching the hilt's black horn scales invoked the hermit's quiet faith, and that calmed her mind.

She reached through the slit disguised as a pleat in her outer tunic and brought out the knife. Right now it was both a weapon *and* a prayer.

Half a dozen spears sailed through the air and squelched into the monster, burying in every case the slim iron head and stopping only at the wooden shaft a forearm's length back of the point. The creature continued to advance. The spears wobbled like tubular wasp larvae clinging to the body of a squat green caterpillar.

A soldier just come from the servants' wing dropped his shield and charged with his javelin gripped in both hands. He twisted at the moment of impact to drive the point in, putting all his strength and weight behind the blow. Half the wrist-thick spear shaft penetrated; sludgy green fluid oozed out around the wood.

The soldier's wordless grunt of effort changed to a scream as tentacles wrapped him. The monster lifted him, pulling his limbs off with the same swift dispassion as a cook plucking a goose for dinner. The screams stopped an instant after the fourth bright flag of arterial blood spouted from the victim's joints.

"Use your swords!" an officer shouted. As he spoke, the monster gripped him. He slashed through one of the feathery tentacles, but another tentacle tossed him with seeming ease twenty feet in the air. He didn't scream until he started to fall back toward the alley. Three soldiers who'd started forward at his order backed instead and raised their shields.

The creature crawled forward on hundreds of cilia each no bigger than a man's foot. It was a plant—it *had* to be a plant; the tentacles were very like fern fronds though huge and hooked with thorns on the underside—but it was a plant from Hell.

Ilna had knotted a pattern from the cords she kept in her left sleeve. She held it up, facing the hellplant.

The creature squished onward, unwrapping a tentacle suddenly to grip a soldier's ankle. He slammed the lower edge of his shield down to cut the frond off against the pavement. Its tip uncurled, leaving a bloody patch above the soldier's heavy sandal. He retreated, his sword up but his face in a rictus of terror.

Chalcus put his left hand on Ilna's shoulder. She tried to shake him off. The sailor kept his grip and shouted, "Come away, dear heart, for you'll do no good here!"

Sharina found herself backing toward the doorway from which she'd entered the courtyard. The hellplant didn't move quickly, but it'd proved it could tear a passage through thick walls.

And thus far, there was no evidence than any human device could stop it.

"LIFT THAT," CERVORAN said to Cashel, pointing at the door set at a slant in the back of the pantry. The housekeeper hadn't been in when her visitors had arrived, and her two assistants had fled with looks of trembling terror when they saw their king.

Or whatever Cervoran was now. Did Protas go back to being a kid that everybody ignored because his father'd returned? There were worse things that could happen, Cashel knew.

"That leads to the bulk storage for liquids, Your Highness," Martous said in a chirpy voice. "We keep the large jars of wine and oil in the cellars so that they won't freeze during the winter as they might in a shed. But there's nothing down there which matters to you."

Whatever other people thought of the business, the chamberlain was sure determined to act as if nothing about Cervoran had changed. Maybe he was right.

"Lift that door," Cervoran repeated, but he could've saved his breath. Cashel had only paused to loosen his sash. He didn't want to rip a tunic if the weight required him to bunch his muscles.

He bent, gripped the bar handle with his free hand, and lifted the panel in a smooth motion. The door was sturdy but nothing that required *his* strength. The air swirling out was cool at this time of year, but Cashel understood what the chamberlain meant. Folk in Barca's Hamlet had root cellars for the same reason, though none—even the inn's—was as large as this one. The darkness had a faint fruity odor.

"Ah, Your Highness?" Martous said. "If you're going down there, should I have a servant fetch a lantern? There are no windows, you see."

Cashel smiled faintly. Anybody looking down the steps into the cellar could see there were no windows; it was dark as an arm's length up a hog's backside.

Cervoran started down, ignoring the chamberlain as he'd done ever since Cashel saw the two of them together this afternoon.

"Follow me," Cervoran said; echoes from the cellar deepened his voice. "Leave the staff; you will need both hands."

Cashel had already started down the sturdy wooden steps behind the king. He paused, trying not to frown, and said, "Sir? I'd rather—"

"It is necessary," Cervoran said.

Whatever else he might be, Cervoran wasn't a fellow who talked for the sake of talking. Cashel sighed and set the quarterstaff against the back wall of the pantry. He'd come this far, so there wasn't much point in starting to argue now.

The cellar was what Cashel'd expected: brick pillars in rows, and big jars lined up against the masonry wall at the back. The ceiling was way higher than Cashel could reach and maybe higher than he could've reached with his staff stretched out above him.

The light that came down the pantry door was enough once Cashel's eyes had adapted. Cervoran seemed to get along all right too, moving at his usual hitching stride down the line of jars. They were two different kinds, Cashel saw, one with a wider mouth and a thickened ridge for a rope sling instead of double handles at the neck like the other.

As he followed, Cashel's eyes caught the least sliver of light from the ceiling in the depths of the cellar. That must be the trap door onto the alley where the jars'd be lowered down from wagons. A cart with solid wood wheels for shifting them here sat beside a pillar.

Cashel grinned with silent pride. If these jars were full of liquids, they'd be work for two ordinary men to shift.

"Your Highness?" Martous called from the pantry. The quaver Cashel heard in the chamberlain's voice wasn't just the echo. "I have a light here if you need one."

"Lift that jar and follow me," said Cervoran, pointing at the first of the wide-mouthed jars in the rank. His fingers were puffy and as white as fresh tallow.

"Yes sir," Cashel said. He looked at the jar and thought about the path he'd be carrying it by. The stairs wouldn't be a problem because the pantry door was hung at a slant, but if Cervoran took him back into the courtyard he'd have to lower the jar from his shoulder to clear the transom. "Is it wine?"

He rocked the jar to try the weight. It'd be a load and no mistake, but he could handle it. The base narrowed from the shoulder, but it still sat flat. The pointy bottoms of the other pattern of jars had to be set in sand to stay upright.

Cervoran walked toward the stairs, ignoring the question. His voice drifted through the dimness, "It is necessary. . . ."

Cashel grinned as he squatted, positioning his hands carefully. He'd taken orders from his share of surly people before, and that'd never kept him from getting his own job done. The others hadn't had Cervoran's good excuse of having been dead or the next thing to it for a while, either.

When Cashel was sure he had the weight balanced, he straightened his knees and rose with the jar against his chest. He had to lean back to center it. There was enough air at the top of the jar for it to slosh as it moved, but he had it under control. It was tricky, but it was under control.

Cashel walked toward the stairs, not quite shuffling. He could only see off to his left side, the direction he'd turned his face when he lifted the jar. He'd had to pick one or the other, of course, unless he wanted to mash his nose against the coarse pottery. He'd be all right unless somebody put something in his way, and anyway he'd be feeling his way with his toes. It was under control.

Funny that Cervoran'd picked him for the job. As best Cashel could tell, the king hadn't set eyes on him till they saw each other through the doorway to the council room. Cashel didn't know another man in the army who could do this particular thing—fetch and carry a full wine jar alone—better than he could, though.

Cashel heard Cervoran climbing the stairs—skritch/*thump;* skritch/*thump.* A moment later he touched the bottom riser with his own big toe. Cashel slid the other foot upward, planted it, and then shifted his weight and the jar's onto it while he brought his right foot up and around to the next tread. He'd thought of leading with his left foot on every step, but he decided he'd be better off climbing with a normal rhythm. He took the steps with ponderous deliberation.

"Oh, my goodness, what's going on here?" the chamberlain chirped from close at hand. "Should I get somebody to help, or—goodness, is that a *full* jar?"

It certainly *was* a full jar. Cashel felt a jolt every time his heart beat.

Judging from the way it got brighter, he must be near the top of the staircase. He hunched forward slightly to make sure the jar was going to clear. It did and he could see the pantry, the shelves and bottle racks and then the chamberlain staring at him in amazement.

Cashel smiled. This jar was a weight, the Shepherd *knew* it was, but nobody was going to learn that from anything Cashel said or showed. Part of the way you won your fights was not letting the other guy know you were straining. Cashel didn't understand quite what was going on, but it was *some* kind of fight. Otherwise Cervoran'd be moving the jar by the usual fashion, a couple of guys and a derrick up through the alley door.

A lot of people thought Cashel was dumb. He guessed they were right: he couldn't read or write or do lots of the other things Garric and Sharina did, that was for sure. But sometimes Cashel thought he saw things clearer than most folk did, just because his brain didn't put a lot of stuff in the way of the obvious.

"Follow me, Cashel," Cervoran said from right ahead. Cashel turned a little to his right so that he could see where he was going. The king was walking out of the pantry with a brass-framed lantern in his white hand; he must've taken it from the chamberlain. Cashel wondered why he'd bothered now that they were upstairs. Light streamed in through the layer of bull's-eye glass set in the wall just below the trusses supporting the floor above.

Cashel had to turn straight on to get through the pantry door with his load, but he sidled again as soon as he was clear. Something was going on ahead of them, out in the courtyard he supposed; shouting and the clang of metal falling onto stone.

There was a scream too, so shrill that Cashel'd have said it had to be a woman if he hadn't heard men sound the same way when the pain was worse than anything they'd felt or dreamed of feeling. Red Bassin sounded like that the time the ox fell on him and thrashed, trying to get to its feet. It was while the ox was struggling that Bassin screamed; he stopped when his thighbone cracked and he fainted instead.

Cervoran led through the indoor kitchen. It was full of people jabbering, all of them looking out onto the courtyard through the big doors.

"Make way!" Cervoran piped. A potboy turned, saw the king with Cashel following, and bawled in terror. Cooks and other palace servants scattered to either side in fright, but they didn't run outdoors.

Cervoran, ignoring the panicked servants the way he seemed to ignore everything that wasn't part of his immediate purpose, marched through the doors to the courtyard. Cashel followed. He heard the battle clearly but he didn't see anything because he was concentrating on not banging the jar. The trusses supporting the portico sloped, so the lower edge of the roof tiles didn't have as much clearance as the kitchen ceiling.

When Cashel stepped off the edge of the pavement and his feet touched grass, he looked up at last. Soldiers stood all around something that was way taller than them and bigger than a full-grown ox.

The thing was green. Its barrel-shaped trunk, thicker than the widest Cashel could stretch with both arms, turned with the slow deliberation of a whale broaching. It started toward Cashel, moving on yellowish squirming roots covered with white hairs like a mandrake's.

"Master Cervoran!" Cashel said. He wasn't scared, exactly, but this wasn't a time he wanted to be standing around with a tun of wine in his arms and his staff somewhere back in the pantry. "Sir I mean! What is it you want me to do?"

The thing crawled toward them in the certainty of a honeysuckle twisting its way along a railing. Except for the fact it moved, Cashel'd have said it was a plant. He guessed watching it that he was going to have to admit it was a plant anyhow, even though it *did* move.

The ring of soldiers'd been keeping a good distance between themselves and the plant, though the blood and mangled bodies scattered over the ground showed that hadn't always been the case. Cashel didn't blame them for backing away a bit now.

"Throw the jar at the Green Woman's creature, Cashel," Cervoran said. He didn't shout, but his voice cut like bright steel through the noisy air.

The plant was definitely coming toward them. Coming toward Cervoran, anyhow, and Cashel stood just behind and a bit to the side of the revived corpse. He shifted the jar, feeling it slosh. He'd have to loft it with his body and right arm like a heavy stone, using his left hand only for balance.

Positioning the jar showed Cashel how much it'd taken out of him to get this far, but he could still manage the throw. He couldn't do it with the troops in the way, though.

"Give me room, you fellows!" Cashel called. "Give me a clear shot!"

One of the soldiers closest to Cashel turned his head back to see who was giving orders. The roots the plant crawled on moved no faster than earthworms, but a feathery tentacle uncoiled like a bird striking. It caught the top of the man's shield while he was looking the other way.

The soldier shouted as the tentacle jerked his shield toward the monster. He dropped the staple at the right rim, but his forearm was through the loop behind the shield boss. The plant slashed side to side, using the screaming man as a flail against the other troops.

"Throw the jar," Cervoran said, standing like a statue with the lantern in his hand. "It is necessary."

The third stroke flung the man loose to tumble onto the ground near the wing on the other side of the courtyard. He lay there moaning. The plant continued to wave the shield for a moment, then flipped it away and started toward Cervoran again.

The man's arm was broken, probably broken in several places, but the circle of ripped-off limbs around the creature showed that the fellow was lucky anyway. Sharina knelt beside him, cutting a bandage from his tunic with her Pewle knife.

Being thrown around that way had been hard on the soldier, but it'd given Cashel the clear path he needed. The plant was about twice his height away. He stepped toward it, bringing the wine jar up and around as he moved.

The strain drew a bloodred mask over Cashel's vision; then the jar was out of his hands and he was falling backward in reaction. He felt light-headed, barely aware of the tentacles uncoiling toward him from either side. His shoulders slammed the ground—if he'd landed on the edge of the pavement he might've broken his neck, but he hadn't—and as his legs rocked down he could see normally again.

The jar squelched into the center of the plant's body without break-ing, then fell back to smash on the ground. It'd been filled with olive oil, not wine. The dent in the great body where it'd hit was bruised a darker, oozing green, but the creature resumed its crawl toward Cervoran.

Cervoran threw the lantern. It broke open, spreading its flames across the oil-sodden ground with a gradual assurance much like the way the plant itself moved. For a moment the plant continued to come on, now shrouded by a pale yellow column. The tiny rootlets burned away from its feet and the tentacles reaching toward Cashel shriveled; the crea-ture stopped.

Heat hammered Cashel's feet despite their thick calluses. He tried to get up but found he was still dizzy. He lifted his torso slightly and shoved himself backward with his hands. When his forearm touched the edge of the pavement, he set his palms on it and managed to lurch into a sit-ting position.

The flames were still too close. He crossed his left hand over his face to keep his lips from blistering, but he continued to watch even though he could feel the hairs on the back of his arm shrinking and breaking in the heat.

A blazing cocoon wrapped the plant. Blackened layers seared off, laying bare the green beneath that charred away in turn. Cashel thought he heard the plant scream, though maybe that was only the keen of steam boiling out of the shriveling body.

Cervoran hadn't moved. Cashel stood and eased him back from the flames. The wizard obeyed with the waxen calm of a sleepwalker. The front of his clothing, the new set of tunic and trousers, was already singed brown.

Civilians had come out into the courtyard to join the soldiers, but more than the heat of the flames kept them at a distance from the dying plant. Sharina looked across to Cashel. Her face was set as she rose from her patient, but now it brightened into a smile. Two soldiers were leading off their injured comrade, his arm splinted with lengths of spear shaft.

The side of the plant's body ruptured, gushing more sea water than would've fit in the jar Cashel had thrown. It poured onto the burning oil, stirring the flames for a moment into greater enthusiasm. Things slithered in the water, swimming or skittering on flattened legs; each held pincers high.

"Crabs!" shouted a soldier and jabbed his javelin at the thing that squirmed toward him through the dying flames. The point missed, sparking on a pebble in the soil. The soldier recovered his weapon, but the pallid creature ran swiftly toward him. He raised his foot to stamp on it, but it sprang upward to fasten its pincers on opposite sides of his ankles where the sandal straps crossed.

It isn't a crab, Cashel thought as he snatched up a javelin lying against the pavement with its slender iron head bent. *It's got a tail, so it's a crayfish or—*

The tail curled into a nearly perfect circle, burying its hooked sting a finger's length in the soldier's knee joint. He fell backward, screaming on a rising note.

Cashel whipped the spear butt around, snatching the flat-bodied scorpion away from the soldier's leg and squashing it on the ground. The yellow horn sting broke off in the wound.

No male peasant was ever without a knife for trimming, prying, and poking, but Cashel wasn't carrying one at the moment because the simple iron tool wouldn't have looked right among all these folk in court robes and polished armor. He knelt and worked the sting out of the soldier's flesh with the point of the man's own dagger.

The knee had turned black and swelled up big as the soldier's head, and his body was thrashing in four different rhythms the way a beheaded chicken does. Well, you did what you could.

Cashel straightened. Sharina was standing beside him. He dropped the dagger and hugged her to him with his left arm. He still held the dripping javelin in his right hand, and his eyes searched the dying fire for any more scorpions that might dart from the charred ruin of the hellplant.

SEVERAL TIMES GARRIC stepped into muck that would've sucked him down if he hadn't jerked back quickly, but he didn't have any real trouble keeping up with Scarface and his companions. The pasture south of Barca's Hamlet had marshy stretches, and there're some sheep that seem determined to bog themselves thoroughly every chance they got.

He grinned. Celondre, one of the greatest poets of the Old Kingdom and of all time, had given Garric a great deal of pleasure. His pastorals of shady springs and gambolling lambs never included the shepherd struggling out of a bog with a half-drowned ewe bleating peevishly on his shoulders, however.

A bird belled like an alarm and shot straight up, almost at the feet of the man who was leading. He cried "Wau!" and jumped backward, tangling his legs and falling over. Garric was startled also, dropping into a crouch. His ancestor's reflex swung his hand to the sword he wasn't carrying.

Scarface at the end of the line was the only one who didn't react. He called a good-natured gibe at the man who'd fallen, then added something in a harsher tone to get the line moving again.

"That one's a hunter," Carus said, assessing the situation. *"The others are fishermen, maybe, or just farmers. Scarface I'd pick for a scout."*

Why isn't he leading, then? Garric asked silently. He wasn't arguing, exactly; just trying to understand what Carus saw and he did not.

"Because they all know where they're going, lad," the king explained. *"I'd guess that means it's not very far. And it also means that they're more worried about what might be following them than they are about what's ahead, which is something to keep in mind."*

As Carus spoke, the path wound around a clump of snake-leafed trees. Ahead rose a series of hummocks some four feet above the general level of the landscape. The hummocks stood in water and were edged with walls made from vertical tree trunks; pole-supported walkways connected them. The surrounding ponds must've been spoil pits from which the dirt had been removed to fill the raised beds.

A man on one of the hummocks saw Scarface's group coming. He waved a hoe and called, "Urra!"

The leading spearman raised his net and spun it in an open circle in response, then looped it back around his waist. Other figures cultivating the raised beds, men and women both, straightened and looked toward the newcomers. A few waved.

"There's the fort," Carus said. *"Well, fortified village."*

He snorted mildly and added, *"It wouldn't be hard to carry, not unless the ones inside are better armed than anything we've seen thus far. And even then it wouldn't be hard."*

It was raining again, but even without that Garric wouldn't have been able to differentiate the stockade from the smaller planting beds spaced in front of it. *We aren't planning an attack, are we?* he thought, amused by his ancestor's focus on the military aspects of any situation.

"No, but somebody *is or the defenses wouldn't be there,"* Carus responded crisply. *"And if that somebody knows what he's doing, those defenses won't be much good."*

The group reached a walkway like those between the beds—and connected to them, Garric saw as he looked ahead in the mist. Scarface clucked something to Garric and took his arm, leading him to the front of the line. The bed, saplings lashed to stringers of heavier timber, was barely wide enough for them to walk abreast.

The gate in the stockade opened. A man standing on the platform above it raised a wooden trumpet to his lips and blew an ugly blat of sound. The people who'd been in the fields started trooping toward the village in response.

An old man wearing a headdress of black feathers stepped into the gateway, acccompanied by a much younger woman. She held the man's left arm, apparently helping to support him. In the old man's hands was a jewel which gleamed yellow even in this dull light.

"Wizardry!" muttered King Carus in disgust.

Well, we knew somebody brought us here, Garric thought calmly. *Now we've got a good idea who it was.*

The feathered wizard raised the giant topaz, a duplicate of the one in the crown of First Atara, and cackled in triumph.

Chapter

4

A DOG RAN out of the gateway and began yapping as Garric and Scarface approached. It was black with a white belly and paws, medium-sized and nondescript. Scarface sent a clod of dirt at it, catching the dog neatly in the ribs. It yelped and bolted back into the village, brushing the wizard on the way. He staggered and might've fallen if the woman accompanying him hadn't tightened her grip.

"*That's the first animal we've seen,*" Carus said with a frown. "*There hasn't been a cow, let alone a horse. There hasn't even been a chicken!*"

Garric grinned. His ancestor knew he could order a battle or site an ambush, things that not even the most educated of peasants could've been expected to know. That didn't mean that peasants knew nothing, however.

Their feet'd rot, Garric explained. *Back in the borough we couldn't pasture the flock in the bottomland for more than a week at a time or their hooves'd get spongy. The clothes here're fiber, not wool, and I'd guess they eat a lot of fish with their vegetables.*

The two men on top of the gate came down a ladder inside the stockade. The trumpeter stepped out of the way, but the fellow wearing a feather robe joined the wizard and his woman. They exchanged brief glances; not hostile, exactly, but cold enough to imply rivalry rather than friendship.

When Scarface reached the mound on which the village stood, he touched Garric on the chest to halt him and stepped forward to talk to the chief. The wizard waited with the big topaz in the crook of his right arm, wearing a disdainful expression. The woman eyed Garric with frank appraisal.

"Well, that one likes what she sees or I miss my bet," Carus said with a chuckle. *"And I don't, because I saw her sort often enough myself back in the days when I wore flesh."*

Garric glanced at the woman, then looked away. He tried to hide his feeling of disgust, but he felt his lip curl despite him.

It wasn't that she was unattractive, but she had a dirty air that went well beyond the simple physical grime inevitable in a village on a mud bank. The woman Katchin the Miller, Cashel's uncle, had married was much the same sort. Katchin had been a boastful, grasping, unpleasant man, but over the years Garric had come to feel that the dance Katchin's wife led him was sufficient punishment for all the man's flaws.

After listening to Scarface for some while, the chief gestured him aside and glared at Garric in what was probably supposed to be an intimidating fashion. Since Garric was taller by half a head, that didn't work very well. The edges of the chief's cloak were worn, and the feathers seemed to be a jumble of anything that could be netted or trapped with birdlime.

The chief raised his hands high in the air and began a speech, his voice cracking repeatedly. He held an edged club the length of his arm, a sort of wooden sword. It could be a dangerous weapon, but the blade of this one was carved with a complex knotted pattern.

Lowering his arms, the chief tapped himself on the chest with his free hand and said, "Wandalo! Wandalo!"

There was a fair chance he was giving his name rather than saying, "It's a nice day, isn't it?" Garric touched his own chest and said, "Garric. My name is Garric."

The wizard spoke, then raised the topaz slightly. He gestured with it toward the chief, who backed a step with an unhappy grimace.

The wizard looked at Garric and said, "Marzan." He touched his own chest and repeated, "Marzan!" He then spoke imperiously to Scarface and turned.

Scarface shrugged uncomfortably. He made a little gesture with his free hand, indicating that Garric should follow the wizard who was stumping back into the village with the woman's help. She looked over her shoulder at Garric.

"This lot don't like wizards any better than I do," muttered the ghost of King Carus.

Fortunately, thought Garric as he strode after Marzan, *I don't have that prejudice myself. Because I can't imagine how we'll get back to our own place and time* without *the help of a wizard.*

The village stockade was a single row of tree trunks sunk into the soil and sharpened on the upper end. An earthen platform on the inside gave defenders a two-foot height advantage over anyone attacking, but there were no towers or arrow slits. Garric realized he hadn't seen bows or any other missile weapon.

Carus snorted when he realized that the palings weren't pinned together. *"With six strong men and a rope I can pull down a hole wide enough to roll wagons through!"* he said. *"I'm not sure I'd bother with anything beyond a straight rush by a company of my skirmishers, though."*

There were about two dozen oval houses with shake roofs and walls of lime plaster on a wicker framework. Each was raised a foot or so on posts; the ground was sodden already, and in a bad storm there must be a serious risk of flooding.

The windows had shutters, but most of them were open. In some birds on long tethers chirruped at Garric, nervous at the sight of a stranger. Fine-meshed fishnets hung under the shelter of the eaves.

The streets—the paths that twisted between the buildings—were paved with clamshells. Shells were probably the source of the plaster too; nowhere since he'd arrived in this land had Garric seen outcrops of stone that could be burned for lime. The quality of the woodwork was impressive, particularly because the people didn't have metal tools, and he thought Ilna would've been interested in their skill with cords and fabrics.

Marzan and the woman led Garric to one of a pair of houses in the center of the village. Both were enclosed by waist-high openwork fences, adornments rather than meant for privacy or protection. Gnarled wisteria grew over one side of the fence around Marzan's compound, but it wasn't blooming at this time of year.

The woman opened the pole crossbar and stepped aside for the wizard to enter. As he shuffled past her into the compound, she looked at Garric and said, "Soma!" She touched her chest, then grinned widely and lifted the top of the thin, waterproof cloth to show her breast before she followed Marzan.

Garric's face was set as he closed the bar after him. He heard Wandalo speaking at a distance and looked back. The top of the chief's head was just visible over the house roofs. He must be standing on the platform above the gate to harangue the villagers whom he'd called from the fields.

Garric wished he knew what Wandalo was saying. Though based on what he'd seen of the man and of rulers of Wandalo's type elsewhere, he probably wasn't missing much.

Garric had to duck under Marzan's doorway, but the hut's ceiling was generously high. Light came not only by the windows but through the roof itself: the shakes were placed in overlapping strips with air spaces between. The design wouldn't work in high winds, so the current vertical drizzle must be the normal state of affairs.

The floor was of planks fitted with narrow gaps between them to deal with roof leaks and tracked-in mud. There were couches on both long walls. In the center of the room a small fire burned on an open hearth of clay laid in a wooden framework. There was no chimney, just the louvered roof: the three of them disturbed the air when they entered, making Garric's nose wrinkle at the swirl of sharp smoke.

Marzan seated himself cross-legged near the hearth and motioned Garric down across from him. Garric squatted, the usual method of sitting in Barca's Hamlet when there weren't chairs. Soma went to the other end of the hut and took baskets from a pantry cabinet made of joined reeds.

The wizard placed his topaz carefully on the floor in front of him where strips of darker wood were inlaid into the planks. They formed a hexagon with the yellow stone in its center.

Marzan smirked at Garric and removed the longest of the three black feathers from his headdress. Using that as a pointer—as a wand—

he touched it to the corners of the figure in turn as he chanted, *"Nerphabo kirali thonoumen. . . ."*

The topaz glowed. The light at its heart was faint but brighter than the dimness of the rain-washed hut. Flaws in the stone became shadows that moved.

"Oba phrene mouno . . . ," the wizard said. He was using words of power, addressing beings that were neither humans nor gods but formed a bridge between them. *"Thila rikri ralathonou!"*

Garric had always thought of the words of power as things which a wizard read. Marzan was illiterate—there was no sign of writing in this community—but he rattled off the syllables in the same sing-song voice as Tenoctris used to chant the spells she'd written in the curving Old Script.

The cultured, scholarly Lady Tenoctris was part of the same fabric as this savage who probably didn't understand the concept of writing. Different from them on the surface but at heart the same nonetheless were Cashel and Ilna. Their mother, a fairy queen or something stranger yet, had passed to them the ability to see the patterns which formal wizardry affected through spells and words of power.

Here in humid gloom lighted by the glow in the heart of a yellow stone, Garric had a brief glimpse of the cosmos interconnected and perfect. *Do Ilna and Cashel always see this?* he wondered; but there was no way to answer the question, and perhaps the question had no answer.

"Bathre nothrou nemil . . . ," Marzan chanted. *"Nothil lare krithiai. . . ."*

The shadows in the topaz moved faster. Garric felt them grip him the way they had when he stared into the diadem on First Atara. Instead of drawing him down this time, the motion sucked a face up from the yellow depths of the stone.

A cat, he thought, but the forehead was too high and the jaw was shorter than a beast's. The image opened its mouth in a silent snarl; the teeth at least were a cat's, the long curving daggers of a carnivore. The eyes were larger than a man's and perfectly round. The pupils were vertical slits.

"Corl," said a voice in Garric's mind. The wizard's mouth continued to chant the words of power.

Marzan's chant was a barely heard backdrop, a rhythm outside the crystalline boundaries of the stone. The cat-faced image drew back to show Garric the whole creature: two-legged and as tall as a man, but lithe and as quick as light playing on the waves of the sea. It wore a harness but no clothing; a coat of thin, brindled fur covered its body. In its four-fingered left hand was a bamboo spear with a point of delicately flaked stone; in its right was a coil with weighted hooks on the end.

The cat man leaped onto a vaguely seen landscape from a fissure in the ground. Garric couldn't tell whether the fog shrouding the figure was real or a distortion of the stone which the wizard used for scrying. A second of the creatures followed the first, then three more. They loped across the sodden landscape, moving in quick short leaps rather than striding like men walking.

The cat men were armed with spears or axes with slim stone heads, along with the hook-headed cords. They formed a widely spaced line abreast as they vanished into the mist. The images faded.

"Coerli," said the voice in Garric's mind as Marzan chanted. "Coerli. . . ."

Garric's mind had never left the boundaries of the crystal. A new image formed around him, a series of planting beds like those around this village. Oats grew on the nearest. The grain was still dark green, but it'd reached the height of the adults' chests and must be near its full growth.

It was late evening, and with their tools in their hands the villagers were moving toward the walkway that led to the walled community. A family—man, woman, and a quartet of children ranging from five to ten years old—had been cultivating the nearest bed. All carried hoes with clamshell blades, but the father had a spear as well.

Coerli came out of a grove of scale-barked trees, their long, narrow feet kicking up splashes of water. Their jaws were open and probably shrieking something, but Marzan's chant filled Garric's ears like the surf roaring in a heavy storm.

The youngest child was in the lead. She stopped transfixed and pointed; the hoe fell from her hand. Her mother clouted her on the side of the head and grabbed her wrist, dragging the girl with her along the narrow walkway.

The two boys and the eldest child, another girl, followed, their light capes flapping like bat wings. The walkway swayed but held, and the people running didn't slip on the wet wood.

The father ran toward the wider walkway the led from the village to the solid ground where the Coerli had been hiding. He got to it just as the cat men reached the other end. There were five of them, perhaps the same band Marzan had shown Garric in the first scene.

Terror drew the skin of the father's face taut over the bones. Villagers who'd been in the other planting beds continued running for the stockade; no one tried to help the family whom the Coerli had chosen.

The human waggled his spear, then hurled it. The leading Corl dodged, then leaped and batted the man into the pond with a swipe of his axe. The motion was swifter and smoother than the spear's wobbling flight.

As the father fell, the Corl made another great leap along the walkway and snapped out his weighted line. It curled over the heads of the older children to wrap the mother's throat, jerking her backward. Her left arm flailed wildly but her right hurled the little girl away from her and the cat men.

The child kept her feet and managed to run three steps before the last of the Coerli sprang onto her as the others were trussing the older children. Twisting her arms behind her back, the Corl thrust a thorn through both wrists to pinion them.

Fog rose to cover the images in the stone's heart. Garric felt a sucking sensation as his mind returned to his own control. His eyes felt gritty, even after he'd blinked several times.

Marzan slumped. He would've fallen across the topaz if Soma hadn't knelt beside him and reached an arm around his torso for support.

When Garric was a boy reading Old Kingdom epics, he'd thought wizardry was a matter of waving a wand and watching wonders occur. He'd seen the reality, now, the crushing effort needed to create visions like the ones Marzan had just shown him.

Garric grinned back at the ghost in his mind. *Aye,* he thought, *the poets didn't give me much feel for how bone-weary I'd be after a battle, either.*

Soma held a drinking gourd to the wizard's lips, tilting it slightly as he slurped the contents. He laid his hand on hers; she lowered the gourd and shifted a little in preparation for lifting him to his feet.

Marzan said something to her, then looked at Garric. He began to speak, not loudly but with hoarse-voiced determination. The only words Garric could understand were his own name and one other: Coerli. He had no context, nor did it help when Marzan gestured or took Garric's hands in his own and raised them.

At last Marzan gave up. He muttered to Soma, who helped him to one of the couches. He was shivering in reaction to his wizardry. Soma tucked a blanket around him with surprising gentleness.

Garric stood, working the stiffness out of his legs. The sun was down. The only light in the hut was an oil lamp—a gourd on a hook near the closed door with a twist of fiber for a wick—and the dull red glow of the hearth fire.

Two terra-cotta pots waited at the edge of the hearth; Soma had cooked a meal while Garric was entranced in the topaz. No wonder Marzan was exhausted!

"Garric," she said and gestured him to her. She sat down, using the hearth as a low table. He joined her, moving carefully. He was tired, not just stiff. It'd been a full day, if he could call it a day. . . .

Soma broke off a piece of oat cake, dipped it into fish stew from one of the pots, and tried to feed Garric with it. He waved her away and took the remainder of the cake himself to dip. The stew was delicious, and so was the mixture of squash and beans that'd steamed in the other container.

"I've eaten harness leather," Carus observed wryly, *"and thought it was fine."*

Garric smiled and nodded to Soma in appreciation. She handed him a gourd of beer, thin but with a pleasant astringence. It cleared the phlegm from the back of his throat.

There was something in what Carus said, but this *was* a good meal. Garric had been unjust to the woman, assuming she couldn't cook just because Katchin's wife Feydra couldn't.

When Garric had finished eating, Soma rose and gestured him toward the other couch. She drew back another thin blanket. He rose, suddenly so tired that he was dizzy, and thankfully walked to the couch. It was covered with a pad of fine wicker rather than a stuffed mattress; it gave pleasantly when he sat down on the edge.

Soma sat beside him and reached between his legs.

"No," Garric said, jumping to his feet again. He made a wiping motion in the air as he'd done when he refused to let her feed him.

Soma tugged at his only garment, the cape he'd borrowed when he met Scarface and his band. The loose knot opened at the pull, but Garric snatched it out of her hand. "No!" he repeated forcefully as he backed away.

Soma stood and lifted her tunic over her head. Garric turned and scrambled out the hut, closing the door behind him. He heard an angry shout; then something hit the panel from the inside.

There were many reasons Garric wasn't interested in Soma's offer. The fact that Marzan was his best chance of returning to his own friends was only a minor one.

It was raining again. Well, that wasn't a surprise. No lights showed in the village and the sky was black. Garric thought of stumbling to Wandalo's compound next door, but nothing he'd seen when he'd arrived here suggested the chief would be a friend. Perhaps in the morning he could find Scarface.

For now, though . . . Garric crawled under Marzan's hut. The clay was damp, but at least there wasn't standing water. Yet, of course.

As Garric turned, trying to find the least uncomfortable position, he heard a whine. A dog snuffled him, then licked his hand and curled up next to him. Back to back with the warm furry body, Garric slept.

He'd been in worse places.

Κing cervoran turned toward Cashel. It was his first action since he threw the lantern. He moved with the deliberation of something much larger: a tree falling or the ice covering the mill's roof slipping thunderously when the winter sun warmed the black slates beneath it.

"Where is the diadem?" he asked in his odd, thin voice. "Where is the topaz?"

"You mean the crown?" Cashel said. "Lady Liane took it after Garric, well, Garric disappeared. I guess it's in the room we were in when you came and fetched me."

Without speaking further Cervoran started across the courtyard. The mess was worse than in fall when sheep were slaughtered so there was enough fodder to winter the rest of the flock. There was blood and frightened bleats then too, but it was sheep, not men.

The oil flames had died, but the remains of the hellplant still smoldered; the air was hazy and rank. Green vegetation always stank when you burned it, but it seemed to Cashel that it wasn't just memory of what the thing was that made this worse'n usual.

Sharina was talking to Waldron and Attaper. Well, they were both talking at her, loudly and not paying attention to what each other said. Cashel started to go to her—but she was all right, he knew that. He

wanted to go back into the pantry and fetch his quarterstaff, but that
could wait too.

He knew in his heart what he ought to do, so he did it even though
it was about the last thing he'd've done for choice: he went after Cervoran, catching up with him in two quick strides and using the spear shaft
to tap folks and make a passage. Anybody who saw Cervoran got out of
the way, but in the noisy confusion people weren't paying attention to
much outside their own frightened imaginations just now.

It wouldn't do to have the wizard trampled and maybe even killed.
He'd been the only one who knew what to do when the plant attacked,
and the fact he'd known what to do even before it happened was important too.

There were guards—again—at the door to the conference room, but
they stepped out of the way with obvious relief when they saw Cashel.
They'd have felt they had to stop Cervoran, and they really didn't want
anything to do with a corpse. Maybe Cervoran'd just had a fit, but even
now he *looked* dead.

"Good to see you, milord," said the officer, a man Cashel didn't
know. "I didn't see how we were going to handle that thing till you took
care of it."

"It was really King Cervoran here," Cashel said, but he opened the
door and followed Cervoran into the room without trying to convince
the soldiers. They'd believe what they wanted to believe, and they *didn't*
want to believe a walking corpse had saved their lives.

Liane and civilians traveling with Garric were busy inside. Lord
Tadai stood in the middle of a whole handful of clerks from his department. Several of Liane's assistants were waiting for a word too, but she
was in a corner of the room talking to a fellow who was dressed like a
servant here in the palace. He was a lot *solider* to look at than you generally saw carrying trays and announcing guests.

Liane had spies all over the Isles; this man must be another of them.
The fact that she was talking with him right out in the open probably
didn't please either her or the spy, but at a time like this you might have
to do lots of things you weren't happy about.

Everybody looked up when the door opened. They kept on looking
when they saw who it was who'd come in.

"Give me the topaz," Cervoran said. His eyes weren't really focused
on anybody, but Cashel had the funny feeling that he saw everybody

around him. "Give me the jewel Bass One-Thumb took from the amber sarcophagus. It is necessary."

"He wants the crown, ah, Liane," Cashel said in the immediate silence. "Ma'am, he was the one who knew to burn that creature outside."

"It is necessary," Cervoran repeated. His voice hurt to listen to, though it wasn't loud or anything. Cashel wondered if the king had always sounded like that.

"Where do you propose to take the diadem?" Liane said. She sounded calm, but her fingers were hidden in a fold of her sash where Cashel knew she carried a little knife.

"What does it matter where this flesh is?" Cervoran said with obvious contempt. "I will use it here if you like. It is necessary."

"Yes, that will do," Liane said, her expression unchanged. She nodded to the assistant sitting with a velvet-wrapped bundle on his lap.

That fellow hopped to his feet and offered the package to her. "Give it to Lord Cervoran," she said sharply. She was generally polite as could be, but it seemed the things going on were affecting her too.

The clerk twitched. Cashel stepped forward, took the bundle, and handed it to Cervoran. The velvet dropped to the floor; Cervoran stared at the yellow stone as if he was trying to see through it to the veins of the rocks beneath the palace.

"Milady?" said the assistant timidly. "Does he *have* to be here?"

"Be silent!" Liane snapped.

Cervoran looked up. "Are you afraid, fool?" he said. His swollen lips spread in a minute grin. "Shall I tell you how you will die?"

The assistant's face went white. He opened his mouth to speak, then toppled forward in a dead faint. Cashel caught him and carried him back to the couch where he'd been sitting.

That was the first really human thing he'd seen Cervoran do since he walked off the pyre. It was a nasty thing to do to the poor clerk, but it was human.

When Cashel turned, Cervoran was looking at the stone again and standing like a wax statue. Tadai and his clerks talked in muted voices, and the spy was whispering to Liane. Nobody was paying Cashel any attention, maybe because he was standing close to Cervoran who nobody wanted to notice.

"Well, I'll go . . . ," Cashel said. "Ah, outside."

Liane nodded as Cashel stepped into the courtyard again, but nobody said anything. He was used to being ignored, of course, though this was a different business from what'd happened in the borough because he was a poor orphan. Everybody here was afraid, and they were afraid to learn anything that they didn't already know.

The bustle around the hellplant was getting organized now. Lord Waldron was giving orders while Sharina looked on at his side and Tenoctris bent over the smoking remains. Ilna was helping the old wizard, prodding layers of sodden greenery apart with the blade of her paring knife.

Cashel would've gone to join them, but his eye caught Prince Protas standing forlornly to the side. The boy's face was formally calm, but he looked awfully lonely. Cashel walked over to him.

"Lord Cashel!" Protas said, suddenly a frightened boy again in his enthusiasm. "Oh, sir, I heard you defeated the monster!"

"Your father knew to burn it," Cashel said. "I just carried the jar. I'll grant it was a big jar."

He spoke quietly, but he knew he sounded proud. He had a right to be proud, but it was true the real credit went to Cervoran.

Though Cashel wasn't completely sure "your father" was quite the right thing to call him now.

"Where did the monster come from, milor—" Protas said. He caught himself and finished, "Cashel, I mean."

Cashel grinned. "I don't know," he said, "but I'll bet if we follow that—"

He pointed the spear shaft toward the hole in the courtyard wall. He wasn't much of a woodsman—picking squirrels off a branch with a hard-flung stone was about as much hunting as he did—but the hellplant's rootlike legs had left a track of slime on the ground behind them. It smelled of salt and sour vegetable matter.

"—we can learn for ourselves. You want to come?"

"With you?" said the boy. "Yes *sir!*"

He sobered and said, "My tutor hid in a clothes chest when he looked out of the window and saw the thing here in the courtyard. When he comes out, he'll want me to get back to my mathematics lesson."

Cashel thought for a moment. He cleared his throat.

"I guess mathematics is important to know," he said. He wasn't sure exactly what mathematics was, though he thought it meant counting without having to drop dried beans in a sack. That was how Cashel did

it when the number got more than his fingers. "But I think this afternoon you can miss a lesson without it being too bad. What with, you
know, the trouble that happened."

Cashel looked at the spear shaft waggling in his hand while he
thought. "But before we do that," he added, "let's get my quarterstaff
back. Just in case."

He and the boy went into the west wing of the palace, through the
kitchens and the crowd of clerks and servants chattering there. Protas
looked around with real interest. Cashel couldn't understand why till the
boy said, "I've never been here before, you know. Is this where the food
comes from?"

"I guess it is," Cashel agreed. "It's fancier than I'm used to."

It must be funny to be a prince. When you're just a boy, anyway.
Garric seemed to be taking to it fine but he had his growth. Though
Garric as a boy would probably have gotten out more than Protas
seemed to've done.

Two servants were in the pantry. The woman looked down into the
cellars through the open trapdoor, but the man had picked up the quarterstaff and was turning it in his hands.

"I'll take that!" Cashel said, tossing the spear away. He hadn't meant
to've shouted but he wasn't sorry that he had. The woman shrieked like
she'd been stabbed; the man dropped the quarterstaff and turned so
quick that he got his feet tangled.

Cashel stepped forward, grabbing the hickory with his right hand
and the servant's arm with his left. The fellow screamed near as bad as
the woman had. Cashel guessed he'd gripped as hard with one hand as
the other, so there'd be bruises on the man's biceps in the morning. That
wouldn't be near as bad as what he'd have gotten by toppling headfirst
into the cellars the way he'd started to do, though.

"What were you doing with Lord Cashel's property, sirrah?" Protas
said. His voice sounded a lot like King Cervoran's, though the boy being
twelve was at least some of the reason.

"What?" said the servant, blinking as he realized it was the prince
speaking. "May the Shepherd save me, I didn't mean—I mean we saw it
and didn't know—that is—"

"It's all right," Cashel said, stroking his staff's smooth, familiar surface. The poor fellow was getting hit from all sides, it must seem like to
him. "You ought to close that cellar door before somebody breaks his
neck, though."

He led Protas back out through the kitchen. The folks there had been looking at the pantry and whispering. One woman got down on her knees and said, "May the Lady bless you, Your Lordship, for saving us from that terrible monster!"

"Ma'am, I just carried the jar," Cashel muttered. Goodness, she was trying to grab the hem of his tunic! He pulled away, striding out much quicker than he normally chose to do. The boy kept up, but he had to run to do it.

The sun was getting low in the sky, but it was still an hour short of sundown. They skirted the soldiers, who probably had a job here in the courtyard; and the civilians, who were mostly just gawking.

As they neared where the back gate had been a voice behind them called, "Your Highness? Prince Protas?"

Cashel turned; Lord Martous was bearing down on them from the other wing of the palace. "He's with me, sir!" Cashel said loudly.

To his surprise, the chamberlain bowed low and backed away. Cashel muttered to the boy, "I thought he'd tell me you had to go off with him anyhow."

"Oh, no, Cashel," Protas said in amazement. "Why, I'll bet even Prince Garric would have to do what you said if you told him something."

"I don't guess he would," Cashel said, blushing in embarrassment. "Anyway, *I* wouldn't do anything like that!"

Close up, what'd happened to the back wall looked pretty impressive. The edge courses were squared stones fitted together, and the rest of the wall was rubble set in concrete which'd cured long enough to be pretty near stone-hard itself. The plant had pushed until it cracked off full-height slabs to either side of the gateway. Besides that it'd broken the transom, a squared oak timber two hand-spans on a side.

"Are there more of the monsters, Cashel?" the boy asked as they followed the hellplant's track back down through the alley. Local people—town dwellers and country folk both, standing in separate groups—talked in low voices and watched as Cashel and Protas walked past.

"I don't know," Cashel said simply. He thought for a moment. "I guess we'd hear shouting if there were more of them close by, though."

The alley led straight to a notch in the seawall; it'd let you back a wagon all the way into the water if for some reason you wanted to. There was no question the hellplant had come up that way: the crushed limestone roadway was still dark with slime.

Two sailors had been talking on the seawall. They went quiet and watched when they saw Cashel and the boy walking straight toward them.

"May the Lady smile on you, good sirs!" Protas said, surprising Cashel. He'd been trying to figure how to open a conversation with strangers who didn't look very trusting. "This is Lord Cashel and of course I'm Prince Protas. Can you tell us how the creature appeared here? Did it come by boat then?"

The pair looked at each other nervously. "We didn't bring it!" said the man whose right arm was so tattooed he looked like he had a long-sleeved shirt on that side.

"Of course not, my good man!" the boy said scornfully. "But you saw it land, did you not? How did it arrive on First Atara?"

"I thought it was seaweed," said the little fellow with three gold rings in his right ear and the lobe of the left one missing. "Just drifting up, you know. And then it come to the wall and started to climb. And I took off running, I don't mind to tell you."

"There's no current could've drifted it to shore that quick," the tattooed man protested. "It had to be swimming, Goldie."

"I don't know what kinda currents there might be!" Goldie said angrily. "What with the Shepherd's slingstone whamming into the sea the way it did. Why, the one wave nigh cleared the seawall, and I've never seen that to happen no matter how bad a storm it is."

"That was this morning!" his companion said. "The sea was calm as calm all the past six hours."

"But you're sure the thing didn't come on a boat?" Cashel said, looking out along the track the low sun plowed glowing on the water. "It just swam?"

"Swam or drifted," Goldie said. "Swam, I guess. But I thought it was just something washed up from when the stone hit the sea."

Cashel looked out to the southwest, through the jaws of the harbor and down the sun's track across the open sea to where the meteor had landed. "You might be right at that," he said at last.

Though fire had devoured the outer layers of the hellplant, it seemed to Sharina that what remained was shrinking further the way frost-killed vine leaves sink into a fetor and ooze away. There was nothing obviously unnatural about this mass, but it was certainly foul and ugly. So was much of peasant life, of course.

Tenoctris had moved from examining the plant to looking at the corpse of one of the three scorpions from inside it. Now she turned and got up, partly supported by Ilna. Sharina smiled at them, hoping Tenoctris had learned something useful—and getting a wan look and shrug that made it clear she hadn't.

Chalcus stood nearby but didn't burden his hands with the weight of an old woman. His lips smiled but his eyes did not, skipping over everything around him. Chalcus' gaze didn't rest any longer than the late sunlight glinting on the edge of his drawn sword. If his eyes had found danger anywhere they danced, that sword would strike with a speed and precision that were themselves just short of magical.

"I've never seen anything like that," Tenoctris said, nodding slightly in the direction of the hard-shelled creature. "It's meant to live in water: its legs are paddles and it seems to have gills instead of lungs. But it's a scorpion and not a crab or lobster."

"Master Chalcus?" Sharina said. "You're a sailor. Do you know where such things come from?"

"Nowhere in the parts of the world I've traveled before now, milady," Chalcus said. He turned his face and his smile toward Sharina, but his eyes continued their restless search. "Which is a good deal of the world. I'd as lief that Mona here had been without the small demons as well, though I wouldn't mind them so much without the mount they rode in on . . . which is new to me as well, I'm thankful to say."

"And new to me," Tenoctris said with a slight nod; she seemed completely wrung out. "Perhaps later, tomorrow. . . ."

"There's nothing of immediate concern that you can see at the moment?" Sharina said. She raised the pitch of the final word to make it a question, but she knew that Tenoctris would've said so if she'd seen something. "In that case, why don't you get some food and rest? I've watched you do five separate divination spells, and I know how much effort that requires."

She smiled at the wizard with real warmth. Tenoctris was one of the strongest pillars on which the kingdom rested, but she was also a friend. In Sharina's mind, that was the more important thing of the two.

"We need you, Tenoctris," she said. "And we need you healthy."

"I did seven spells, not five," Tenoctris admitted with the same wan smile as when she'd risen to her feet. "And as for resting, I might've been asleep in bed for anything useful I gained from any of them. But yes, I'll see if I can't do better in the morning."

She dipped her chin in the direction of the plant's remains. The gesture was as quick and businesslike as a hatchet stroke. She added, "Don't allow this to be removed, if you will."

"Lord Waldron," Sharina said in a tone that was about as crisp as the wizard's nod. "Place a guard on this mess, if you please. Don't let anyone but Lady Tenoctris come near it."

The army commander barked a laugh. "As Your Highness wishes," he said. "Though I wouldn't worry about thieves myself. And if any of the palace staff are devoted enough to their duties to clean it up, that'll surprise me too."

"One of your own officers might've taken care of it, milord," said Attaper. His brief smile rang like a hammer. "Or mine, of course. Better safe than sorry."

Waldron snorted as he gave the orders. The two senior officers were in a surprisingly good mood. A creature that was physical if not exactly flesh and blood had attacked; the creature had been destroyed. That was how things were supposed to work in the soldiers' world, and by now the fact that something was unusual didn't bother them so long as it wasn't wizardry.

Soldiers tended to take a sharply limited view regarding what was their business, too. In the present case, that permitted both men to ignore the question of how a giant plant could've come to walk into the palace *without* wizardry. Sharina found that puzzling, but they were very good at their jobs.

A Blood Eagle, one of the squad Garric had detailed to guard Tenoctris, picked up the satchel in which the old wizard kept the paraphernalia of her art. He tramped along beside her, offering his free hand if she needed support on the way to her room and bed.

Most of the troops—like most civilians—were uncomfortable dealing with wizardry. There were a few, though, who didn't mind. All the Blood Eagles were ready to guard Tenoctris with their lives; this particular trooper was also happy to carry a bag filled with spells and potions, and to treat the wizard as though she were no more than an old lady with a pleasant personality.

Sharina was suddenly tired also, though she hadn't done any serious work today. It was the tension, she supposed. She giggled.

"Milady?" said Chalcus with a hard smile. "If there's a joke in all this business, I'd be pleased to hear it."

"When I got up this morning," Sharina said, "I was worried that my tongue would get tangled when I offered the hand of fellowship to Marquess Protas on behalf of the citizens of Haft. As it turned out, I needn't have worried since the coronation didn't take place. So many of our fears are empty."

She shook her head, grinning wryly. She looked around and added, "Does anyone know where Lady Liane's gone?"

"Not gone but stayed," said Ilna. "In the conference room Master Chalcus took me to when I proved useless here."

She glanced at the knotted pattern she held between the fingers of both hands, then grimaced and looked up again. Ilna was short and dark and slim; pretty or at least handsome, but likely to be overlooked when she was in the company of her friend Sharina, a lithe blond beauty. If Ilna resented that, she kept the feeling well hidden—even from Sharina herself.

"Then let's go talk with Liane," Sharina said, offering Ilna her arm and starting toward the council chamber. "She may know something about this even if Tenoctris doesn't."

The chamber was unexpectedly dim. The sky wasn't dark yet, but it didn't send much light through the clerestory windows. Nobody'd lighted the lamps in the wall sconces. The guards hadn't let servants in to do that, Sharina realized.

Sharina stepped back outside. The guards had a lighted lantern dangling from the edge of the portico. The hook supporting it normally held a polished marble "sparkler" that threw sunlight onto the interior as it rotated.

Sharina lifted down the lantern. "I'll borrow this if I may," she said, twisting the base away from the barrel to expose the burning candle. She walked into the council chamber with it.

"Your Highness?" said the puzzled officer behind her. Of course nobody objected to Princess Sharina taking a lantern if she wanted to, but he was probably surprised that she knew how to take it apart.

Sharina knew how to light lamps too. She walked from sconce to sconce, holding the candle flame just below the wick of each oil lamp in turn. The Lady only knew how many winter evenings she'd done this same thing at the inn, though generally using a splinter of lightwood instead of a candle.

She turned, righting the candle in her hand. One of Lord Tadai's clerks stood at her elbow, looking nervous.

"Jossin here will take that back to the guards, Your Highness," Tadai said. "I was remiss in not dealing with the situation myself earlier."

"It's not part of your job, milord," Sharina said. "And it has been part of mine."

She turned her attention to Liane, saying, "Do any of your sources know where the creature might have come from, Liane? Or who sent it?"

Cervoran moved. He held the uncut topaz, and it threw foggy highlights across the room as he lowered his hands. He'd been so still that Sharina hadn't noticed him until then.

"Not yet," said Liane, "though—"

"The Green Woman sent it," Cervoran said. "She made it in her Fortress of Glass and sent it to attack me."

His voice was rising in pitch and volume. The oil lamps gave his complexion a yellow tinge and brought out blotches beneath the skin that daylight had concealed. Neither Sharina nor Liane moved away from the recent corpse as most of the others in the room did, but Liane had her right hand between the folds of her sash.

"She will attack me while she lives and I do," Cervoran said.

"There'll be more of those hellplants?" Sharina asked sharply. Waldron and Attaper with their aides had entered the chamber behind her; the soldiers' faces were taut with the instinct to attack or flee.

"There will be many more!" Cervoran said. His fingers moved over the topaz like maggots crawling on a yellow corpse. "But I will prevail!"

ILNA LOOKED AT the man she'd saved from death on his own funeral pyre. If he was still a man, of course; and if she'd saved him.

"A meteor struck the sea yesterday," Cervoran said. "We must find it. The Green Woman is there, and I will defeat her."

"The slingstone struck, right enough," said Chalcus with cheerful bravado, the backs of his wrists against his hipbones and the fingers turned outward like flippers. "And I or anybody who was with the fleet can show you where, easily enough; any sailor, at least. But it won't do you any good, I fear."

Cervoran looked at him. Ilna had begun picking apart the pattern she'd knotted from lengths of twine as the hellplant slithered across the courtyard.

"Take me to the meteor," Cervoran said. Only his squeaky voice and the muffled breaths of the others in the room could be heard. "It is necessary. I will defeat her!"

The pattern would've frozen a man in his tracks. A man's eyes don't see: they gather patterns that his mind turns into sight. The patterns Ilna wove in fabric had a greater reality in the minds of those who saw them than a mountain or the blazing sun above.

"I can take you there right enough, my friend," Chalcus said. He feared the Gods—he didn't worship but he *feared*. He feared no other thing in this world as far as Ilna could tell, beast or man or wizard. "But the place I'll take you is the deepest trench in the Inner Sea. A full league down a wizard said, or so the rumor has it. If your Green Woman's on the bottom of that, then you'll not be going to her unless you're a fish, not so?"

Ilna's pattern hadn't stopped the plant. Now she was beginning to wonder what effect it would have on the recent corpse.

"Do you think to mock me, little man?" Cervoran said. It was odd to hear so shrill a voice speaking as slowly as a priest praying while the villagers came forward with their offerings during the Tithe Procession. "Take me to the place. It is necessary!"

"Your Highness?" Chalcus said, looking past Cervoran to Sharina. "This is a thing I can do well enough in the *Heron,* should you wish it. But . . . ?"

"It is necessary!" Cervoran repeated shrilly.

Cervoran, king or man or corpse, took Cashel out of this room and brought him back with a jar of oil in time to destroy the hellplant— which nobody else had been able to do, Ilna herself included. That didn't make Cervoran a friend to the kingdom and its citizens, but at least it made him an enemy of their enemies.

"Master Chalcus . . . ?" said Sharina. From the set look on her face she was thinking the same way as Ilna was. "Would a larger ship be better? I could send him out on the *Shepherd* or one of the triremes."

Chalcus snorted. "And what could a fiver do that my handy little *Heron* could not, eh, milady?" he said. "We can turn twice around in the time it'd take a cow like the *Shepherd* to change course by eight points only. We'll take him."

"At once," said Cervoran.

"Indeed not," said Chalcus. "In the morning. I'll find the spot by the angles on the Three Sisters east of here and Mona Headland itself, but I can't do that till sunrise."

"In the morning, then," Sharina said, giving an order rather than commenting. "And Master Chalcus? Don't set out until I've had a chance to learn Lady Tenoctris' opinion on the matter."

"Master Cervoran?" Ilna said. She'd reduced the knotted pattern to the cords it'd started as. She held them in her right palm and stroked them with the fingers of her left hand. "There was a slingstone, a meteor, hitting the sea as we approached the island yesterday."

"Yes," said Cervoran. "But I will go to her and defeat her."

"There was a second stone, *meteor,* this morning," Ilna said. She had the odd feeling that she was standing outside herself and hearing someone else speak. "During your funeral. It burst in the air above us. What did that meteor mean?"

"It means nothing," said Cervoran, his voice becoming even more shrill.

"It exploded in the air," Ilna repeated, "and then you rose from your bier. What does that mean?"

"I am Cervoran!" the former king cried. He lowered his eyes to stare into the topaz again.

"What?" said Ilna.

But Cervoran remained as motionless as a statue; and when Chalcus murmured, "We'll be up betimes, dearest. Best to get some rest now," Ilna left the chamber with him.

"There's a pattern too big for me to see the ends of it," Ilna whispered. Chalcus listened, but she wasn't so much speaking to him as to the cosmos itself. "But we're part of it, like it or not. And I *don't* like it at all!"

Chapter

5

SHARINA AWAKENED IN shocked awareness that something was wrong. She sat bolt upright, hearing low-voiced chanting nearby. She didn't know where she was, and the sun was already up behind the shutters.

She was out of bed, gripping the hilt of the Pewle knife with her right hand and its sealskin sheath with her left, when she remembered. She relaxed with a sigh, then giggled at what a fool she'd have looked if there'd been anyone to see her.

There wasn't, of course. Sharina had been an inn servant herself too long to want anybody serving her when she didn't need it.

The bedroom of the queen's suite where Sharina slept had a door to Cervoran's chamber of art. Tenoctris had that room now, sleeping on a simple cot and rising at intervals in the night to browse Cervoran's collection of books and objects by lamplight. That's what was happening now.

Sharina shot the knife back in its sheath, but she didn't hang it on the bedpost before she walked to the connecting door and opened it. Tenoctris sat on the floor, chanting over a flattened bead of green glass that'd been in the late king's curio cabinet.

Cashel stood close by, his quarterstaff planted firmly on the floor. He'd turned his head when he heard the door open. He didn't speak because that might've disturbed Tenoctris, but his smile was as warm as sunlight on the meadow.

A sparkle of blue wizardlight dusted the air above the glass bead, then vanished like a puff of warm breath on the polished face of a mirror. The old wizard sagged, setting down the split of bamboo she'd used for a wand. She disposed of each sliver after she'd used it once, because she said otherwise the influences it'd absorbed from previous spells would affect later ones in directions she couldn't foresee.

Most wizards made wands and athames, dagger-shaped implements of art, from materials chosen to concentrate power; then they covered the tools with symbols of art to increase the effect still further. Those folk could perform far greater wizardry than Tenoctris could . . . but as Sharina herself had seen, eventually they did something they hadn't intended. A very great wizard had brought down the Old Kingdom a thousand years past—and was drowned in a reaction to his spell which he hadn't predicted and couldn't control.

Tenoctris' smile had a hint of fatigue. She put her right hand on the floor to brace her as she rose, but Cashel instantly squatted and supported her. For the most part Cashel ambled along at the pace of the sheep he'd spent most of his life caring for, but he moved with amazing speed when he needed to.

"This comes from the moon," Tenoctris said, dipping a finger toward the glass bead she'd left within the five-pointed star drawn in powdered charcoal. She wasn't using the figures Cervoran had inset in the floor any more than she was using an athame carved from a dragon scale. "It'd fallen into the sea, struck off the moon's surface by a meteor. Cervoran located it through his art and sent divers to bring it up for him."

"What does it do, Tenoctris?" Sharina asked, looking at the vaguely greenish bead with greater interest. "Does it increase your powers?"

"It doesn't do anything at all, dear," the old woman said, smiling faintly. "But it's from the moon."

She gestured toward the shelves and bookcases which covered the workroom's outside wall. They were a hodgepodge of objects, codices, and (in pigeonholes) scrolls. None of the jumbled contents were labeled.

"That's generally the case with Cervoran's collection," she explained. "Many of the objects I've examined are quite remarkable, but they're not really *good* for anything. They're not important."

Sharina cleared her throat. "Tenoctris," she said, "King Cervoran wants to go out to where the meteor fell as we approached the island. Chalcus is ready to take him if I agree. Should I let him go?"

Tenoctris stood motionless for a moment; then she dipped her head three times quickly like a nuthatch cracking a seed. "Yes, I believe so," she said. "But I'd like to go along."

"To see what Cervoran's searching for, Tenoctris?" Cashel said. "Or to watch Cervoran?"

Tenoctris chuckled. "A little of both, I suppose," she said. "He's a greater puzzle than any of the objects in his collection. The divinatory spells I've attempted haven't helped me to understand him better."

Sharina's right hand touched the Pewle knife. The cool horn scales settled the gooseflesh that was starting to spring up on her arms.

"I wonder if he was always like he is now?" she said. "I don't see how he could've been. I think he changed during the time he was, well, the time he *seemed* dead."

"I don't know, dear," Tenoctris said in a regretful tone. "The wizard who amassed this collection was of considerable power but no real focus. He was a scholar of a sort, one who preferred to use his art to learn things rather than to search them out in books as I've always done for choice. But he wasn't a man with interests beyond his studies, and he certainly didn't have an enemy who would send a creature like that plant to kill him."

She gave Sharina one of the quick, bright smiles that took twenty years off her apparent age. "And before you ask, no, I don't know who the Green Woman is either."

"Maybe we'll learn today," said Cashel. He looked at Sharina.

"I know you have to stay here and, well, be queen," he said. "But do you mind if I go with Tenoctris? I think there ought to be somebody with her that was, well, hers."

"I think that's a good idea," Sharina said. She stepped quickly to Cashel and hugged him, careful to hold the knife out in her hand so that the sheath didn't prod him in the back. "We need Tenoctris. But Cashel?"

"Ma'am?" Cashel said, his voice a calm rumble like the purr of a sleeping lion.

"Be careful of yourself, too," Sharina said, still holding herself tight against his solid bulk. "Because I need *you,* my love."

ꝿARRIC AWAKENED IN shocked awareness that something was wrong. *Somebody shouted!* he thought.

Somebody screamed, but Garric was already worming his way out from under Marzan's house. The dog was gone and an angry yapping sounded from the direction of the village gate. That was where the scream'd come from, too.

It was dark: cloud-wrapped, moonless, starless *dark*. Even so the house had a presence in the darkness.

Garric reached up the sidewall, groping. The fishnet hung where he remembered it. He jerked it down, pulling a wall peg out in his haste. The size of the house showed that Marzan was a great man for this village, but that didn't save him or his wife from having to catch their own fish. He wondered if they had to work in the raised fields as well, or if wizardry at least saved them from that backbreaking drudgery.

Heartbeats after the scream, a dozen or more *things* shrieked from around the whole eastern circumference of the village. They weren't human and they weren't in pain: they were beasts, hunting.

"Coerli," the ghost of Carus said in Garric's mind. "*They looked very quick.*"

Neither he nor Garric had any doubt about what was going on, though thus far they'd seen the cat men only in silent topaz visions. This must be a larger band than the five who'd raided the field before, though.

Garric stepped to the fence, moving by memory and instinct. He felt along the top rail to an upright and gripped it firmly. The railings were cane, but the support posts were wrist-thick and of a dense wood probably chosen to resist rot.

Garric half-squatted, then straightened his knees and pulled the post up with a squelch of wet clay. The railings were bound on with cane splits. A quick shake right and left snapped them free.

A sword'd be better, but even that probably wouldn't be good enough. The Coerli were inhumanly quick, impossibly quick; but you did what you could.

Marzan's door opened and fanned out light, shocking in the previous darkness. Garric risked a glance over his shoulder. Soma stood in the doorway with a rushlight: a reed stripped to the pith, dried, and soaked with oil or wax. It lit quickly and wasn't as easy to blow out as a candle, though the flames didn't last long either. In her right hand was a knife made of horn or ivory.

There were more screams in the night, all of them human. A pair of yellow-green eyes flared in the rushlight's circle, ten or a dozen feet from Garric. He spun the net out as though he were casting for minnows, keeping hold of the drag. He couldn't reach the Corl with it, but he saw the spinning meshes bell as the cat man's own hooked line tangled with them.

Garric pulled his left arm back *hard* while swinging the sturdy post outward, a crushing blow directed at the empty air in front of him. He felt the weight as the slack came out and the net brought the Corl with it.

The beast shrilled in startled fury. Like the cat men Garric had watched in the topaz, this one had wrapped the end of its casting line around its wrist for a more secure grip. Racing charioteers regularly did the same thing with their reins—and were regularly dragged to their deaths when they fell or their vehicle broke up beneath them.

The cat creature was lithe and muscular, but its slight frame weighed less than a human female; Garric's furious strength could've overmastered an opponent twice as heavy. When this one realized it couldn't resist the pull, it twisted in the air and leveled its delicate spear at Garric's face. Garric's club brushed the light shaft out of the way and smashed the Corl's left arm and ribs.

The cat man slammed to the ground, instantly curling faceup despite its injuries. Garric kicked at its face with his heel. He missed because the Corl ducked its head aside faster than a human could've thought.

Garric spun the net widdershins. Despite its speed, the wounded creature couldn't completely avoid the spreading meshes. It yowled again and—Gods! it was fast—stabbed Garric in the thigh with its spear. His club stroke had broken the flint blade straight across, but this thrust was a strong one and tore into the muscle.

Garric swung the club a second time. The Corl would've dodged but Garric scissored his arms, tugging the net toward him at the same time he brought the club down. The cat man's skull was large to give the strong jaw muscles leverage, but the bones were light and crunched beneath the powerful blow. The creature's saw-edged scream died in the middle of a rising note.

There were glowing eyes to right, left, and center. Garric flattened and heard the spiteful *bwee!* of a thorn-barbed line arcing through the air above him.

He started to roll. A Corl landed on his back and looped his neck with a garrote.

Garric's throat was a ball of white fire. He gripped the Corl's calf with his left hand, then swung the creature like a flail into the ground beside him. It bounced with a moan of pain, losing both ends of the garrote.

Garric stabbed with his pole, using it as a blunt dagger instead of a club. Ribs cracked under the Corl's brindled fur.

Garric's arm went numb; he saw the post drop from his hand though he couldn't feel his fingers release. The Corl standing above him raised its stone axe for a second blow like the one that'd already stunned his right shoulder.

Garric kicked sideways. The Corl leaped over the swift attack with no more difficulty than Garric would've made in hopping from rock to rock in crossing a stream. Garric had saved his skull for a few moments, but perhaps only that.

Soma threw her rushlight at the Corl in a blazing whirl. The cat man wailed, its eyelids blinking closed and its arms crossing in front of its face. The pithy stalk bounced away in a shower of sparks.

Garric lunged upward, still seated but his torso straight and his left hand spearing out to grab the Corl by the throat. It struck clumsily with the axe, but he jerked its face down onto the anvil of his skull. A fang gouged Garric's forehead painfully, but the Corl's nose flattened with a crackling of tiny bones.

Garric tried to lift his right hand to twist its neck like a chicken's; the muscles of his bruised arm didn't respond. He shook the Corl one-handed, showering blood from its ruined face for the instant before the world flashed in negative: charcoal shadows on a sepia background becoming white on pearl.

I've been hit on the head. . . .

Garric turned and rose like a whale broaching from the depths. His world was silent and without feeling but he could move, did move. A Corl half again the size of the others faced him with a ball-headed baton lifting for another blow. This creature had a lion's mane and prominent male genitalia. Behind him Soma was being born down by another cat man.

Garric lurched toward the big Corl, stumbling from weakness. The club's shaft rather than the knobbed end cracked him across the head.

Light flashed. Garric saw the mud rushing up, but he didn't feel the smack of it against his face.

Then there was nothing at all.

Cashel stood on shore beside Tenoctris and Ilna, waiting for word to board. Chalcus walked down the line of oarsmen, chatting in friendly fashion but looking each man over as carefully as Cashel would the sheep walking out of the byre past him in the morning.

"Is he worried about the men?" Tenoctris said. "They're his regular crew, aren't they?"

Ilna looked at the older woman but didn't speak. Cashel nodded in understanding. His sister wasn't one to repeat things that she and Chalcus talked about in private, not even to a friend like Tenoctris.

Cashel had only what he'd seen and what he knew from experience. Tenoctris was very smart, but she'd lived in a different world from that of men whose work took them into places they might not come back from. Cashel understood that sort of thing better.

"I don't guess he's worried about the men rightly," he said. "But they've been on shore and living pretty hard, I guess. If anybody's so hung over he'll be dragging on his oar, or he's got his head cracked in a tavern, Chalcus'll leave him ashore this time."

He cleared his throat. "It's not the men he's worried about," he added. "It's where we're going."

"Ah," said Tenoctris. "Yes, I see that. I regret to say that I share his concern."

They all three looked where the sailors were determinedly *not* looking, at King Cervoran standing alone with a case of age-blackened oak on the sand beside him. Cervoran's complexion was so waxen that Cashel had a vision of him melting in the bright sunlight.

"He's bringing objects from the collection in his workroom," Tenoctris said quietly. "Nothing of real power or significance, except for the diadem. There *isn't* anything else really significant in the palace."

"He brought the big topaz?" Ilna said as her fingers knotted and picked out patterns. She glanced out through the mouth of the harbor to where a plume of vapor rose on the horizon.

"Yes," Tenoctris said. "He said it was necessary . . . the way he does, you know."

She shrugged and added with a faint smile, "I'm not sure what the stone is. It's important, but I can't find the key to how to use it. I've been reading the documents in Cervoran's library. I've learned many interesting things, but thus far nothing about the topaz."

"All right, buckos!" Chalcus called in a cheerful voice. "Let our fine passengers board and we'll take them to visit a hole in the deep sea."

He turned and flourished his right arm toward Cervoran and beyond. "Master Cervoran, Milady Tenoctris, and my dear friends," he said. "If you'll cross the gangplank and stand steady, we'll be shortly under way."

Cervoran was stumping forward at the first words. Cashel was ready to help him across the narrow boarding bridge that ran from shore to the bireme's central catwalk, but he shuffled along without hesitation.

That didn't mean he wouldn't fall off, of course. The *Heron* was pulled up on the beach, and the catwalk was a full man's height above the sand.

"A man could break his neck if he fell from that," Cashel murmured.

"Yes," said Tenoctris. "And perhaps Cervoran could also, though I'm by no means sure that's true."

She paused and added, "I may be being unjust."

"We can go aboard now, I guess," Cashel said quietly.

Ilna looked at Tenoctris. "Do you think I shouldn't have saved him?" she asked with a touch of challenge.

"I'm not sure Cervoran is an enemy," Tenoctris said. "He's certainly not our only enemy at present. You did what was right at the time."

Ilna gave a little dip of her chin in acknowledgment. "I'm sure some of the people I hurt when I was doing evil's will were evil themselves," she said. "I suppose it's only fair that I save a few of them now to make up for it."

She was joking but completely straight-faced. Well, maybe she was joking.

Cervoran'd reached the deck and gone forward. It was intended for the steersman, the ship's officers, and seamen handing the sails when they were set.

Chalcus had told Cashel that although the *Heron* didn't carry marines, the oarsmen had swords or spears and wicker shields under their benches. The *Heron* had a ram, but if they found themselves locked to an enemy vessel the crew'd leap over the other's gunnels with wild cries and their weapons out.

Chalcus said that was how the pirates fought; and from the scars Cashel saw on the fellow's body, he should know. Cashel smiled: Chalcus was good for Ilna, and that was all that mattered now.

Ilna led the way up the gangplank. Tenoctris followed, one hand gripping Ilna's sash. The older woman wasn't prickly about doing everything for herself; she knew she could lose her balance. Cashel was last in line, the satchel and quarterstaff in his left hand so that his right could grab Tenoctris if she slipped.

The plank wasn't much, but even so it was for the landsmen only: Chalcus and his sailors would swarm aboard like so many monkeys. Cashel would just as soon of done that himself—he wasn't a sailor, but with his strength and the quarterstaff to brace him he could climb a sheer wall twice his own height—but he'd come for Tenoctris' sake, and that meant staying close to her.

When the passengers were on the central catwalk, Chalcus shouted an order. A double handful of men scrambled onto the outriggers and thrust their oar looms down to brace the narrow hull. The steersman loosed the hawsers tying the sternpost to the mast and yard, rammed into the sand as bollards while the ship was out of the water. Chalcus was leaving the sailing paraphernalia on shore, since the *Heron* was going no farther than they could see on the horizon.

When the men aboard were set, Chalcus called, *"Pay me or go to jail!"* in a singsong voice. *"Pay me my money down!"* The crew on shore surged forward, lifting and shoving the *Heron* into the harbor.

"Pay me master sailorman!" Chalcus sang and the men ran the ship the rest of the way out. *"Pay me my money down!"*

The *Heron* bobbed briskly, light without the weight of her crew to steady her. The oarsmen swung themselves over the outriggers from both sides, balancing the hull and sliding quickly onto their assigned benches to unship their oars.

Cashel put an arm on Tenoctris' shoulder. It seemed to him the old woman was gripping the rail harder than the pitching really required.

"All the sailing I did in the age in which I was born . . . ," Tenoctris said. She was standing between Ilna and Cashel on the narrow deck, so she turned to touch both of them with her wry smile. "Was on merchantmen, and generally old tubby ones besides. I sometimes thought how much nicer it would be on a sleek, swift warship."

She didn't put the rest of the thought into words, but she didn't have to. Cashel and his sister grinned back.

The flute player in the stern with Chalcus played a pretty farandole as the rowers fitted their oars into the rowlocks. Then at a quickening two-step from the flutist, they began to stroke in unison. The *Heron* slid forward, steadying as she moved. The wobbliness of the raised catwalk became a slick, slow yawing as the hull moved into and through the swells.

Tenoctris relaxed slightly. Cashel took his hand off her shoulder, but he stayed ready to grab her any time.

The *Heron* passed between the jaws of the harbor and into open sea. The surface was a bit choppier, but the rowers had the beat and the short hull didn't pitch. Chalcus walked forward, whistling a snatch of the chantey he'd sung to launch the ship.

"Milady Tenoctris," he said with a bow that was affectionate rather than mocking. "I have them on an easy stroke, one the boys could keep up all day needs must—which they won't, given how close the thing is."

He nodded toward the plume of vapor off the bow. A light breeze bent the column eastward to thin and vanish, but already Cashel could tell it was rising from a single patch of surface.

"A volcano under the sea, do you think, milady?" Chalcus added in what somebody who didn't know him well might've thought was a nonchalant voice.

"I don't know," Tenoctris said simply. She smiled for fellowship, not because there was anything funny. "I don't think so, but I really don't know."

"Ah, well," said Chalcus, putting his arm around Ilna's waist and hugging her close for a moment. She didn't respond, but she smiled and didn't pull away either. "We'll all know shortly, will we not?"

Cashel followed his eyes, not toward the vapor this time but to Cervoran standing motionless in the bow.

"That one knows, though he won't tell us, eh?" Chalcus said.

Ilna continued working her knots as she looked at Cervoran. She looked coldly angry, but for Ilna that didn't mean a lot.

"He thinks he knows," Ilna said. "For most wizards, that isn't the same thing as knowing."

Chalcus nodded curtly. He set his hands on his hips and stood arms akimbo. "Master Cervoran!" he called. "I'm going to halt a bowshot short of the smoke and bring us around."

Cervoran turned, giving Cashel again the feeling that the bits and pieces of the wizard's body weren't working together quite the way they ought to. "I must be close," he said. "It is necessary."

"You'll be as close as I'm willing to come and pretend the ship's safe," snapped Chalcus. "Which is a bowshot out!"

He walked back to the stern, moving more like a cat than a cat does. Cervoran didn't do anything for a moment. His eyes remained fixed on where Chalcus'd been instead of following the sailor away.

The cloud of steam was getting close. It covered a considerable patch of the sea, enough to swallow the *Heron* if they'd gone into it. Cashel was just as glad they weren't going to, but he'd trust Chalcus on something like that if he'd said it was all right—or Tenoctris did, of course.

Tenoctris hadn't argued with Chalcus.

Chalcus shouted an order that didn't mean anything to Cashel. The stroke oars on both levels called something too, and the flute player changed his rhythm. The rowers all lifted their oars together; then the ones on the port side backed water with a measured stroke while those to starboard pulled normally. The ship began to slow and turn like a fishhook.

"That isn't steam," Ilna said. "The water's not boiling, and besides the color's too yellow."

They had a good view of the column now. Cashel could even see it wobbling up from the depths, twisted by currents but curling back like a corkscrew for as far down as he could follow it. Far below even that was a speck of light. It must be really bright and big to be seen, but it didn't have any more detail than a star does.

Cervoran opened his oak case. First he placed the topaz crown on his head, then he brought out a small brazier made of filigreed bronze. He pointed at the brazier and spoke an unheard word. A scarlet spark popped from his finger, striking the sticks of charcoal instantly alight.

Cashel moved a trifle to put himself between the two women and the man in the bow. Cervoran took a bowl out of his case and held it out to Cashel. "Fill this with seawater," he said. "At once."

Cashel glanced at Tenoctris; she nodded. Cervoran opened his mouth again as Cashel handed his staff to his sister to hold. He didn't often speak sharply, but this time he said, "Don't say that, if you please, Master Cervoran. I don't care if it's necessary or not, I'm coming t' do it!"

Cashel took the cup. It was bone, mounted in silver but the top of a human skull beyond doubt. He'd handled dead men's bones, and he'd cracked bones to kill men if it came to that; but Cervoran having such a thing for a toy wasn't a thing to make Cashel warm to the man, that was a fact.

He gripped the railing and swung himself over, feeling the narrow hull rock. Chalcus shouted in a voice like a silver trumpet, "Bonzi and Felfam, get to port *now*!" The two men closest the bow on the starboard outrigger jumped from their benches and shifted to the other side as Cashel let himself down where they'd been.

Only a few men on either side were rowing now, slow strokes to keep the ship from drifting back into the column of smoke. It smelled like brimstone. There were fish floating on their sides around it, a lot of them kinds Cashel had never seen before. There should've been gulls and all kinds of seabirds, but the sky was empty.

He bent over the outrigger and dipped the skull full. The sea looked pale green, but the water in the cup was just water, nothing different to the eye from what bubbled up in the ancient spring-house where most of Barca's Hamlet fetched its water.

Cashel stood and raised the cup in his hand. Cervoran had taken the crown off and was looking into the topaz again. His lips were moving, but no sound came out.

"Master Cervoran?" Cashel said. He couldn't climb up holding the cup, not without spilling the most of it. Didn't the fellow see—

Tenoctris took the skullcap from Cashel and held it out to Cervoran. He didn't react until she raised it so that it was between the topaz and his eyes; then he took the cup and replaced the crown on his head. As Cashel lifted himself onto the catwalk—the sturdy railing squealed and the *Heron* bobbed violently—Cervoran held the cup over the charcoal fire and chanted, *"Mouno outho arri. . . ."*

Cashel took his staff. He didn't exactly push the women back, but he kept easing toward them and they in turn moved down the catwalk to the middle where the mast'd been. They could hear Cervoran chanting there, but as a sound instead of being words.

"Do you know what he's doing, Tenoctris?" Ilna asked. She seemed curious, not frightened, and she spoke like she didn't have a lot of use for the fellow she was asking about. Pretty much normal Ilna, in fact.

"He's gathering power to him," the older woman said. "And channeling it onto the surface of the sea. I don't know why or what he intends by that. And I don't know what the thing in the abyss is, though it's more than a simple meteor."

She smiled. "We knew that before we came, I suppose, didn't we?" she added.

"Could you say a spell yourself and learn, ma'am?" Cashel asked. He kept his face half toward the women, but he made sure he could watch Cervoran out of the corner of his eye.

The water in the cup was bubbling, which it shouldn't've been without the bone charring—which wasn't happening. No man Cashel knew could've kept holding the cup like that close above a charcoal fire. No matter how brave you were, there was a time that the heat was too much and your fingers gave way. Cervoran's seemed to be sweating yellow fat.

"Perhaps I could," Tenoctris said, her eyes on the other wizard, "but I think I'm better off seeing what my colleague is doing. If I concentrate on my art, I'd be likely to miss things. I'm also concerned that—"

She met Cashel's eyes. "I'm afraid that if I sent my mind down to that light," she said, "either I wouldn't be able to get back or I'd bring something back with me. Cervoran may not be our friend, but I'm quite sure that the thing he's fighting, the Green Woman, is our enemy and mankind's enemy."

"*Kriphi phiae eu!*" Cervoran shouted. The sea was suddenly glazed with red light. The ship jolted upward. When the light faded, the surface had frozen to ice the hue of the wizard's topaz crown.

The rowers shouted in terror and jumped from their benches. The *Heron* trembled as the floor of an inn would when men were struggling on it, but it didn't heel and pitch: the hull was set solidly in the ice.

Cervoran dropped the skullcap. Still chanting, he lifted himself over the railing and slid down the bow's outward curve to the ram. He landed like a sack of oats, but he got up immediately and stepped onto the ice.

"*Iao obra phrene . . . ,*" he chanted as he walked stiffly toward where the smoke had risen.

The light in the depths shone through, despite the thickness of the ice.

W HILE ILNA WATCHED the former corpse stumping across the yellow ice, her fingers knotted lengths of twine and her mind danced along the vast temple of connections that her pattern *meant*. People thought that things stood apart from each other: a rock here, a tree here, a squalling baby here.

They were wrong. Everything was part of everything else. A push at this place meant a movement *there*, unimaginably far away; without anyone knowing that the one caused the other.

Ilna knew. She saw the connections only as shadow tracings stretching farther than her mind or any mind could travel, but she *knew*. And she knew that the pattern of action and response centered on this point—on Cervoran, on the thing beneath the sea, and on Ilna os-Kenset—was greater and more terrible than she could have imagined before this moment.

Cervoran stood in the near distance with his hands raised; the jewel on his brow pulsed brighter than the pale sun hanging at zenith. The rhythm of his chant whispered over the ice like the belly scales of a crawling viper.

The frightened oarsmen shouted angrily. Ilna could see the men brandishing swords they'd taken from beneath their benches. One fellow jumped out of the ship and began hacking at the ice. He'd have done as much good to chop at a granite wall; the ice was thicker than the *Heron* was long. The oarsmen couldn't tell that, but Ilna knew.

Chalcus spoke to calm his crew, then asked Tenoctris a question with a flourish of his hand. She answered and Cashel said something as well, calm and solid and ready for whatever came.

Ilna's ears took in the sounds, but her mind was focused outside the ship, outside even the universe. She saw the shadows merge and link. The light in the depths swelled and wove its own pattern across the cosmos. She understood what Cervoran was doing, and she understood that he would fail because what he faced was more powerful than he knew or could know.

Ilna understood. Cervoran was a part of the pattern created by the light and the thing within the light. Very soon it would be complete.

She couldn't block the play of forces any more than Cashel could stand between two mountains and push them apart. She and her brother were powerful in their own ways, but the present battle was on a titanic scale. All Ilna could do was protect herself, wall herself off from the struggle.

She raised the pattern her fingers had knotted, holding it before her eyes. Then—

A flash of blue wizardlight penetrated the sea and sky, clinging to and filling all matter. Motion ceased, and the universe was silent except for the voice of Cervoran shrilling, *"Iao obra phrene. . . ."*

He was trapped in his own spell, weaving the noose to hang him and hang all the universe with him. Everything was connected. . . .

Ilna tucked the cords into her sleeve and climbed over the railing. The pattern was fixed in her mind, now. She no longer needed the physical object, and she didn't have time to pick out the knots.

The oarsmen stood like a jumble of statues, frozen by the spell and counterspell. Ilna hung on the outside of the railing for a moment to pick a spot to fall. She dropped to the outrigger between a man caught shouting desperately to Chalcus and one praying to the image of the Lady he held in his hands. She stepped down to the ice.

"*Akri krithi phreneu . . . ,*" Cervoran said.

Ilna walked toward him, taking short paces on the slick footing. The ice humped and cracked the way the millpond in Barca's Hamlet did during a hard winter.

"*Ae obra euphrene . . . ,*" Cervoran said.

The ice groaned in an undertone that blended with the wizard's voice. He'd been a fool to match himself against the thing beneath, but Ilna had been a fool herself many times in the past . . . and perhaps now. She loathed fools. *All* fools.

As the light flooding up through the ice grew brighter, the sky blurred gray and the scattered clouds lost definition. Ilna wasn't sure whether the spell had formed a cyst in time around Cervoran and those with him, or if the whole world was being changed by the pattern woven in words of power.

"*Euphri litho kira . . . ,*" cried Cervoran or at least Cervoran's lips.

Ilna was wearing suede-soled slippers because city custom, court custom, demanded that she not be barefoot. Nobody could've ordered her to wear shoes, but people might have laughed if she hadn't.

Part of Ilna would've said that she didn't care what other people thought, but that wasn't really true. The truth was that she'd do what she thought right no matter what anyone said or thought; but it was true also that if it was simply a matter of wearing shoes needlessly or being laughed at, she'd wear shoes.

That was a fortunate choice now. She'd walked barefoot on ice in the past when she had to, but the layer of suede was less uncomfortable. She hadn't dressed for deep winter this morning.

The light beneath the sea throbbed in the rhythm of a beating heart. As the syllables fell from Cervoran's lips it glowed brighter, faded, and grew brighter yet.

"*. . . rali thonu omene. . . .*"

Ilna reached the chanting wizard. She was a weaver, not a wizard. She could do things with fabric impossible for anyone else she'd met, perhaps impossible for anyone else who'd ever lived. But any bumpkin in the borough could slash across one of Ilna's subtle patterns, destroying it and its effect completely.

Ilna grasped the golden wire and twisted the topaz diadem off Cervoran's head.

The wizard shrieked like a circling marsh hawk. His hands fell and his body went limp. She caught him as he slumped, then pulled his arms over her shoulders and turned, dragging him with her toward the ship. Cervoran was silent and a dead weight, but she'd done this before.

Breaking the spell had freed the crew of the *Heron*. Ilna heard the men shouting and praying, all at the top of their lungs for the joy of being able to speak again. Someone called her name, but she saved her breath for what she *had* to do.

The ice was breaking up, crackling and groaning underfoot. A great slab tilted vertical close by Ilna's left side, then slipped back with a moan. Salt water shot up from the fissure in a rainbow geyser; the whole ice sheet undulated in a web of spreading cracks.

Water as warm as blood sluiced ankle-deep across her feet. She paused, then stamped onward when the flow ceased. The ice, already slick, now glistened mirror-bright and smooth. She paced on because there was no choice and no other hope.

The snapping grew to a roar and the ice began to shiver. A chasm was opening, rushing toward Ilna faster than she could walk away from it. She didn't run because she couldn't run with Cervoran's weight to carry; and if she tried she'd fall; and if she fell, she'd fail.

She was blind with effort. Her breaths burned as she dragged them in through her open mouth.

Ilna had no God to pray to because she didn't believe in the Gods, and no one to curse because her own choice had brought her to this. Curses would be as empty as prayers, and anyway she wouldn't curse.

Cervoran lifted away from her. Her eyes focused. Cashel was beside her, striding for the ship again with the once-dead wizard over this shoulder. Chalcus caught Ilna around the waist and snatched her overhead with an acrobat's grace and a strength that belied his trim body. Together the men ran the last few steps back to the ship and handed their burdens aboard. A burly crewman took Ilna and lowered her to the hollow planking beneath the outrigger.

She turned. The ice sheet was pulling apart in a torrent dancing with great yellow chunks. The split reached the *Heron*, lifting the ship and shaking it like a dog before dropping it to wallow freely in open water.

"To your benches, buckos!" Chalcus shouted. "Panshin, give us the stroke on your flute! On your *lives*, my lads!"

Ilna stepped up to a bench and jumped, catching the railing around the raised deck. Chalcus was mounting in a single smooth motion, swinging his feet over with a twist of his shoulders. Ilna wasn't an acrobat or a sailor, but she heaved herself onto the rail, balanced, and rotated her body to stand upright. Tenoctris was beside her, holding the quarter-staff vertical in both hands.

Cashel, methodical as always, lifted Cervoran to the deck like a sack of grain and pulled himself up. The ship pitched and yawed, but that always happened when oarsmen shifted back to their places.

Cashel took his staff with a smile and a murmur of thanks. He looked past Cervoran toward the island.

Tenoctris said, "May I look at the diadem, Ilna?" In a warmer tone she added, "You saved our lives, you know. At least our lives."

Ilna looked down in surprise. She was holding the crown in her right hand, the gold wire twisted into a knot by her grip. The big topaz winked, reminding her of the ice now shattered about the *Heron.*

"I . . . ," said Ilna. She wasn't sure what to say next, so she just handed the crown to Tenoctris. It wasn't really damaged. Pure gold was nearly as flexible as silk, so the band could easily be bent back into its original shape.

The ship was getting under way. Only half the oars pulled water on the first stroke, but the remaining rowers were sliding onto their benches and picking up the rhythm. Chalcus called, "Aye, lads, your backs or your necks. Put your backs in it, sailors!"

Tenoctris was examining the crown, turning it by the band but eyeing the play of light in the heart of the stone. Ilna wondered if she should've thrown the jewel into the sea, but if she'd done that. . . . It must've had something to do with Garric's disappearance, so it was the best chance they had for returning the prince to his kingdom and Garric to the friends who needed him just as surely as the kingdom did.

Cashel kept his back to the two women; his quarterstaff stood upright like a supporting pillar. Cervoran sprawled ahead of him on the catwalk, his eyes open but unseeing. *He might have been dead,* Ilna thought; and smiled grimly. *Dead again, that is.*

The sea leaped with violent ripples centered on the place in the near distance where Cervoran had stood to chant. Violent blows hammered the *Heron's* keel. Oars clattered as a few of the rowers lost the stroke, but they picked it up again almost instantly. When Ilna looked down on the benches she saw faces set in fear and stony determination.

Water bubbled, mounded, and finally climbed to the sky in the *Heron's* wake. The rowers faced backward, so all of them could watch. This time they kept the rhythm, taking themselves farther from what was happening behind them with every stroke.

The roar filled the sky and flattened the chop. The sea mounded in a huge circle, spreading outward from the rising dome. Fish and flotsam and yellow foam danced in the churning water.

A gleaming, turreted crystal mountain rose from the surface, throwing shattered sunlight back in as many shards as the stars of a winter night. The sea heaved, exposing or distorting three legs that shimmered into the depths.

The deepest trench in the Inner Sea, Chalcus had said. *And this thing came out of it.*

"The Fortress of Glass," Tenoctris said wonderingly. Ilna remembered the words from Cervoran's mouth as he rose from his trance in the depths of the topaz. "There's nothing in any of my records, but here it is."

Ilna put an arm around the older woman's waist and gripped the railing with her other hand; Cashel knelt and grasped a handful of Cervoran's collar. The spreading wave lifted the ship and flung it forward, but neither wizard went overboard.

There was confusion on the benches but at least half the crew kept their oarlooms and at least a semblance of the rhythm. Blades cracked together, but not badly; the men who'd been thrown down returned to their seats and their duty. They were trained men, picked men; men fit for a leader like Chalcus.

The *Heron* drove back toward harbor. Chalcus gestured to Panshin; the flute-player increased his tempo. They were drawing away from the fortress, but it was high enough to be seen even from the island's shore.

Things slipped from the crystal battlements and splashed into the sea. *Flotsam,* Ilna thought. *Scraps of seaweed and muck from the abyss, lifted when the fortress rose.*

Instead of bobbing at the base of the crystal walls, the blobs moved outward. They were hellplants like the one that had attacked the palace, and they were swimming in the *Heron*'s wake.

"Captain Chalcus!" Cashel called. He'd gotten to his feet again and was looking over the bow. "Look ahead of us, sir!"

Ilna bent outward to look also. Ahead of the ship, rising from the depths like foul green bubbles swelling from a swamp, were more hellplants. They moved toward the *Heron* on strokes of their powerful tentacles.

Chapter

6

CHALCUS SNATCHED A boat pike from one of the stern racks; the shaft was half again his height. Using it for a balance pole, he jumped to the rail. Looking out, he called "Hard aport!" sharply. The steersman leaned into the tiller of the port steering oar.

The *Heron* heeled toward the oar, making the blade cut deeper into the water and tightening the turn. Chalcus shifted his footing slightly, leaning further for a better view past the hull; the pike in his hands moved inboard to balance him.

The show was as good as any troupe of the acrobats who'd entertained at palace dinners, but here it was in dead earnest. The rail was the only place where Chalcus could both conn them through the gauntlet of swimming monsters and be sure the steersman could hear his orders instantly in the likely tumult of the next minutes.

"The plants ahead of us must've been going to attack the palace,"

Tenoctris said, pursing her lips. She spoke loudly enough for to be heard, but it seemed to Ilna that she was organizing her own thoughts rather than informing her friends. "The person, the thing in the fortress must really control them to send them against us instead."

"The Green Woman," Ilna said, though the name was only a sound without meaning. Did even Cervoran know what she was?

"Tenoctris, can you do something?" Cashel said. "To fight the plants, I mean."

He gave the staff a trial spin overhead where he wasn't going to hit anybody, then lowered it. They'd all seen the plant attacking the palace. A quarterstaff wouldn't be much good against more creatures of the sort.

Ilna's fingers had been busy with the cords while her mind was on other things, hopeless things. When she looked at what she'd knotted, her lips pursed with surprise. She knew her patterns were useless as weapons against the hellplants, but this was no weapon.

"I'll try," Tenoctris said. She grasped the railing with one hand and lowered herself to the catwalk. "I don't have a great deal of power, though."

Cervoran was extremely powerful. He hadn't been able to destroy the fortress in the depths, but saving the *Heron* from the creatures attacking was surely a smaller thing.

"Cashel, let me by," Ilna said. "To get to Cervoran."

Cashel stepped aside with the powerful delicacy of an ox lowering itself onto the straw. He didn't ask what she planned to do; he knew she'd tell him whatever she thought he needed to know.

Ilna smiled, though the expression barely reached her lips. Her brother had more common sense than most of the people who thought they were smarter than he was. In fact, thinking Cashel was stupid proved you didn't have common sense.

There was a sucking *thwock* from forward; the *Heron* staggered. A swatch of vegetation spurted up from the ram's curve before falling back into the sea.

"Stroke, lads!" Chalcus shouted. "A cable's length and we're through the devils!"

Ilna squatted at Cervoran's head and spread her knotted pattern before his staring eyes. For a moment nothing happened; then a shudder trembled the length of the wizard's body. The design had penetrated to his stunned consciousness and wrenched him back to the present.

Cervoran closed, then opened his eyes again. His irises were muddy and stood in fields of pale gold. The swollen lips moved, but no sound came out.

"Stroke!" Chalcus shouted. As the word rang out, oars on the port side clattered together and the ship slewed toward them.

Ilna glanced to the side, continuing to hold the tracery of fabric in front of the wizard. The *Heron*'s hull had cleared the nearest hellplant, but the creature grasped an oarblade as the ship drove past. The tentacle held, dragging the oar back into all those behind it in the bank.

"Overboard with it!" Chalcus bellowed, springing from the deck to the outrigger. "Shove it out, we don't need the bloody oar!"

Chalcus' dagger, curved like a cat's claw, flashed; he bent and cut through the twist of willow withie that bound the oar to the rowlock. The rower pushed his oar through the port, but the hellplant's tentacles had grabbed more blades. The *Heron* wallowed: the starboard oars were driving at full stroke, but half those on the other side were tangled. The hellplant's bulk tugged at the ship like a sea anchor.

Cashel stood amidships. He'd picked up the pike Chalcus dropped when he jumped from the deck railing. Some of the shepherds in the borough carried a javelin instead of a staff or bow, but Ilna didn't recall having seen her brother with a spear of any sort in his hand before.

Cashel cocked the pike over his shoulder, then snapped it forward as though it was meant for throwing instead of having a shaft thick enough to be used to fend the ship's fragile hull away from a dock. The pike wasn't balanced: the rusted iron butt cap wobbled in a wide circle.

The point and half the long shaft squelched into the hellplant, tearing a hole the size of a man's thigh. The barrel-shaped body quivered, but the plant continued to pull itself up the oarshafts toward the ship.

Half a dozen more oars slid through the ports as crewmen jettisoned anything the plant's tentacles had caught. The *Heron* was under way again, limping but moving forward. The steersman had his starboard oar twisted broadside on, fighting the ship's urge to turn to port where the hellplant lashed the water in a furious attempt to renew its grip.

"Where is the jewel?" demanded a voice that drove into Ilna's mind like a jet of ice water. "I must have the topaz from the amber sarcophagus."

Ilna looked at Cervoran, whom she'd forgotten for a moment. He'd raised his swollen body onto one elbow. His eyes had returned to the febrile brightness that'd been normal for them at least since she brought him off the pyre.

"I'll get it," Ilna said. She put her knotted pattern in her left sleeve; it'd served its purpose by bringing the wizard out of his coma. Now the question was whether Cervoran would serve *his* purpose, and they'd know the answer to that before long.

Tenoctris had set down the crown when she started her own spell. Ilna leaned past the three-cornered figure her friend had drawn in charcoal on the pine decking. Grabbing the wire band she drew it to her, trying not to disturb Tenoctris.

The stone was awkwardly heavy; she couldn't imagine wearing such a thing herself. Nobody was asking her to, of course. She gave the crown to Cervoran with a cold expression.

Oars rattled. The *Heron* twisted, then shuddered to a stop. Two more hellplants had swum close enough to grab the leading oars on either side, binding the ship to them hopelessly. A third creature, the one that they'd struggled clear of moments before, swam up in the *Heron*'s wake and would catch the stern in a matter of seconds.

"All right, lads!" Chalcus cried. "Swords out and show these vegetables what it means to play with men!"

Cervoran rose to his feet. The great topaz winked on his forehead as if it was alive too. He picked up the silver-mounted skullcap that lay where he'd dropped it after the earlier spell froze the sea into yellow ice.

A sailor screamed. A flat green tentacle started to lift him from the ship. Chalcus scampered down the outrigger like a squirrel, slashing with his incurved sword. The slender blade slit the tentacle neatly, leaving only the leafy fringe remaining. The sailor twisted with desperate strength and tore that apart also, tumbling back aboard the *Heron*.

"Master Cashel!" Cervoran piped. "I have need of you!"

CASHEL WAS FROWNING, not because of the situation but because there didn't seem to be anything for him to do. The quarterstaff was no use on plants, though it felt good in his hands. It reminded him of the days he sat with his back against a holly tree, watching the sheep on the slope below him and listening to Garric play a pipe tune. Cashel couldn't sing or make music himself, but he loved to hear it when others did.

Feeling good wasn't going to beat these plants nor would happy memories. The spear he'd thrown didn't seem to have done much good either. Besides, the plant that'd attacked the palace had looked like a pincushion from the soldiers' spears by the time he and Cervoran came up from the cellars, and it didn't even slow down till the fire got burning good.

Regretfully, Cashel laid his staff on the catwalk. The wicker mat hanging from the rail would keep it there unless the ship sank. *Until* the ship sank likely enough, but the crew'd fight till then and Cashel *sure* would be fighting.

A sword'd really be the best thing, but Cashel was hopeless with them. He hadn't seen any call to learn to use one despite not liking them the way he'd done with other things.

A broad-bladed hatchet with a square pein stood in a hole in the mast partner—the piece where the mast would be stepped. Cashel drew it out. He'd rather have a full-sized axe, but the hatchet would do. The haft was short but it'd let him grip with both hands; if he had to get close, well, he'd get close. He'd been in fights before.

Hellplants pulled themselves toward the bow from either side, using their grip on the leading oars like men crossing a span hand-over-hand by a pole. It wouldn't have done any good for the crew to cast the oars loose the way they'd done before, since this time the monsters were in front of the ship. Backing water wouldn't help either, since the plant they'd gotten past was swimming up in the wake.

The one behind was the one Cashel'd probably try to deal with, see-ings as Chalcus was in the bow—one foot on the outrigger, the other on the ram—waiting for whichever of the front pair came in range of his sword first. Cashel stayed where he was for the time being. He figured his job was to protect Ilna and Tenoctris the best way he could, and just now he wasn't sure what that'd be.

You didn't win fights by being too hasty. Of course this time Cashel didn't expect to win, but he wasn't going to change ways that'd served him well so far.

"Master Cashel!" Cervoran said. That high voice was as nasty to hear as a rabbit screaming, but like the rabbit it sure did get heard. "I have need of you!"

Cashel hadn't thought about the wizard since he'd carried him aboard. Cervoran was holding out that piece of skull again. "Fill this with seawater," he said when he saw Cashel was looking at him.

Ilna nodded agreement, but Cashel hadn't been going to hesitate anyhow. Nothing he'd come up with for himself to do was going to be much good. The first plant he got close to would've known it'd been in a fight, but the monsters were the size of oxen. They didn't have a head or a heart you could split with an axe, either.

Cashel took the cup and dropped it down the front of his tunic. He could climb down one-handed, but just now he figured the other hand had better be holding the hatchet.

He swung over the railing, pushed a couple standing crewmen aside with his feet, and dropped. The bench he came down on creaked angrily and threatened to split; he'd landed heavier than he'd meant.

The *Heron* dipped like a lady doing a curtsey: a hellplant had grabbed the outrigger with more tentacles than a hand has fingers and was pulling its huge body out of the water. Chalcus slashed, his sword twinkling like lightning in the clouds. Feathery tufts of green fluttered up.

The ship's bow lifted, but another tentacle snaked around Chalcus' ankle from behind. Without seeming to look, the sailor jerked his leg up against the plant's strength and flicked his dagger across. The plant's tough fibers parted, and the curved sword whirled in an arc of its own through a couple more gripping tentacles.

The plant behind them had reached the stern. Crewmen there started hacking at it. Most used swords, though one fellow shoved in a pike. He was still holding the shaft when two tentacles lifted him screaming into the air and pulled his limbs off one by one.

In the bow, chips flew from the outrigger as oarsmen swung their swords with more enthusiasm than skill. Somebody was bound to cut a friend's hand off the way they were acting, though Cashel didn't suppose it'd matter much in the long run.

Cashel fished the cup out, then dipped it full. He turned to lift it to Ilna's waiting hand. His sister was one of those people who didn't wait around wondering what was going to happen next. Cashel could never figure why there were so few folk like her, but that made him happier for the ones he did meet.

With one hand on a deck support and the other holding the hatchet against the top railing, Cashel lifted himself up to where the women were. Tenoctris chanted over her little triangle on the decking. Cashel could see an occasional rosy gleam of wizardlight in the air, but anything else happening was beyond him.

Ilna had her paring knife out. Its blade was good steel, not like the knives forged from strap iron that every man back home in the borough carried. Cashel figured the tricks Ilna did with twine didn't work on the hellplants or she wouldn't have taken the knife from her sleeve. That was too bad, though he didn't doubt she'd give as good an account of herself with the little knife as any of the sailors would with their swords.

He grinned at her. She sniffed, looking peevish but resigned to a world that didn't work the way it ought to. That was so much his sister's normal expression that Cashel guffawed loudly. It took more than a whole army of plants to change who Ilna was.

Cervoran held the cup over his brazier and started chanting again. The charcoal hadn't gone out with all the tossing around it'd gotten, though the sticks were just ghosts of what they'd been, nested in a mound of white ashes.

Cashel couldn't figure how the wizard stood the heat that rippled the air above the cup in his hand. Maybe he just didn't have any feeling in his fingers.

Cashel looked down at the fight. He was itching to mix into it, but he knew there'd be time aplenty. They'd all get their bellies full of fighting today. . . .

Timbers were crackling and the *Heron* rode way deep in the water, but it was next to impossible to make wood really sink. Chalcus cut like a very demon. He was bloody in a dozen places and'd lost his leather breeches; pulled clean off by a tentacle, Cashel supposed, but it hadn't slowed him a mite. Ilna'd found herself a man and no mistake.

From the height of the deck Cashel saw plants in all directions. There was a lot of seaweed floating in the Inner Sea. Once back home when the winds and currents were just right, he'd seen the whole bay on the other side of the headland from Pattern Creek filled with slowly turning greenness. This was the same, only the green swam toward them.

Cervoran's eyes were open but they weren't focused on anything, as best Cashel could tell. Thinking about previous times he'd seen the wizard, he wasn't sure there was a difference. Cervoran was alive, no question about that; but Cashel got the feeling he was *riding* in his body instead of living in it the usual way.

A hellplant dropped away from the starboard bow. Chalcus had hacked its tentacles off, however many there were. That was a wonderful thing, but the plant on the port side was struggling with the crewmen there. Chalcus sat on a bench with his head bowed forward to make it easier for him to drag breaths in through his open mouth.

Cashel knew better than most what fight took out of you, even when you won. Chalcus'd be back in it soon, but nobody could keep up for long what he'd been doing.

Cashel looked critically at his hatchet. The blade was straight and as broad as his palm; it had a good working edge, put on with a stone some time since it was last used. Rust flecked it, which pleased him. Steel rusted quicker than iron did, he'd found.

The haft was hickory like his quarterstaff. He grinned. Hickory was a good wood for tools, hard but with more spring to it than cornelwood or elm. Besides, he liked the feel of it.

The sea around the *Heron* was solid green, a mass of waving fronds and bodies like fat barrels. There were more plants than Cashel could count with both hands, many more. Chalcus was back in the fight. Men cut and screamed and died in the grip of arms stronger than any animal's.

A hellplant had grabbed the outrigger to starboard. It'd driven the sailors back, and now a tentacle waved toward the raised deck. Cashel couldn't wait any longer. Instead of cutting at the arm—the plant had who knew how many more?—he lifted one foot to the railing. He'd leap on top of the plant and with the hatchet—

"*Phroneu!*" Cervoran cried, his voice stabbing through the ruck of noise. Cashel glanced instinctively toward the wizard. The water in the skull was at a rolling boil, frothing over the silver lip.

Cervoran's case was open at his feet. In his free hand he held a small velvet bag, the sort of thing a woman used to store a fancy ring or brooch. Cervoran shook the contents, a dancing and glittering of metal filings, into the water. They burned with a savage white glare, and around the *Heron* the sea burned also.

Cashel slitted his eyes and turned to cover Tenoctris. The brightness was beyond imagining; it was like being put next to the sun. *Beyond imagining. . . .*

The blaze—it wasn't flames so much as hot white light—mounted higher than the mast would've been, higher than the tallest tree of Cashel's memory. Hellplants shriveled. Bits of them lifted and spun into the air, black ashes disintegrating into black powder and vanishing.

The hammering glare stopped abruptly. Cashel opened his eyes and lifted his body off Tenoctris. He'd supported most of his weight on the railing, but he was still glad when she looked up and him and said, "Thank you. *Thank* you. Are you all right, Cashel?"

While the light blazed Cashel hadn't been aware of any sounds, but now people were screaming or praying or just blubbering in terror and pain. The air stank with a combination of wet straw burning and cooked meat. The sea as far as he could tell was black with drifting ash.

Men who'd reached over the side of the ship had burned too. Most of them'd been dead already or next to it, snatched out of the *Heron* by a plant's crushing tentacles. Some had probably been pushing forward to fight, though.

Well, it'd been quick. And it was done, so that was good.

Tenoctris was all right. Ilna was down in the bow, wrapping a bandage over the torn skin on Chalcus' right forearm. Cashel looked at Cervoran, not exactly his business to protect the way the women were; but maybe Cervoran was his business too.

The wizard stood like a wax statue, neither smiling nor concerned. The empty velvet sack was in his left hand, but he'd dropped the skull to the deck again.

Cashel bent and picked up the cup. There was no telling when they'd need it again.

$\mathcal{G}$ARRIC'S HEAD HURT. The blinding surge of pain every time his heart beat was all his universe could encompass just now. He wasn't sure how long he lay like this, he wasn't sure of anything but the pain.

Then he noticed that other parts of his body hurt also.

"It means you're alive," noted the ghost in Garric's mind with amused dispassion. *"There came a time I couldn't say that, so be thankful."*

I'm not sure I'm thankful, Garric thought, but he knew that wasn't true as the words formed. He grinned and immediately felt better. Carus, who during a lifetime of war had been hurt as often and as badly as the next man, grinned back in approval.

Garric opened his eyes. He was being carried under a long pole, lashed by the elbows and ankles. His head hung down. Two women from the village had the back of the pole; when he twisted to look forward he could see two more in front. It was raining softly, and there was only enough light for him to tell there were people in the group besides the women carrying him.

A Corl warrior bent close to peer at Garric, then raised its head and yowled a comment. Other Coerli answered from ahead in the darkness. The women supporting the front of Garric's pole stopped and looked over their shoulders.

The cat man slashed the leading woman with his hooked line, held short and jerked to tear rather than hold. The woman cried out in pain and stumbled forward again.

Two Coerli walked toward Garric from farther up the line, a female wearing a robe of patterned skins and the maned giant who'd knocked him unconscious. The male was twice the size of the ordinary warriors, taller and about as heavy as the humans in this land. The female was as big as the warriors but unarmed. A crystalline thing sat on her right shoulder. It was alive.

"Can he walk?" the big male asked. Garric's ears heard a rasping growl, but the question rang in his mind.

"You!" said the female Corl, looking at Garric. She had four breasts, dugs really, under the thin robe. "Can you walk?"

"I can walk," Garric said. He wasn't sure that was true, but it seemed likely to get him down from the pole. With his legs freed and maybe his hands as well, who knew what might happen? "How is it you can speak my language?"

"We can't," the female said. "The Bird speaks to your mind and to ours."

The crystal thing on her shoulder fluffed shimmering wings. Well, they might've been wings. It wasn't really a bird, but Garric supposed that was as good a name as any.

"Where do you come from, animal?" the big male demanded.

"My name is Garric," Garric replied. "I'll answer your questions as soon as you've let me down from here to walk on my own. Otherwise, there's not much you can do to me that'll hurt worse than I feel already."

"That's not entirely true," noted Carus. *"But a little bluster at a time like this can be useful. It's the best you can do till you've got a hand loose, anyway."*

Now that Garric was fully awake, the jouncing ride was excruciatingly painful. The Coerli must have better night vision than humans; they moved with complete assurance, avoiding puddles and trees fallen across the trail. The women carrying Garric couldn't see much better than he did, though. Somebody slipped at every step, and once both of those in front fell to their knees. The jerk on Garric's elbows made his mind turn gray.

"All right, put him down," the big male said. "But keep him tied. Nerga and Eny? Walk behind the big animal and kill him if he tries to run."

"Female animals, put the male Garric down," the female Corl said. She looked at Garric and added, "I am the wizard Sirawhil, beast Garric."

The carriers stopped abruptly. Presumably they'd heard the big male just as Garric had, but they hadn't reacted till they got a direct order from the wizard. Now they more dropped than lowered Garric onto the muddy ground.

The big male glared at Garric, fondling the knob of his wooden club. "I am Torag the Great!" he said. A warrior cut Garric's ankles away from the long pole. "No other Corl can stand against me!"

A flint knife sawed Garric's elbows free. His wrists were still tied in front of him by thin, hard cords, but one thing at a time. He rolled into a sitting position and looked at his captor.

Let me get my hands on you and I'll show you what a man *can do,* he thought. Aloud he said, "Why have you attacked me, Torag? I was not your enemy."

Torag looked at him in amazement. He turned to Sirawhil and snarled—literally from his own mouth, and the tone of the words ringing in Garric's mind was equally clear—"What is this animal saying? He's a beast! How can he imagine he's an enemy to the greatest of the Coerli?"

"You hit him on the head," Sirawhil said with a shrug. "Perhaps he's delusional. Though—"

She glanced back; Garric twisted to follow the line of her eyes. Women from the village carried the bodies of two warriors. The cat men's corpses were light enough that a pair of bearers sufficed for either one.

"—while he's only an animal, he's a dangerous one."

"Resume the march!" Torag ordered. In a quieter though still harshly rasping voice he added to Sirawhil, "We can't get back to the keep by daylight, but I'd like to put more distance from the warren we raided. Just in case."

He prodded Garric with the butt of his club. "Get up, beast," he said. "If you can't walk, I'll break your knees and have you dragged. Maybe I ought to do that anyway."

Garric rolled his legs under him, rose to his knees, and then lurched to his feet without having to stick his bound hands into the mud to brace him. He wobbled and pain shot through his body—ankles, wrists, and a renewed jolting pulse in his head—but he didn't fall over. He began plodding after the Corl warrior who was next ahead in the line. Torag and the female wizard fell in beside him.

"*He's not a great thinker, this Torag,*" Carus said. "*He's too stupid to hear a good plan even when it comes out of his own mouth.*"

He's not really afraid of me, Garric thought.

Carus laughed. The king's good humor was real, but it was as cold and hard as a sleet storm.

"Why are you so big, beast?" Torag said. "Are there more like you back in the warren where we captured you?"

"Its name is Garric," Sirawhil said to her chief. "Sometimes using their names makes them more forthcoming."

Garric looked at the Corl in amazement. Didn't they realize that he could hear what they said to one another?

"The Coerli think only what they say directly to you will be translated," said an unfamiliar voice in Garric's mind. "It's never occurred to them to test their assumption. They're not a sophisticated race."

Neither of the Coerli had spoken. The Bird on Sirawhil's shoulder fluttered its membranous wings again.

"I don't come from around here," Garric said. "I'm a visitor, you could say. All the members of my tribe are as big as me or bigger."

Torag looked at Sirawhil, his face knotting in a scowl emphasized by his long jaw. "Is the beast telling the truth?" he demanded.

"I don't know," Sirawhil said. "Usually they're too frightened to lie, but this one does seem different."

In a sharp tone she added, "You beast women! Is the male Garric a stranger in your warren?"

"I know where he comes from," called one of the woman carrying the dead warriors. "My husband Marzan brought him. Make somebody else take the pole and I'll tell you all about him."

Garric turned. He understood the words only because the Bird translated them in his mind, but the tone of the speaker's voice identified Soma more clearly than he could see through rain and darkness.

"Nerga, discipline that one," Sirawhil said offhandedly to the nearest warrior. Nerga lashed out with his line. Soma tried to get her hand up, but the Corl was too quick: the hooked tip combed a bloody furrow across her scalp.

Soma wailed in despair but didn't drop the pole. Head bowed and her left hand clasped over the fresh cut, she stumbled on.

"Speak, animal," Sirawhil demanded with satisfaction.

"My husband sent men out to find the stranger," Soma said in a dull voice, no longer bargaining. "The stranger is a great warrior and was supposed to protect us."

She raised her head and glared at Garric. "Protect us!" she said. "Look at me! What protection was the great warrior?"

"Does she tell the truth, animal?" Torag said to Garric. He wore a casque of animal teeth drilled and sewn to a leather backing. As he spoke, he rubbed them with his free hand.

From the chief's tone he was trying to be conciliatory, but he hadn't taken the wizard's suggestion that he call his prisoner by name. Indeed, not a great intellect . . . and the fact Torag rather than somebody smarter was in charge of the band told Garric something about the Coerli.

"*I* told you the truth, Torag," Garric said. "I'm a visitor here. Why did you attack me? My tribe has many warriors!"

Walking had brought the circulation back to Garric's legs. That hurt, of course, but he'd be able to run again.

If there'd been anywhere to run to. And he knew from seeing the Coerli move that at least in a short sprint they could catch any human alive.

"Where does he come from, Sirawhil?" Torag asked, scowling in concern. "If there's really many like him . . ."

"I can do a location spell," Sirawhil said. "We need to stop soon anyway, don't we? It's getting light."

"I'd like to go a little farther . . . ," Torag grumbled. Then he twitched his short brush of his tail in the equivalent of a shrug. "All right, if he's alone. If there was a whole warren full of them close, I'd keep going as long as we could."

"I'm hungry, Torag," whined Eny, the second of the warriors told to guard Garric specially.

The chief spun and lashed out. He used the butt of his club rather than the massive ball, but it still knocked the warrior down. Eny wailed.

"You'll eat when I say you can eat, Eny!" Torag said. "Watch your tongue or I won't even bother to bring your ruff back home to your family!"

Eny rolled to his feet almost before his shoulders'd splashed on the muddy ground, but he kept his head lowered and hid behind Nerga. Torag snorted and called, "All right, we'll camp here till it gets dark again."

He looked at Sirawhil. "Learn where the animal comes from," he said forcefully. "And learn how many there are in his warren. That could be important."

"Sit here, Garric," Sirawhil said, pointing to a hummock: a plant with fat, limp leaves spreading out from a common center. "You and I will talk while the warriors make camp."

It looked a little like a skunk cabbage. The best Garric could say about it as a seat was that it wasn't a pond. He didn't have any reason to argue, though, so he squatted on one edge facing the Corl wizard squatting opposite him.

"If they call this light," said King Carus, viewing the scene through Garric's eyes, *"then they must see better in the dark than real cats do."*

Garric nodded. The eastern horizon was barely lighter than the rest of the sky, but even full noon in this place had been soggy and gray. Dawn only meant it was easier to find your footing between ponds.

Warriors began trimming saplings for poles and stripping larger trees of their foliage. The Coerli hands had four fingers shorter than a human's; the first and last opposed. They looked clumsy, but they wove the mixed vegetation into matting with swift, careless ease.

After staring silently for a moment, Sirawhil opened her pack of slick cloth and took out a bundle of foot-long sticks polished from yellow wood. They were so regular that Garric thought at first they were made of metal.

"Don't move," she said. She got up and walked around the hummock, dropping the sticks into place as she went. Only once did she bend to adjust the pattern they made on the ground, a multi-pointed star or gear with shallow teeth.

The Bird shifted position slightly on her shoulder to keep its place. Its eyes, jewels on a jeweled form, remained focused on Garric as Sirawhil made her circuit.

Garric watched for a moment, then turned his attention to what the rest of the party was doing. He wondered how the warriors were going to build a fire on this sodden landscape. Perhaps there was dry heartwood, but most of the trees he'd seen were pulpy. They'd be as hard to ignite as a fresh sponge.

"The Coerli don't use fire," said the Bird silently. Its mental voice was dry and slightly astringent. "They don't allow their human cattle to have fires either. In the villages the Grass People keep fuel under shelter to dry out and light their fires with bows."

"Do you come from here, Bird?" Garric asked. He flexed his legs a little to keep the blood moving. He was used to squatting, but being trussed to the pole had left the big muscles liable to cramping.

Sirawhil looked up as she finished forming her pattern. "We captured the Bird when we first came here to the Land," she said. "Torag and I are the only ones who have such a prize. The other bands can't talk to the Grass Animals they capture, so it's a great prize."

"I am Torag the Great!" the chieftain roared, looking over at Garric and the wizard. "I've torn the throats out of two chiefs who thought they could take the Bird from me!"

Nobody moved for a moment. His point made, Torag surveyed the camp. The warriors had raised matting around a perimeter of a hundred and fifty feet or so. Though the sun still wasn't up, it'd stopped raining and the sky was light enough for Garric to count a dozen Coerli and about that number of captive humans. All the latter were females.

Torag gestured toward a plump woman. She'd been one of those carrying Garric when he was tied to the pole. She moved awkwardly; she seemed to have pulled a muscle in the course of the raid and march.

"That one," Torag said.

The woman looked up, surprised to be singled out. Eny grabbed her by the long hair and jerked her into a blow on the head from his stone-headed axe. The woman's scream ended in a spray of blood. Her arms and legs jerked as she fell.

Eny and two more warriors chopped furiously at her head for a moment, sending blood and chips of skull flying. The rest of the band growled in delight. The Bird didn't translate the sound; it was no more than hunger and cruelty finding a voice.

The three killers stepped back. Another warrior threw himself on the twitching corpse, his flint knife raised to slash off a piece. Torag roared and lifted his club. The warrior looked over his shoulder but hesitated almost too long. He leaped sideways with a despairing snarl; the chief's club hissed through the air where the warrior's head had been. It made a sound like an angry snake.

Torag knelt, raised the dead woman with his left hand, and tore her throat out without using a weapon.

Garric stared at Sirawhil to keep from having to look at the butchery. "You eat *people*?" he said in disgusted disbelief. He saw it happening, but part of his mind didn't want to believe what was perfectly clear to his eyes.

"Torag doesn't usually let the warriors have fresh meat," Sirawhil said nonchalantly. "They begin to mature if they do, and he'd have to fight for his position. In the keep they eat fish or jerky. Here on a raid, though, there's no other food so he'll share the kill."

The big Corl leaned back. His muzzle was red and dripping. He stared around the circle of longing warriors with a grin of bloody triumph, then took a flint knife from his belt. He stabbed it into the woman just below the left collarbone, drawing the blade the length of the chest. The edge ripped through the gristly ends of the ribs where they joined the breastbone. Placing one furry hand on either side of the incision, he tore the chest open.

"Flint's sharp, that's true," Carus said, grim-faced. *"But he's a strong one, Torag. I wouldn't mind showing him how much stronger I was, though; or you are, lad."*

In good time, thought Garric. He'd seen women and children killed by beasts—and by men, which was worse. There was a particular gloating triumph to the way Torag tore out pieces of the victim's lungs and gulped them down, though. *In good time. . . .*

Sirawhil squatted on the hummock opposite Garric, within the figure of sticks. She began chanting. The sounds weren't words or even syllables in human terms, but Garric recognized the rhythms of a wizard speaking words of power.

The spell helped to muffle the crunches and slurping from the other Coerli. Torag had eaten his fill and allowed his warriors at the victim. The sound was similar to that of a pack of hunting dogs allowed the quarry of their kill, only louder. The captive women huddled together, whimpering and trying not to look at what was happening to their late companion.

Garric closed his eyes, feeling a wash of despair. A lot of it was physical: he was wet and cold, and his body'd been badly hammered. But this was a miserable place and situation. He didn't see any way to change it, and especially he didn't see any way out. What had brought him here?

"The wizard Marzan summoned you," said the Bird's voice. Garric's eyes flew open. "Summoned one like you, that is. He knew the Grass People, his race, can't stand against the Coerli, so he used his art and the power of the crystal to bring a hero to help them."

I haven't done much good thus far, Garric thought; but the weight of hopelessness had lifted. He'd killed two cat men, and so long as they kept him alive there was a chance of doing better than that. Ideas were forming below the surface of his mind. His experience and that of his war-rior ancestor were blending to find solutions to a very violent problem.

"Where do the Coerli come from?" Garric asked. He spoke aloud though he obviously didn't have to. It didn't seem natural to look at something, some*one,* close enough to touch and talk to him without moving his lips.

"This place," the Bird said. "This Land. But from the far future. There's a cave in a chasm some fifteen miles from where we are now. It's a focus for great power. Coerli wizards have learned to use it to carry them back to this time to hunt."

"They're trying to conquer their own past?" Garric said, hoping to gather enough information that he'd be able to make sense of it . . . which the fragments he'd heard thus far certainly didn't permit him to do.

"The Coerli don't make war," the Bird said. "They skirmish over boundaries with neighboring bands, and they hunt. They've hunted out their own time, so they come here for game. Torag and other chiefs have built keeps in this time. Many more will follow as their own world be-comes more crowded, but they don't think of it as conquest the way your people would."

Torag wiped his muzzle with a hand which he then licked clean. He and the other cat men were lost in their own affairs, though some of the captive women watched in puzzlement as Garric talked. Unless the Bird translated them, his words were as meaningless to them as to the Coerli.

"They have no reason to overhear," the Bird said. "Don't think that because you're the same species that your fellow slaves are your friends."

It stretched one wing, then lowered it and stretched the other. They were small, no bigger than Garric could span with one hand, but when he looked into the light that shimmered through them he had a momen-tary vision of infinite expanses.

Garric grinned. "I'm not a slave," he said quietly.

He lifted his hands slightly to indicate his bound wrists. "For the mo-ment I'm a prisoner," he said. "But they'll never make me a slave, Bird."

Sirawhil stopped chanting and slumped forward. Garric was so used to helping Tenoctris that he reflexively reached out to catch the ex-hausted wizard. Even without full use of his hands, he kept her from rolling off the hummock as she'd started to do.

The motion drew Torag's attention. He was on his feet, raising his club with the sudden snapping movement of a spring trap releasing.

"I'd wondered what would happen if we jumped him while he was full of food and relaxed," Carus observed with a wry smile. *"Your knees broken is what'd have happened, I suppose."*

In good time, Garric thought. Aloud he said, "Your wizard worked a great spell, Torag. Should I have let her drown in a puddle?"

The warriors looked up also. They'd finished their meal for the most part, though one was still gnawing a rib. The corpse was reduced to scattered bones and a pile of offal on a patch of bloodstained ground.

Instead of replying to Garric, Torag growled, "You, Sirawhil! What have you learned?"

The wizard lifted herself upright, but she splayed her legs on the hummock instead of making the greater effort to squat. She rubbed the back of a hand over her eyes and tried to focus on the chieftain.

"I'm not sure, Torag," she said. "He comes from very far away. There's a great deal of power involved in his presence."

"There's no chief in the Land more powerful than I!" Torag said.

"It's not that kind of power," Sirawhil said wearily. "It's wizardry, Torag, and it's greater wizardry than I can fathom. It isn't—"

She glanced toward Soma, who tried to burrow out of sight behind the other captives. The women had learned what it meant to be singled out in this company. . . .

"—anything that the wizard in the warren we raided could've done by himself. I think we should take him back home for the whole Council of the Learned to examine."

"Are you mad, Sirawhil?" Torag said. He sounded more amazed than angry, the way he had when Garric treated him as an equal. "If I leave here, some other chief will take my keep. Or—"

And here the growling threat was back in his tone.

"—do you think I'll let you and the Bird go back without me? *And* take a valuable animal?"

"Torag," said the wizard, "this thing is too big for me. We need to take this Garric to someone who can understand him, even if there's a risk."

"It's not too big for me," Torag said complacently. "We'll go back to my keep and I'll decide later."

He looked at Garric, his ruff lifting slightly. "Nerga and Eny, tie him up again. Tie all the females too, just in case. I'm not taking any chances till I have him in the pen with the other animals."

You're taking a big chance, Garric thought as the warriors came toward him with coils of hard rope. *You're taking the last chance you'll ever take. But in good time....*

Sharina stood on the seawall of Mona Harbor, watching the *Heron* ease toward the quay on the stroke of ten oarsmen. The trim bireme that'd rowed off at midmorning was now a shambles, the outriggers broken in several places and the hull scorched by the sky-searing blaze Sharina had seen leap from the sea about the ship.

She'd been ready to die when she saw the fire, but it'd vanished as suddenly as it'd appeared and the *Heron,* though at first wallowing, still had figures on her deck. Cashel, big and as solid as a rock, was obvious among them, and Sharina'd breathed again.

Admiral Zettin had manned and led out ten ships as soon as he saw something was happening to the *Heron*. They now passed back and forth at the harbor mouth.

You couldn't keep warships at sea for long periods—there wasn't room for the crews to sleep aboard, let alone food storage and a place to cook. For now, though, it was important to Zettin to be seen to be doing *something;* a notion that Sharina understood perfectly. She only wished there was something she could've done besides wait and pray to the Lady—silently, because it wouldn't do for the Princess Sharina to show herself to be desperately afraid.

She smiled. Attaper, leading her personal guard at this dangerous moment, saw the expression and grinned back. Did he realize that she was smiling at the fact that her duty was to be seen to be unconcerned? Perhaps he did; but maybe even that experienced, world-wise soldier thought Princess Sharina really *had* been confident, no matter how confusing and dangerous the situation seemed to others.

Lady, make me what I pretend to be, Sharina prayed in her heart; and smiled more broadly, because she seemed to be fooling herself as well.

Cashel used his staff to jump ashore while the *Heron* was still several feet out from the quay. It was a graceful motion but completely unexpected, though Sharina'd seen Cashel clear gullies and boggy patches that way frequently in the borough. Here it called attention to him, which Cashel never liked to do; but Sharina stepped toward him and he folded her in his arms. At last she could fully relax for at least a few moments.

"Tenoctris is all right," Cashel said in a quiet rumble. "Ilna's sitting with her on the deck because she's so, you know, tired; and maybe you couldn't see with the wicker matting in the way."

"I knew they were all right," Sharina said, simply and honestly. "Because you are."

She stepped back and gave the battered bireme a real examination. The crew was climbing out, some of them helped by their more fortunate fellows or by men waiting on the dock. The benches and hollow of the ship were splashed with blood—*painted* with blood on the port bow where the fighting must've been particularly intense. It seemed to Sharina that nearly half the crew was missing, and many of the survivors had been injured.

Cervoran was trying clumsily to get down from the deck. He held his wooden case in one hand.

"Your pardon, mistress," Cashel said with impersonal politeness. "I better get that."

He jumped from the quay to the *Heron*'s outrigger and took the case in his left hand. "Careful or you'll fall," he said to Cervoran. "Would you like me to lift you—"

Sharina supposed he was going to say "down," but the former corpse simply let go of the railing and dropped. He landed on his feet but toppled forward. He didn't raise his arms to catch himself, but Cashel shifted to put his body in the way as a living cushion.

Cervoran steadied himself, then stumped to the ladder up to the quay without speaking. Several sailors who'd been waiting to climb up made way for him, though with respect rather than the frightened hostility Sharina'd seen in their expressions previously.

"Plants like the one that came here yesterday attacked us," Cashel said, looking from Cervoran to the crewmen, then back to Sharina. "There was any number of them, swimming all over the sea. Master Cervoran made the water burn and saved us."

The *Heron* hadn't been backed onto the beach in normal fashion: the surviving sailors were too few and too tired to accomplish that. A replacement crew was boarding to handle the job. Ilna'd started to help Tenoctris down from the deck, but fresh men under Chalcus' direction grabbed the old wizard and passed her hand-over-hand to their comrades on the quay.

Sharina's face stayed calm, but her first notice of Chalcus since the *Heron* left harbor explained why he hadn't carried Tenoctris to land himself in the sort of flashy, boastful gesture he was used to making.

He'd lost most of his clothing in the fight, and the hooked tendrils that'd torn it off him had gashed runnels across the many existing scars. He must've bathed himself in the sea since the fight because otherwise he'd have been completely covered with blood, but many of the fresh wounds were still leaking. The worst'd been bandaged with swatches cut from Ilna's own tunics, but the wool was now bright scarlet.

Chalcus hadn't bothered replacing his trousers, but he'd twisted a length of sailcloth around his waist for a sash. That gave him a place to thrust his sword and dagger. He'd lost the sheath for the latter, and the point of patterned steel winked like a viper's eye.

Tenoctris, looking weary but determined, joined Sharina. She nodded to the glitter on the horizon and said, "That's the Fortress of Glass that I was wondering about. What you see looks like crystal, but it's really the intersection of many planes of the greater cosmos."

She took a deep breath. "I've never seen such a nexus of power, Sharina," she added. "I never imagined that anything like it could exist. I've seen so many marvels since I was ripped out of my time and brought to yours."

Sharina took the older woman's hand in hers. "If you keep saving the world as you've done in the past," she said, "I'm sure we'll be able to show you still more wonders." Her tone was affectionately joking but the words the simple truth.

Cervoran had climbed the short ladder, moving one limb at a time instead of lifting a leg and an arm together. He walked toward Sharina with the awkward determination of a large insect. Cashel, who'd followed the wizard off the ship, now stepped past him. His presence forestalled the pair of Blood Eagles who'd otherwise have put themselves between Cervoran and Princess Sharina.

"Princess," Cervoran squeaked. "In her fortress, the Green Woman is too strong for me. I will enter by another path, but to do that I must take her attention off me. At dawn tomorrow I will go to the charnel house when they bring the fresh corpses and pick the one that best suits my needs."

Liane stood at Sharina's elbow. She'd stayed at a discreet distance while Sharina was praying for Cashel's safe return. Liane, better than most, understood what it meant to wait for the one you love. . . .

"People of property here cremate their dead," Liane said, speaking to Sharina with the same unobtrusive precision that she'd used to inform Garric in the past. Her finger marked a passage in a slender codex, but she didn't need to refer to it. "The poor in Mona are placed in a cave at the eastern boundary of the city. In rural districts they throw the bodies into the sea with stones to weight them."

"It is necessary," Cervoran said. "She is too strong in her fortress, so I must deceive her."

Ilna and Tenoctris joined them, the older woman leaning on the arm of the younger. "Tenoctris?" Sharina said. "Master Cervoran wants to use a fresh corpse for, for his art."

Tenoctris looked at her fellow wizard with the sharp, emotionless interest that she showed for any new thing. "Does he?" she said.

Cervoran didn't look around or otherwise acknowledge the newcomers' presence. Tenoctris shrugged and gave Sharina a smile tinged with sadness. "I've practiced necromancy myself, dear," she said. "When it was necessary. When I *thought* it was necessary."

"Yes, all right, Master Cervoran," Sharina said. "Tenoctris will accompany you on behalf of the kingdom."

She raised an eyebrow at the older woman, since she hadn't actually asked if she was willing to go. Tenoctris nodded agreement.

"She may go or stay," Cervoran said. He took off the diadem he was wearing and concentrated again on whatever he saw in the depths of the topaz. "It makes no difference. She has no power."

Tenoctris nodded. "That's quite true," she said, "in his terms."

Her voice was pleasant, but there was the least edge in the way she spoke the words. Tenoctris was both a noblewoman and the most accomplished scholar Sharina had ever met. There were various kinds of power, but knowledge was one kind—as Sharina knew, and as Tenoctris certainly knew.

Chalcus, limping slightly but wearing his usual expression of bright insouciance, sauntered up from the ship. He'd tied a portion of sail into a linen breechclout, and he'd found a red silk kerchief to twist into a replacement for the headband he'd lost in the fighting.

Cervoran looked up from the topaz. He pointed a fat white finger at Cashel. "You will come with me, Cashel," he said. "At dawn, as soon as the night's dead have been brought in."

He rotated his head toward Ilna, though his pointing hand didn't shift. "And that one, your sister," he said. "Your name is Ilna? You will come, Ilna."

Chalcus didn't seem to move, but the point of his curved dagger hooked into Cervoran's right nostril. "Now I wonder," Chalcus said in a light, bantering voice, "what there is about common politeness that's so hard for some folk to learn? There's places a fellow'd get his nose notched for treating Mistress Ilna in such a way, my good fellow . . . and you're in one of those places now. Would you care to try again?"

Ilna smiled faintly and placed her fingertips on the hand holding the dagger. "I sometimes fail to be perfectly polite myself, Captain Chalcus," she said. "But I appreciate your concern."

"Master Cervoran?" said Sharina. When the wizard spoke, she'd had an icy recollection of white fire enveloping the sea where the *Heron* was floating. "You don't give orders to my associates."

She paused to consider, then went on, "Nor, I think, do you give orders in the kingdom I administer in my brother's absence. Your ignorance has already cost the lives of citizens and endangered the lives of all those accompanying you on the *Heron*. I'll arrange for an escort of soldiers—"

"That's all right, Sharina," Cashel said. He was rubbing the shaft of his quarterstaff with a wad of raw wool, working the oils into the pores of the wood. "I don't guess that thing—"

He dipped the staff toward the glitter on the horizon, the Fortress of Glass.

"—was Master Cervoran's fault. And anyhow, he was a big help out to sea. We wouldn't've got back without him."

"Master Cervoran was the reason we were at sea in the first place," Ilna said waspishly. "Still, I see no reason why I shouldn't go with Tenoctris and Cashel in the morning. I can't imagine what I could do that would be more useful."

She looked out at the fortress also. "And it's obvious," she added, speaking as crisply and precisely as she did all things, "that *something* has to be done."

Chapter

7

TORAG ROUSED HIS band and their captives at dusk. It'd rained at least three times during the day, and the shelter of twigs and brush the warriors'd woven was meant for shade, not to shed water. Part of Garric's mind doubted that he'd slept at all, but he knew he was probably wrong. The pain of his injuries, the drizzle, and the growing discomfort of his tight bonds kept him from enjoying rest, but there'd doubtless been some.

Growling among themselves—Coerli voices sounded peevish to a human, even when they weren't—four warriors set off in the lead. Torag and Sirawhil paced along beside Garric, with Eny and Nerga on guard immediately behind him. The women, bound together by the necks, followed. Two warriors were with them, more to guide than to guard them: they obviously weren't a danger to anyone.

That left four warriors. Garric supposed they were the rear guard, though he was well out of sight before they'd have left the temporary camp.

"*What are they worried about, do you suppose?*" Carus wondered mentally. "*I didn't see anything in the village that'd concern me—nobody even able to lead a rescue attempt except maybe Scarface. Do these cat creatures prey on each other?*"

The Bird on Sirawhil's shoulder turned its glittering eyes toward Garric. "Every band is a potential enemy of every other band," it said silently. "They only attack if they have an overwhelming advantage, which isn't likely when every band is always on their guard against every other."

You hear my ancestor, then? Garric asked, this time silently. *As well as hearing my thoughts?*

The Bird said nothing. Garric grimaced. That'd been a stupid question: *obviously* the Bird 'heard' everything that went on in his head. He wasn't in good shape.

They slogged on in the sopping darkness. Garric's wrists had been tied since capture, and when they camped the Coerli had lashed them to his waist as well. Garric worked at his bonds for want of anything better to do, but apart from wearing his wrists bloody he didn't accomplish anything.

Because he couldn't throw out his arms for balance as he instinctively tried to do, he stumbled frequently and occasionally fell. The Coerli didn't help him. Once when he was slow getting up—he'd braced his hands on a log which collapsed to mush, skidding him on his face again—one of the warriors kicked him with a clawed foot.

Garric heard the captured women whimper occasionally, but they seemed to be having less trouble than he did even though they were tied together. They couldn't have night vision like the Coerli, but at least they were used to starless nights and constant overcast.

"*That makes these cat beasts easy meat in daylight, lad,*" Carus noted. His image had a quiet smile. "*Even what passes for daylight in this bloody bog.*"

Meat, perhaps, Garric amended, but he smiled too. Perhaps he and Carus were being wildly optimistic, but it was better than resigning himself to a gray future ending in butchery.

A plangent *Klok! Klok!* rang across the marsh. Torag lifted his great maned head and roared a coughing reply.

"Are we being attacked?" Garric asked Sirawhil sharply.

Too sharply, apparently. A guard slapped him across the head with the butt of his spear and snarled, "Silence, beast!"

It wasn't a serious blow—the spear shaft was no more than thumb-thick—but Garric's head still throbbed from the stroke that'd captured him. He staggered, dropping to one knee in a blur of white light; his skin burned. With an effort he lurched forward and managed to keep going so that the Corl didn't hit him again.

In its own dry voice, the Bird said, "We're approaching Torag's keep. The warriors left as a garrison have given the alarm, and Torag has announced himself in reply."

"The Coerli can see any way in this?" Garric said. He spoke aloud but without the harshness that'd gotten him swatted a moment earlier. He couldn't be sure of the distance, but the gong note was dulled by what seemed like several hundred yards of drizzle and darkness.

"The distance is close to a quarter of one of your miles," the Bird said, answering both the question Garric had asked and the one he'd only thought. "While the tower guard might have seen movement, it's more likely that he heard the party returning. The Coerli have keen hearing, and you humans make a great deal of noise in the darkness."

I can't argue with that, Garric thought. *I wonder if I'll get to be at least as good as the Grass People are?*

"*I hope we're not here long enough to learn, lad,*" said the ghost in his mind. Carus grinned, but there was more than humor in the expression.

Garric heard a gate creak, followed by the scrape and slosh of people doing something in the bog. The ground here was wetter than most of what they'd marched through on the way from Wandalo's hamlet; the Coerli were sinking to their fetlocks because there were no firm patches to step on.

Instead of a stockade, a high wicker fence loomed out of the night. A number of warriors were pushing what Garric first thought was a fascine, a roll of brushwood to fill a gully. In fact they were unrolling a coil of wicker matting to cover the ground up to the open gate. It served the same purpose as a drawbridge.

"*There's six of them,*" Carus noted, always professionally detached in assessing an enemy. "*That's sixteen warriors we know about, plus Torag. And Sirawhil, I suppose, though I don't count her as much.*"

"Torag left six warriors to guard the keep and control the existing slaves," the Bird said. "He has three sexually mature females in his harem as well, but female Coerli do not fight."

Garric looked at the Bird. There was a great deal about the situation that he didn't know and which he suspected Torag hadn't even wondered about.

"The Coerli are not a sophisticated species," the Bird said, repeating an early comment. It turned its sparkling eyes toward the compound without speaking further.

Torag led the procession through the gate. Garric glanced at the wall as he entered, expecting to find it was double with the interior filled with rock. Well, filled with dirt: he'd seen no stone bigger than Marzan's topaz in this whole muddy world. In fact the wall was a single layer of heavy basketry, sufficient for a house but certainly not a military structure in human terms.

"*It's to keep animals out, I'd judge,*" said Carus. "*Cat beasts like the ones that built it. They wouldn't know what a siege train was if it rose up and bit them on their furry asses. Which we may be able to arrange, lad.*"

He chuckled and added, "*In good time.*"

Torag raised his muzzle into the air and sniffed. The interior of the compound was ripe with the sharp stench of carnivore wastes, but that was only to be expected.

"Ido!" said Torag. "You've butchered an animal while I was gone!"

Five of the six warriors who'd been left to guard the keep edged away from their chief. The remaining one, taller and visibly bulkier than the others, straightened. He held a spear, but he kept its bone point carefully toward the ground as he growled, "We were hungry, Torag. We didn't know when you were coming back."

Torag snarled and leaped, swinging his club. Ido hesitated for a fraction of a second between thrusting and jumping away. The knot of hardwood crushed his skull, splashing blood and brains across the surviving members of the garrison. They scattered into the interior of the compound with shrill cries; some of them dropped their weapons as they fled.

Torag roared, a hacking, sawtoothed challenge that echoed through the night. The Coerli warriors hunched, their long faces toward the ground. Sirawhil stood silent, and the captive women huddled together. Several were blubbering in despair.

Garric got down on one knee, keeping his eyes on Torag's short, twitching tail. He hoped his posture looked submissive, but he'd chosen it to give him the best chance of grabbing Torag if the chieftain swung around in fury to strike again.

Breathing in short, harsh snorts, Torag did turn, but he lowered his blood-smeared club. The fighting was over—to the extent there'd been a fight.

"Sorman, Ido was your sibling," the chief growled. "Throw his carrion into a pond where the eels will eat it."

A warrior, bending almost double, squirmed from the fringe of the gathering and gripped the corpse by the ankles. The victim had stiffened instantly when his brain was crushed; one arm stuck out at a right angle. Sorman dragged the body through the gate and into the darkness. He didn't lift his gaze from the mud, at least until he was out of Torag's sight.

Torag raised his head and roared, but this time he was just sealing the reality that everybody around him accepted. Garric half-expected him to urinate on the gatepost, but apparently the Coerli were a little less bestial than that.

When Torag turned, he'd relaxed into his usual strutting self. Licking the head of his club absently, he said, "Get the fresh catch into the pens. And see to it that they're fed and watered. I don't want them dying on me after they cost me so much."

"What about the big one?" Sirawhil asked as the escorting warriors used spear butts to prod the captives toward the back of the compound. "I'll need to examine him further. Though I wish you'd let me take him home to the council."

"Faugh, the council," Torag said. "I don't care what happens at home anymore. *This* is my world, Sirawhil. Put him in the same pen as the rest of them."

He looked at Garric, the club rising slightly in his hand. Garric kept his eyes on the leather belts that crossed in the middle of the chief's chest; he didn't move.

"If he breaks out," Torag said after obvious consideration, "he'll give us good sport. That's probably the best use for him anyway."

"Torag, he's important," the wizard said, then cringed away before the chieftain even raised a hand to strike her. In a less forceful tone she went on, "He could be valuable. We need to know more about him before, before . . ."

"As breeding stock, you mean?" Torag said. "Well, we'll see. Get him in the pen and we'll talk about it after I eat."

Either Nerga or Eny—the pair was indistinguishable to Garric—raised his spear as a prod. Garric stepped forward quickly, joining the coffle of women being marched through the compound by their escorts.

A thought struck him. He turned and called, "Sirawhil? If you want me to settle in properly, you'd better come along with your Bird. I can't speak the language of the villagers here."

By chance he was near Soma. She put her arm around him and called in a loud voice, "Garric is my man, you women! I will let you share him, but *I* am his first wife."

Garric shook her arm away. "Soma," he said, speaking to be heard by the entire coffle. "I am not your man, and you will never be my woman. Your shamelessness disgusts me!"

That was more or less true, but Garric had better reasons for speaking the words. He wanted allies for whatever plan he came up with, but Soma was the last person of those he'd met in this world whom he'd be willing to trust.

Sirawhil joined them. She glanced over her shoulder to see that Torag was entering the longhouse and no longer looking at them, then whispered, "Garric, you must not run! Torag and his warriors will hunt you down easily. If you'll stay quiet and not anger the chief, I'm sure I can get you home with me soon. Whether or not he agrees! You can live your life in safety, then."

"I don't want trouble," Garric said. That was a lie or the next thing to one. "If you'll help me, Sirawhil, I'll do what I can to help you too."

And that was a flat lie. Garric didn't make the mistake of thinking the Corl wizard was his friend just because she wasn't as likely to kill and eat him as her chief was.

The longhouse had a thatched roof. Its walls were wicker, waist-high for two-thirds of its length but solid at the back except for small windows covered with grilles of some hard jointed grass like bamboo. Three Corl faces were crowded at the nearest window, watching Garric and the other prisoners file past. That must be Torag's harem.

"Yes," said the Bird's silent voice. "If Torag allowed his warriors to eat fresh meat regularly, they'd become sexually mature and he'd have to fight every one of them. Just being close to females in estrus may bring males to maturity. That's what was happening with Ido and why he risked killing meat for himself."

To either side of the longhouse were circular beehives big enough for two or three warriors apiece. Members of the raiding party split up among them, growling to one another and to members of the garrison who were coming out of hiding now that Torag's temper had cooled.

A single Corl climbed a tower supported on three poles, disappearing into the thick darkness. Garric couldn't imagine how a watchtower was of any use in these conditions, but the fact the guard had called the alarm at Torag's approach proved otherwise.

Behind the Coerli dwellings was another woven fence, this one only half the height of the fifteen-foot wall surrounding the compound. The gate could be barred, but at present it stood open. A human male and female stood in the gateway watching the newcomers. Patterns of deeper darkness behind the fence suggested others were looking out through gaps in the wicker.

The man in gate was squat and burly; his arms were exceptionally long for his modest height. "I am Crispus!" he shouted. "I am the slave of great Torag! All other Grass Beasts are *my* slaves! Bow to me, all you who enter my domain!"

The coffle of women stopped. Garric stepped forward. Sirawhil was speaking, but though the Bird translated the words in his mind, they were a meaningless blur.

Garric had met his share of bullies at the borough's annual Sheep Fair: merchants' bodyguards, muleteers, and sometimes one of the badgers who'd drive off the sheep that a drover had purchased. He'd learned that you could deal with the bully immediately or you could wait, but waiting didn't ever make the situation better. Therefore—

"I'm Garric or-Reise," he said, his voice rising. "I don't need to be your master, but I'll never be your slave!"

Crispus raised the hand he'd held concealed behind the gatepost; he held a cudgel the length of a man's forearm. Garric lunged forward and smashed the top of his head into Crispus' nose. Crispus bellowed and staggered backward. Garric drove at him again, catching Crispus with the point of his shoulder and crushing him against the gatepost. Garric felt the air blast out of Crispus' lungs, but he didn't hear ribs crack as he'd hoped he might.

Crispus went down. Garric kicked him twice in the face with his heel. He'd been wearing boots or sandals since he became prince so his feet weren't as callused as they would've been when he still lived in Barca's Hamlet, but the blows would've broken bones in a less sturdy victim. As it was, Crispus' head lolled back and his body went limp.

Garric was breathing hard. He hadn't had anything to eat since the evening before he was captured; that was part of the reason he was suddenly dizzy.

He bent and picked up Crispus' cudgel. It wasn't much good to him with his wrists bound together and tied to his waist on a short lead, but he didn't see any point in leaving it for Crispus when he woke up.

"Does anybody else think he'll make me his slave?" he shouted into the darkness beyond the gateway.

The woman who'd been standing with Crispus stepped forward and touched the cords binding Garric's wrists. She held a hardwood dowel no thicker than a writing stylus. She thrust the point into the knots and worked them loose with startling ease.

"I am Donria," she said. She was young and shapely. "Until now there were no men here except Crispus."

She looked up at Garric and added, "Now that I've seen you, I don't think there were any men here at all—until now."

CASHEL FIGURED THE road to the charnel house wasn't any worse than the one that led west out of Barca's Hamlet, but nobody tried to take a carriage down that one. He, Chalcus, and Ilna had gotten out and were walking with the escorting soldiers, but Tenoctris stayed in the open vehicle of necessity.

Cervoran stayed for reasons Cashel wasn't sure about. Maybe Cervoran didn't notice the bumping around.

"Sister take this track!" said the Blood Eagle stumbling along beside Cashel. The guards had their equipment to carry besides watching out for enemies. "You can tell from the ruts how much traffic it gets. How come they don't grade it smooth, hey?"

As soon as the party'd got into the valley north of Mona, the road'd become limestone—living rock, not crushed stone laid over mud. That sounded better than it was: some layers were harder than others, so the carriage's iron tires bounced and skidded from one swale to the next. It made a terrible racket and must've felt worse, though Tenoctris didn't let it show and Cervoran, well, he was Cervoran.

"I don't guess it bothers most people who ride this way," Cashel said after thinking about it for a little while.

They came around a corner. The valley floor widened here, not much but enough to turn a wagon if you swung the outside wheels up onto the slope. The entrance to the cave was a man's height up the east wall. A heavy wooden frame'd been built against the limestone to support a double-leaf gate.

A slate-roofed hut stood above the cave mouth where the slope flattened into a ledge. An old man sat on the hut's porch, cutting an alder sapling into a chain of wooden links. He must've heard the carriage far back down the route, but it wasn't till he saw it was a carriage with the royal seal instead of a wagon carrying corpses that he jumped to his feet. He half-ran, half-scrambled down to meet his visitors. He dropped the shoot he was whittling, but he was waving his short, sharp knife until one of the Blood Eagles stopped him and pried it out of his fingers.

"May the Sister help me, dear sirs and ladies!" the fellow said. He spoke the name of the Sister, the Queen of the Underworld, as a real prayer rather than the curse it'd been in the mouth of the soldier a moment before. "Has something gone wrong? Was the delivery this morning not a pauper after all? Oh dear, oh dear!"

"We're here for other reasons," Tenoctris said as Cashel helped her out of the carriage. "There has been a recent interment then?"

"Why yes," the caretaker said, backing slightly. "A woman, it was. I didn't hear the cause of death. They found her dead in the night, was all I was told."

Cashel handed Tenoctris off to one of the soldiers and stepped quickly around the back of the vehicle to get Cervoran. The Blood Eagles knew Tenoctris well enough that they treated her like a friendly old woman instead of a wizard, but the recently dead man bothered them.

Cashel didn't blame them for feeling that way, but Cervoran'd showed how useful he was when he made the sea burn. Cashel wouldn't say the fellow was necessary; nobody was so necessary that the world was going to stop without him. But Cervoran knew more about the present trouble and how to fix it than anybody else Cashel'd met, Tenoctris included by her own words.

"I must have the body," Cervoran said, tramping toward the gate. The slope'd been cut and filled into a ramp instead of a flight of steps. That'd make it easier for fellows carrying a body. The weight wasn't much, not for two men, but you were likely to trip on steps for not seeing your feet.

"Ah, may I ask why, sirs and ladies?" the attendant said. He stood stiffly, wringing his hands together. He wasn't as old as Cashel'd thought first off, maybe no more than thirty. It was hard to judge with bald folks.

Cervoran ignored him, not that "It is necessary" would've helped much if the fellow'd been what was for him talkative. Tenoctris followed on Ilna's arm, with Chalcus behind looking as tense and alert as an eagle.

"There are dangers to the kingdom, sir," Tenoctris said. "Perhaps you heard about the fortress that rose from the sea? The body will help us, help my colleague that is, deal with the threat."

Cervoran turned on the platform at the top of the ramp. "The Green Woman's creatures are landing even now," he said. "Human weapons may delay their advance, but I alone can defeat the Green Woman."

He paused, then added at a pitch even higher than his usual squeak, "I am Cervoran!"

The attendant looked at Tenoctris and blinked three times quickly, trying to get his mind around the thought. "*King* Cervoran?" he said in disbelief.

"It seems so," said Tenoctris, not putting any opinion into her tone. Cashel grinned. He'd probably have said, "I guess so," and meant the same thing: that they weren't sure.

Cervoran took hold of one of the doors' long vertical handles. The panel quivered when he tugged, but it didn't open. Something buzzed a loud, low note.

"I'll get it," Cashel said, stepping past the two wizards and gripping the handle. The door didn't have a bar or even a latch; nobody was going to break in or out, after all.

Cashel pulled. The door was heavy and fit tightly, but it swung sideways with a squeal.

A flood of flies curled out of the cave and back, like sparks when the roof of a burning building collapses. The stink was the worst Cashel'd smelled since the summer the body of a basking shark cast up on Barca's Hamlet, so rotten that the lower jaw had fallen off; the cartilage of the gill rakers had rotted into what looked like a horse's mane. He was used to bad smells, but he stepped back by reflex because he hadn't expected this one.

Tenoctris threw a hand to her face, then turned and bent over. "Tenoctris, are you—" Cashel started to say, but right then the wizard opened her mouth and vomited. She retched and gasped and tried to throw up again. Cashel stepped toward her but his sister was already there, supporting Tenoctris by the shoulders so she didn't fall on her face from sheer weakness.

It didn't affect Cervoran. Well, Cashel hadn't expected it would. He stepped into the cave and said, "I will use this body. Remove it from the cave for me."

Cashel pulled the other panel open to give better light than there'd be if his body blocked the half the doorway that was already open. Flies were whirling around like anything, brushing Cashel's face and even lighting on him. It was pretty bad and the stink was still worse, but he didn't let any of that show in his face.

From the entrance the cave sloped down for as far as Cashel could see. The stone floor was covered with bodies, bones, and the slick, putrid-smelling liquids that a body turns into if you just let it rot. The corpses near the entrance weren't as far gone as the ones farther in, which'd probably slid or leaked downward as they rotted. The one just inside the door was a middle-aged woman who might've been asleep if you didn't know better.

Cashel squatted beside the body, judging how best to pick it up. It'd stiffened since she died, which'd make it easier to carry. It was a good thing the carriage was open, though, because with her arms spread like this he'd need to break something to get her in through the usual little carriage doors.

"Where d'ye want me to set her, Master Cervoran?" he asked, looking over his shoulder.

It'd have been a side panel of the carriage that got broken if it'd come to that. The woman wouldn't mind and what nature was going to do to her body shortly was a lot worse, but Cashel would still've broken the side panel.

"Carry her outside and put her on the ground," Cervoran said. "The presence of so much death aids my work, but I need more room."

Cashel glanced toward Tenoctris; she lifted her chin just a hair's breadth in agreement. Her face was tight and would've been angry if she'd allowed it to have any expression.

"All right," said Cashel, sliding his hands under the shoulders and hips of the corpse and lifting it. The dead woman wasn't heavy, but she stuck to what'd soaked into the stone. He had to rock her back and forth carefully so that he could pick her up without tearing her skin. He stood, turned, and set her down just clear of the arc the doors swung through.

In the cave it didn't bother Cashel that all the bodies'd been stripped before being thrown there. The sun was high enough now to shine on the little entrance plaza, though, and the woman looked different. It made Cashel feel like a bully to treat her this way, even though she was dead.

He shrugged, but his expression didn't change. Well, it had to happen.

Ilna stepped past and swung the doors shut. She didn't have any difficulty moving the heavy doors, though some of that was just knowing how to use your weight. Still, she was stronger than most people would guess.

Cervoran followed her with his dull eyes. "There was no reason to close the cave," he said.

"I choose to close it," Ilna snapped. "Just as I chose to pull you off the pyre. You may call it my whim, if you like."

Cervoran looked at her for a further moment, then bent and opened his oak case. He had no more expression than a carp does, sucking air on the surface of a pond in high summer.

Cashel grinned. Ilna was a lot of things that most people wouldn't guess. She hadn't said, "Tenoctris is a fine lady, not a peasant like me'n my brother, so the smell bothers her." That might've embarrassed Tenoctris, and Ilna wasn't one to lay what she did on somebody else anyway.

Cashel was proud to have her for a sister. She felt the same way about him, which made it even better.

Cervoran put on the topaz crown, then took other things out of his case. He hadn't started chanting a spell, but Cashel could feel his skin prickle the way it always did around wizardry. That was what they'd come here for, after all.

Cashel looked at his friends: Ilna and Tenoctris and also Chalcus, who'd backed against the rock face so he could look all the other directions without worrying that somebody was coming up behind him.

The sailor flashed Cashel a grin in response, but he was tense and no mistake. Chalcus wasn't afraid of wizardry, exactly, but he was nervous because he knew his sword and dagger were no use against it.

Cashel checked to make sure he had space, then started his quarterstaff in a series of slow circles, first in front of him and then over his head. There was a *lot* of power around this place. The ferrules on the ends of the hickory shaft twinkled with sparks of blue wizardlight.

Cashel smiled as he moved. This quarterstaff had saved him and those he was watching over lots of times; and some of those times he'd been facing wizards.

ILNA WATCHED CERVORAN draw a knife from his box and turn toward her. She knew it was an athame, a wizard's tool used to tease out incantations. The curving symbols cut into the blade were words written in

what educated people like Garric called the Old Script. Ilna could recognize them as patterns, though she couldn't read them any better than
she could the blocky New Script folk used today to write in.

Wizard's tool it might be, but this athame was a real knife also. The
hilt and blade were forged from a single piece of iron, and the double
edges were raggedly sharp.

"You, Ilna," Cervoran said. He stepped toward her, raising the
athame. "I must have a lock of your hair for the amulet which controls
my double."

Chalcus flicked his sword out and held it straight. The point didn't
touch Cervoran's right eye, but it would run the wizard through the
brain if he took another step forward.

"Let's you take a lock of somebody else's hair, my good friend," the
sailor said in his falsely cheerful voice. "A lock of your own, why not?
You'll not want to pay the cost of raising that ugly blade of yours to
Mistress Ilna."

"Do you think your steel frightens me, man?" Cervoran said. His
head turned toward the sailor. "There must be a lock of my hair in the
amulet to animate the simulacrum. The hair of Ilna is to control it. Do
you think to build a double of me and free it uncontrolled?"

"Why hers, then?" Chalcus said. "Take hairs from my head if you
like!"

He was angry in a way Ilna'd rarely seen him. Normally anything
that disturbed the sailor as much as this did would've given him the release of killing something. The humor of the situation struck Ilna,
though nobody seeing her expression was likely to know she was smiling.

"The clay was female, therefore the control must be female," Cervoran said. "And there are other reasons. If the clay had been male, I would
have used Master Cashel as my control."

His tone was always peevish, but perhaps it was a little more so just
at the moment. Despite the way the wizard had sneered at the sword, Ilna
noticed that he hadn't tried to move past it.

"Tenoctris, is this true?" Chalcus demanded. He flicked his eyes toward the old woman, then locked them back on Cervoran. "Does he
need Mistress Ilna's hair as he says?"

"It may be true, Chalcus," Tenoctris said carefully. "To be sure of
that, I'd have to be a much greater wizard than I am."

"You'll do," said Ilna. She stepped forward and plucked the athame
from Cervoran's pulpy fingers. He tried to keep hold when he realized

what she was about, but she had no desire to let Cervoran's hand hold an edge that close to her throat. She shook him free easily and raised the blade to her head.

Ilna pinched a lock of hair from in front of her ear with the other hand, then sawed the athame through it. Though the iron hilt had been in Cervoran's hand, it remained icy cold. She didn't like the feel of the metal, but she used the athame rather than her own paring knife because it might have a virtue she didn't understand herself.

Ilna's mother, Mab—her mother and Cashel's—had been a wizard or something greater than a wizard. Ilna'd never met Mab, only seen her at a distance, and she wouldn't have understood much more—about Mab or about the things she herself did with fabric—even if they'd spoken, she supposed. But as Tenoctris said, there were reasons a wizard *might* use Ilna or her brother to increase the power of his spell.

"Ilna?" said Tenoctris. "I'm sure you realize this, dear, but there are dangers to the person whose psyche controls the simulacrum of a wizard."

"Thank you, Tenoctris," Ilna said. It felt odd to realize that she had friends, that there were people who cared about her. "There's danger in getting up in the morning, I'm afraid. Especially in these times."

She handed the pinch of hair to Cervoran; he took it in the cup of his hand instead of between thumb and forefinger as she offered it. Ilna rotated the athame to put the point up and the hilt toward the wizard, and he took that also.

Ilna watched Cervoran use the athame to draw an oval around the corpse, leaving more space at its feet than at its head. His point scored the soft stone only lightly, but he never let it skip.

She was glad to be shut of the athame; she'd rather put her hands in the stinking muck of the charnel house than to touch that cold iron again. But she'd do either of those things and worse if duty required it.

Ilna smiled and, without looking, reached out to the back of Chalcus' wrist. He'd sheathed his blades again, but the hilts were never far from his hands. She wouldn't pretend she was happy, but she was glad to be the person she was instead of somebody too frightened or too squeamish to do things that had to be done.

Cervoran stepped into the figure he'd drawn, standing at the corpse's foot. He pointed the athame at the woman's face. Someone had closed her eyes, but her mouth sagged open in death. She'd lost her front teeth in both upper and lower jaws.

"*Ouer mechan . . . ,*" Cervoran said. Azure wizardlight, a blue purer than anything in nature, sparkled on the point of the athame. "*Libaba oimathotho.*"

Ilna looked dispassionately at the woman's corpse, wondering what her name had been. Cities were impersonal in a way that a tiny place like Barca's Hamlet never could be, but Mona wasn't large as cities go. People on the woman's street, in her tenement, would have known her by name.

Now she had nothing. Even her corpse, her *clay* as Cervoran put it, was being taken for another purpose. It was that or the maggots' purpose, of course, but perhaps the maggots would've been better.

"*Brido lothian iao . . . ,*" Cervoran chanted. The topaz on his brow flamed with more light than the sun struck from it; his athame sizzled and chattered as though he'd pent a thunderbolt in its cold iron form.

Ilna's fingers were working a pattern. She didn't recall taking the yarn from her sleeve, but for her it was as natural as breathing. The dead woman had no name, and shortly there would be nothing at all left of her. . . .

"*Isee!*" Cervoran said. A crackling bar of wizardlight linked his athame to the bridge of the corpse's nose. "*Ithi! Squaleth!*"

The dead woman's features slumped. *Melting away,* Ilna thought, but instead they were melting into the shape of Cervoran's own face. Wizardlight snarled and popped, molding flesh the way a potter's thumbs do clay. *The clay is female,* the wizard told Chalcus, and he'd meant the words literally.

Cervoran's mouth moved. Perhaps he was still chanting but Ilna couldn't hear words through the roar of the wizardry itself. The woman's mouth, now Cervoran's mouth, closed. The eyes blinked open, filled momentarily by a fire that was more than wizardlight. The corpse folded its hands and sat up slowly as the spluttering light spread down through its changing body.

The blue glare cut off so abruptly that for an instant the sun seemed unable to fill its absence. Cervoran staggered out of the oval he'd scribed. He might've fallen if Cashel—Ilna smiled: of *course* Cashel—hadn't put a hand behind his shoulders.

What had been the corpse of an unknown woman stood up with the deliberation of a flower unfolding. It was no longer dead, it was no longer female, and in every way but size it looked exactly like Cervoran. He was a bulky man though of only average height, while the corpse—

the clay he'd molded his double from—had been both shorter and slighter.

The only thing the double wore was the bag hanging from its neck. Cervoran had put the locks of hair and probably other things into it, to judge from the way it bulged. Both the bag and cord were linen rather than wool. Ilna was far too conscious of the powers that fibers held to think the choice of vegetable rather than animal materials was chance.

Ilna turned and pulled the door of the charnel house open a crack; she tossed the pattern she'd just knotted inside, then pressed the doors closed.

It was a monument, of sorts; a distillation of the woman's presence. It wasn't much, but it was what Ilna could do.

Chalcus cursed savagely under his breath. His cape was sewn from red and yellow cloth in vertical stripes. He unfastened the gaudy garnet pin clenching it at his throat and laid it over the double's shoulders.

"Cover yourself, damn you!" he snarled, his face turned away from the creature and the wizard who'd created it.

"We will return to my palace now," Cervoran said. "I have work to do."

Ilna couldn't be sure, but she thought there was a smirk on his purple lips.

A HORSE TAKES up as much room on shipboard as a dozen men, so when Garric embarked the royal army he didn't take horses. The courier panting in front of Sharina had run the whole distance back from the battle. He'd stripped off his armor and weapons before setting out, but he still wore military boots. He was bent over with his hands on his knees, shuffling slowly to keep from stiffening as he sucked air into his lungs.

The tablet's wax seal was impressed with a bunch of grapes: the crest of Liane's family, the bor-Benlimans, not Lord Waldron's two-headed dragon. Sharina broke the tablet open, unsurprised. That's why she'd sent Liane along with the army, after all; or better, allowed Liane to accompany the army. Lord Waldron regarded reporting back to be somehow demeaning, and in the present instance he probably had his hands full.

Waldron *definitely* had his hands full. The note inked on white birch in Liane's neat uncials read: APPROXIMATELY 300 HELLPLANTS ASHORE IN CALF'S HEAD BAY SEVEN MILES WEST OF MONA. NO MORE APPEARING AT PRESENT. ATTEMPTING TO FIGHT PLANTS WITH FIRE BUT WEATHER DAMP. LBB FOR LD WALDRON.

"Your Highness?" said Attaper. "Lord Cashel and the others're back."

He'd formed the available Blood Eagles around Sharina in the palace courtyard. That was about a hundred and fifty men, scarcely a "regiment" even with the addition of the troop in Valles guarding King Valence III and the troop who'd escorted Cashel, Ilna, and Tenoctris to the charnel house. The royal bodyguards had taken heavy casualties ever since they'd begun accompanying Prince Garric. There was no lack of volunteers from line regiments to fill the black-armored ranks, but selection and training took more time than Attaper'd had free.

Sharina looked up. Her brush was poised to reply on the facing page of the tablet, using red ink because she was the acting ruler of the kingdom whether she liked it or not. She'd been so lost in organizing a response to what was happening miles away that she hadn't noticed the return of Cashel with Tenoctris and the others. Things had been happening so fast. . . .

Her friends were coming toward her one at a time through the narrow aisle the guards had opened for them. Cashel was in front. Seeing him made Sharina feel calmer than she had since the woman ran into the palace screaming that something had happened to her boy. The child, a nine-year-old, had been chasing crows out of the family barley plot. When hellplants crawled out of the sea and began crushing their way across the field, he'd tried to stop them by flinging stones.

The boy's mother had come out of their hut in time to see the boy snatched by a tentacle. Fortunately she'd been too far away to comprehend what Sharina knew must've happened next, and she'd run to Mona for help instead of going out into the field to join her son.

Sharina'd dispatched Lord Waldron with the three regiments billeted in the city to deal with the attack. She hadn't gone herself because she wasn't a warrior like her brother. She couldn't *lead* an attack the way Garric might well have done, so rather than being in the way of the fighting men, she'd stayed in the palace to command the whole business.

The rest of the army and fleet was scattered across First Atara so that no district was completely overwhelmed by the numbers of strangers it had to feed and house. Those units had to be alerted, and somebody had to make decisions if a second attack occurred while Waldron was involved with the first.

It was possible that a second or third or twentieth attack would occur. Sharina knew their enemy was powerful, but not even Tenoctris could guess *how* powerful.

Cashel smiled as warmly as an embrace, but instead of putting an arm around her he stepped to the side and let those behind get through also. Tenoctris followed, then Ilna, and Chalcus with his usually cheerful face looking like a thunderhead ready to burst forth in hail and lightning. Cervoran was the last.

Sharina's eyes widened in surprise. The person immediately behind Chalcus wasn't Cervoran—it was a slightly smaller copy of Cervoran, dressed in a rag breechclout and the short cape that Chalcus had worn when the group left in the morning. Cervoran, the real Cervoran, was in back of his double.

"I will create the necessary devices in my chamber of art," Cervoran said. The other members of the party were tensely silent, but the soldiers who'd escorted them talked in muted voices to colleagues who'd stayed at the palace. "I cannot breach the Fortress of Glass directly, so I will enter it from another place."

Sharina glanced at Tenoctris, who sucked her lips in and shrugged. "I can't judge what Lord Cervoran can do or should be permitted to do, Your Highness," she said with quiet formality. "I'm trying to follow the various currents of power about us, but I haven't been able to do so as yet."

"You have no choice, fools," Cervoran squeaked. "The Green Woman has sent her servants against one place at present. She will attack other places, all the places on this island. Unless they are stopped, her creatures will advance until they have killed me. Then they will conquer this island and all islands. Only I can stand against the Green Woman, and I must have my chamber of art!"

"Yes, all right," said Sharina calmly. She didn't like Cervoran's tone, but she didn't see any useful result from trying to teach him manners. Whatever he'd been in his earlier life, since Ilna dragged him off the pyre he'd acted less like an adult than like a child—or perhaps like a storm, howling and whistling and sizzling with ungoverned power.

"Cashel must help me," Cervoran said. "And Protas, who is clay of this clay."

"*Prince* Protas?" Ilna said, the words coming out clipped and hard. "Your son, the child?"

"It is necessary," Cervoran said. "His clay, his *flesh* is of this flesh."

All the time Cervoran was speaking, the near-copy of him stared at the original with cold black eyes. Sharina wondered what the double's voice would sound like if he spoke.

Aloud she said, "I won't order a child to help in wizardry. I won't order anybody to help your wizardry!"

She looked at Cashel, opening her mouth to repeat her words in a more personal fashion, but Cashel was already giving her a slow grin. "It's all right, Sharina," he said quietly. "If I can do something to help, I will. And I guess Lord Protas feels the same way. He's a good boy, though he's, you know, younger than I was or Garric was."

"Find him and ask him, then," Sharina said, suddenly tired from making decisions for other people that meant life or death; for them, perhaps for everyone in the kingdom. "But I won't order him!"

She knew Protas would go anywhere that Cashel was willing to take him: the boy would've accompanied the group to the charnel house if Tenoctris had permitted it. And Sharina understood that more than the life of one boy hung on Cervoran's wizardry. The child who'd been watching the field at Calf's Head Bay had been younger than Protas was when he fell victim to the hellplants.

But as she watched Cashel leave with Cervoran and the lesser copy of Cervoran, she was glad Liane wasn't here to listen. Liane wouldn't have allowed Cervoran to use Protas, no matter how critical the boy's presence might be to the survival of the kingdom.

Liane's father had been a wizard too; and in the end, he'd been ready to sacrifice his daughter's life to complete an incantation.

Chapter

8

CASHEL OPENED THE door of the chamber and stepped through first. He held his staff at the balance in his right hand. He wasn't exactly poised to bash anybody waiting inside to attack them, but—

Well, if somebody inside was waiting to attack them, Cashel would bash him. There were people who jumped at shadows and that was silly, but recently some shadows had been doing the jumping. Cashel wasn't going to let anything happen to his friends because he hadn't watched out for them. That's what a shepherd did, after all.

There was pretty much nothing inside, just the cases of books and oddments along the back wall. The windows were shuttered and the door to the rest of Sharina's suite was closed. Light bled through the cracks, but not enough to properly see the figures laid into the floor. The tapestry on the west wall was a square of shiny blackness.

While the others came in, Cashel walked across the room to throw back the shutters. Protas had scooted up right beside him, which was all right now. The boy'd had the good sense to stay out of the way when Cashel got ready to open the door, though, which not every adult would've done.

"Leave the windows as they are!" Cervoran said. His voice didn't get any deeper in here, but it echoed in a funny way. "There is light enough for my art."

Cashel didn't say anything, just turned. "Light enough" he'd grant; but that was different from saying more light would be a bad thing. Creatures that scuttled when light fell on 'em generally weren't good company in darkness, either.

He didn't like this room. There wasn't anything specific wrong, it just felt like all sorts of things were pushing for space. Which was funny since it was near as empty as a barn in springtime, but Cashel guessed that meant there were more things here than his eyes were seeing. That stood to reason.

Sharina came in with Attaper and a double handful of guards standing so close that Cashel could scarcely see her through all the black-armored bodies. *What did they think they were going to do that I couldn't of?*

But Cashel held his tongue. That was something he'd learned young and never forgotten, even after he'd got his growth and pretty much could say what he pleased.

Cervoran raised his hand. He wasn't holding the athame, but the topaz crown winked in a way that made him look bigger than he had in full sunlight.

"Stop!" he said. "No one may be present while I build a portal. I and Cashel and the clay will perform the rites without interference."

"What does he mean, 'the clay,' Cashel?" Protas whispered.

Cashel touched a hand to the boy's shoulder to reassure him, but he kept his eyes on Cervoran. The way the wizard talked wasn't much to Cashel's taste, but words weren't enough to get upset over.

"Lord Cervoran?" Tenoctris said quietly. A couple of the soldiers were probably her guards, but they gave her more space than Attaper did Sharina. "I would—"

"No one!" Cervoran said. He always sounded angry or at least out of sorts, but there was more than usual of it now. "I and Cashel and the clay Protas, no one else!"

Sharina must've said something testy to her guards, because a couple of them moved sideways to let her step between them and face Cervoran directly. "Milord," she said, "I remind you again: you do not give orders in this kingdom."

She looked at Cashel. He drew himself up another fingertip of straightness. Sharina was so very beautiful. His Sharina. . . .

"Cashel," she said. "I know you're willing to do this. I want your opinion as a friend: should I allow the ceremony to go ahead with only the three of you present? I'm asking because I trust your instinct."

Cashel thought for a moment. "Ma'am," he said, formal because it was a real question she was asking. "I don't see how it could hurt. I mean, it may go wrong but nobody else being near could help, right, Tenoctris?"

Tenoctris gave a quick dip of her chin. "I agree," she said simply.

"We must be alone," Cervoran said shrilly. He didn't bother to turn to look at Cashel behind him. "It is necessary!"

"All right," said Sharina. Cashel felt the emotion that she kept out of her voice. "We'll wait in my suite."

There was a bustle as folks, mostly soldiers, got turned around and shuffled into what'd been the queen's bedroom. Chalcus, smiling on the surface and as angry underneath as Cashel'd ever heard him, said, "And your copy that we went to the tomb to get you, Master Cervoran? Does that one go or stay?"

"I go," the double piped, sounding exactly like Cervoran himself. "My time is not yet come, but soon."

They left the room. Sharina turned in the doorway and said, "Cashel? May the Lady be with you."

Then she shut the door behind her. *She's so very beautiful. . . .*

"Come here," Cervoran said, walking heavily across the room. He stopped and bent, placing the crown on the floor.

Cashel's eyes had adapted well enough he could see the lines inlaid on the stone floor. The jewel was in the center of a triangle, and a circle scribed the triangle's three points.

Cervoran shifted so he was standing in the scoop of floor between the inside of the circle and one flat side of the triangle. He pointed—with his hand, he still wasn't using the athame or another pointer—at the side to his left and said, "Cashel, go there. Protas, clay of this clay—"

He pointed with his other hand.

"—go there. Kneel, Cashel and Protas, and put your fingers on the talisman."

Protas hesitated. Cashel squatted, keeping the staff against the floor as a brace. He didn't ordinarily kneel and he wasn't going to now unless Cervoran said he absolutely had to do it that way. If Cashel had a choice, he wasn't going into this business in a posture that made him uncomfortable.

He smiled at Protas as he touched the topaz with his fingertips. It felt warm, which surprised him a little.

Protas squatted also, then had to bob up and pull some slack in his trousers to give his knees room. The boy wobbled for a moment, then had to touch the floor to keep from falling backward.

"Just go ahead and kneel, Protas," Cashel said, trying not to smile. "I'm used to squatting, but you ought to do what you're used to."

Protas knelt. He looked doubtful, but Cashel knew that the boy would try if he told him to stand on his hands. He touched the back of Cashel's fingers, then slipped his fingers down onto the topaz.

Cervoran dropped to one knee, then the other. He moved like a doll on strings. Cashel didn't flinch when the wizard reached out, but he was just as glad their fingers didn't touch.

"*Horu wo awita . . . ,*" Cervoran chanted. "*Siwa sega sawasgir. . . .*"

The room went completely black, as black as soot on fire irons, but the topaz kept the same slight glitter as before. Cashel could see the tips of his own fingers and the others' too, but he couldn't tell where the windows were except from memory. Protas' hand trembled, but the boy didn't whimper or jerk away.

"*Phriou apom machri . . . ,*" said Cervoran. "*Alchei alchine cheirene . . .*"

The topaz blazed with yellow fire that didn't light anything. Cashel couldn't see his hands anymore; he couldn't feel Protas or the staff. His body tingled all over.

MONZO MOUNZOUNE, thundered a voice. It wasn't Cervoran speaking because Cashel was completely alone in a universe of pulsing yellow light. *IAIA PERPERTHOUA IAIA!*

The light was sunlight. Cashel fell onto his side in a meadow because he'd lost his balance during the incantation. Flowers growing in the short grass scented the air.

"Cashel!" Protas cried, jumping up from his sprawl. The crown lay between them. The topaz was its usual yellow color with muddy shadows from the flaws inside the stone. "Cashel!"

Instead of answering, Cashel rolled to his feet and slanted the quarterstaff crossways before him. In a grove of trees nearby a woman with a horse's skull for a head played the harp. Accompanying her on a lute was a rat standing upright; it was the size of a man. Their music screeched like rocks rubbing hard against each other.

A winged demon with tiny blue scales for skin and a tail as long as its body faced Cashel. It was standing where Cervoran had been in the room during the incantation, but Cervoran was nowhere to be seen now.

"You are Cashel and Protas," the demon said. It was so thin it looked like the blue hide had been shrunk over a skeleton, but its voice was a booming bass. "By the decision of one who has the power to command me, I am to escort you to the next stage of your journey."

The demon threw its head back and laughed thunderously. "I would rather tear the flesh from your bones!" it added, and it laughed again.

Protas had jumped around behind Cashel, closer than he ought to be if there'd been a fight; but there wouldn't be a fight. Cashel raised the staff upright in one hand and put the other on the boy's shoulder.

"Better pick up the crown, Protas," he said.

"Cashel?" said the boy. The demon had stopped laughing, but the lute and harp continued to make their ugly sound. "He said he was going to eat us?"

"He said he'd like to," Cashel explained. "But somebody bigger 'n him is making him help us."

"All right, Cashel," Protas said. He ducked down and grabbed the crown, but he didn't look at the demon again till he'd skipped back to Cashel's side.

"Anyway," Cashel said, speaking for the boy's sake and not just to brag, "what he means is he'd *try* to eat us. Folks've tried that in the past, and some of them—"

He smiled at the demon, the sort of smile he'd used lots of times just before a fight started.

"—were a good bit bigger than that fellow is."

Donria took garric through the gate while the neck-bound women waited uncertainly. Beyond was a single long hut and, in the gray distance, either a number of larger buildings or more likely raised beds like those the people of Wandalo's village used to drain the roots of their crops.

"You lot, pick up the other male and drag him in with you!" one of the escorting warriors said as the women started through after Garric. The line shuffled to a stop.

"Bend down!" Soma said. "Bend down, you fools!"

By half-dragging the women nearest her in the coffle, Soma got enough slack in her neck ropes to get her arms under Crispus. She rose, holding the groaning man's right arm over her shoulders and clasping him about the waist with her left hand. The line resumed moving.

Soma's strength was impressive, though that didn't surprise Garric since he'd grown up in a peasant village. Women in Barca's Hamlet worked as hard as the men did and often for longer hours.

Women who'd been waiting inside the wall crowded around Garric. He couldn't be sure of the number in this foggy darkness, but there were at least twenty and perhaps half again as many. They chattered among themselves and threw comments and questions at him as well: *Where did you come from, Garric?/You're so big, I've never seen such muscles/Oh, your hair's all bloody, did Crispus hurt you?* Fingers plucked at him, testing and caressing.

The last of the coffle moved through. The gates groaned shut on their rope hinges. A bar squealed into place on the other side, where Nerga and Eny stayed. Sirawhil was outside also, but the Bird gave a chirrup and flew from her shoulder to settle in a glitter of wings on the ridgepole of the longhouse.

"*It wouldn't take much to open the gates,*" Carus observed. "*Just cut the hinges. Even without a proper knife that wouldn't be hard to arrange. Of course there's the guard in the watchtower. . . .*"

He was just thinking aloud, not planning anything for the time being. It wasn't *idle* speculation, though. Garric had learned that the way Carus always thought about the military possibilities of a situation meant he reacted instantly to threats that would've taken most generals completely by surprise.

"Give us room here!" Donria said. "Newla, if you touch him again, I'll break your fingers. Do you hear me? Move *back!*"

The women moved a little, enough that Garric could shift into a wider stance without stepping on somebody. Donria's authority had to be based on more than the physical threat she'd just made: she was a small woman, and though she was obviously fit it would've been remarkable if that weren't true of most of the others. He'd seen in Wandalo's village that the Grass People didn't have enough surplus to keep fine ladies in pampered leisure.

"Here, Newla," Donria said, giving her pointed dowel to a raw-boned woman half a head taller than she was. "Get the new arrivals loose, won't you? You know what it's like when you're first brought here. And Brosa? You and the other girls in your section, start dishing food out. Bring Garric's to the headman's room, he'll stay there now."

"What about Crispus, Donria?" asked a woman Garric couldn't see in the crowd.

"Well, what about him?" Donria said sharply. "*You* saw, didn't you? Garric's our headman now!"

Garric let Donria walk him along, guided by her hand on his shoulder. He wasn't sure that he wanted to be headman of this slave community, but he was very sure that he didn't want Crispus to be headman over him.

The longhouse was similar to the houses in Wandalo's village, built of thatch instead of shakes, wicker, and a floor of puncheons—logs flattened only on the top side. The construction was cruder, though, and the design was nothing like what the Grass People built on their own. This was a copy of the Coerli chieftain's hut, constructed by slaves from common materials.

Donria led him inside. Garric hadn't been able to see much in the open air; here he was stone blind. The floor had been roughly shaped with a stone adze but smoothed only by those walking on it. Garric's feet didn't pick up splinters, but it felt as though he were stepping onto the shingle beach of Barca's Hamlet.

"Donria, I can't see inside," he said, stopping where he was.

"Your room is right here, Garric," Donria said. She pressed against him, a reasonable way to direct him to the left. More was going on than that, of course, but Donria seemed considerably more intelligent than Soma was.

But—Donria had to be aggressive or she wouldn't be leader here, and she knew she wouldn't remain leader without the support of the headman. Garric smiled faintly. The ram of the flock. The concept wasn't new to him, but its application to human beings certainly was.

Donria opened a door and led him into a separate room. His eyes must be adapting a little, because the open gable was noticeably brighter than everything around it. There was a flutter as the Bird landed there, a blotch of shadow and highlights.

"Here's the couch," Donria said. He heard withies creak as they took her weight. He eased himself down also, then regretted it. The bolster was damp; probably damp with the former headman's urine, judging from the smell pervading the room.

Garric jumped up. He wasn't fastidious by the standards of city folk, but his father had kept a clean inn. Besides, well-rotted waste from *all* animals was the best manure you could put on a field: Crispus was not only a pig, he was a wasteful pig.

"Get this out of here!" he said, jerking the bolster off the bed. It was coarse sacking stuffed with straw. Donria'd gotten up when he did, backing slightly away till she learned what was bothering him. "If there isn't a clean one, I'll sleep on the slats."

Donria pulled open the inner door and hurled the bolster into the main hall. "Newla, bring our headman a fresh mattress. Quickly, before he gets angry!"

"I'm not angry," Garric said quietly. "Well, not at you. This is a terrible way for people to live!"

There were slave pens in the Kingdom of the Isles too. Not officially, but the lot of a tenant farmer on Sandrakkan or in the east of Ornifal could be very hard if he fell behind to the landowner . . . and they all fell behind to their landowners in a bad year, which meant forever after. That was something he'd deal with as soon as he got back. . . .

A pair of women appeared in the doorway with a wooden bucket and a platter. Either could've carried the load by herself, but the way other women crowded behind them in the open hall showed that Garric was a matter of general interest.

Garric wondered how long it was till dawn. He couldn't get a feeling for his surroundings till there was more light.

"The sky will brighten in three hours," said the Bird silently. "Full sunrise is another hour beyond that. It still won't be as bright as you're used to, of course."

Of course, Garric agreed, *but I'll never accomplish anything if I wait for perfect conditions.*

Which left open the question of what he planned to accomplish. Well, getting out of this slave pen as a start, and then getting back to his own world as quickly as possible. He didn't have any idea how he was going to accomplish that, but he'd find a way or die trying; which wasn't a figure of speech in this case.

"Let me past!" someone called. "Make way or I'll make one!"

The big woman, Newla, shoved her way through the spectators with not one but two bolsters to lay on the bed. They had the smell of fresh straw, a hint of sun and better times in Garric's memory.

"Donria?" she said, a hint of hopefulness in her voice. "Could I stay tonight too? For after you, I mean."

"Please," said Garric, trying to be firm without sounding angry. He could only hope that the Bird translated tone as well as it did words. "I want to be alone. I need to be alone. I've got to rest. And I will rest."

Donria had taken the food from the women who'd brought it. She looked at Garric, though he couldn't read her expression in this light.

After a moment she said, "You are our headman, Garric," and put the pail and platter on a ledge built out from the interior wall. "Your will is our will."

She motioned Newla out of the room, then added quietly, "But Garric? Torag won't keep a headman who doesn't service his herd. The Coerli will eat any of us, but they prefer infants."

She closed the door behind her.

Garric took a deep breath, then sampled the food. What he'd thought was porridge was a mash of barley bruised and soaked but not cooked; the Coerli didn't allow their herd to have fire. The fish on the platter had been air dried.

And the Coerli ate their own food raw.

I'll find a way out, or I'll die.

"*Aye, lad,*" said the warrior ghost in his mind. "*But right now I'm more interested in killing cat beasts first.*"

W IZARDLIGHT AS RED as the heart of a ruby shot through Ilna's soul and the universe around her. She'd been squatting as she knotted small patterns. She wished she'd brought a hand loom, since it was hard to judge how long they'd be.

The light and the thunderclap which shook Cervoran's chamber of art jolted her to her feet. She folded the fabric back in her sleeve and uncoiled the noosed cord she wore in place of a sash.

"Cashel!" Sharina cried.

Lord Attaper and the under-captain with him kicked the connecting door together, as smoothly as if they were practiced dancers. It was a light interior door whose gilded birch panels were set in a basswood frame. The hobnailed boots smashed it like a pair of battering rams. The soldiers rushed through, drawing their swords.

Impressive, Ilna thought dryly, but scarcely necessary. The door hadn't been locked or barred.

The interior was still dark. As Ilna and Chalcus slipped through in the midst of more soldiers, Attaper wrenched a set of shutters down with a crash, frame and all. The guard commander was angry and taking it out on the furnishings. Garric had disappeared, fighting was taking place a few miles away while Attaper's duties kept him from the battle, and three more people had vanished more or less under his nose.

Because there was no doubt that the room was empty. Cashel, Protas, and the wizard who'd said he was "opening a portal" were gone.

Guards in the foyer opened the other door. "Did they go out past you?" Attaper shouted at them, and their blank looks were proof of the obvious.

The air had a faintly sulfurous smell. Ilna touched the floor in the middle of a triangular inlay where the stone looked singed. It was warm, at any rate.

"Do you see anything, Ilna?" Sharina murmured. Her face remained aloof, but she'd wrapped her arms tightly around her bosom.

"Nothing useful," Ilna said, straightening. "What do I know of wizardry?"

She cleared her throat. "My brother doesn't know anything about wizardry either," she said. "But I'd trust him to take care of anything that could be taken care of. He's proved that many times."

"Yes of course," said Sharina and hugged Ilna, hugged her friend. In their hearts they both knew that it wasn't really "of course" that Cashel would come safely through wherever Cervoran was taking him.

The copy Cervoran had made of himself entered the chamber, walking with the same hitching deliberation as the wizard himself had done. He silently stared around the chamber. Men edged away from him and dropped their eyes to avoid his gaze.

Ilna deliberately glared back at the fellow, angry even at the *thought* that she might be afraid of him. The copy's lips smiled at her, though his eyes were as flat as mossy pools.

"Where is the topaz?" he said. "Where is the amulet that Bass One-Thumb found?"

Nobody else seemed disposed to answer, so Ilna said, "Cervoran had it with him when he came into this room. He and it both have vanished, so common sense suggests he still has it."

The copy smiled again, this time toward a blank patch of wall. He turned his head to Sharina and said, "You are the ruler. You will take me to where the creatures the Green Woman makes from seaweed are coming ashore. I must see them to defeat them properly."

"The princess doesn't *take* you anywhere, creature!" Attaper said sharply. "If she decides you can go, we'll arrange an escort to get you there."

"Milord?" Sharina said. "I'd already decided to view the invasion for myself. We'll set out as soon as I've arranged a few details with Lord Tadai. And if the . . ."

She paused, her face expressionless as she looked at the copy.

". . . person here wishes to accompany us, I can see no objection."

"As Your Highness wishes," Attaper said. He looked away and shot his sword into its sheath with a squeal and a clang.

Tenoctris appeared at the door behind Cervoran's double. Instead of rushing into the chamber of art with the rest of them, she'd remained in Sharina's bedroom. Apparently she'd worked a spell there, since she was holding one of the bamboo splits she used for her art. She tossed it to the floor when she noticed it.

"What is your name?" Tenoctris said.

The copy turned to face her. "Who are you to ask?" he said.

"I am Lady Tenoctris, once bos-Tandor," Tenoctris said clearly and forcefully. "My line and my very epoch have perished utterly. What is your *name*?"

"Do you think I fear to tell you?" the copy said. "You have no power, old woman. I am Double. I will be Cervoran."

Double gave a horrible tittering laugh. He said, "I will be God!"

ᴛ ᴇɴᴏᴄᴛʀɪs ᴄᴏᴜʟᴅɴ'ᴛ ʀɪᴅᴇ as far as Calf's Head Bay on horseback and arrive in any kind of condition, so Lord Martous had found her a light carriage. Tenoctris could *drive* the single horse herself, though— that was a proper accomplishment for a noblewoman, along with fine needlework and accompanying her own singing on the lute.

Sharina rode with the old wizard. Horses had been rare visitors in Barca's Hamlet when she was growing up, and the training she'd gotten since then didn't make her either a good rider or a comfortable one.

"I smell smoke," Tenoctris said as the gig climbed a track meant for hikers and pack mules. She gave a quick twitch to the reins. "It's making the horse skittish."

"They'll be burning the hellplants," Sharina said. "That's all they can do, I suppose. I wonder if—"

She started to glance over her shoulder at the similar gig following theirs, but she changed her mind before her head moved. "I wonder if Double will be able to help?" she went on quietly. "Is he really a wizard himself, Tenoctris?"

A second gig followed theirs, driven by Attaper's own son. The Blood Eagles were a brave and highly disciplined body of men, but Attaper hadn't been certain that any one else in the unit would've obeyed an order to drive the vehicle in which Double rode.

The guards who'd watched Double being created had described the experience to their fellows. The story had gotten more colorful when they'd passed it on, though the bare reality that Tenoctris described was horrible enough.

"Yes, dear," Tenoctris said. "Easy, girl, easy. Lord Cervoran created a true duplicate of himself to hold his enemy's attention while he himself left this world. Double has to be a wizard to succeed as a decoy; and besides, I can see the way power trails from him."

It took Sharina a few heartbeats to realize that, "Easy girl, easy," had been directed to the horse. Nervous from the smoke and perhaps other things—the hair on the back of Sharina's neck had begun to rise—the animal was threatening to run up the backs of the soldiers immediately in front of them on the narrow track. The hills framing Calf's Head Bay weren't high, but they were steep.

Three troops of Blood Eagles marched ahead of the gigs, and another troop brought up the rear. The soldiers were on foot but trotting along the rutted track double-time. Sharina hadn't thought that they could keep up the pace with three miles to cover, but with a few exceptions—men recently wounded and not fully recovered—they did. The royal bodyguards had been trained to be soldiers equal to any they might meet, not just a shiny black backdrop for the king on public occasions.

Sharina looked at the older woman. "I don't trust Cervoran," she said. "That means we can't trust Double either, if he's the same as his creator."

"They each have their own agendas," Tenoctris said, her eyes on the bay mare she was driving. "And as you say, their purposes aren't ours. But when I said Double was the same as Cervoran, I didn't mean they're allies. Double is as surely Cervoran's rival as each of them is opposed to the Green Woman. That gives us some . . ."

She let her voice trail off, then glanced at Sharina with a wry smile and went on, "I was going to say that it gives us some advantage, dear, but that isn't correct. It gives us a certain amount of hope, though."

Sharina laughed and squeezed her friend's shoulder. Despite the situation, she felt more comfortable than she had for longer than she could guess. She'd changed into a pair of simple tunics under a hooded military cape, and she wore the Pewle knife openly in its heavy sealskin sheath. At the moment, being able to move—and fight if necessary—was more important than impressing people with the majesty of the Princess of Haft.

The leading guards disappeared over the top of the ridge. A man shouted. Sharina touched her knife hilt, but the cry had been startlement rather than fear and there was no clash of weapons with it.

Tenoctris clucked the horse over the rise. They drove out of bright daylight into a dank gray mist and the smell of rotting mud; the change was as abrupt as going through a door. No wonder a soldier had called out in surprise.

"Hold up!" somebody called angrily. "Hold up! And by the Lady, what're civilians doing here!"

Tenoctris was already drawing the horse around to get the gig off the track. A Blood Eagle ran back to them and called, "Your Highness? Lord Attaper says not to take the cart any closer, if you please."

Attaper was talking to—shouting at—one of Lord Waldron's aides. The topic probably involved the respect owed to Her Royal Highness Sharina, Princess of Haft. That wasn't fair: the mist blurred details, and she and Tenoctris really were civilians, after all.

"Milord Attaper!" Sharina said, jumping down from the gig while Tenoctris was still maneuvering it. "As I've heard my brother say, worse things happen in wartime. Where is Lord Waldron?"

And where's Liane, who'd be more forthcoming and probably more knowledgeable. Liane and the army commander were probably together; if not, Sharina could make further inquiries.

The shoreline and the barley field a hundred double-paces inland crawled with hellplants. Liane's estimate of three hundred seemed reasonable, but the gray undulations of mist prevented certainty.

A hundred fires burned on the curved plain below; some had dimmed to red glows. All had bodies of troops behind them. Through the swirling mist Sharina saw thirty men march forward carrying what'd been a full-sized fir tree, possibly one of those whose stumps grew in a circle where Tenoctris had halted the gig.

Under other circumstances the tree would've made a good battering ram. This one had a torch of oil-soaked fabric, probably a soldier's cloak, wrapped around the small end of the pole. On command, the troops slammed their weapon into a hellplant. The flames billowed, then sank beneath a gush of black smoke roiling from the point of contact.

The hellplant staggered back. Two of the tentacles that curled to wrap the pole shrivelled in the flame, but a third gripped closer to the men carrying the weapon. Squads of waiting infantry darted in and hacked the tentacle to green shreds.

Hellplants advanced with greasy determination on either side of their smoking fellow. The troops holding the pole retreated; the flame had sunk to a sluggish ghost of what it had been. Other soldiers came closer and threw hand torches which bounced off the barrel-chested plants. The creatures changed their course to avoid torches burning on the ground, but they continued to advance.

For a moment, the injured plant remained where it was, the wound steaming and bubbling thick fluids. Then that hellplant too advanced, though it was slower than its fellows.

Like trying to fight the sea, Sharina thought. Her guts were tight and cold.

"Your highness, my sincere apologies!" the aide said. "I didn't see—"

"Understood, Lord Dowos," Sharina said. The name had come to her unexpectedly, but at a particularly good time. "Now there are real problems. Where's Lord Waldron?"

"Lord Drian," Dowos snapped to one of the boys at his side to carry messages. Drian was probably Dowos' relative or the relative of some noble friend. "Lead Her Highness to the commander immediately."

To Sharina he added, "They're down by the pile of timber, Your Highness. Well, what used to be a pile. Most of it's been burned, I'm afraid."

The second gig pulled in beside the first. Double sat next to the driver, who was as stiff as the statues of the Lady and Shepherd which priests from Valles drew through the borough during the annual Tithe Procession.

Tenoctris joined Sharina, her arms over the shoulders of the two soldiers who were carrying her. Their shields were strapped to their back and they used their spears butt-down in their free hands as walking sticks. That wasn't necessary here, but it would be as they descended the slope which thousands of cleated boots had already chewed to slippery mud.

A third man, Trooper Lires, carried the satchel with the wizard's equipment in it. Sharina beamed at him and said, "I thought you'd been discharged wounded, Lires. After the fight in the temple in Valles."

The Blood Eagle grinned, delighted to be recognized. "Well, ma'am, I'm on light duty," he said. "But I figure a sword, that's not very heavy; and I guess Captain Ascor, you remember him, don't you? He felt the same way. Because he's here too."

In truth, she'd thought Lires had been killed in the wild slaughter while the guards protected Tenoctris as she closed the portal from which creatures would otherwise have overrun the Isles. It was amazing that a man could survive such serious wounds, but that he'd willingly return to the same dangers was more amazing yet.

Thank the Lady that men did. And thank especially the Shepherd and all the human shepherds, with their swords and their quarterstaffs and their courage.

Laughing in relief, Sharina followed the impatient Lord Drian, a thirteen-year-old who showed signs of growing out of his gold-inlaid armor. The situation was just as bad as it'd been when she was in despair a moment ago, but if ordinary men soldiered on cheerfully, how could their leader do less?

The slope wasn't as bad as Sharina'd feared, though she was glad Tenoctris was being carried. The mist smelled of salt and decay, like a tidal flat but worse. It didn't get thicker as she went down the way she'd expected, and the whorls and openings in it didn't seem to be connected with the light breeze off the water.

"Your Highness!" Waldron said. "Your Highness, I don't think this is a safe place for you. Though we're holding them at present, as you see."

"I've given directions in your name to Lord Tadai, Your Highness," said Liane in a cold, flat voice unlike her usual pleasant tones, "to scour building sites in Mona for quicklime and to start burning any limestone he can find. Marble statues as well."

"Will quicklime be more effective than using the same fuel in open flames, the way you're doing here?" said Sharina.

She kept her voice calm, but she couldn't help feeling a twinge of regret at the notion of statues being reduced to the caustic powder that was the basis of cement. The only statues in Barca's Hamlet had been simple wooden ones of the Lady and the Shepherd in the wall shrines of the better houses. Sharina's first view of lifelike humans carved in marble was a treasured memory of her arrival in Carcosa.

"We can use pots of quicklime in our ballistas," Waldron said. He nodded at Liane. "It was her idea. Stones don't do much, and we can't shoot firepots at full power or it blows out the flame through the air holes. Before now I haven't had much use for artillery except for sieges, and I haven't had much use for sieges either; but quicklime driven into those plants to where they're full of water, that'll take care of them!"

"Admiral Zettin is taking the ballistas from the ships and sending them here also," Liane said. "The problem's transport, getting enough wagons and baggage animals together in Mona Harbor."

Three fit-looking men in civilian tunics stood nearby, separate from the aides and couriers around Waldron. Lady Liane bos-Benliman was the kingdom's spymaster. She alone controlled the movements of the agents and received their reports. She'd based the operation on her father's banking and trading contacts, and she paid for it entirely out of her considerable personal wealth.

When something more than information gathering was needed, Liane had men—and perhaps women for all Sharina knew—to accomplish that too. The trio waiting here looked like they knew as much about weapons as any soldier.

In anybody else's hands, the spy apparatus would be a huge potential danger to the kingdom. Under Liane, it along with the army and Tenoctris were the three pillars on which Garric's rule rested.

And on which Princess Sharina's rule rested, for what Sharina hoped would be a very short time.

"Why can't the warships stand offshore and bombard the plants?" Sharina said. She frowned. "In fact, why weren't there warships here before the attack started? I'd have thought there'd be a squadron at least on the beach, it's so close to Mona."

"There's a mud bar at the mouth of the bay, Your Highness," said a young soldier Sharina didn't recognize. The short horsehair crest on his helmet was dyed blue, indicating he was one of the fleet officers under

Admiral Zettin. "We're looking into dredging it so that warships could get through, but with the creatures swimming . . ."

"I see," said Sharina. She looked at Liane and Lord Waldron, feeling her guts freeze tightly again. "That means the person sending the hellplants knows the terrain, and knows at least something about war."

Double joined the group, helped by Lord Attaper himself. The guard commander had no expression as he withdrew his arm from the wizard's grasp.

Another time Attaper would be able to order one of his men to perform the service—because they'd seen him do it this once. Sharina knew that Attaper would rather face death than touch a wizard, but he'd done his duty regardless. Courage came in many forms.

"The Green Woman knows the shape of this world because she intends to rule it," Double said. "She will fail, because I will defeat her."

Waldron looked at Double with distaste, then said to Sharina, "Your Highness, I've summoned a section of the phalanx from where they're billeted on the east coast. Ordinary spears don't do any good against the creatures, but I hope that the mass of long pikes will kill them, destroy them. Fire works to a degree, but there are so many of them that we're forced back when we attack one."

"I saw that," Sharina said. She took a deep breath. "What do you need from me?"

"Your Highness?" said Liane in a careful voice. "I carry Prince Garric's signet, as you know, and I've been giving orders in what's now your name. If you acquiesce—"

"Yes," said Sharina, "I do. Lord Waldron, do you have any requests?"

"They've stopped coming out of the sea," Waldron said, getting to the question indirectly. "We can take care of the ones here in the bay if that's all there are. It'll cost men, but that's what an army's for."

"She will send more of her creatures," Double said. His voice was a sharper—and if possible, more unpleasant—version of Cervoran's own. "She will send her creatures till they have killed me, or I kill her, or weed stops growing in the sea, and the weed will never stop growing."

"Then we'll keep on killing them!" Waldron said. He was partly angry and partly afraid of the wizard; and because he hated fear, especially in himself, he was becoming more angry.

"Look at the land her creatures hold," said Double, stretching out his left arm toward the bay. "The sea swallows it down. Every day more hellplants will attack, and every morning this island will be smaller with fewer men to protect what remains. Only I can defeat the Green Woman!"

Sharina followed the line of the wizard's arm. Knots of soldiers battled hellplants with fire and their swords, trying to destroy the creatures by force of numbers before the lashing tentacles could destroy them all. Occasionally they succeeded, but the hills behind the plain echoed with despairing cries. Sharina saw bodies and body parts fly into the air.

Close to the shore . . . Double was right. Rows of barley were sinking into the marsh. Sharina had never seen Calf's Head Bay before, but she knew that even salt-resistant barley couldn't have grown with seawater gleaming in the furrows as it did now. The hellplants were a material enemy, but they weren't the only threat the Green Woman posed.

"Tenoctris?" Sharina said. She tried to keep her voice neutral, but she was afraid that there was a hint of pleading in the word.

"No, dear," said the old woman. "Though I'll try, of course."

"I must go back to my chamber of art," Double said. He touched the amulet hanging around his neck. "I must have the help of Ilna os-Kenset and her companions. I will defeat the Green Woman."

"Liane?" Sharina said. "Lord Waldron? Is there anything I can do here that you want me to stay for?"

Liane shook her head minusculely. Her face was as still as a death mask of the cheerful, smiling woman she had been.

Waldron said, "I have a regiment throwing up earthworks on the slopes. I'm not worried during daylight, but if they attack at night, I, well, I want a barrier even if it takes time to shift troops to the point that's threatened."

Double looked at him. "Her creatures will not advance in darkness," he said shrilly. "They will wait in the marsh and attack again when the sun rises."

They're plants, Sharina realized. *With the weaknesses of plants as well as plants' lack of a vulnerable brain or heart.*

She nodded. "All right," she said, "we'll go back. Tenoctris, will you come or . . . ?"

"Yes," Tenoctris said. "I have a manuscript that might be useful; I'll read it carefully."

She smiled wistfully. "It's a manual of spells and potions to aid crops," she said. "There might be something."

Double laughed. He turned and started up the track toward the gigs.

Sharina felt an urge to slap the creature and keep slapping him until she'd worked off the wash of anger and frustration that suddenly filled her. After a moment she sighed and said, "Carry on, Lord Waldron. Tenoctris, we'll return to the palace."

At least there'd be sunlight as soon as they got out of this *accursed* plain.

Garric awakened slowly. He ached in many places and this bed was the most comfort he'd felt since he came to wherever he was now.

He opened his eyes. The sun was well up, making the room reasonably bright. Though the roof thatch was opaque, the walls were wicker without mud and plaster to make them solid. The eaves sheltered the triangular vent at the top, but quite a lot of light—as Garric was learning to judge things here—came in that way.

The wall separating his room from the hall was woven bark fabric on a lattice of finger-thick poles. Garric heard women speaking in normal tones on the other side of it. With a smile at the incongruity he realized that he couldn't see through the inner wall the way he could through the much thicker outer ones.

He carefully raised his torso, then swung his legs out of bed. He wrapped the coverlet around him and stood.

His head didn't throb as badly as he'd expected, but it felt odd. He touched his scalp, expecting to find hair matted with his blood, and found instead a linen bandage holding a pad where Torag's mace had cut him. The nurse—Donria beyond reasonable question—must've sponged him clean while he was asleep, because he remembered his face'd been crusted with a mixture of mud and his own blood despite the frequent drizzle he'd marched through.

"Not all of it your own blood," said King Carus. The balcony on which the smiling ghost stood might never have existed in reality, but for now its sunlit stone was a memory to cherish. *"Some of the other folks in those fights were bleeding pretty freely, remember."*

Garric reached for the latch, a simple rotating peg that held the frame of the door panel to the jamb. There was no lock. It bothered him that he'd been so exhausted that he hadn't thought to *try* to lock it, though. He had Crispus for an enemy here and no certain friend except Donria.

"She's your friend while it suits her purposes," Carus said. *"That may not always be true."*

I think she's my friend regardless, Garric said firmly. *As it is with Cashel, or Ilna; or me.*

The ghost laughed, but there was more sadness than humor in his voice as he said, *"The only thing I ever trusted was my sword, lad. You're in a better place; you are, and the kingdom is with you ruling it."*

A flutter behind Garric threw highlights over the room. He spun, realizing what'd happened even before he saw the Bird perching in the vent as it had the night before. By daylight—and it wasn't even raining—the Bird looked more like the scrap pile at a glass foundry than it did anything living. This time the creature balanced on one glittering foot and grasped a cord and some wood in the other.

"It's midday," the Bird said silently. "You've slept long. Are you able to fight and run, Garric?"

"I'm able," Garric said. "I don't expect to do either of those things for at least another day or two, until I have a better idea of the circumstances."

The Bird made an audible *cluk/clik/clik/clik* with its beak. In Garric's mind it said, "Wait and learn, then."

Garric didn't know where he'd run to. All he could think of now was to run away from Torag's keep. That was all very well, but Torag had captured him once and could quickly capture him again. Unless, of course, he happened to stumble into the arms of another band of the Coerli who were spreading into this land.

Sirawhil wanted to take him to the place the cat men came from. It was at least possible that Garric'd find it easier to get home from there than from this gray swamp. Aloud he said, "Where is Sirawhil, Bird?"

"The Coerli are asleep, all but the guard in the watchtower," the Bird said. It fluffed its wings into a rainbow shimmer like the play of light on a dew drop. They were thin crystal membranes, not really wings like a bird's or even a bat's. "Torag slaughtered another of the recent captives. His folk feasted except the warriors who were here with Ido. They had to eat fish, and they're keeping watch today while Torag and his raiders sleep with full bellies."

Was it Soma who'd been eaten? Garric thought. The whole business of the cat men butchering people for food disgusted him, but since it'd happened he could hope that Marzan's wife was the victim. That might make his life in Torag's keep—and escape from it—considerably simpler.

"The victim was named Jolu," the Bird said. "She was seventeen, plump, and had a high laugh. She was unmarried, but Horta whose wife had died in the spring planned to ask her father for her. Horta died in the raid, though Jolu never knew that."

Garric felt a wash of dizziness. Jolu was a complete stranger to him. Hundreds of people like her must die every year back in the Kingdom of the Isles: drowned or carried off by fevers, dead in childbirth or any number of other ways. Death wasn't horrible in itself; it was part of life.

But Jolu had been eaten by catlike monsters. If somebody didn't stop them the Coerli would eat many more people, until they'd eaten all the people there were in this world. . . .

"I'm going to get something to eat," Garric said, reaching for the door latch again. He needed to know more before he could act, because based on what he knew at the moment there was nothing he could do. Except, he supposed, throw his life away with nothing to show for it except taking a few Coerli with him.

"Killing cat beasts isn't a small thing," Carus murmured. *"And maybe we could get more than a few of them."*

The latch turned before he touched it. "Garric?" said Donria, pulling the thin panel open. "Did you call?"

"Thanks for cleaning me up last night," Garric said. It was disconcerting to hear the woman's words clearly in his mind while at the same time seeing her lips form completely different sounds which came to his ears in the same tone as those in his mind. "Ah, can I have something to eat? And I'd like to see things outside."

He had only the vaguest notion of the compound's layout. It'd been dark, he'd been woozy from the fight and the march, and when he arrived murderous violence had pretty quickly absorbed his whole attention.

Donria took his hands and pulled him gently toward the door. "Whatever you wish, Garric," she said. "Newla! The headman wants food! Bring him porridge from the smaller tub. I put the herbs in that one."

Half a dozen women were in the open hall of the large building. Two were villagers Garric had seen in the coffle captured with him in the raid. Newla was watching as they cleaned the far end of the hall where the food was prepared. The new arrivals went to the bottom of the pecking order, here as in any society.

Though here the hierarchy could be disrupted at any moment by Torag's choice for a meal. Which, thinking about it, was how chickens lived in the inn yard too.

Garric's whole youth had involved the care and feeding of domestic animals, but he was getting a different view of the process now. He smiled, because his discomfort wasn't primarily because of the risk he'd be killed and eaten.

They walked outside. Behind them, Newla shouted gruff directions to the slaves she was managing.

It surprised Garric to see thirty or forty women sitting or lounging in the relative sunlight. Many were weaving on hand looms, but it looked to him like a friendly activity rather than work imposed by the Coerli.

There were a number of children as well, girls of all ages but no boys old enough to walk on their own. Behind the first longhouse was a separate building. Pregnant women and mothers must be relegated to that one, explaining why Garric hadn't seen children the night he arrived.

Soma sat at the kitchen end of the first longhouse. She met Garric's eyes without expression. He didn't see Crispus. That was good in itself, but it made him wonder where the other man was.

Fishnets hung beneath the eaves, just as they had in Wandalo's village, and a separate thatched shelter covered hoes, rakes and sickles set with chips of clamshells. Nobody seemed to be working in the raised fields north of the dwelling, though, nor fishing in the surrounding moats.

Donria followed Garric's glance. "We get a holiday when the masters feast," she said. "We take one, anyway. They're all asleep except the one in the tower. And anyway, they're not hungry."

"I see," said Garric. The mud in front of the gate to the Coerli side of the compound had been raked since the rain stopped. Blood still showed at the edges of the patch. The cat men must've killed and gutted Jolu there before carrying the carcass out to be devoured.

Garric looked up at the watchtower, a platform on thirty-foot poles. Two of the three poles were supports for the fence dividing the Coerli from their slaves. A warrior glared down at Garric.

When Garric held his eyes, the Corl snarled and shouted, "Go on about your business, beast!" He looped his thorn-toothed cord down and up again in a quick arc.

"Come this way, Garric," Donria said, leading him around the end of the longhouse. Under the eaves they were out of sight of the tower, and vice versa.

Garric squatted with his back to a support post, breathing deeply and trying to wash the anger out of his system. There was nothing to be done at the moment. Maybe there'd never be anything he could do!

He balled his fist to slam it into the wall, but he realized how silly he was being. He opened his hand and laughed instead. The sun was shining—all right, above the overcast, but it was shining—and so long as the Coerli kept him alive he had a chance of escaping and maybe even doing something about the plague of monsters overrunning this land.

Women congregated around him and Donria in a polite arc, the way students did in Valles before their teacher. There were no schools in Barca's Hamlet. Most children learned basic letters and how to count from their mothers, but the only books in the community were those Reise had brought with him from Carcosa.

Reise perhaps would've been willing to teach other children while he taught his own, but none of the other parents valued the sort of education he was giving Garric and Sharina. What did it matter who were the rulers of the Old Kingdom and what wars they fought?

It mattered to Reise's son, who'd become ruler of the Isles. It mattered not only because Garric didn't have to repeat mistakes a thousand years old, it meant that he could relax with the simple beauty of *"Oh Bandusian spring, shimmering like glass; worthy of being mixed with sweet wine at a party. . . ."*

Garric laughed, suddenly able to focus on what he *had*: youth, strength, friends, and a good mind. And also he had the Bandusian spring, gleaming as clearly in his mind as it had in the eyes of the poet Celondre a thousand years before. As long as Garric lived he'd have the Bandusian spring, one of Reise's greatest gifts to his children.

"Donria," said the Bird from the transom above them, "come to the headman's room immediately."

Donria jumped up, looking around in amazement. "Who said that?" she cried.

"Donria, what's wrong?" a spectator called. Other women were getting to their feet, looking surprised and fearful. Surprises in Torag's compound were generally going to be unpleasant, Garric supposed.

"The Bird spoke, Donria," Garric said, wondering if he should get up too. "Haven't you heard him before?"

From the look Donria gave him, that was one of the sillier things Garric had said since he came to this place. "The Bird?" she said, looking up and gaping at the glittering distortion.

"Yes," said the Bird. Its mental voice was as mechanically crisp as the tick of a metronome, but Garric thought it held an undertone of impatience. "Come into Garric's room immediately. Newla can feed him without your presence."

"I didn't know . . . ," Donria said, staring at Garric again. "Headman, did you make it do this?"

"Do as it asks, mistress," Garric said. "The Bird isn't one of our enemies here."

He grinned at the Bird. "I don't think so, at any rate."

The Bird clucked audibly again. "I do not have friends or enemies," it said in Garric's mind. "Only purposes. Your present survival benefits my purposes, Garric."

"Go along with him," Garric said, giving the trembling Donria a gentle pat. She bolted around the corner of the building, almost colliding with Newla and her two flunkies holding pails and a trencher of dried fish.

Did Donria think the Bird was a God? Hmm; was *the Bird a God?*

The Bird had hopped with its assortment of sticks and cord into the interior of the building. Though unseen its words rang with tart clarity in Garric's mind: "I am not a God."

Garric stood out of courtesy for the women bringing the food, then settled again. The pails were cut from the stems of a jointed grass—bigger than bamboo from the island of Shengy, but something like that. The smaller pail held a sour fermented beverage. It had a reddish cast, so he supposed it was wine rather than beer. His lips puckered when he sipped it, but it was better than water polluted by runoff from human slaughter.

Crispus stepped around the corner. He held a wrist-thick log the length of his forearm. It was cruder than the cudgel that he'd tried to use on Garric the night before, but it'd do.

Garric scrambled to his feet, holding the pail. He'd left the cudgel behind in the headman's room. He thought of shouting to Donria to throw it through the vent to him, but the chances were he'd lose the fight if he turned away from Crispus to grab a wildly flung weapon.

The women scattered like frightened chickens, though Garric saw them only as motion at the corners of his eyes. He didn't blame them. This wasn't their fight, and he was a stranger with no claim on their loyalty anyway.

Crispus shuffled forward, holding the club vertical in both hands.

He hadn't spoken. His nose was purple and swollen, and his eyes were bloodshot.

What would happen if I ran? Garric wondered. He wouldn't, though. There was the risk his leg'd cramp because of the way he'd been tied on the march from Wandalo's village, and anyway he didn't like the thought of running.

In the back of his mind King Carus weighed options with the cold skill of a born warrior. Crispus wasn't going to get a third chance to kill the man who'd supplanted him as headman. . . .

"Hey, what's going on down there?" the tower guard called. The Corl couldn't see him or Crispus either because the building was in the way, but he'd noticed the women fleeing and could guess what it meant. "Torag will decide when you'll be allowed to fight!"

Crispus ignored the guard, edging closer by a dragging step. Garric smiled disarmingly. He was crouching, but instead of tensing he let his body rise slightly as though he'd relaxed.

Arms clutched his torso from behind and lifted him off the ground. *"Now, Crispus!"* Soma screamed. She was as strong as an octopus.

Crispus strode forward, bringing his club down in a whistling arc. Garric kicked back at the post he'd been leaning against, throwing himself and Soma both to the right.

The club smacked the woman's shoulder hard enough to stagger Garric too. Soma shouted and lost her grip. Garric sprang up, grabbing Crispus' left wrist and the shaft of the club.

Crispus bawled in fear and tried to pull away. Garric let go of his wrist and used both hands to wrench the club free. Crispus turned and ran around the corner of the building. Garric sprang after him.

The gate between the slave and Coerli portions of the compound was open. The guard stood in it; he'd come down from the tower to end the fight. His weighted cord curled around Crispus' neck, choking him silent.

Garric's left hand jerked Crispus back by the hair as he raised the club in his right. Crispus gave a strangled bleat. The Corl snarled and leaped the ten feet separating him from Garric, furious that the beasts were continuing to fight even after he'd immobilized the nearer one.

Garric's club slashed down. He wasn't quick enough to follow the cat man's action, but King Carus' instinct had allowed him to anticipate it. The business end of the club cracked the Corl's skull.

Garric jerked the stone-headed axe from the warrior as he convulsed. Crispus began to thrash also; the cord in the Corl's right hand was tightening on his neck. Garric didn't have either the time or the inclination to worry about that. He hadn't been thinking, just reacting as Carus would've reacted. That was the reason he was still alive.

He drew in a deep breath and sneezed violently: the longhouse was on fire. Flames curled out of the transom, and the wet thatch was gushing smoke.

Donria ran out of the front door of the building. She held the sticks and cord the Bird had appeared with. Linked as they were now, Garric recognized a firebow. He'd seen others light a fire by friction when flint and steel weren't available, though he'd never had occasion to do it himself.

"Come, Garric!" she cried. "There's a hole at the back of the stockade!"

"But—" Garric said, then turned to follow Donria. Action might save him; argument certainly wouldn't.

A glitter at the corner of his eye drew his attention as he ran. The Bird whirled out of the smoke with a tag of burning mattress in its claws. It dipped to set the fire under the eaves of Torag's longhouse, then sparkled through the white billows to join Garric and Donria as they fled.

Chapter

9

THE SUN WAS just below zenith when the gigs and the soldiers guarding them pulled up in the plaza behind the palace. Tenoctris hadn't spoken on the way back except for brief, vague replies to the few questions Sharina'd asked. Though the wizard's eyes were on the horse and the road before them, her mind was obviously other places.

Sharina'd ridden in silence most of the way also. It seemed likely that whatever Tenoctris was considering was more important than answering questions about Double and the hellplants that Sharina suspected didn't have real answers.

A groom gripped the horse's cheekpiece. Two Blood Eagles reached up for Tenoctris, but Sharina helped the old wizard dismount herself. She was a princess and for the moment regent of the kingdom, but that didn't mean she couldn't lend a hand to a friend.

"Your Highness!" said Lord Martous, bustling toward her—and

stopping at the line of guards. "Lady Merota and her caretakers were nowhere in the palace, nowhere at all! One of the servants thought they'd gone down to the harbor so I've sent for them, but they're not here yet!"

"I'm sure they're coming," Sharina said. "When they arrive, direct them to my suite. Double—"

She used the simulacrum's name for itself. It was accurately descriptive, and they had to call the creature something.

"—will be in the adjacent workroom."

"I wouldn't want you to think I'd disobeyed your request to summon the parties!" the chamberlain said. He put enough high-pitched anxiety in his voice to make it sound as though he were reporting a disaster. Just as well he wasn't delivering dispatches from Calf's Head Bay. "As soon as your note arrived, I—oh! Here they come!"

"Yes, thank you, milord," Sharina said, turning to smile at her friends as they approached the paved walkway beside the palace. Chalcus smiled back and gave Merota, hanging from his arm, a delighted twirl. Ilna's lips curved slightly, which was quite cheerful for her.

"We're loyal citizens of the kingdom here on First Atara!" Martous said determinedly. "You have but to request—"

By the Lady's mercy, will the man never shut up? Sharina thought. Aloud she said sharply, "Milord, speaking of requests—I requested that the remains of the pyre be cleared off the plaza here. The work doesn't appear to have been started."

When the pyre collapsed, some of the hurdles had fallen clear of the flames and broken open when they hit the ground. That was merely messy, but the ashes swirling from the great pile in the center smutted everything. If it rained, they'd mix with the dirt in a gray, clinging mass.

"Ah," said the chamberlain in a muted voice. "Ah, the truth is, Your Highness, that since King Cervoran, ah, regained consciousness on the pyre, the common people have tended to keep their distance. I'm afraid they're a superstitious lot, you know. Perhaps your soldiers could take a hand?"

"I'm afraid the kingdom has better use for the royal army just now," Sharina said, feeling a sudden chill as she heard her own words. It put Double's equation too clearly into focus: the kingdom would run out of soldiers before the sea ran out of weed.

Chalcus shifted Merota to his left hand, putting her between him and Ilna at the same time he made sure Double would have to go through him to get to the women. The sailor was still smiling, but he had survived by being a careful man.

"The *Heron*'s been repaired, Your Highness," he said with a sweeping bow that kept his eyes on Double, hitching his way toward them from the other gig. "Just a matter of replacing some scantlings and cleaning her, you see. Would you have called us to take her off somewhere?"

"I have need of you," Double said. His swollen lips were formed in a smirk, though that might've been a chance of his condition like the unpleasant voice he shared with Cervoran. "Ilna, you will come with me onto the roof of the palace and view the sea."

"We'll all view the sea, then," said Chalcus heartily. He set his knuckles on his hipbones and stood arms akimbo, grinning falsely. "I dare say I've more experience of looking at the sea than any two other folk within bowshot, not so?"

Double looked at him. "I have other uses for you and the child Merota," he said. "There is a tapestry in my chamber of art. There are animals woven into the pattern of the maze. You must count those animals, both of you, and come to me on the roof when you are sure of their number."

"That'll be easy!" Merota cried, looking up at Chalcus in delight. He was exchanging glances with Ilna; both of them showed hints of concern under studiously blank expressions.

"I don't need a chaperone to look at waves," Ilna said with sudden brusqueness. "Tenoctris, will you be with us, or . . . ?"

"I was planning to examine Lord Cervoran's library again," the old woman said. "Though I could join you if—"

"No," said Ilna. "I'd rather you were with Merota and Master Chalcus. I haven't had time to look over that tapestry properly, but it does more than just keep drafts from coming through the walls. I'm not sure. . . ."

"Count your waves, dear one," said Chalcus. He leaned forward, miming an attempt to kiss Ilna's cheek. She jerked back in scandalized surprise as he must've known she would; that broke the tension in general smiles. "Lady Merota and I will count woven beasts the while. We'll see who has the more fun, will we not?"

Quite a number of clerks, aides, and couriers were gathering just beyond the line of guards, waiting to talk with Sharina. The number was growing the way a lake swells behind a dammed stream. Lord Tadai was keeping the civilians in his department under tight control, but a number of the military personnel—particularly the younger nobles—would start raising their voices for attention shortly.

"Lord Tadai," Sharina said. "I'll begin seeing petitioners in my suite as soon as I get up there. Please determine the order of audience among civilians at your best discretion. And who's the ranking military officer present?"

Three men—a cousin of Lord Waldron, a regimental commander, and the deputy quartermaster—all spoke at once, then stared at one another in confusion. "Very well," Sharina went on, jumping in before the soldiers could sort matters out, "Lord Tadai, take charge of ordering *all* the petitioners."

She grinned at Tenoctris and said, "Let me give you my arm. I'm going to be regent for the next I-don't-know-how-long, so I'd like to be Tenoctris' friend Sharina till we get up to the second floor."

Tenoctris laughed as they walked along in a cocoon of Blood Eagles. The petitioners—the smarter ones, anyway—had turned their attention to Lord Tadai so the guards didn't even have to shove their way through a crowd.

Sharina grinned at human nature: some of the black-armored soldiers probably regretted not having the chance to knock civilians down. That didn't make them bad men, exactly, but it was fortunate for the kingdom that they'd been smart enough to find duties where external discipline controlled their aggressiveness.

On this side of the palace a broad staircase led to the royal suites. Sharina helped Tenoctris up the left-hand flight to the king's apartments and into the chamber of art, then walked through to the suite she was using. Tenoctris glanced at the tapestry on the shaded wall before going to the bookcase. Her steps were as purposeful as those of a robin hunting worms in the grass.

Several of Lord Tadai's ushers were already in the queen's suite, arranging tables and notebooks for the influx of petitioners who'd be coming up the interior stairs. They nodded respectfully to Sharina but went on with their work. Tadai had sent them ahead with his usual efficiency. He and Waldron were as different as two rich male aristocrats could be—save in their ability and their sense of honor.

"Shall I close this, Your Highness?" said a Blood Eagle officer at the door to the chamber of art.

Sharina opened her mouth to agree, then heard Chalcus and Merota calling back to Ilna as they entered the chamber. A recent brick extension continued the outside stairs to the roof. The palace didn't have a roof garden but Cervoran must've found the tiled surface useful, perhaps for viewing the stars.

"Leave it open," Sharina said. "In case I need to say something to my friends."

"Your Highness?" Tadai announced from the door to the foyer. "If you're ready?"

"Yes," said Sharina, settling on a backless stool in front of a table arranged as a barrier between her and the enthusiasm of those who wanted, *needed*, something from the regent. "Send them in."

Three clerks took seats to the right and slightly behind her, ready to write or locate information as needed. All together they probably weren't the equal of Liane, but Liane was better placed with the army.

Sharina felt a sudden twist of longing. She hoped Cashel was where the kingdom most needed him to be also, but she desperately missed his solid presence. *Lady*, she prayed silently, *let my Cashel serve the kingdom as he best can; and let him come back safe to me.*

The first petitioner was a middle-aged female clerk, part of the financial establishment under Tadai. She had a series of cost estimates for damage done in the course of Liane's lime-burning operation. The figure was astoundingly high—fees for stone, transport, and particularly the fuel which Liane had ordered to be gathered with minimum delay. That meant tearing apart buildings for the roof beams in some cases, and cutting down orchards that would take over a decade to grow back to profitable size.

Sharina suspected Tadai wanted her to rescind some of Liane's more drastic measures. Instead she signed off on them. The cost was very high, but the cost of failure would be the lives of every soul in the kingdom. Liane thought speed was of the first importance, and nothing Sharina'd seen made her disagree.

"Oh, look at this one, Chalcus!" Merota called happily. "It's a unicorn!"

Her voice was as high-pitched as Cervoran's, but Sharina found it as cheerful as birdsong. It wasn't a surprise to realize that timbre wasn't why she found the wizard—and his double—unpleasant.

The second petitioner, an officer with the blue naval crest on the helmet he held under his arm, opened his mouth to speak. In the next room Merota screamed, "Chalcus, I'm—"

"What're ye—" the sailor cried. His voice cut off also.

Sharina was on her feet and through the connecting door, slipping by the guard who'd turned at the shouts. The table she'd bumped with her thigh toppled over behind her.

Chalcus was a flicker of movement, reaching for *something* with his left hand and the curved sword raised in his right. She didn't see Merota, and as Chalcus lunged his body blurred into the tapestry on the wall. Then he was gone also.

"Ilna!" Sharina shouted, running toward the tapestry. "Ilna, come here!"

D OUBLE STOOD ON the parapet chanting words of power, his face to the sea and his pudgy arms spread out to the sides. He'd thrust an athame from Cervoran's collection under his sash, an age-blackened blade carved from a tree root, but he wasn't using it for the spell.

If there really was a spell. Ilna, standing to the side as Double had ordered her, felt if anything angrier than usual. She couldn't understand the words the wizard was using—of course—but she did understand patterns. Double's chant was as purposeless as a snake swallowing its own tail.

She grinned slightly. Double reminded her of a snake in more ways than that. But if the fact she disliked a person doomed him, the world would have many fewer people in it. It wouldn't necessarily be a better place, but it'd be quieter.

From here Ilna could see the waves beyond the harbor mouth. Double'd said they were coming to the roof to do that, to watch the waves, but she suspected that was a lie. Certainly his incantation wasn't affecting the sunlit water, and yet . . .

And yet there *was* a pattern in the waves. Ilna couldn't grasp the whole. It was far too complex, for her and perhaps any human being, but it was there. Perhaps she was seeing the work of the Green Woman spreading from the shining fortress on the horizon, but Ilna thought it was greater even than that.

Ilna's smile spread a little wider; someone who knew her well might've seen the triumph in it. She was glimpsing the fabric of the cosmos in the tops of those few waves. She saw only the hint of the whole, but no one she'd met except her brother Cashel could've seen even that.

That didn't make life easier or better or even different, but she granted herself the right to be proud that she *almost* understood.

She felt herself sliding deeper into contemplation of the waves, following strands of the cosmos itself. Things became obvious as she viewed them from nearer the source. Double had brought her here: not to work a spell but to trap her the way a clover-filled meadow traps a ewe. The sheep could leave, but the pleasure of her surroundings holds her for a bite, and another bite, and just another—

Merota screamed.

Ilna's concentration was a knife blade, smooth and clean and sharp. The pattern of the waves and the cosmos was for another time or another person. She jumped from the parapet to the stairs directly below her, though that meant dropping her own height to the bricks. To start down the stairs where they opened onto the roof, she'd have had to go past Double. . . . He stopped chanting, but he didn't try to restrain her.

Chalcus called something, his voice blurring with its own echo. He sounded as if he'd stepped into a vast chamber.

Ilna reached the marble landing and the entrance to the king's suite; the guards there jumped back to let her by. Her hands were empty. If she needed knife or noose or the cords whose knotted patterns could wrench any animate mind to her will, she would take that weapon out. First she had to learn what the threat *was*.

"Ilna!" shouted Sharina. "Ilna, come here!"

The entrance to the room where Cervoran did his wizardry was by a full-length window. The casement was open. Ilna stepped through, looking not at Sharina but to the tapestry on which Sharina's eyes were focused.

It was a panel as tall as she was and half again as long. Warp and weft both were silk; they'd been woven with a sort of soulless perfection.

Normally a room's rugs or hangings would've been the first thing Ilna examined, but this piece had been an exception. Bad workmanship merely made her angry, but the coldness of this undoubtedly artful tapestry had caused her to avoid it the way she would've stepped around the silvery pustulence of a long-dead fish.

If she'd looked at the panel carefully, Chalcus and Merota might be at her side right now. *If.*

Sharina and some soldiers were speaking, explaining that the child and Chalcus had vanished into the tapestry. Ilna ignored them, concentrating instead on the fabric itself.

The design was of a garden maze seen from three-quarters above. Greens and black shaded almost imperceptibly into one another, just as foliage and stems do in a real hedge. There were fanciful animals: here a cat with a hawk's head, there a serpentine creature covered in glittering blue scales, many others. They were what Double had sent Chalcus and Merota to count, but Ilna realized that they didn't really matter. What mattered was—

The maze had no exit: the outer wall formed a solid cartouche around the whole. The inner hedges twisted and bent, creating junctions and dead ends which seemed to blur from one state to the other as Ilna shifted her attention. In the center was a lake fed by tiny streams that zigzagged from the corners of the fabric; in the lake was an island, reached by a fog-shrouded bridge; and on the island was a circular temple whose roof was a golden dome with a hole in the middle.

But the temple was only the end. Ilna needed the beginning, and she found it in the shape of the hedges. Their twists gripped the mind and souls of those who looked hard at the tapestry, making them part of its fabric. Ilna could've stepped back, but she knew now what had happened to her *family*, her real family, and she had no choice but to join them.

"Double, what do you know about this?" Sharina shouted in the near distance. "Chalcus and Lady Merota walked into the wall! I saw it happen!"

"Why do you ask me?" said the wizard's double, a wizard itself.

Ilna had no time for Double at the moment. He'd laid a clever snare. He'd known he couldn't catch her in it, but he'd known also that she'd follow those she loved. Loved more than life, some would say, but Ilna'd never loved life for its own sake.

She saw the pattern. She took a step forward, not in the flesh but between worlds that touched at a level beyond sight.

"Ilna!" Sharina said.

As Ilna's fingers brushed the prickly branches of densely woven yew, she heard the wizard pipe from a great distance, "I was Double. Now I am Cervoran."

And then very faintly, "I will be God!"

GARRIC REMEMBERED HOW depressing he'd found this land when he first arrived in the rain. It was raining again, generally a drizzle but off and on big drops slashed across the marsh. Nonetheless his spirits were as high as he ever remembered them being.

He laughed and said, "Donria, we're free. That's better than being an animal on somebody's farm in sunlight, even if we're kept as pets rather than future dinners."

Donria gave him a doubtful smile, then looked at the Bird fluttering from stump to branch ahead of them as a bright moving road sign. "Where are we going, Garric?" she asked.

"We are returning to Wandalo's village where Garric has friends," the Bird said in its dry mental voice. "The Coerli will track us, but not soon. Smoke blunts their sense of smell and anyway, fire disconcerts them. It will be days before they pursue."

And what next? Garric thought, suddenly feeling the weight of the future again. It'd felt so good to escape that he hadn't been thinking ahead.

A tree had fallen beside the route the Bird was choosing. A dozen spiky knee-high saplings sprang from its trunk. As Garric trotted past, he became less sure that it wasn't simply a tree which grew on the ground and sent its branches upward. Several blobs—frogs? insects?—slid from the bole into the water. If they hadn't moved, Garric would've thought they were bumps on the bark.

"Bird?" Garric said aloud. "Where do you come from?"

"I come from here, Garric," the Bird said. "My people are coeval with the land itself, created when the rocks crystallized from magma. We lived in a bubble in the rock, all of us together. When the rock split after more ages than you can imagine, we continued to live in what was now a cave. We could have spread out but we did not, because that would have meant being separated from our fellows."

He laughed, the audible clucking sound Garric had heard before. It sounded like a death rattle in this misty wilderness.

"Was the cave near here?" asked Garric. He didn't care about the answer; he'd spoken instinctively because of the sudden rise in emotional temperature. He was asking what he hoped was a neutral question to give the Bird the opportunity to change the subject. Garric would've done the same out of politeness if he were speaking to a human being he didn't know well.

"I was the different one," the Bird said, apparently ignoring the question. "The daring one, a human might call it; but we are not human. To my people and myself, Garric, I was mad."

The rain had stopped and the sun was a broad bright circle in a dove-gray sky. The Bird fluttered above a creek too wide to jump. The water was black and opaque. Garric tried it with his foot; Donria simply strode across.

Garric followed feeling a little embarrassed. The water was mildly cool and only ankle deep. *Well, I didn't know what might be living in a stream like that.*

"I went into the depths of the cave," the Bird continued. "This is the shape I wear now—"

It fluttered its gauzy wings.

"—but I can take any shape I choose. I followed the fracture into the rock until I was a sheet of crystal with granite pressing to either side. I wanted to experience separation, you see. I was mad."

Garric's lips shouldn't have been dry in this sodden air. He had to lick them anyway.

"I could barely feel my people," the Bird said. "They missed me, but they did not object to my choice. My people did not coerce: they were part of the cosmos and lived in their place and their way. They had no power because using power would have been out of place and therefore mad. As I am mad."

"Were," Garric said. He didn't amplify the word or put any particular emphasis on the way the Bird had used the past tense in referring to his people.

"Before I decided to return to the bubble and my fellows, my birthmates, my other selves," the Bird said, "two wizards arrived. My people ignored them, continuing to contemplate the cosmos and their place in it. The wizards killed them and took away their bodies to use in their art."

Garric licked his lips again. "I'm very sorry," he said. When you're told of a horror, words may not be any real help to the victim; but words, and the bare truth, were all there was. "Who were the wizards?"

"They were not of this world," the Bird said. "They were not human; they were not even alive as humans judge life. They came and they killed my people, then they left with our crystal bodies. I wanted to sense separation. For five thousand years now I have known only separation."

He gave his terrible rattling laugh again. "Is it a wonder that I am mad?" he asked.

A breeze bringing a hint of cinnamon rippled the standing water to either side, clearing the air briefly. Ahead was a solid belt of cane waving ten or twelve feet in the air. The stems were as thick as a big man's finger, and the bark had scales. *We'll have to go around,* Garric thought; but the Bird fluttered into the cave, weaving between the closely spaced stems.

Donria continued forward without hesitation, plowing into the wall of vegetation, breaking the canes like so many mushrooms. Either there were no windstorms in this place—and Garric hadn't experienced any, now that he thought about it—or these plants grew to full height in a day or two. Perhaps both things were true.

"Bird," he said aloud. "You've helped me escape from Torag. If I can help you, I'll do my best."

"I have purposes, Garric," the Bird said. "Your survival suits my purposes. I am not human."

A stone's throw down the path was a plant whose trunk looked like a pineapple with four leaves crawling from the top and across the ground. The Bird lighted on it and rotated its crystalline head to face back at Garric.

"Thank you for treating me as though I were human, however," the Bird said. "It does not matter to my people, but it speaks well of you and your race; and perhaps that matters to me after all. After so many years alone I am no longer wholly one of my people."

"I smell smoke," said Donria abruptly.

"Yes," said the Bird, shimmering back into the air again. "Before sundown we will reach Wandalo's village."

In a mental voice that wasn't attenuated by distance, the Bird added, "The cave in which my people were created and died still focuses energies. The Coerli wizards use that cave to come to this place far in their past where they hunt. Someday I will revisit it myself."

The Bird clicked its laugh. "I have purposes, Garric," it said.

CASHEL BACKED A step and raised his staff as the demon leaped into the air, beating its wings strongly. Something so big—and all right, the demon was thin as a snake, but it was still man-sized—shouldn't have been able to fly on wings no longer than Cashel could span with his arms spread, but it did.

Hanging like a hummingbird over Cashel and the boy, it called angrily, "Fly, then! You can fly, can't you?"

"Cashel, what do we do?" Protas said desperately.

He's afraid of failing, Cashel thought. *He can't do what the demon just told him to.*

Knowing that, and knowing that the demon didn't really believe they could fly—it was bullying them, making them feel guilty—Cashel said harshly, "Come down, you! You're to guide us, you say. Stop playing the fool and come do your job."

"You can't command me, human!" the demon said, still hovering.

"Maybe not," Cashel agreed. "That's between you and whoever set you to guide us. But as Duzi's my witness, you can't give us orders. If you won't come down and do what you're told, we'll go our own way."

"Fools!" said the demon, but it cupped its wings and landed beside them. "We'll go on foot, then. But it'd be easier to fly."

The business'd gotten Cashel's back up quicker than it ought to've, maybe because of the noise the musicians were making. He wouldn't call it music, not a bit.

Instead of letting the demon's posturing go, Cashel reached out quick with his left hand and pinched the flat scaly nose between his thumb and forefinger. The demon shrieked on a climbing note and tried to jump backward, which it had no more chance of doing than a snared rabbit has until Cashel opened his hand.

"Remember who set you the job of guiding us, fella," Cashel said, breathing deeply to calm himself down. He'd had his staff poised in his right hand so that he could use the short end as a cudgel if the demon'd tried to bite him. "And remember I'm Cashel or-Kenset, so keep a civil tongue in your head when you talk to me and my friend."

"Yes, yes," said the demon, sounding conciliatory now. A man would've massaged his bruised nose with a hand, but the scaly blue thing just shook its head. "Let's get it over with, then. There's risk for me too in this, you know."

They set off walking—eastward, judging from the way the sun'd moved in the little while since Cashel had come here. Protas put the crown on his head. It fit there, which surprised Cashel a good deal. It'd fit the much larger Cervoran as well.

When they got a bowshot away from the grove and the musicians, Cashel felt a little embarrassed at the way he'd gone after the demon. All it'd been trying to do was save face.

A fellow as big as Cashel got a lot of that, people pretending they weren't going to fight him just because they didn't feel like it. He'd learned to let it go, mostly from temperament but also because if you humiliated or knocked silly everybody who got too much ale and started mouthing off, you got the reputation of being the sort of man Cashel didn't like.

This time the demon'd gone after the boy, though. Bullying kids was the wrong thing to do. Doing it in front of Cashel was *really* the wrong thing to do.

"Master Demon?" Protas said. He was a courteous little fellow, which wasn't true of every nobleman's son Cashel'd met since he left the borough. "How far are we to go?"

"An hour, walking," the demon said. It turned to glower over its narrow shoulder at Cashel and Protas. "If nothing happens."

Cashel nodded, just showing he understood. He figured the demon might be trying to scare them over nothing, but in this place it wasn't hard to imagine there were real dangers. He'd have been keeping his eyes open regardless.

The ground was dry red clay. Grass grew on it in a sere yellow blanket; seed heads scratched at Cashel's knees. Trees were sparse, and their gray leaves curled around their stems.

Because Cashel was busy looking in all directions, it was Protas who first saw the town on the southern horizon. "Look, Cashel," he said, pointing.

At first Cashel thought it was a range of low hills, but as they walked along a little further he decided the humps were just too regular to be natural; they must be domed buildings. Something glittered on top of one, but it was too far away for even Cashel's excellent eyes to tell any more than that something was shining.

"Who lives in that city, Master Demon?" Protas asked. At least for as long as they held up, his trousers were better for this country than Cashel's tunics and bare legs.

The demon looked back again. "We have no business with them," it said. "You'd better hope that they have no business with us, either. If you believe in Gods, boy, pray that reaching toward them doesn't call them to us!"

Protas jerked his hand down. Cashel frowned, then decided to let it pass. From the way the demon turned its sharp-featured face away it'd seen the frown and knew what Cashel'd been thinking. Maybe it'd remember to be more polite the next time it warned Protas.

A grove of trees lay close by to the left of the line they were taking.

They were bigger than those Cashel'd seen when they arrived here, but they were dead instead of just dry: most of the bark had sloughed away from the trunks and branches.

Something could still be hiding behind the trunks, though. Cashel didn't let the trees keep his whole attention, but he made sure his eyes flicked back to them often enough that nothing could rush out unnoticed even when they were within a stone's throw.

A woman's hiding in that hollow trunk!

"Halloa, mistress!" Cashel called, bringing his staff up crosswise. In a lower voice he growled, "Protas, get clear of me but don't go too far!"

She was clutching the trunk with her hands, her body pressed against the wood. She lifted her face in surprise, then smiled broadly. *She's not wearing any clothes!*

"Who are you, stranger?" she said, speaking to Cashel and completely ignoring his companions. She moved a step out from the hollow. "My, today blesses me as I never thought to be blessed again in this life!"

Duzi, the tree's been making love to her! Or likely she's been . . .

Cashel turned away. "Demon," he said, "let's walk on. This is no place for decent people."

"Where are you going, stranger?" the woman said. Her voice'd started out a pleasant coo like doves in a cote but it went all shrill. "You've come here and you'll not leave until you've pleasured me!"

"Demon, I said go on!" Cashel said, because their guide was standing on one leg with the other foot resting against his knee. He had clawed toes like a bird's.

"Go ahead and service her," the demon said. "We're not short of time, and it's too dangerous not to now that she's roused."

"I said go *on!*" Cashel said, thrusting the iron butt of his staff at the demon's face. It jerked back or its nose'd have gotten a knock and no mistake.

"Are you mad?" the demon cried incredulously. It sprang into the air again, hovering like a sparrow over a sunflower. "If you're killed, what will happen to me?"

Cashel poised the quarterstaff to prod again. The demon flapped higher, then turned and flew off in the direction they'd been going.

"You must run, then," it shrilled over its shoulder. "You're a fool and worse than a fool!"

"I guess we run, Protas," Cashel said. "It shouldn't be too far to where we're going, given what he said at the start."

"Yes, Cashel," the boy said. He put a hand up to hold the crown and started sprinting, though before Cashel could say anything he'd slowed his pace to a gentle lope.

They didn't *know* how far it was; lying on the ground throwing up at the end of your strength was the wrong way to be if something really was chasing them. Though Cashel figured his staff could deal with the woman if he had to.

He looked back. The circle of dead trees were pulling their roots up out of the ground. The one she'd been making love to had bent down a big branch and lifted her up in it.

"It's too late now!" the demon cried. "You'll regret this for the rest of your short life!"

"I don't guess I will," Cashel said as he stumped along beside Protas. "Short or long, I don't guess I will."

He concentrated on running. It wasn't something he'd ever been good at, though he could move quick enough when he had to. Not for long, though; he wasn't built for it, and watching sheep hadn't given him practice.

Cashel looked over his shoulder, just a quick glance. He faced front again so he wouldn't stick his foot in what might be the only gopher hole in shouting distance.

There wasn't much he wanted to see going on behind them anyway. There were more trees than he could count on both hands. They didn't seem to move fast, but their roots were each longer than he was tall. They were covering ground as fast as Cashel did trotting, and maybe covered it a little faster.

He glanced back again. Faster for sure.

"Run!" the demon called. "Run! You have to reach the rocks!"

There was an outcrop up ahead, a lump roughly a man's height in diameter every way. It looked natural, but the top and one side were flattened. Most of it was pebbly gray, but the hot sun'd flaked a slab off. Where that'd happened, the surface was pale yellow.

It wasn't far away, but it was too far for Cashel to make before the trees reached him. Well, he didn't much care for running anyhow.

"Keep going, Protas!" Cashel shouted. The boy was pulling ahead anyway; he ought to be fine.

Cashel turned and faced the oncoming trees, spinning his quarterstaff in front of himself. Each of the however many trees there was had branches thicker than his hickory staff, but he'd do what he could. They squealed low like a forest flexing in a windstorm.

The trees'd strung out some on the chase, but the big one that the woman rode on was closer even than Cashel'd feared. She stood in the crotch, laughing and gesturing as the tree loped along. Its long branches had twice the reach of his staff.

The demon let out a screech like a hog being gelded. Cashel didn't look over his shoulder; the trees were plenty to occupy his attention. As he readied to step forward and bring his staff straight out of its spin into the tree bole, the demon swooped in front of him.

The demon swept its arms apart. Blue wizardlight streaked from its fingertips to draw a blazing arc between Cashel and the tree. Grass flashed into soft orange flames. The roots skidded the tree to a stop, plowing furrows in the hard soil. Dirt and gravel sprayed over Cashel's feet.

"Begone!" the demon screamed toward the trees. "I will! I must preserve them!"

Which it hadn't said before. If Cervoran was the reason this was happening, then he was a powerful enough wizard to scare even demons.

The woman swayed awkwardly when the tree stopped the way it did. She likely would've fallen if it hadn't reached up a branch to give her something to grab on to. The rest of the grove was dragging to a halt too. Cashel didn't relax, not yet, but he drew in a deep breath. He hadn't seen any good way for things to work out.

The crouching demon poised with its arms still spread. It turned its head and cried, "Get on, then! To the top of the rock. You can do that, can't you, climb onto the rock?"

Cashel turned and started jogging again. He wobbled for the first couple steps; he'd been closer to being winded than he knew. Stopping something and starting up again was a lot harder than just to keep going the first time.

Protas was waiting with his back to the rock. Cashel thought the boy was clenching his fists in fear, but when he got close he saw he had a stone in either hand.

Cashel grinned broadly. Sure, flinging rocks wasn't going to do much good against trees the size of the ones chasing them, but neither was the quarterstaff he'd been ready to use himself. He was glad to see the boy thought the same way he did.

"What do we do now, Cashel?" Protas said. His voice was higher than it had been, but he was being brave just the same.

"Drop the stones and let me boost you up!" Cashel said. He ought to've leaned the quarterstaff against the rock to free both hands, but instead he used just his left to grab Protas by the back of his garments—tunic, sash, and trousers all together in a tight handful—and swing him up the side of the boulder. When Cashel let go, he realized he'd swung harder than he'd meant to, but the boy managed to grab on and not go sailing off the back side as he'd nearly done.

Cashel looked back as he planted his staff arm's length out from the boulder. The trees stood in a tight arc just beyond where the grass still smoldered. When the demon saw Cashel and Protas had reached the rock, it spun and sprang into the air. The trees surged forward again, at first looking like they were bending in a storm.

Cashel jumped with a twist of his shoulders on the staff to swing his feet to the top of the boulder. There he straightened and brought the staff up across his body again. The stone'd been scribed with a star so long ago that the grooves were the same dirty gray as the flat surface.

He grinned. Mounting that way was a neat piece of work. It took timing as well as strength, but it took more strength than most any two other men could've managed.

The demon circled them, glaring fiercely. "You've cost me a kalpa of torment to save you as I did!" it cried. "But better that than all eternity. Get on with you and bring misery to some other wretched creature!"

Hovering, it stretched out its clawed hands toward Cashel and the boy. Cashel tensed, remembering the blast of blue flame that'd halted the grove now rushing down on them again; dust rose in a dirty plume as their roots scraped over the ground.

The star on the boulder glowed azure. The surface within that boundary vanished and the world beyond as well. Cashel was falling through starry space, conscious only of Protas' desperate grip on his belt.

Chapter

10

"Oh chalcus!" merota cried. "It's all right! Ilna's here!"

It certainly isn't *all right,* Ilna thought. Merota hugged her and she patted the girl's shoulder, but she was ready to act if there was need.

Which there didn't seem to be. She'd stepped from the wizard's chamber into a maze with broad aisles. The hedges, twice her height, were holly, but trees and fruiting bushes grew among the interwoven, spiky branches.

Underfoot the grass was soft and curly. The ends were pointed so it hadn't been cropped, but the blades were only high enough to brush Ilna's ankles.

Chalcus was a double pace away, as close as he could be to Merota and still have room to swing his curved sword with reflexive speed. He didn't have his back to a hedge, either, which surprised Ilna till she noticed faint rustlings and the way leaves occasionally quivered in the still air.

That might be ground squirrels, of course. It might also be a viper hunting ground squirrels, and it wasn't hard to imagine worse things than vipers here.

"I heard the child call," Chalcus said. His mouth smiled but his cheeks were set in hard planes and his eyes went every direction in quick jumps like a bird hunting. "I tried to follow her, but I got dizzy. Do you know where it is we are, dearest?"

"We're in the tapestry Double set you to look at," Ilna said. "It's a trap, or at least Double used it as one. The pattern the hedges make draws you into it if you concentrate. Which of course you did."

Poking through the holly beside her was what looked like blackberry canes with the usual mix of purple, red, and pink fruit on them. She picked a ripe one and tasted it. It was an ordinary blackberry, tart and tasty.

She looked at her companions. "It was my fault," she said. She stood as straight as she'd have done if she was about to be hanged. She'd rather be hanged than to have made the mistake she had. "I should've looked at the tapestry myself. I would've known."

"Dear one," said Chalcus with real affection, though his eyes continued to search. Under other circumstances he'd have touched her cheek with the back of his hand, but now each held a naked blade. "When I think I need you to scout before I look at a wall or a field or it may be a stretch of sea, I'll drown myself. I'll have lived too long to be a man."

He stepped toward the next angle of the maze; the path branched left and right. "What I don't see . . . ," he said, looking down both paths. "Is why Double would want to catch me that way. I wasn't a particular friend to him, but I wasn't his enemy either. Not then."

He glanced back and gave the women a hard grin. "That will change when we return," he added.

"He didn't care about us, Chalcus," Merota said. She wasn't looking at the ground or the hedges either, it seemed to Ilna. "He used us to draw Ilna here. He knew she'd follow us, don't you think?"

"He wouldn't need to be a wizard to see that," Chalcus agreed. "But how is she his enemy?"

"The *amulet*," Merota said. "Lord Cervoran sent Ilna to control Double. Double sent Ilna away so that he isn't under Cervoran's mastery anymore."

There was a tiny note of frustration in her voice. Merota was a courteous and respectful child, but this was a strain for her as surely as it was for the rest of them. She clearly felt that what was obvious to her ought to be obvious to other people, at least when she'd pointed it out.

Ilna smiled coldly. The child might learn better, or she might not. Ilna'd never quite learned that lesson herself.

"Ah," said Chalcus with a wry smile. "I see, I'd been getting too full of myself, thinking I was the target. A flaw I'm prone to, milady, and I'm thankful to you for catching me."

He spoke lightly, but he wasn't being ironic. Chalcus wasn't the man to deny his faults. Now he turned to Ilna and said, "Is there a way out, then, dear one?"

"Probably," Ilna said. That was the first thing she'd considered, of course; the thing she'd been puzzling over even as she stepped into tapestry. "Almost certainly. It's a complex knot, but there's no knot without an end somewhere. I haven't found it yet, is all."

She took another blackberry, realizing that she hadn't eaten in longer than she wished was the case. Food wasn't a great pleasure to her, but without it she was more apt to make mistakes. Lack of food, lack of sleep, cold weather or to a lesser extent hot weather—they all made her less effective than she liked. She regarded those requirements as weaknesses and disliked herself for them, but she wasn't the sort to deny that she was weak.

"Is it best we stay here, dearest?" Chalcus said. "Or is there a direction you think we should go?"

"I don't know anything about this place," Ilna said, irritated to be asked questions she couldn't answer. She'd known *where* they were, no more. "We'll need food and there's little enough here. Water too, I suppose. There were fountains and streams on the tapestry."

She cleared her throat. To take the sting out of her previous tone she added, "Though the blackberries are good. Will you have one?"

Merota was standing primly with her hands tented together. Ilna glanced at her, then looked again: the child was terrified. Ilna reached into her sleeve for the twine she kept there. It'd be a simple thing, a few knots and a pattern to spread in front of Merota's barely focused eyes to calm her. . . .

Ilna paused, put the twine away and instead hugged Merota. The child threw her arms around Ilna and squeezed hard before relaxing and stepping back.

"Thank you, Ilna," she said formally. "I'm all right now."

"There's an apple tree to the right, Master Chalcus," Ilna said, pretending nothing had just happened. "Since we have no better direction, let's go that way. Perhaps we can see something from its branches, too."

Her cheeks were hot. She hated embarrassment, *hated* it, and being around other people was one embarrassment after another.

"There's little men in the hedges," said Chalcus with a lilt as he led with his sword and dagger angled out in front of him like a butterfly's feelers. "Brown and not so tall as my waist, short fellow though I am. But there's a lot of them."

He sounded cheerful, and perhaps he was. Ilna smiled grimly. Chalcus wasn't a cruel man, but he regarded the chance to kill something that deserved it as the best sport there was.

What Ilna really hated was emotion. At least now she had some emotions besides anger, but a life spent suppressing anger left her uncomfortable with the softer feelings as well.

Insects buzzed and fluttered in the foliage, but Ilna didn't see birds. There were sounds that might've been bird calls, but she thought they were more likely insects also—or frogs. They could've been frogs.

Her fingers began plaiting a fabric for occupation. Though she didn't see the little men that the sailor had, she could *feel* movement in the way leaves trembled or the grass lay: everything was part of an interwoven whole.

Including of course Ilna os-Kenset. She knew that another person in her place might've learned how to leave this tapestry before following her friends into it; but that other person wouldn't have been Ilna and very probably wouldn't have been able to see the patterns that Ilna saw.

Ilna grinned to think what she'd never have said aloud: she hadn't met anybody except for her brother who saw patterns as clearly as she did. Cashel would've gone bulling straight ahead just the way she'd done, if he'd known how to.

They'd reached the ground beneath the apple tree's spreading limbs. The trunk was hidden within the hedge, but the branches reached out from above the holly.

Apple cores lay scattered on the grass. Some were so fresh that though the flesh had browned it hadn't started to shrivel. The mouths that'd nibbled the fruit were no bigger than a young child's.

"The little people eat apples," said Merota, meaning more than the words.

"So do we," said Ilna tartly, "but that doesn't mean we'd turn down meat."

She'd snapped at the child's foolish hopefulness before she could catch herself—and regretted it as the words came out. Chalcus glanced at her with a hint of pain and probably irritation, completely justified. *Of course* the girl was being foolish, and *of course* the girl knew that as surely as Ilna herself did.

"Merota," Ilna said, "I'm nervous; I'm afraid, I suppose. This makes me more unpleasant to be around than usual. Even more unpleasant. I apologize."

"You're not unpleasant, Ilna!" Merota said. She probably even meant it. She was a sweet child, truly nice, and she couldn't understand what a monster her friend Ilna really was.

Chalcus cleared his throat. "I might be able to jump to the lowest branch," he said, looking at the tree above them. "But I don't think I can get through the prickles without leaving more of my skin behind than I'd choose to. The little folk have skills I do not."

"I'll go up," said Ilna, slipping loose the silk rope she wore around her waist in place of a sash. "You stay with Merota."

You and your sword stay here, but there was no need to say that.

She eyed the branches. The lowest, less than her own height above her, wasn't as thick as she'd like but she'd try it for a start. She cocked the rope behind her, then sent it up in an underhand cast. It curved over the branch and dropped.

"Ah!" cried Chalcus, sheathing his dagger to grab the dangling end in his left hand. He'd been frowning, obviously wondering what Ilna expected to catch with the loop. There was nothing for a noose to close over, but it'd weighted the throw nicely.

Ilna scrambled up the rope with the strength of her arms alone: the silk cord was too thin for her feet to grip it well, but the present short climb didn't require that. She pulled herself onto the branch, then stood and surveyed their surroundings.

"It doesn't help," she called, keeping the disappointment out of her voice. "The hedges are as thick as they're tall. I can't even see into the next passage. And in the distance there's fog."

The fog might be ordinary water vapor, but Ilna doubted it. She hadn't imagined that they could get back to their own world by walking to the edge of the tapestry, but perhaps . . .

Ilna smiled grimly. She hadn't consciously allowed herself to hope for anything, but obviously the part of her mind she couldn't control had been hoping. The human part of her mind.

"No matter, dear one," Chalcus called. "At least we've the apples."

The branch swayed gently, but Ilna was comfortable with its support. She lifted the skirt of her outer tunic into a basket and plucked fruit from the branches above her into it. The apples were small but sweet; apparently they were fully ripe when half the skin was still green. Many were wormy, but she had no difficulty gathering sufficient for the three of them.

Because the hedge was so thick, the branches in the interior had leaves only on the tips. Ilna'd walked some way out in that direction to complete her foraging. As she turned, she saw faces staring up at her from among the knotted gray stems.

They were visible only for an instant, but she'd gotten a good look at a trio of naked brown-skinned people, adult in proportion but no bigger than a six-year-old. One was a woman. Their large dark eyes reminded her of rabbits, and they'd vanished like rabbits leaping into a brush pile.

Ilna walked back to where her friends waited and spilled the apples onto the ground. She hung from the branch by one arm and dropped. While Merota picked the apples up, she looped the rope back around her waist.

Chalcus continued watching in all directions. He hadn't ceased to do that even when he was belaying the rope for Ilna to climb.

"I saw the little people," she said quietly. "They don't seem to have weapons. Or any tools whatever."

"Aye," said the sailor. "They're a fleeting, fearful lot and likely harmless. But it strikes me, dear heart, that they wouldn't be *so* fearful were there nothing here in this garden to fear, not so?"

He stepped around the next corner of the maze, munching an apple in his left hand as his sword quivered like a dog scenting prey. Merota followed, holding the apples in her tunic with both hands, and Ilna brought up the rear as before.

Several trees grew in the opposite wall of the hedge. One was a walnut, she thought. Nutmeats would be a good addition to the apples, though the capsules holding the nuts would stain her hands indelibly when she shucked them. Perhaps—

A fat-bodied snake stepped on two short legs from the opposite end of the aisle. The creature was the size of a man, pale red in front and its back and tail covered with vivid blue scales. It raised a neck frill as Chalcus lunged forward.

"Look away!" Ilna shouted, closing her eyes. Her fingers knotted a pattern that she understood perfectly though she couldn't have described if her life'd depended on it. Words were for the world's Lianes; Ilna had her own way of communicating.

Merota's scream muted into the desperate wheeze of someone drowning. Ilna lifted her pattern of cords and looked.

A shock lashed her. It felt like what'd she'd gotten from touching metal after walking across wool on a dry day. Merota stood paralyzed with her mouth open; Chalcus had fallen as if his legs were wood. His sword was outstretched and his eyes stared in horror.

Instead of a snake's jaws, the creature had a blunt, bony beak like a squid's. A forked blue tongue trembled from it in a high-pitched hiss. Ripples of blue and red played across its broad frill in a sequence as wonderfully perfect as a nightingale's song. The pattern caught every eye that fell on it and gripped with the crushing certainty of a spider's fangs.

The creature, taking one clumsy stride forward, saw the open fabric in Ilna's hands. The rhythm of color in its frill broke, bubbled, and subsided into a muddy blur.

"Basilisk!" Merota shouted. She flung an apple at the creature. It bounced harmlessly away. The rest of the harvest fell to the ground.

Chalcus rolled to his feet. The creature leaped backward. The sailor was still off-balance, so his sword notched the frill instead of skewering the long snake neck.

"My pardon!" the creature cried. It leaped onto a limb of the walnut tree; the stubby legs were as powerful as a frog's. "My pardon, I didn't realize you were Princes! The One hasn't added new Princes in an age of ages!"

Chalcus jumped upward, his sword flickering left to right. The creature sprang over the hedge and into the aisle beyond.

"I beg your pardon, fellow Princes . . . ," it called, its voice trailing off behind its hidden flight.

"It was a basilisk!" Merota said, staring at the scars the creature's claws had left in the bark.

"What did it mean by calling us Princes?" Ilna said, trying not to gasp.

Chalcus shot his sword and dagger home in their sheaths. He leaned forward, resting his hands on his knees to breathe deeply.

"What I'd like to know . . . ," he said to the ground in front of him, "is who the One is?"

IT WAS SO dark that Garric couldn't see his own hand at arm's length, but he knew they were being stalked. He didn't hear the predator, but changes in the sounds other marsh creatures made showed that something was disturbing them.

"Donria," Garric said quietly. He slid the axe out from under the sash that was his only garment for the time being. He hoped that mud he'd splashed on the grip wouldn't make it slippery. "Something's moving up on us from behind. I want you to take the lead, but don't make a fuss about it."

"You'd have made a good scout, lad," Carus whispered in his mind.

Perhaps, but what Garric had been was a shepherd. He'd learned to absorb his surroundings: the color of the sky and the sea, the way light fell on the leaves or the swirls of fog over the creek on cool mornings. Garric didn't exactly look for dangers. He simply noticed things that were different a few minutes ago or yesterday or last year.

He'd heard a shift in the pattern of trills, chirps, and clicking. The little animals he and Donria'd disturbed were remaining silent after they were well past. Previously the chorus of frogs and insects had resumed as soon as they went on.

"There's a human following us, Garric," said the Bird. "His name is Metz, but you think of him as Scar. He's been lying in wait on the route Torag used to attack Wandalo's village twice in the past."

Garric stopped and straightened. He couldn't see a thing. Besides darkness, the rain was falling as it had more hours than not during the day. He and Donria'd been moving since they broke out of Torag's keep, and fatigue was taking a toll on him.

"Metz!" he called. "Scar! This is Garric! I've escaped from the Coerli and I'm here to help you!"

He'd come back to join Wandalo and his people, at any rate. He might or might not be able to help, but he was going to try.

Nothing happened for a moment; then Metz sloshed up from the darkness and came forward. He held what'd started as a fishing spear. A single hardwood spike now replaced the springy twin points intended to clamp a fish between them.

"How did you learn to speak our language?" he asked, obviously doubtful. Then, frowning in real concern he added, "And how did you see me? Nobody could've spotted me, not at night!"

"I listened to the frogs," Garric said. "I've spent a lot of time out-doors too."

He didn't say that he'd been a shepherd. That wouldn't have meant anything to Metz, since the only large animals he'd seen here were humans and their dogs.

The Bird landed on Garric's shoulder. Its feet were solid pressures, but the glittering creature didn't seem to *weigh* anything. "I am helping you speak to one another, but I can speak to you as well."

"Master Garric?" said Donria. "Is this man the chief of the village?"

"No, the chief's named Wandalo," Garric said. "This is the man who found me when I came here from my own land."

"Wandalo's dead," Metz said. It was too dark for Garric to be sure of the hunter's features, but his voice sounded tired and worn. "Nobody's really chief now."

He turned to look back in the direction Garric had come from. "My uncles and I decided we'd better watch the way the Coerli came from," he continued. "Nobody else was willing to. If we don't have any warn-ing, they'll keep snatching us up until nobody's left. I said I'd watch nights; I'm better at it than Abay or Horst."

Garric had thought a club hung from Metz's belt; it was actually a wooden trumpet. Garric looked at it and looked up at the man again. Metz might be able to hide from a raiding party as long as he kept silent, but as soon as he blew a warning on that trumpet the Coerli were going to kill him. Unless they captured him to torture at leisure at their keep.

"Well, what else could I do?" Metz said angrily. "Somebody had to watch!"

You could've done what the rest of the villagers did, Garric thought. *Hide in your hut like a frightened rabbit till the cat men came to wring your neck for dinner.*

Aloud he said, "The village must be close, then. We'll go there and call a town meeting. There's a way to deal with the Coerli if we stay to-gether and work fast."

"Torag won't be coming tonight," the Bird said. "Nor tomorrow night, I think; but soon he will come. Garric will act before then."

Metz led the way sure-footedly through the marsh to the village gate. Donria had never been this way before, but she had less trouble with the slick wood rods of the catwalk than Garric did.

"Marzan said he was summoning a hero to destroy the Coerli," Metz said. "That's why my uncles and I were waiting for you—Marzan told us where you'd come. He's a great wizard. But you didn't seem . . ."

"I can't do much about the Coerli by myself," Garric said quietly. "With your help—the help of everybody in the village—I think there's an answer."

The village walls loomed up before them. Metz lifted the trumpet to his lips and blew a surprisingly musical tone, clear and wistful.

"Open the gates, Tenris," he called. "I've brought friends back with me."

"Is that you, Metz?" called a man from the gate platform. There'd been no sign that the guard had been aware of their presence, even though Garric thought he'd been slipping and splashing enough to wake the dead. "All right, I'm opening the gate."

"And call the villagers to assemble!" the Bird said in what would've been a tone of command if the words were audible. "We must prepare immediately."

"Who's that?" cried the guard in sudden alarm.

"Never mind, Tenris, it's a friend," Metz snapped. "And do as he says. The Bright Spirit knows we need all the friends we can get in these times."

Wood squealed on the platform and the bar shifted on the inside of the gate. There was apparently a lever and cord, a large-scale equivalent of the ordinary latch string. Metz pushed open one of the gate leaves, then lifted his trumpet and blew it again in harmony with the three blasts of the guard's deeper horn.

Lights, dim and yellow, began to wink through the fog. Villagers were lighting oil lamps from embers on their hearths. Garric heard a woman begin to wail in high-pitched despair.

"There is no danger," said the Bird, dropping down from the stockade to perch on Garric's shoulder. "You are not being attacked. You must assemble and do as Garric orders, because the Bright Spirit has sent him to save you."

Garric frowned and started to turn his head, but the Bird was too close for him to focus on it with both eyes. He faced front again and said quietly, "How many of the people in the village can hear you?"

"All of them," said the Bird with a hint of satisfaction. "Every one of them. But they will not follow me, Garric. They will follow *you*."

That remains to be seen, Garric thought, but cynicism didn't suit him. Natural optimism lifted his spirits as he saw villagers coming toward the gate with whatever weapons had come to their hands. *Just maybe . . .*

The sky had brightened from pitch black to dark gray. That'd make it easier to address the villagers, though he still wasn't clear about what he was going to say. He grinned: maybe he could claim his arrival at dawn was a good omen.

"Get up on the platform where they can see you," Carus directed. *"And make sure Metz comes with you. It'll work, lad."*

It would or it wouldn't, but Garric was going to try regardless. "Come along, Metz," he said to the hunter. "We're going to tell them how to defeat the Coerli."

"How are we going to do *that*?" Metz muttered, but he looked up and called, "Get down from there, Tenris. Me and the hero who Marzan brought us need the room."

Tenris dropped from the platform with real enthusiasm. "There's no chief," Metz had said; because nobody wanted the job in the face of inevitable disaster. The villagers were terrified, so anybody could become chief just by saying he wanted to lead.

Which was different from saying anybody would follow him; but maybe . . .

The ladder and platform were lightly built, but they weren't as flimsy as Garric had expected. The Grass People lacked arts that everybody in the Isles took for granted, but they had very highly developed skills nonetheless. Woodworking, including the ability to weave withies into solid structures, was among the latter.

"What's going on, Metz?" called one of a pair of husky men in the growing assembly below. It wasn't bright enough yet for Garric to be sure of faces, but the voice sounded like one of the men who'd met him—captured him—with Metz when he arrived in this land.

"Garric escaped from the Coerli," Metz said. "Nobody's ever done that. He's going to talk to us."

"He's the hero I summoned to save us!" cried Marzan. A girl of seventeen or so had been helping him along the path from his house, but now the old wizard stood with only his staff to support him. The feathered crown waggled on his head. "See how my foresight has been repaid?"

Well, not yet, thought Garric, but that was a good opening for him. In a loud voice he said, "People of the village. Fellow humans!"

That was a nice touch. He'd given enough speeches by now that he was getting the feel of the task.

"The Coerli can be defeated!" he said. "My return proves that. But we, the rightful owners of this world must act together and we must act *now*. We must arm ourselves. I'll teach you the tactics I've used to kill cat men already. Instead of waiting for them to attack again, we'll go to them. Tomorrow evening we'll set out for Torag's keep, the chief who's been raiding you, so that we arrive at dawn. We will destroy Torag and free his human captives!"

"You're a demon, sent to destroy us all!" cried a woman. "Metz, come down here now! Better yet, throw that madman off the walls and close the gate!"

"That is Opann," said the Bird; to Garric alone, he supposed, though there was no way of telling. "She is Metz's wife. Her father was chief before Wandalo."

"The chief of my village was Paltin!" called Donria from the base of the ladder. "I am Donria who was Paltin's wife. Torag and his warriors came to us, snatching folk from the fields by day and entering our walls at night. At first they took a handful, then another handful. At the end we *were* only a handful, and they took all of us but those they slew. Listen to Lord Garric!"

"Metz Scarface!" Opann said. "Get down here at once! The madman lies, and the foreign slut lies as well. Our only safety is to hide behind our walls. The cat men can't be killed!"

"I've killed them myself!" Garric said. "I killed two warriors the night they raided this village, and—"

He brandished the axe he'd taken from the Corl guard.

"—I killed another when I escaped to come here. Join me and together we can—"

"He lies!" Opann said. Was she simply frightened, or was she ignoring the Coerli threat in her concern about Garric becoming her husband's rival for leadership of the village? "No human can kill a cat man!"

"Some of you saw me do it!" Garric said. *That probably isn't true in the darkness and confusion of the raid. And the Coerli carried off their dead.* . . . "Together we can—"

"You lie!" said Opann. "I—*uhh!*"

Donria stepped away from her. Opann fell forward as though her joints had all given way. The hilt of a knife projected from just beneath her rib cage. From the angle, it'd been driven upward through her left kidney. Wooden knives couldn't cut very well, but they'd take enough of a point to be good poniards. . . .

"Duzi!" said Garric aloud. "Donria killed her!"

"What?" said Metz. Garric put his hand on his shoulder, but Metz didn't seem so much angry as confused. "What? Did that really happen?"

"Our only safety lies with Lord Garric," Donria called in a ringing voice. "He will save us if we give him complete obedience. He tore his way alone out of captivity, bearing me on his shoulders, and with our help he will destroy the monsters entirely."

"I, Marzan the Great, brought the hero from the far future to save us!" the wizard said. "My power and the hero's power will join to rout the cat men."

The old man's cracked voice wasn't loud, but the words were vivid and compelling in Garric's mind. He didn't doubt that the Bird was projecting them to the villagers as well.

"You are correct, Garric," the Bird said, adding an audible cluck of laughter.

"Abay?" Metz said. "You and Horst, you're with me, right?"

"Why, sure, Metz," one of the bulky men said. "You've always been able to see as far into a mudbank as the next fellow."

"Right," said Metz with satisfaction. "Idway, Mone, Granta? You men trust me too, don't you?"

"Well, I guess," a man said. "If you want to be chief, I'll back you, but yesterday you said you didn't. Didn't you?"

"I *don't* want to be chief, that's right," Metz said. "But I want Garric here to be chief. He knows how to fight the Coerli and I sure don't. Does anybody want to argue that?"

The uncle who'd spoken before, Horst or Abay, turned to look back at the crowd. "You're arguing with me if you do," he said in a tone of low menace.

Nobody spoke for a moment.

Unexpectedly Donria's clear voice called, "Chief Garric, I have a boon to ask of you. Grant me to your deputy Metz, the greatest of our warriors except yourself!"

Garric froze with his mouth open. Then he cried, "To Metz, the first of my warriors, I give Donria, a wife fit for a warrior and a chief. May they be happy together!"

Very quietly he added, "Metz, you may not always thank me, but you're better off with her than you'd be against her."

"*And that,*" said the laughing ghost in Garric's mind, "*is the truth if truth was ever spoken!*"

*C*HREE-WICK OIL LAMPS hung from stands to Sharina's right and left. Before her on the long table spread reports and petitions. These ranged from a ribbon-tied parchment scroll in which the high priest of the Temple of the Plowing Lady objected in perfect calligraphy to the destruction of a shrine to the Lady by lime-burners, to a note scratched by those same lime burners on a potsherd. The shrine's walls were brick and useless for their purpose, but the roof beams and the wooden statue itself had provided fuel to reduce lumps of limestone to fiery quicklime.

Sharina tossed the parchment to a clerk. The Temple of the Plowing Lady was on the spine of hills in the middle of the island. It, rather than one of the temples in Mona, was the head of the cult on First Atara.

"Request that they send a formal statement of damages to Lord Tadai for examination," she said. "Add the usual language about sacrifices in this hour of the kingdom's need."

Sharina slid the potsherd to a second clerk. "Noted and approved," she said, then paused to rub her eyes.

About a hundred documents remained. Long before she'd worked through them, messengers'd bring in that many more new ones. This was her third trio of clerks, but all they and the earlier shifts did was to transmit the decisions Princess Sharina alone could make. Sharina knew what Liane was doing now was necessary, but she remembered with wonder the smooth way in which this sort of task had vanished when Liane attended to it.

Lord Attaper had been talking with a messenger at the door of Sharina's suite. "Lady Liane's back, Your Highness," he said quietly.

"Lady, you have blessed your servant," Sharina whispered. The prayer was heartfelt and spontaneous. Then, louder, "Send her in please, milord."

She knew that Liane would be as tired as she was, but at least they could talk for a moment. The thing Sharina missed most in being regent was the chance to chat with equals. Garric was gone and Cashel was gone; and Ilna as well, though Sharina'd always felt restraint with Ilna.

With Ilna you were always aware that you were talking to someone who judged herself by standards harsher than those of the most inexorable God. Sharina had to suspect that Ilna in her heart of hearts applied the same standards to everybody else as well, no matter how good friends they were.

Liane looked worn. Her clothes were smudged and wrinkled, and the suggestion of fatigue in her posture would've been visible a bowshot away.

Sharina embraced her friend, feeling a rush of sympathy. She was embarrassed to've complained—even silently—about the stream of work she herself faced.

"The plants retreated to the plain as the sun set," Liane said. "They'd carried the first line of earthworks and were starting to fill them in, but now they're just standing in a circle. Waldron's going to attack when the moon rises."

She slumped into a straight-backed chair beside the door. It was one of a set of four whose ornate bronze frames matched that of the bed. Sharina'd thought the chairs looked terribly uncomfortable. Perhaps they were, but Liane was too tired to mind.

"More of them came from the sea after you left, Sharina," she said. She pressed her fingertips together, then straightened with a noticeable effort of will. "More hellplants. Still, Waldron's hopeful that tonight's attack will destroy those already ashore, and if more appear tomorrow we should have the artillery with quicklime projectiles in position. So long as they become torpid at night, we should be able to contain the attacks for the time being."

Till the kingdom runs out of soldiers, Sharina translated silently. That would happen eventually, but not soon. Not for the time being.

She'd planned to ask Liane to help with the petitions, but that was obviously impractical. Though Liane would try, she was sure.

"You need sleep," Sharina said. "Come, why don't you use the servants' chamber of the suite here? I'll wake you if there's anything that you should know about."

Particularly if Garric reappeared as unexpectedly as he'd vanished. *Oh, Lady, bless me and the kingdom by returning my brother!*

"Yes," said Liane, closing her eyes as she tensed her body to get up again. "I'll sleep for—"

"Do you wish to see the attack?" Double's scraping, squealing voice called from the chamber of art. "I can show you what your human forces can do, better even than the generals leading them see. Then you can decide whether your powers are sufficient to scotch the Green Woman!"

The doorway between the rooms was empty, but the pair of Blood Eagles on the other side hid Double from Sharina's eyes. One of the men advanced his shield slightly, a psychological attempt to fend the wizard away.

"Come into the chamber, Princess!" the wizard said. It giggled, a sound as unpleasant as the whistle of gas escaping from a bloated corpse. "Come and see how human might succeeds against the Green Woman!"

"Your Highness," said Attaper forcefully. "We don't know what happened to Mistress Ilna and her friends, but it happened in that room. It's too dangerous for you to enter. And I don't trust that one—"

He nodded his helmet fiercely in the direction of the doorway and beyond it.

"—a bit. Not a bit!"

"If the princess is afraid," said Double, "let her send a lackey to observe and report to her. Is the great Attaper afraid of me also?"

"I'll go," said Liane, rising to her feet. "I wanted to stay and watch the attack anyway, but Waldron said I'd only be in the way."

"We'll both go," said Sharina. She looked around the room. Clerks and guards and courtiers all watched her in silence. "Anyone who likes can come with Lady Liane and myself. Those of you who prefer to avoid wizardry stay here."

She grinned wryly. "And I won't blame you. Believe me, I won't."

Attaper took a deep breath. "Yes, I suppose . . . ," he said.

He looked at Sharina with an expression of bleak humor that she didn't recall seeing on the guard commander's face before. "My father was sitting at table, no older than I am now," he said. "He'd just reached for his cup of wine. He shouted, 'Sister take me!' and jumped up; and died right there. She did take him."

Attaper took a deep breath and forced a smile. "There's no certainty in this life, your highness, except that we'll die someday."

Sharina laid her hand on Attaper's armored shoulder as they walked into the chamber of art together. "Perhaps, milord," she said. "But I expect to live considerably longer because of your care than I would without it."

The room's only light was a single oil lamp hanging from a central chain. Double had moved away from the door; he now stood beside one of the symbols inlaid in the flooring. Tenoctris joined Sharina with a nod and a crisp smile.

Sharina glanced over her shoulder. Half the staff from her bedroom was joining them, far more than she'd expected.

Double's lips twisted in an oily sneer. The figure he'd chosen was a triangle with a circle of the largest possible radius drawn within it. Words of power were written along each side in yellow chalk, though Sharina couldn't read them well enough to pronounce in the present light. A piece of cloth, probably a dinner napkin, lay over something slight in the center of the enclosed circle.

"He has a length of seaweed there," Tenoctris said quietly. "And a bone which I presume is human; I'm not an anatomist. He's using them as a focus."

Nothing in the old woman's dry voice suggested horror or disgust that Double was using human bone. Tenoctris was a wizard, and she'd used necromancy when that was the only way to get information which the kingdom needed. Sharina had *asked* her to use necromancy, though she'd been too squeamish to watch the incantation.

Remembering that morning, not so long before, Sharina gripped Tenoctris' hand and squeezed it. Friends did things you couldn't or wouldn't do for yourself. Tenoctris was a friend to the kingdom, and a friend to Good; and very certainly a friend to Sharina os-Reise.

Double drew the ancient athame from his sash and lifted it above the figure. "Watch, Princess," he said, then chanted, *"So somaul somalue. . . ."*

At each slow-spoken syllable he dipped the black blade, shifting the point from one angle to the next. The lights dimmed or seemed to dim. *"Zer ze-er zeruesi. . . ."*

A clerk dropped her slate tablet with a clatter and ran sobbing from the room. Nobody else moved.

"Lu . . . ," said Double. *"Lumo luchresa!"*

The lamp went out completely. Instead of plunging the room into darkness, a circular lens as bright as the full moon appeared above the center of the figures. In it was a marshy landscape on which every object showed as sharply as they would if carved on a triumphal relief.

Double stepped back. His hand trembled slightly as he lowered the athame, but he managed an oily smile and said, "You see *my* power, Princess. Now you will see the power your human forces have against the Green Woman."

Instead of staring into the lens as everyone else was doing, Tenoctris bent to peer at the words chalked around the figure. Sharina gave her friend's hand a final squeeze and concentrated on the image Double had created. She supposed Tenoctris was more interested in details of another wizard's art than she was of what was happening on a battlefield miles away. The first was her job, come to think of it.

In the lens Sharina saw the hellplants wedged as close together as sheep in a blizzard. Their bulky green shapes formed an arc with both flanks anchored on the bay. Though a heavy mist blanketed the valley, she could see every detail of the creatures with a clarity that would've been impossible at arm's length in bright sunlight.

She frowned. Her subconscious mind was sure the image was real. She wondered if Double was bringing distant events close or if instead he was merely tricking the minds of those watching. She could get details from Lord Waldron after the battle and see how well they jibed with what she thought she'd seen.

A trumpet called, thin and unimaginably distant. "Where's that coming from?" said Attaper, looking around angrily. "That's *Charge!* Are we hearing commands from Calf's Head Bay?"

"Watch and learn, brave soldier," Double said in a deadpan sneer. He gestured with his athame like a pastry chef teasing icing into a delicate spire; the image in the lens shifted to the earthworks on the surrounding slopes. Soldiers climbed out from the defenses with their swords drawn. In ragged groups of six to ten they marched toward the plain. Generally one man of each group had a torch and the others carried fagots of brushwood to use when they reached the hellplants.

The torches were pinpricks of yellow light; fog swirled around the troops like the tide rising in a mangrove swamp. Sharina could see the men clearly, but from the way they splashed and stumbled they themselves were almost blind.

"They're sinking above their ankles," Sharina said, frowning. "I thought the valley was sown in barley. You couldn't plow ground that soft, let alone get crops to sprout in it."

"It wasn't that wet this morning," Liane said. "It kept getting boggier as the day went on. I think the tide may be rising, but there's the fog as well. Local people say they've never seen anything like it, even in the dead of winter with the wind from the southwest."

"The Green Woman's minions are reclaiming the land for her," Double said. "As they advance, the marsh will also advance."

He turned his white, swollen face slightly. Light from the lens glinted on his bulbous eyes.

"If you kill the hellplants, soldier," Double said, "will you then drain the soil with your sword?"

Attaper met the dead glare. "Creature," he said in a tight, controlled voice, "you have no friends in this room. Don't push your luck! The way I see it, it's not murder to cut apart something that's already dead."

Staggering, tripping; often grabbing one another so as not to fall in the muck, the soldiers pressed their attack. Sharina could faintly hear the angry, blasphemous murmur of the advancing army. A few of the men had kept their spears; they used them to probe the fog-blurred darkness.

The hellplants were as silent as a rank of haystacks. Sharina was tense, expecting the massive forms to rush forward now that they'd lured the troops close, but the men continued to advance against a motionless enemy.

A soldier screamed on a rising, piercing note. Twenty more soldiers echoed his cry with nearly identical ones.

Double pointed his athame and twisted it. The image shrank to a full-sized image of the marsh: a soldier's right leg stepping forward in muck in which half-grown barley lay matted. Though dismounted for the moment, the man was from a cavalry regiment; he wore knee boots instead of hobnailed sandals as the infantry did.

A scorpion like the ones that'd spilled from the hellplant in the palace squirmed through the gooey earth. Its pincers caught the man's calf and the tail arched up to strike.

The soldier shouted in terror and brought his long sword down sideways, crushing the scorpion against his boot. The creature's sting stayed in the leather, still twitching even though it'd been torn from the tail.

"Demons!" the soldier screamed. "Demons're coming out of the ground!"

He slashed wildly in front of him. Probably he'd imagined that a waterlogged furrow was moving, because the unnatural clarity of Sharina's vision didn't indicate any danger where the blade splashed muck.

Instead of assuming that his sword didn't kill another scorpion because there was no scorpion present, the soldier turned with a despairing cry. The bundle of brush on his back wobbled as he ran, forgotten in his panic.

"He's not a coward," Liane whispered in sick horror. "He's from Lord Waldron's personal regiment and they've been fighting all day. It's the darkness and the fog, that's all. . . ."

She's probably right, Sharina thought. *But conditions are never going to be better than they are tonight, and tonight is a disaster.*

Double gestured with his athame, drawing back the apparent viewpoint so that his audience could see the panorama of the attack. Here and there a bonfire blazed, but it seemed to Sharina that some had been lighted at a distance from the hellplants instead of being laid up against the creatures as intended.

The troops were retreating in more or less order all across the plain. Generally less order. They couldn't see their attackers, and the paddle-legged scorpions were as agile as seals in the flooded field.

A circle of dismounted cavalry kept good discipline. Every other man had a torch made from the fagots they carried. With those for light, the other half of the squadron stabbed and cut at the scorpions curling toward them from any direction.

Lord Waldron was part of the defensive circle, not within it protected by his troops. His sword dripped with the ichor of at least one scorpion, and his chief aides stood to either side with torches.

But even these men were pulling back to the temporary safety of the hills from which they'd sallied. In the morning the hellplants would attack again, and more of the creatures would come from the sea, as surely as the tide and the sunrise.

The lens faded, then regained clarity as it shrank to half its size.

"*Lamsucho!*" Double said in a high-pitched snarl. He sliced his athame through the air, wiping the lens away. The oil lamp blazed, seemingly brighter than it'd been before the incantation darkened it to Sharina's eyes.

"You have seen!" Double said. The strain of his art must've greatly weakened him, but only those familiar with wizardry would've seen that beneath Double's bravado. "You have seen human strength against the Green Woman."

"What do you offer instead, milord?" said Liane. Her face was calm, her voice cool. She was poised lady to every hair's breadth of her body, and that too was bravado.

"In the morning I will show you," said Double. "First I will destroy the Green Woman's minions, then I will destroy her. I will be God!"

"One thing at a time, Lord Wizard," Sharina said. Her mind was as hard as glass. "One thing at a time. . . ."

CASHEL STOOD ON ground covered with leaf litter; the forest around him was silent. Winter had stripped the trees of foliage, but a swath of them had been blasted to dead gray stumps by something more sudden than the cold.

Protas let go of Cashel's belt and stepped away. He cleared his throat. Cashel guessed he was embarrassed to be frightened when the boulder they stood on seemed to fall away.

"It's cold here," Protas said formally. He took off the crown and polished the big jewel on his sleeve; just to have something to do with his hands, Cashel supposed. "Do we just wait, Cashel, or . . . ?"

"I don't know which way we'd go if we walked on ourselves," Cashel said quietly. This landscape was nothing like the one they'd left. The shape of the land was different from where they'd been, not just one being sunbaked waste and this a forest late in the year.

The boy was right about it being cold, though for a matter of pride he hadn't hugged his arms around his thin tunic to cover himself from the wind. Above, the sky was gray with streaks of pale blue; a winter sky, promising worse in the future if not now, not quite now. A flock got restive and peevish in this weather, though you had to know sheep pretty well to realize they were in a bad mood.

Cashel tapped the ground with his bare toes. Leaves rustled slickly; the soil beneath was firm but not frozen. He and Protas were just standing *here* instead of *there* in the place where the trees were running toward them.

He focused on the forest as a whole again instead of the dirt at his feet, though he hadn't ever really lost track of the general landscape; a shepherd doesn't dare do that. *These* trees, even the ones that were still alive, weren't attacking anybody. It was a terrible waste of timber to smash so many trees this way and just leave them scattered about.

Something was jingling toward them through the trees. Cashel turned and faced the sound, his staff lifted. It wasn't loud, but it sure wasn't trying not to be heard.

Without being told, Protas stepped to where he wouldn't be in the way. "Is somebody driving a carriage through the woods?" he asked. "It sounds like harness, almost."

"Hello there!" Cashel called to the bare trunks. "I'm Cashel or-Kenset and I'm just passing through!"

From the sound being so slight he figured it must be far off, but around the shattered trunk of a chestnut came—

"That's a helmet!" said Protas. "It's rolling along the ground!"

That wasn't quite true: the helmet was walking on little jointed metal legs, and it had two short arms besides. One held a butcher knife, notched from cutting things it shouldn't have been used on.

"Hello?" Cashel said again, not so loud as before. He started spinning his staff, not hostile exactly but bringing it into motion in case he needed to use it suddenly.

He wasn't a bit surprised to see little dustings of blue wizardlight trail off behind the butt caps. His skin'd been prickling ever since he and Protas stood with Cervoran back in the palace.

"Hello yourself," the helmet said in a voice that seemed to come from the grating under the front of the flared brim. "Since you've been fool enough to come here, I'm the poor devil tasked to guide you out again."

It gave a nasty laugh and added, "Poor devil indeed!"

The helmet sounded angry but not angry at anything in particular. Cashel relaxed a little and smiled to find something familiar in this strange place. He knew a number of people who acted that way too, waving their ill temper like a flag they were proud of.

"Thank you, then," he said politely. "I'm Cashel and this is Protas. We'll be out of your way as soon as you show us how."

"Come along," the helmet said. It'd kept on walking as it talked, but it wasn't coming *toward* them Cashel realized. It trundled past, heading for a goal that they'd been standing in the path to. "And be ready to hide if I tell you to. It isn't far, but it could take your whole life to get there if we're unlucky."

Cashel motioned Protas ahead of him and walked along at the rear himself, a trifle to the left of the line their guide was taking. He didn't have to run to keep up but those little legs clinked and jingled along like a centipede's. The helmet covered ground faster than he'd figured it could.

There wasn't a path but the going wasn't too bad. In summer the trees shaded out undergrowth, so the saplings they came across were spindly and easy to push aside. The worst trouble was stones covered with leaves, slippery and easy to stub your foot on if you weren't used to it.

Protas *wasn't* used to it, but he never quite fell on his face and he didn't complain. The boy didn't know a lot of things, but he made a better companion than plenty of folk who might not've stumbled so much.

The helmet was muttering. To itself, Cashel figured, but then in a louder voice it said, "You, boy! You have the Great Talisman. Why have you come to this benighted Hell?"

"We're passing through, Master Helmet," said Protas easily. "Do you get many visitors to your world?"

He was the funniest combination of little boy and gracious prince. It was the prince who seemed to do most of the talking to strangers.

"Visitors!" grated the helmet. "No, we don't get many visitors, boy! No one comes here but fools and men who like to kill more than they want to live. Or those who want to die, of course. Which are you, eh?"

"I've been called a fool often enough," said Cashel, figuring it was time for him to take over. Their guide wasn't talking, he was pushing, and if there was pushing to be done then it wasn't for a boy to take it un-aided while Cashel was around. "The folks who called me that maybe were right, but looking back on it they weren't themselves people I'd trust if they said the sun would rise."

He cleared his throat. "And we're not either of the other two things," he went on. "Though if somebody figures he just has to have a fight, I'll give him one."

"Faugh," muttered the helmet, suddenly tired and dejected instead of angry the way he'd been from the first. "I'm a fool myself, so why should I complain about what you two do?"

They'd been going more or less uphill ever since they met their guide, not steep but noticeable. Because of the slope there were more bare rocks poking out; the helmet's feet clicked and sparked on them, which set things ringing inside its body too. That was what Cashel and Protas'd heard coming toward them like a miniature carriage.

The trees in this stretch weren't knocked about like the ones were back where they'd met their guide. A lot of them were pines on this thin soil, but there were near as many chestnuts, some of them huge trees with boles thicker than Cashel standing with his arms spread straight out to either side.

Cashel heard a buzzing that seemed to come from the treetops. He looked up, trying to find the source. It was way too late in the year for bees to be swarming, and there wasn't anything else that—

The helmet turned lizard-quick and said, "Stand against a tree trunk and don't move! Don't hide, just get against a tree. They'll see move-ment, but you're all right if you keep still!"

Protas opened his mouth to ask a question. Cashel gripped him by the shoulder and backed against a big spruce whose branches didn't start till several times Cashel's own height up the trunk. He didn't know what was going on, but he didn't doubt that they'd be better off doing what they were told just now instead of arguing about it.

The helmet hunkered down among the rocks, drawing in its legs like a box turtle closing up. It held the blade of the butcher knife under its body.

When Cashel was sure the boy wasn't going to jump he relaxed his grip, though he didn't move his arm away. Protas swallowed stiffly, but he didn't so much as turn his head. There were lots of things the boy didn't understand because he hadn't been raised in places where those sorts of things happened, but he was a quick learner. That was certain sure.

The noise was getting louder. Cashel didn't move, just waited, and sure enough something high up in the air swam into sight. It looked a lot like a white bird, but it was the size of a ship and its stubby wings were rigged as sails. Black smoke oozed from the bird's open beak, rising only with difficulty.

Cashel couldn't tell for sure—the bird was near as high as the clouds—but it looked like people in armor stood in the open back half of the body. He thought about their guide. There was armor, anyway, and maybe it had people in it.

As Cashel watched, the wings canted and the creature started to come about. The figures in the stern turned also, raising round metal shields. They shouted in ringing, angry voices, too thinned by distance for Cashel to understand the words.

"Don't move," the helmet grated. "On your lives, don't move!"

The bird was silent except for the creaking of cordage and the cries of the crew. The buzzing didn't come from it, so—

Three saucers with silvery wings burred down from the clouds, curving toward the bird. In the belly of each saucer rode what looked like a man-sized frog holding a lance. The frogs were trying to point their lances toward the bird, but as they gestured their mounts wobbled awkwardly.

The leading saucers almost flew into each other. As they jerked apart wildly, flame shot from the bird's beak in a great, arching jet that briefly enveloped the third saucer that trailed the others. The wings melted like ice in a furnace.

The saucer flopped onto its back and the frog tumbled out, blackened and burning. From its wide mouth came a scream like steam jetting from under a pot lid. The bird's crew shouted in triumph.

One of the surviving saucers dived away, but the other looped up over the bird. The rider was actually upside down when his lance sent a bolt of crackling lightning into the open back. Several armored crewmen flew apart, helmets and segments of limbs spinning away from the bird in smoking arcs.

The survivors sent arrows sailing after their attacker. They didn't hit the rider, but at least one stuck in the saucer's glittering gossamer wing.

The bird was rising. Its outlines blurred in the overcast, then faded entirely. For a time Cashel could still hear the buzzing sound, but the saucers didn't come into sight again. At last the sky fell silent.

"We can go on now," the helmet said. "And quickly—we were lucky this time that they stayed high. You saw in the valley what happens when they fight closer to the ground!"

"Aye, we did," Cashel said. He understood the blasted trees, now.

"You mean that we might have been hurt by accident if the ships had stuck to the forest instead of each other, Master Helmet?" Protas said.

The route they were following was steeper than it'd been. Sometimes it was simply steep, places where Cashel used the quarterstaff as a brace to lift him up to the next firm footing. The helmet flowed over whatever was in the way like a centipede climbing a wall, not slowing down a bit. Protas scrambled along right behind it, putting a hand down for a grip whenever he needed to.

"No, I don't mean that, boy!" the helmet said. "I mean if they'd been lower they might've seen us—and they'd have killed us if they had. You're easier prey than their usual enemies, you see. Perhaps you think the talisman would save you—and perhaps you're right, it would. But it wouldn't help me!"

Or me either, it sounds like, Cashel thought. Well, he hadn't expected their guide was the sort who worried much about what happened to other people. "Other people" if you wanted to call a walking helmet a person, that is.

The top of the ridge was a bald with only small plants clinging in crevices filled with leaf litter. Part of it was bare even of that: a blast of fire had not only scoured the surface but fused the rock to a glassy polish. Half caught in that but untouched by heat that'd melted dense granite on both sides of the line was a star with as many points as the fingers of one hand.

"Stand in the pentacle," the helmet ordered. "And be quick about it. There's no cover here, and if they see me they'll hunt me down even if I get back into the forest."

The wind whipping up the back side of the bald was fierce, strong enough that even Cashel had to lean into it to walk to the center of the star. Cashel put his left arm around Protas; the boy'd done all right with the wind, but his trouser legs and the hem of his tunic were flapping fiercely.

"Master Helmet?" Cashel said. "What are they fighting about? The frogs and the folk in the bird?"

"Fighting about?" said the helmet. "There's no about. They fight to fight, that's all. It's the same as in your world."

"No sir!" said Cashel, surprised at how hot that made him. "There's fighting on our world, that's so; but there's good and evil fighting at the bottom of it!"

"Do you think so?" the helmet said. "Well, I'm a fool too, just as I said."

Laughing in a nasty, knowing way, it pointed the jagged butcher knife toward Cashel and Protas. Light as red as a sunstruck ruby sprang from the blade. Again solid stone vanished from under Cashel's feet, and he felt the illusion of falling through a starless void.

Chapter

11

Torag's keep loomed like a gray lump out of the green/gray/black marsh. The sun had been up for two hours and it wasn't raining.

Garric grinned. In this land it passed for a bright morning. He'd wanted to arrive promptly at dawn to have the full day for their business with the Coerli, though.

"I hope we've got enough time to finish the job in daylight," he said to Metz as they came out of a grove of trees whose foliage dangled like sheets of moss from the spreading branches. "If we don't, we'll none of us survive the night to come. Torag isn't much of a general, but even he's smart enough to know that he has to kill any Grass People who've learned to fight before the danger spreads."

"The Coerli kill without being smart," Metz said in a distant tone. "They only have to think if they don't intend to kill."

He looked at the sky. "There's enough time," he said. "If we can do it at all."

Every adult in the village was with them. Everybody whom Garric'd judged was capable of making a seven-mile march, that is. There were about fifty in all, as many women as men. They were burdened with bundles of brush, every fishing net in the community, and the rolled-up wall of a house. Unrolled, the wicker mat would let them cross the bog surrounding Torag's keep without sinking knee-deep at every step.

Then the hard part would begin.

The Corl in the watchtower finally saw them and blew a warning on his trumpet. After a moment he blew twice more, nervous blats of sound that were as much fright at the unexpected as an attempt to rouse his fellows.

"With the cat beasts," King Carus said, *"now is better than right at dawn."*

The ghost's voice was calm and analytical, but underneath it was the leaping delight of a warrior about to enter battle. He went on, *"Their own folk wouldn't attack in daylight, and till now there's nobody else in their minds who might. The guard wasn't alert, and the rest of the animals have had time to go to sleep."*

"All right, everybody!" Garric called. He raised his voice by reflex, though he knew the Bird would project his words to the villagers at heightened volume regardless. "Keep close to each other but not so tight you can't move. Be ready to raise the nets when I say so. Just keep marching on. And remember—this world is for humans!"

He'd hoped for a ringing cheer in response, but apparently that wasn't part of the political process among the Grass People. He grinned wryly. At least they didn't freeze in panic where they stood. That might've happened if they'd been a little more sophisticated and thus knew what they were getting into.

"Metz?" Garric said as he and the scarred hunter struggled through the belt of furze bushes around the bog. Coerli raiders had passed back and forth often enough to mark a path, but the cat men moved with such delicacy that the path wasn't wide enough for human beings. "It's time for you to go to the rear like we planned. We'll need a leader back there if they get around us."

"*You* planned," Metz said. All the villagers wore broad-brimmed hats of linen stretched on a wicker frame. They were meant for rain covers, but they ought to give reasonable protection against overhead blows. "My uncles can take care of the back. I'm staying where I am."

Turning, he said, "Get that mat up to the gate, Kimber! Come on, you kin of Wandalo! Remember what the cat people did to our chief!"

The four men and two women carrying the house wall staggered toward the bog. They dropped the loose wicker roll sooner than they should have, starting to unroll it a good ten feet back on firm ground. Garric judged that the mat wasn't going to reach all the way to the walls unless—

"Fill in the last with firewood!" Carus ordered. His practiced eye had measured the gap with a certainty Garric couldn't match. *"And move it! You'll need it sooner than you can get the wood carriers up from where they're marching!"*

"Bring up rolls of brush!" Garric shouted. "Quick, before they figure out what they're going to do!"

Torag and half a dozen of his warriors mounted the step inside the wall and looked down on the attacking humans. The chief himself seemed stupefied by the event, unable to grasp it even though he watched it happening. One of his warriors gave a rasping shriek, a sound of wordless anger that the Bird couldn't and needn't translate.

The walls of Torag's keep—even just the part the Coerli themselves inhabited—were far too long for fifty humans to encircle, even if they'd all been trained soldiers. The alternative was to keep the attacking force together and smash through the stockade at a single point. The cat men could come at them from any direction, or they could flee beyond any chance of human pursuit.

"If Torag were smart enough to run now, lad," Carus said, his hand resting on the pommel of his sword, *"then he'd have been smart enough to've chased you down the night you escaped. No, lad; it'll be a fight."*

He spoke with the cheerful satisfaction of a gambler about to collect his winnings. The sword on the ghost's hip was merely an image like every other physical attribute of the king today, but the enthusiastic readiness to fight was just as real as it'd been a thousand years before.

Sometimes a mind like that is a good thing to have on your side and the kingdom's side. Right now it was a good thing to have on the side of the Grass People. . . .

The crew—the family group—pushing the matting got to the end of the roll and rose from their stooped posture. They were still a dozen feet from the base of the wall.

"Go on back!" Garric ordered, walking just behind them with the axe in his right hand and a minnow net spinning overhead in his left. "Get the firewood up here *now!*"

The flattened wall wobbled underfoot, but it didn't sink out of sight in the muck. Not only did it spread the weight of the people standing on it, the buoyant wicker resisted being forced under the surface.

The shrieking warrior leaped from the wall onto Garric. Garric did the only thing he had time for in the second it took the Corl to drop: release the thread-fine net already spinning in his hand. The pebble-weighted mesh wrapped the warrior, binding the barbed blade of his outthrust stabbing spear to his right thigh.

The warrior crashed into Garric, knocking him off his feet. The Coerli weighed no more than half-grown human children, but that was still a solid mass hitting from twenty feet up. Garric rolled, trying to raise the axe that he'd managed to drive straight into the bog when he went down.

The warrior dropped his tangled spear and drew a flint knife from his harness. The movement was a single blur.

Duzi they're fast! but Garric's left hand closed on the cat man's wrist. The ghost in Garric's head had started his arm moving well before the Corl had decided to act. The warrior's thin bones crunched like chalk breaking. He shrieked in pain and tried to bite; Garric slammed him back against the matting.

Metz brought down his stone-headed mace. He'd aimed the blow at the Corl's head but the blow landed at the base of the creature's throat instead, crushing the collarbones and windpipe both. The cat man's nostrils sprayed blood as he spasmed into death.

"Raise your nets!" Garric screamed. He grabbed his axe hilt with both hands to pull it out of the muck, but his left hand threatened to cramp. The hysterical strength he'd used to crush the Corl's wrist came with a price. "Raise your nets!"

The gate started to open inward. Garric glanced up. Torag and his warriors weren't looking down from the wall anymore. *Duzi! Are they going to sally straight out the main gate? Are they that stupid?*

The gate jerked the rest of the way open; sure enough, the wicker bridge was there, ready to be spread over the bog. The Coerli *were* that stupid, or at any rate they were that ignorant. The Grass People didn't know what war was, but neither did their enemies. The Coerli were hunters and raiders, not soldiers, and they'd just met a soldier. . . .

Garric got to his feet. He smelled smoke. Villagers back in the line must've started a fire already. Garric'd meant to burn a gap in the stockade when they got up to it, but what were they thinking of to start one now?

The mat was crowded. Villagers with brushwood were coming forward. They got tangled with the nets their fellows stretched high on fishing spears whose springy, two-pronged heads were ideal for lifting the mesh.

The nets were supposed to form a barrier on both sides of the mat. That was more or less how it worked, but inevitably some of those holding the nets managed to tilt their spears inward, narrowing the walkway from its original six feet or so. There wasn't enough space for all the people and their gear unless everybody was careful—which would've been a greater marvel under the circumstances than the Lady coming down from the sky and declaring peace.

"Throw the—" Garric began, but caught himself. "Throw the wood into the bog to get it out of the way," he'd meant to say, but that wouldn't work with the nets in place. He hadn't thought it through. The plan was falling apart and it was his fault!

The cat men's wicker bale lurched forward awkwardly, pushed by warriors rather than by their human slaves. They weren't used to the work, and their narrow pads didn't grip as well as human feet on the wet ground churned by past traffic; the roll jammed in the gateway.

Torag gave a great snarling roar and vaulted over the bridge. Warriors followed him in quick succession, each spanning the gap like a pouncing leopard.

Metz spun the minnow net he carried. Torag twisted in the air, avoiding the fine mesh but bowling the hunter over with his feet instead of braining him with the wooden mace as he'd intended to do. Metz fell back into the woman holding up one end of a heavy gill net, one of those the villagers used to drag their ponds; Torag tumbled on past into the bog.

Garric brought his axe around in a swift, slashing diagonal. Carus' instinct told him he couldn't miss the warrior leaping at him—but he did; it was like trying to cut a wisp of smoke. The Corl's long legs rotated away from the stroke; still in the air, the creature stabbed Garric through the right shoulder. His spear had barbs on the end of a stiff wooden point. It burned like a hot wire as it pierced the muscle.

The creature landed on its feet. Garric grabbed the Corl's right elbow so it couldn't bound away as it'd thought to do. He drove his right fist at the long cat face, using the butt of the axe helve because they were too close for him to swing the weapon normally. His whole right arm was afire, but the Corl's skull deformed at the blow and it lost its grip on the spear.

Garric hurled aside the twitching corpse and lifted his axe to strike again. Several humans were down, but besides the warrior he'd killed there were three more struggling in the bog and a fourth tangled on the inside of the gill net. Two women were methodically beating that one to death with their loads of firewood. The individual sticks were too light to make effective clubs, but the women were using their whole bundles end-on like giant pestles on the cat man's ribs.

"Throw them!" shouted Donria. A shower of burning brands spun over the fighters to land in the gateway. They'd been cut from an oily brush that lit easily and burned even when green, though with low, smoky flames. They were only sticks, not dangerous as missiles, but the Coerli, already uncomfortable to be fighting in broad daylight, feared and hated fire.

A warrior poising to leap from the wicker hurdle instead sprang backward with a howl. Those behind him shoved the rolled wicker out of the way and began pushing the gate leaves closed.

"Get 'em!" Garric cried. He jumped forward and tripped to splash at the end of the villagers' own mat; his foot was tangled in a net.

The butt of the spear wobbling from Garric's shoulder hit the ground end-on, driving the point all the way in till the thicker shaft stopped it. He lost his grip on the axe and shouted in fury.

Torag dragged himself onto the matting; the strength in his shoulders was remarkable. He'd lost his mace. Metz cut at him with a sword edged with jagged teeth of shell. Torag avoided the blow easily and drew his hardwood knife. Donria stepped forward, swinging a torch in a smoky arc.

The Corl chieftain let out a despairing wail that was nothing like the other sounds Garric had heard from his throat. Instead of finishing Metz, he vaulted back through the gates of the stockade as they closed.

Garric looked around, trying to get his breath. His eyes blurred in and out of focus.

Three warriors were half submerged in the bog. Villagers, the ones who'd been holding up the net barriers, were now using the long spears to worry the Coerli to death. The springy fishing points weren't very suitable for the purpose, but enthusiasm and trapped victims were accomplishing the task. There's nothing neat about a battle. . . .

Someone gripped Garric's arm from behind. He started to turn.

"Hold still!" Donria ordered. With her free hand she held the spear shaft firmly where it touched his shoulder. She bent and he felt her cheek against his back.

"What in the Lady's name are you—" he said. As he spoke, Donria twisted the shaft; he heard a crunch behind him.

Donria drew the spear out of his flesh almost painlessly. She brandished it in triumph: she'd bitten off the barbs and now spat them into the bog.

Garric took a deep breath. The gates were closed and the surviving cat men weren't showing themselves on the step of the stockade; the fighting was over for the moment.

"Now," said the ghost in Garric's mind, *"we finish them!"*

ILNA FOLLOWED HER companions onto a stretch of wet meadow, not very different from the tidal marsh near the mouth of Pattern Creek. She recognized many of the flowering plants—turtleheads, the great blooms of rose mallow, and sprays of joe-pye weed. All the flowers were rose pink. It wasn't a color that much appealed to her, though—

She smiled at evidence of her own vanity.

—that might be because she'd never found a lightfast dye that would match it. Well, she didn't care for dyes anyway, even the best indigo. In Ilna's ideal world everyone would wear natural browns and grays and blacks; and whites too, white fleeces were natural, though white wasn't a favorite of hers personally.

She smiled again, amused at herself.

"Ilna, what time is it?" Merota asked in a small voice. "I'm getting tired."

Ilna glanced at the sun. At this season—late summer, judging by what was in flower—it should be about the second hour of the afternoon.

It'd been about the second hour of the afternoon when the three of them arrived in the garden, quite a while ago. She glanced at Chalcus.

"Aye," he said. "Not a bad time of day as such things go, though I might've chosen a later hour if I'd been asked. At least—"

He smiled to make the bald truth sound like a jest.

"—we needn't worry about things creeping up on us in the darkness, eh?"

He turned and jabbed his left hand into the hedge behind him with the speed of a striking cat. Quick as the sailor was—and Ilna had never seen a man quicker—his fist closed on air; the slender brown figure melted like liquid through the holly branches.

Chalcus sighed and drew back his hand. The spiky leaf tips had clawed narrow trails the length of his forearm, but he hadn't jabbed the end of a twig through himself.

"Master Chalcus, what would you have done with it if you *had* caught it?" Ilna asked tartly. "I'm certainly not that hungry."

"Asked the little fellow some questions, is all, dear heart," Chalcus said. He gave her a broad grin and added, "And to be truthful as behooves the honest sailor that I am today, it gripes my soul that the little demons think they can snoop and scamper and spy on us and we can do nothing to let or hinder them."

"Can they really do that, Chalcus?" Merota said doubtfully.

"They can indeed, my darling girl," said the sailor. "Did I not just prove it?"

Ilna took a few steps out into the narrow meadow, looking about her. The vegetation was soft enough to make a good couch, but her bare toes squished water up from the soil. They'd best find a drier spot to rest.

"There's one!" called Merota, pointing with her right forefinger. A brown figure quivered from the east side of the meadow to the shaded hedge on the west, merging the holly as easily as the breeze that faintly ruffled the garden.

Ilna made a sour face. The little people were harmless, but so were the midges fluttering around her face and landing at the edges of her eyes. The insects tickled and distracted her. If there'd been a way to make them all vanish, she'd have—

The little brown man screamed like a leg-snared rabbit. He tried to leap back into the meadow, but the shadowed interior of the hedge closed about him. He screamed again, but faintly. His body was becoming misty. He turned his large eyes on Ilna in a look of desperate entreaty—

What does he think that I can do to help?

—and faded completely away. For a moment Ilna thought she saw the little man's bones, as delicate as those of a dead goat picked clean by ants; then the skeleton too vanished. The knotted stems of the holly remained unchanged.

A cat the size of a horse stalked into the meadow from the aisle at the other end. Gossamer wings were folded tightly on its back; they were marked like oil-patterned paper and gave the impression of being feathered.

Growing from the cat's neck were a pair of viper heads on an arm's length of serpent body. They looked small compared with the cat, but Ilna didn't recall ever seeing another snake as big as these were.

Her fingers were knotting a pattern that instinct told her would be effective. She brought her hands up. The great cat spread a wing before its eyes. Soft pastel smudges distorted the creature's appearance to Ilna's eyes, and they would also distort the effect of Ilna's pattern of mastery.

"Wait!" the cat said in a deep rumble. "I have no quarrel with Princes! If you wish to hunt in this meadow, you're welcome to it. Though—"

It sounded not so much hostile as aggrieved.

"—it's been part of my territory since the One brought me here."

"It's not hunting we're after doing, friend cat," said Chalcus in a lilting challenge. The dagger in his left hand drew fanciful little curlicues in the air. The glitter of the point drew an opponent's eye away from the sword in his right, rock steady and ready to thrust. "But it's not prey that we are either, do you see?"

"I think he's a chimaera, Chalcus," Merota said in a tiny schoolgirl voice. She was terrified and therefore going back to the routines of normalcy, of tutors and knowledge from books. "Only not exactly."

"I know you're not Prey," the cat—the chimaera?—said with a touch of irritation. "I'll back away and leave the meadow to you, if you like. What could be clearer than that?"

"Wait," said Ilna, folding the knotted fabric into her left hand. She walked forward, past where Chalcus had stationed himself. He frowned but wisely held his tongue. "If you've lived here for a time, then you can answer a question."

For an instant she'd been considering ways to modify her fabric so that the effect would pass the creature's veiling wing. That was merely a competitive reflex, a desire to prove to the chimaera that it couldn't escape Ilna os-Kenset by a trick like that.

And perhaps it couldn't, but life had brought Ilna enough real enemies that she didn't need to fight something which didn't want to fight her. The chimaera was ugly and probably dangerous if it wanted to be, but if it didn't threaten her or hers, then it could live or die without Ilna's involvement.

"Perhaps," the chimaera said. "We Princes owe one another courtesy. For the sake of quiet lives, if nothing else."

It partially folded its wing. Ilna wondered if the creature could really fly. Was it possible to fly out of the tapestry?

"One of the little people just ran into the hedge there," she said, gesturing—not quite pointing—with her left hand. She kept her eyes on the great beast.

"Yes, the Prey," the chimaera said. "Are you having trouble catching them? I'll willingly help fellow Princes, of course."

"That won't be necessary," Ilna said. Her voice sounded grim in her own ears; but then, it generally did. "What concerns me is that the little man vanished. Seemed to dissolve. There was nothing there that I could see, but . . ." She shrugged.

"Ah!" said the chimaera. Its head jerked toward where Ilna indicated, and it started sideways into the opposite hedge. "Ah. You saw that, did you? Well, it's safe enough now. It doesn't stay around after it's fed . . . or it doesn't seem to, anyway."

"Yes, but what *was* it?" Ilna said, trying to keep the irritation out of her voice but not succeeding especially well. "I didn't see anything, just the man disappearing."

"We call it the Shadow," said the chimaera, "but . . ."

The big creature made a rumbling sound deep in its chest, apparently the equivalent of a man clearing his throat before he was ready to speak.

"It never comes for Princes," the chimaera went on, "or almost never. But most of us, certainly myself . . . we prefer not to use the name. Sometimes you call something to yourself by naming it, you know. Or they say so."

"They say a lot of things," said Ilna tartly, but her irritation was more at the situation than this great cat's fearful mumbling. "Is the—"

She waved her left hand in a quick circle. Using the word "Shadow" wasn't going to help in getting information from the cat; and anyway, the concern might be correct. She knew very little about this place, and she knew nothing about the Shadow save that she didn't want to meet it. There was no point in using a name that could be harmful to herself and her friends.

"—darkness, whatever, it is—is it a wizard, then? Did it make this place?"

"It?" the chimaera said. "Oh, certainly not. The One created the Garden and placed us in it. The other that you refer is a resident like the rest of us Princes. Like yourselves, that is."

"Not, I think," said Chalcus, "like ourselves; but we'll let that pass. Is there a way out of this garden, friend cat?"

"Out?" the chimaera repeated in a puzzled tone. "Why, no. The One sealed the Garden for his perfect pleasure, or so they say. Anyway, why would you want to leave it? The weather is perfect and there's plenty of Prey. It's a paradise."

"Chalcus?" Merota said primly, her hands folded before her. "Ilna? I don't like the way he talks."

Then the child cried, "They aren't Prey, they're people! Real little people!"

"Yes," said Ilna. "I think they are too. Master Chimaera, you said you were leaving when I called you back. I won't trouble you further."

"Well, you know that I have just as much right to—" the creature said.

Chalcus stepped in front of Ilna, his blades out. Her fingers were knotting yarn, visualizing the shimmer of the wing in her mind's eye and shifting the sequence of her fabric in ways that only she could understand. Even her understanding was at the muscle level, not in her conscious mind.

"All right!" cried the chimaera. Its hind legs hunched as it turned, then launched itself into the air. Its gossamer vans spread and stroked, driving a gust backward. The great creature vanished over the tops of the hedges.

"This garden isn't so bad a place," said Chalcus judiciously. "But barring present company, I don't much care for the neighbors I'm sharing it with. I'll be glad when you find us a way out, dear heart."

"Yes," said Ilna. "So will I."

Her nostrils flared as she breathed out. "So will I!" she repeated.

Cashel held protas and his quarterstaff firmly as the void coalesced into a world beneath their feet again. He looked around quickly. Midges rose in a cloud from black water. They'd come from an upland forest to a swamp.

Cashel sniffed: a tidal swamp. The air had a salty sharpness in addition to the usual smell of decay.

The air was also full of the midges. He'd breathed in a flock of them, and he'd doubtless breathe more before he was gone from this place. They tickled the back of his throat but at least they didn't seem to be the biting kind.

"There isn't anywhere we can go, Cashel," Protas said, taking his hand down from the topaz crown. "It's all mud and water. Do you think a boat will come for us?"

A boat couldn't get through this, Cashel thought. Cattails grew all about, but he could see the roots spreading over the surface of the mud. *There's not a hand's breadth of water in any direction from us.*

Aloud he said, "We may have to get muddy, Protas. You'd best take your slippers off now, because—"

A figure came through the cattails toward them. Rose up from the cattails, it seemed to Cashel, though the fellow was hunched and maybe could've walked this close unnoticed. Not really—but Cashel could tell himself it might've happened.

"You're the ones with the gem," the fellow said. He raised a lens of rock crystal in a gold frame and through it studied first Cashel, then Protas and the topaz. "I'm to guide you to the next stage. Yes, I am. . . ."

He was a little fellow with no hat and a head that'd been shaved bald except for a thin circle of fine brown hair just above his ears. He carried a heavy book in his left hand; it had a medallion on the spine and iron clasps to lock the covers closed. His jaw was long, too long for a man's, and the nostrils in his little flat nose were perfectly round.

Cashel cleared his throat. "Ah," he said, "we're pleased to meet you. I'm Cashel and that's Prince Protas."

"Yes," said their guide. He wore a fine red robe with sleeves, though the hem was muddy as any garment must get in this place. Over it was a cape of gray satin covered with sequins. "Protas. And the gem."

His eye, swollen through the crystal lens, focused again on the boy. "So, Prince," he said softly, drawing out the *ess* sounds in a way Cashel didn't like. "You have the gem; do you know how to use it?"

"I'm not here to use it, sir," Protas said. He spoke calmly but he stood very straight at Cashel's side. "Master Cashel and I are carrying the amulet to where we're going, and I don't believe we've yet reached that place."

"Believe what you want, boy!" their guide said with a nervous titter.

"Things are or they aren't regardless of what you believe; and sometimes they are *and* they aren't."

"Time to be going, I'd judge," Cashel said. He didn't say *how* he judged that: it was by deciding that every heartbeat of time he spent in this place was one longer than he'd have been here if he'd had his choice. The sky was blue and clear, but thick fog had wrapped his mind ever since he and Protas arrived.

"Do you think you can give me orders because you're a big man?" their rat-faced guide said, slipping into anger with the suddenness of an icicle cracking off the slates in winter.

"You're here to guide us," said Cashel, adjusting his hands slightly. "If you're not willing to do your job, then just say so and point us the direction we're to go. But you're not much of a man if you do that."

"Not a man?" said their guide. He gave out a screeching sound. Cashel recognized it as laughter, but not until his hands had tightened on the staff. "Not a man, do you think? Well, perhaps so, but I'll guide you nonetheless."

He walked past them, splashing in the muddy water. From behind Cashel saw that the fellow's back had been cut open, likely with an axe. The ends of the ribs stuck out the gash. Inside, the organs pulsed in a general red mess, but a loop of sliced intestine oozed black liquid in a smear down the lower part of the cloak.

Protas walked straight off after their guide. His eyes were glazed in the short glimpse Cashel got of the boy's face, but he didn't hesitate. Two steps into the swamp, he'd lost both of his fine slippers with the toes curled up in tassels.

Cashel reached down and retrieved them even before Protas realized the mud had pulled them off. He sloshed them through a tongue of deeper water that reached up toward the ankle-deep path they were following, then handed them back to the boy.

"Oh!" said Protas when he realized what Cashel was reaching over his shoulder to give him. He took the slippers and said in embarrassment, "I'm sorry, Cashel. I forgot what you said."

"Keep them for later," Cashel said. "I don't think they'd do much good in this mud anyway."

"Cashel?" said the boy without turning around again. "Did we die? Is this the Underworld where we're being punished for our sins?"

"I don't think so, Protas," Cashel said. "But I'll be glad to be another place too."

"So you say!" said their guide, turning his narrow rat face to look back over his shoulder at them. "So you say, as though you knew already where you were going."

He laughed, not in a nice way. "But maybe you're right at that," he added. "No matter what place it is you're going to!"

The cattails to the left of the path shuddered. Cashel eyed them as he strode past. Something smooth and rounded rose through the black water. A bubble, he thought; the mud belching out decay.

It continued to rise, gray and gleaming above the surface: a huge fish, its head alone the size of a brood sow. The bulging eyes stared at Cashel with a malevolence that he thought was more than his imagination. He shifted his staff slightly as he passed, but the fish remained where it was: half out of the mere, but only half.

"Follow me and you won't be harmed," the guide said. "Unless I've made a mistake, of course."

It sounded to Cashel like the fellow was taunting them instead of being reassuring. This wasn't a place for a decent man to be. Whatever their guide had started as, living here for a long time would make the best man peevish.

"Carry out your duties, Master Guide," said Protas in the haughty tone Cashel'd heard from him before when he was afraid. "We understood there'd be risk in our undertakings."

The cattails were behind them. Nearabout in all directions were sloughs of dark water and mudflats mottled with slimy green algae. The only other plants were ferns whose fronds curled to knee height like feathers. Many of them were a deep maroon. On the horizon were mountains, but in this steam-hazed air Cashel couldn't guess how far away they were.

He looked behind. On bare ground their footprints were filling with water and smudging away even as he watched. When they'd stepped in the black water, they'd swirled the mud beneath, but that was settling as quickly.

Eyes watched them. Sometimes Cashel could see the head and back of the fish also, sometimes not.

He turned and cleared his throat. "Protas?" he said. "I have some bread and cheese in my wallet, and there's a bottle of ale besides. Would you like something to eat?"

This wasn't a good place for it, but none of the places they'd been

were any better. They'd been a long time since standing in the room with
Cervoran, and Cashel didn't know when the boy'd last eaten anyway.

"I'm not hungry, Cashel," Protas said carefully. "But, ah, thank you."

He's scared to death but too much a man to say so, Cashel thought, smiling inside. Aloud he said, "Well, maybe later then, after we've gotten
where we're going."

Then because it was his nature, he added, "Ah, Master Guide? Would
you care for something yourself? It's coarse fare, but it keeps me going
on the road, I've found."

"Eat your food?" the fellow said, turning his long face with a sneer.
"No, not that. But perhaps you'd like to share my meals? Shall I offer
you that? That would be in keeping with my obligation as your fellow
man, wouldn't it? *Shall* I offer you food?"

"Carry out your duties, sirrah!" Protas said sharply. "We want no
more of you than that!"

There was a deep rumble through the ground, then in the air as well.
The surface of the water ahead of them puckered. Their guide stopped,
his face frozen into a half-snarl.

"Come along!" he said, splashing onward at a quicker pace than before. His feet left narrower tracks than those of Protas following behind
him, though the mud was so soft that Cashel couldn't be sure of the details.

"What's that sound?" said Protas. "Is it thunder?"

A second shock trembled across the landscape ahead of them. This
time the ground lifted ankle high, whipping the ferns violently. A line of
shattered white foam burst over the water.

"*Come along!*" the guide shrieked, raising the hem of his tunic in order to run. The book in his left hand rocked and wobbled, but it didn't
fall into the muck as Cashel thought it might.

Cashel started running also. He didn't like it and he wasn't any good
at it either, but for a lot of reasons he didn't want to fall too far behind
the others. Fortunately the guide setting the pace was even less of a runner than Cashel.

Over these flats Cashel could follow the wave as it lifted on the horizon and spread toward them at the speed of a galloping horse. He judged
his time, then jumped to have both feet in the air when the ground rose
beneath him.

The ground settled with a gelatinous quiver as the wave passed on.

Cashel landed and sank in deep. Protas had tangled his feet and gone down, while the guide had fallen forward with a despairing shriek. His cloak and tunic had flown up; he smoothed the garments back over his tail with his right hand before rising and turning to glare at the humans he was guiding.

Cashel helped Protas to his feet. The boy's face had gone into the mud, but he'd clutched the crown to his temples with both hands.

"It's not done," said Protas in a small voice. He pointed with his right hand.

Cashel looked ahead. The third wave spreading toward them across the flats was taller than he was.

With the staff vertical in his right hand, Cashel wrapped both arms around Protas and lifted him. He kept his own legs slightly flexed. He thought of telling Protas to keep hold of the crown, but the boy'd been doing that fine the whole while he'd been carrying it. Telling him to be careful would be slighting him, and Protas didn't deserve that.

The wave threw Cashel in the air with a roar as deep and loud as a building falling. If his balance hadn't been perfect the shock would've spun him head over heels like a pinwheel. Cashel had jumped across streams from one wet rock to the next while carrying a ewe on his shoulders; he didn't tumble this time either, just rode the wave up and came down again as smoothly as if he'd stepped from a bank onto soft ground.

Very soft ground. The shock'd shaken the mud to nearly a liquid, like well-sifted flour only more so. Again Cashel sank in, this time almost to his knees.

He set Protas down, then pulled his legs out—the right and then the left. He looked around first to see if there was a rock or a log or something he could butt the quarterstaff against to push on; but there wasn't, not anywhere in this world that he'd seen so far.

The thunder of the wave rolled off in its wake. Ahead, the direction it'd come from, there was a wasteland even more barren than it'd been when Cashel first saw it. The smears of algae were now mixed unrecognizably with the mud they'd covered, and the shallow roots of the ferns had been ripped up as the plants were flung in windrows like seaweed at the tide line.

Their guide got to his feet. His dirty brown eyes had a look of fear, like a dog who'd been kicked often and expects to be kicked again, only harder.

"I can't help you now," he said. Then, angrily, "It isn't my fault! Even if I'd known she was going to act, what could I have done? If I had *that* power, would I be here?"

"We're all right," Cashel said. He nodded in the direction they'd been heading. "It'll be harder walking with this muck all stirred up, but we can do it. I'll carry you if I must. And anyway, it's settling already."

Their guide's feet were narrow so they might sink in worse than Cashel's, but the main trouble was that hauling your feet through a bog was work about as hard as anything Cashel remembered doing. But he *had* done it, and he was ready to do it again if he had to.

"You don't understand!" the guide said. "She's cut the path to the portal, I'm sure of it! And I'll be punished even though there was nothing I could do, nothing!"

"Let's go on and see what things look like," Cashel said quietly. He didn't really doubt what the rat-faced man was saying, but he'd learned long since that there could be a big difference between what people thought'd happened and what'd really happened. "Then we'll decide what to do."

"There's nothing to do!" the guide shouted. "Didn't you hear me? I'm doomed!"

"You are our guide," said Protas in a funny tone that Cashel hadn't heard from him before. The boy had his left hand on the jewel even though nothing was going to jiggle him just now. "Guide us as you're compelled to do."

"I know my duty!" the guide said peevishly. "All right, since you're so sure of yourself."

The mud was shaking down inside itself, just as Cashel'd figured it would. A skim of water formed on top and drained sluggishly toward the inlets on either side. He could see fish lifting their heads from the muddy water every once in a while. Occasionally one took a gulp of air before sinking out of sight.

The guide set off at a good pace. The sun was brighter, burning through the haze as a distinct disk instead of being a smear of light beyond the overcast. The flats reeked before the earthquake, but the shocks had stirred them to worse. Death, very old death, was so present that Cashel thought he ought to be able to see it.

Protas stumbled along with his arm over his face so that his sleeve covered his nose. Cashel doubted that helped, but the boy wasn't complaining.

The guide didn't seem to notice the smell, which was about what you'd expect. Cashel tried not to look at the tear in the fellow's back, but he couldn't avoid seeing the gnats curling from the wound and back like a cloud of smoke.

"I see something," said Protas, lowering his arm to speak. "Cashel, I see a rock!"

"Yes, a rock and on it the portal that would take you to where you'd trouble me no more!" said their guide. "And the water that cuts you off from it, do you see that too? You'll never reach it, and you've doomed me by your failure!"

Cashel didn't say anything till he'd reached the new shore. The shocks that'd stirred things up came from the land slipping here to let the water through. The channel wasn't terribly wide, no more than a bowman could span with a good chance of hitting his target on the other side . . . but it could've been the whole Inner Sea and not been a worse barrier.

"Cashel, I can't swim," said Protas in a small voice.

"Nor can I, lad," said Cashel. "So we'll have to find another way."

He turned to their guide and gestured toward the channel. He said, "Is there a way around this?"

"How would I know?" the guide snarled. "It just appeared, didn't it? But even a louse should be able to guess that if She cut the pathway once, She can do it again—if that's even necessary."

Cashel smiled. The little fellow had a right to be sarcastic. Besides, it reminded Cashel of his sister. He thought about how Ilna was doing, and especially he thought about Sharina; but he had other things to deal with before he was back with them.

There wasn't anything to build a raft out of. They could maybe make floats out of their clothes and buoy Protas up, but Cashel knew from experience that he himself'd sink like a stone without more than that. People tended to think a lot of his bulk had to be fat, not muscle; but they were wrong.

Of course if the new channel was shallow enough to wade—

A fish lifted its head from right in the middle, where the path to the rock must've gone before the land sank. It was the biggest fish Cashel had seen in this place; apart from whales, it was the biggest fish he'd seen ever.

Its mouth gaped open, showing a long arched tunnel with the bright red pillars of the gill rakers to either side at the back. The mouth closed.

The fish sank back slowly, leaving a swirl of water that lapped at Cashel's feet.

The fish didn't have teeth. If it hadn't been the size of a good-sized ship and had a mouth that could swallow a wagon, that might've been reassuring.

"Master Guide?" said Cashel, his lips pursed as he thought. Ordinarily he'd have said "friend" when he didn't know a fellow's name, but not here. "Is there a place anywhere around that we can find trees to build a raft?"

The forest might be a month away and besides, that wouldn't solve the problem of the fish, but—

"There are no trees here," said their guide. "There are cattails and there are ferns; and there is mud, that is all."

"Well, we'll gather cattails, then," Cashel said, nodding as he worked the business out in his head. "They'll float, and with enough of them we can—"

"That would take too long," said Protas in his funny voice. His left hand was back on his head again. He stretched out his right arm with the fingers tight together.

"It's the quickest way I can come up with, Protas," Cashel said, not loud but making it clear to anybody listening that he wasn't looking for an argument. "The fish is another thing, but maybe if we set the raft on fire at one end—"

The boy's lips didn't move, but somebody started chanting words of power in a voice like a cicada shrilling. Cashel couldn't hear the sounds as words, but the rhythms were unmistakable to anybody who'd heard wizards in the past. He looked at Protas in surprise and started to speak.

He shut his mouth again. Whatever the boy was doing and however he was doing it, interrupting him wasn't going to change things for the better.

Their guide stared in wide-eyed horror. Cashel had wondered if maybe he was doing the chanting, but the expression on the fellow's nasty little face proved that wasn't so.

"Do you know what's happening, then?" Cashel asked. The guide didn't seem to have heard the question.

Wizardlight as bright and blue as a sunstruck glacier shivered over the surface of the channel. The water stirred and humped as the great fish started to rise again. The keening insect voice shouted a syllable that Cashel almost could hear.

A blue flash lighted the channel to its muddy bottom, showing the fish as a shadow with its bones as darker shadows. It was even bigger than Cashel had guessed. It dove toward the bottom with a convulsive flip of its serpentine tail.

The water was opaque for a moment. Then it froze into yellow ice.

Protas swayed; Cashel caught him in the crook of his left arm. He'd had a lot of experience with the way wizards wore themselves out with their art, but he hadn't had a hint of Protas being a wizard himself. . . .

The boy opened his eyes. "What happened, Cashel?" he said. Hard as he tried to hide it, he sounded scared.

"We've got a way across the channel now, Protas," Cashel said. He looked at the guide. Try as he might to be charitable, he loathed the foul little man. "That's right, isn't it?" he demanded.

"You didn't tell me you could control the talisman," their guide whispered. "You should've told me. I didn't think anyone could. . . ."

Cashel's expression was getting harder. "Yes, I heard you," the guide said. He licked his lips; his tongue was forked. "Yes, you can cross. We must cross, yes."

He walked onto the ice without speaking further. Cashel patted the boy's shoulder. "Let's go, Protas," he said. "We've got our path."

"Yes, Cashel," said the boy. "Ah—is it safe?"

"Safer than staying around here, I'd judge," Cashel said, stepping onto the cold, hard surface. The ice was a maze of cracks, not slippery and not even unpleasant to walk on after the warm mud.

Protas winced as he followed. His feet didn't have Cashel's calluses, but this short hike wouldn't give him frostbite. They walked across quickly. Cashel glanced over his shoulder to make sure nothing was following them; the mudflats were the same steaming wasteland they'd been before.

The rock was just that: one rock, a spike of basalt sticking up like a fingertip from the mud on the other side of the ice bridge. It was chest-high on Cashel and a little above the boy's head. There was a symbol on the top of it, but this time it had one more angle than a hand has fingers.

"We're to get up on this?" Cashel said politely, pointing.

"Yes, unless you plan to stay here," snapped the rat-faced man. Then he wrinkled his short nose and said, "Get up there, of course! Leave here before you cause me even more trouble."

Cashel lifted the boy onto the rock. He prodded the ground with his big toe to find a suitable spot to butt his staff. It was firmer here than it'd been anywhere on the other side of the channel.

Their guide looked back. The ice was already turning to slush, and bits were breaking off the edges.

"I don't know how I'll return," he said. "And I don't care! You'll be gone, that's all I ask!"

"That's all we ask too, Master Guide," Cashel said. With his left hand on top of the stone and his right braced on his quarterstaff, he lifted himself to sit beside Protas, then got to his feet.

"You should have told me you commanded the talisman," the guide whispered. He held out the book in both hands. *"Methan meruithan man!"* he boomed in a voice whose resonance didn't seem to come from his narrow, broken chest.

The points of the figure lit like rubies and the light spread rapidly through the lines connecting them. Protas clung tightly to Cashel's belt with one hand and the crown with the other.

"You should have told me. . . ." The guide's voice came as a ghostly murmur. The stone underfoot vanished.

SHARINA KEPT HER right arm around Tenoctris as the convoy jerked and squealed up track into the hills surrounding Calf's Head Bay. A Blood Eagle officer drove the gig this time. Tenoctris had protested at first, but she'd agreed when Sharina pointed out that her strength was better conserved for her art.

"Lord Waldron planned to have his soldiers improve the road," Sharina said as the gig jounced around a particularly bad switchback. It'd be a wonder if all the wagons behind them made the corner without losing a wheel or overbalancing. "I suppose he needed them too badly against the plants."

As much as anything, she was speaking to take her mind off the thoughts that swirled about in her mind. The last minutes before dawn could be a bad time. Sharina's fears didn't have faces or even forms, but in the gray dimness they were all too real.

"I wish there were more I could do," Tenoctris said. "I've had fine opportunities to observe and study, though. The forces Cervoran and the Green Woman are arraying are . . ."

She turned to Sharina. The lantern held by the groom leading the gig threw just enough light back for Sharina to see her friend's wan smile.

"They're like the Outer Sea," Tenoctris said. "Each of them is. I find it hard to imagine two such powerful wizards being perfectly balanced in strength, and yet that's their weakness as well. Because I can see their structures while I remain outside them, I could undercut either one and bring him down."

She grinned, this time with her natural good humor. "Or *her* down, I suppose," she added. "Though I'm not sure gender is really a valid concept with Cervoran and the Green Woman."

"While they both exist," Sharina said, filling in what Tenoctris had left unsaid, "they control one another. But if one destroys the other, we have nothing but our own devices to oppose the remaining wizard."

They'd reached the top of the ridge. The new track led north and west along the curve of the hills; their wheels bumped over stumps. The crest had been wooded a few days ago, but the trees had been cut for fuel during the fighting. In the darkness to their left, soldiers were putting on their armor and forming ranks with muted grumbles and clanking.

"Yes," said Tenoctris. "And while Cervoran claims to be our only defense against annihilation by the Green Woman, I don't trust his good faith so far that I'd choose to be the instrument of giving him unbridled power."

In the gig ahead, Double pointed toward a place on the summit of the final hill of the range. The ground beyond sloped raggedly toward the sea, visible now as lines of foam picked out by the graying sky. The driver, a Blood Eagle who never let his eyes rest directly on his passenger, obediently pulled up. Sharina noticed with a smile that he immediately jumped out of the vehicle, almost certainly without direction.

"Pull in beside them," Sharina said to their own driver, raising her voice as the wheels bounced them noisily over rock from which the soil had been worn by recent traffic. To Tenoctris, more quietly as they swayed together with the gig, she said, "You say Cervoran, Tenoctris. You mean Double, don't you?"

The gig rocked to a halt; the women waited. Their horse backed a step as Double lurched in their direction as he got down from the other vehicle.

"Double *is* Cervoran," Tenoctris said in a dry undertone. "Is Cervoran or is the mirror image of Cervoran. I don't know whether or not another Cervoran exists, but I'm sure of what's in our presence now."

The six heavy wagons following the gigs pulled in one by one, guided by Double's imperious gestures. Five carried long posts, most of which had until the previous day been the roof trusses and ridgepoles of houses in Mona. Many of the city's residents now lived in stunned misery under tarpaulins in the ruins of what had been their dwellings. After the crisis was over they'd be paid compensation and perhaps they'd understand the necessity of what'd happened to them; but perhaps they wouldn't understand even then.

If matters went the wrong way, the army of hellplants would destroy them in those same ruined houses and it wouldn't matter if they understood why. Sharina didn't understand why herself.

"Tenoctris?" she said. "The plants, the Green Woman . . . Cervoran even, all the things that have threatened the kingdom over the past two years. Surely there's someone behind them, some *thing* behind them. Something that hates Mankind. Doesn't there have to be?"

"Because human beings are so uniquely important?" Tenoctris said. "Because anything that happens in the cosmos has to be directed by men or at Mankind?"

"I don't mean that," Sharina said, flushing. The wizard's smile took some of the edge off the words, but it was there nonetheless. "I know it's not that, but so many things are happening. . . ."

Tenoctris gestured toward the sea below them to the south. The sky to the east was orange, slanting color across the wave tops.

"How many waves would you say there are?" Tenoctris asked. "Too many to count, at least. And they keep coming."

Crews of laborers, civilians who'd hiked up with the wagons, were lifting the materials out of the beds. The last wagon had an escort of soldiers. In it were rolls of sailcloth and the silver service from the royal palace.

"Yes," agreed Sharina. "But they always did. That's nothing to do with—"

She waved her hand, indicating not the sea but the mass of hellplants beginning to stir as the sky brightened. Around them were ripples in the marshy ground. The scorpions were returning to the reservoirs in the barrels of the plants where they sheltered while the sun was up.

"—those things. Wizards. Monsters!"

"No, dear," Tenoctris said. "But if a storm struck this coast, the waves would be a thousand times stronger. They'd eat away the shoreline, they'd flood the fields. Ships would be swamped, people drowned, and it'd all be normal. Nobody would think anything was wrong, except that it was a bad storm; perhaps the sort of storm that arises only once in a lifetime."

She nodded down at the fields and the ranks of hellplants starting to advance again. "What we're seeing here, what we've seen in the past two years and will see for another year still, happens only once in a millennium. But it's just as natural as the waves and the storms. Only very much worse."

Sharina put her arms around herself and hugged them tight. She wished Cashel were here. She wished—

Tenoctris laid her hand over Sharina's. Neither woman spoke, but the touch was a reminder that Sharina had friends and that the kingdom had defenders.

Horns and trumpets were signaling. The troops were in place behind earthworks and trenches; the day before some units had built stockades, but all the wood had been burned in the course of the fighting.

Waldron had sited the catapults and ballistas just below the hillcrest. Sharina guessed there were forty or fifty of them all told. They were high enough on the slope to shoot over the infantry positions, but they weren't on the ridge where they'd block the road. The army artillery was on wheeled carriages, but the naval weapons were mounted on bases that'd obviously been knocked together quickly, generally from house beams. The crews of the larger weapons were cranking back their levers against springs made from the neck sinews of oxen.

Captain Ascor commanded the company guarding Sharina this morning. He was going from one man to the next, checking equipment and talking quietly to his troops. If everything went as it should, the Blood Eagles were above the battle and would have nothing to do but watch. If matters went badly wrong, they might not be able to save the princess's life—but they would certainly die before she did. They had their duty.

Sharina smiled: Princess Sharina had her duty also, to stand on the battlefield as a symbol to the royal army of what it was fighting for. The kingdom couldn't watch the army's sacrifice, but the regent would.

The sun wasn't quite above the horizon, but the sky was bright and the hellplants were moving forward on the plain below. Their smooth, slow progress reminded Sharina of slime oozing down an incline. The plants were actually moving uphill, but the comparison to slime was still valid. Behind the earthworks, officers called orders to their men in hoarse voices.

The workmen on the ridgeline were digging in the posts at intervals of ten or a dozen feet, tamping earth in around them to hold them upright. They looked like the stakes of a crude fence running generally east to west along the hilltop. Other men were carrying bolts of sailcloth and dropping them between pairs of posts, but what that was in aid of was beyond Sharina.

"Do you know what they're doing?" she said quietly in Tenoctris' ear.

"I do not," said the older woman. Her attention was on Double, though he seemed simply to be standing with his head bowed. He held the wooden athame point-down before him. "I will say that at the moment there's a . . . a gap, a hole almost. Surrounding Cervoran. There's a stupendous concentration of forces here, and none of it is touching Cervoran."

Sharina licked her lips and glanced down at the plants. They were spreading slightly apart as they advanced toward the fortifications. She looked back at Tenoctris and said, "Why? Why isn't he—defending himself?"

"I think he's conserving his strength," Tenoctris said simply. "And he has strength, dear. He's a *very* powerful wizard."

An artillery officer bawled an order; his subordinate jerked the lanyard of a big catapult. The slip-hook flew back, clanging on the frame, and the long vertical arm crashed forward into the padded bar. A missile shot down toward the plain.

The nearest plants were still a quarter mile from the breastworks and farther than that from the artillery on the ridge. Sharina frowned; she knew a big catapult could throw its ball that far, but she didn't think it could hit a target as small as an individual plant.

The projectile, a sealed jar, was light-colored and easy to track against the black fields. It snapped out in nearly a straight line, quite different from the high arc that Sharina'd expected a catapult projectile to describe.

The missile smashed squarely into the body of a hellplant and shattered into pale fragments. It took a noticeable length of time for the sound of the impact, a hollow *whop*, to reach the top of the hill. An instant later the quicklime burst into snarling, spitting tendrils of white fire, shriveling the plant's dark bulk.

"How did they do that?" Sharina said in amazement. "How did they hit a target so far away?"

She was speaking toward Tenoctris, but of course she didn't expect an answer. To her surprise an artilleryman, part of the crew of a small ballista which wasn't powerful enough to shoot yet, turned and called out, "We set range stakes last night, Your Highness. The ground-pounders, they got smoked good when they attacked, but we went along behind 'em putting white spears in the field every fifty paces. For this morning, you see."

"Oh!" said Sharina. "I'd seen them. I didn't know what they were."

In fact she'd thought the white poles were stripped saplings or some vestige of the farms that'd been in the bay before the plants invaded. She looked down to her left to where Lord Waldron had planted his standard. The army commander was narrow-minded, stubborn, and a stiff-necked aristocrat . . . but he was either smart enough to have made preparations to use the artillery accurately, or he was smart enough to listen to a junior officer who'd come up with the idea.

The kingdom was well served by its army in more ways than the fact its soldiers were willing to die for the civilians who paid their wages. But it was well served in that as well.

More weapons, catapults and ballistas both, were shooting now. The crash of their arms against the stops echoed around the bowl of hills. Crewmen grunted as they bent to the bars of the windlasses that slowly recocked their weapons.

Not all the jars of quicklime hit plants, but many did. The hiss of lime slaking in plant tissue, devouring both the hellplants and the scorpions swimming in their central tanks, became a noticeable backdrop to the shooting and human voices.

Even the missiles that missed splashed long fiery smears across the wet fields. They caused advancing plants to hesitate and raising the spirits of the soldiers watching. Men who'd been crouching nervously behind the breastworks began to cheer.

The sun was throwing the plants' shadows onto the hills to the northwest. By its light, Sharina saw fresh forms humping up out of the surf. More of the creatures were arriving on the beach. Sharina swallowed. The troops would fight hard, but . . .

As the sun climbed, mist rose from the fields. That was more disconcerting to Sharina than the fact that plants were walking. Every clear cool morning in Barca's Hamlet she'd seen mist form over standing water, but then it burned away as the sun rose higher. Here in Calf's Head Bay she watched the opposite: it was as if the sun were wringing water from the soil and spreading it as a shroud over the advancing monsters.

The Green Woman had formed her creatures by wizardry. At least here within the half-circle of hills, her art ruled the weather also.

The hellplants had come within range of the smaller ballistas, which began to fire with sharp cracks. They were loaded with quarrels whose usual square bronze heads were replaced by small jars of quicklime. Sharina had wondered how effective they'd be, but she saw a missile from the weapon just below her plunge into the barrel of a hellplant. For a moment there was no response; then the creature's body ripped open in a gush of steam, and the remainder sank into a smoking pile.

"That's what he's doing with the silver!" Tenoctris said.

She was probably speaking to herself, but the delight in her tone jerked Sharina's head around to look. The last of the posts had been dug in on the ridgeline and the crews had almost finished hanging the sail-cloth between them. It formed a long canvas screen across the north side of the bowl. It wouldn't stop a galloping horse, let alone a plant that weighed more than an ox, so it had to have something to do with Double's wizardry. Whatever his ultimate purposes, Sharina'd be glad to see him to unleash something against the army of plants right now.

Workmen were carrying loads of silver—urns, salvers, ewers, and in one case a huge bowl for mixing wine with water—from the wagon and placing it on the ground in front of the canvas screen. Each load went more or less between a pair of support posts.

A soldier followed each laborer, guarding him and more particularly guarding the silver. Was anybody likely to run off with a cup now, when on the plain below men and monsters battled for the fate of the world?

Sharina grinned. Yes, of course somebody was likely to do that. Given half a chance the workmen might abscond with *all* the silver, even if they were told it was the only thing standing between mankind and the inhuman army advancing on them. Many people took a very short-term view of things—and prospered.

Short-term thinking wouldn't work this time, though, but Lord Tadai or whoever'd turned the silver over to Double had taken precautions. Soldiers weren't notably more honest than civilians, but they *were* disciplined.

"Tenoctris?" Sharina said. "I see what they're doing with the silver, but I don't understand why."

"It's a contagion spell, dear," Tenoctris said. She probably thought she was explaining. "The wood and cloth simply create a material framework by which Cervoran will form the silver."

The last of the plate had been arranged in front of the screen and the workmen were walking back to the wagons. The soldiers gathered under their officer, talking in quiet, worried voices and looking toward the plain. They'd carried out their orders by delivering the silver, but there were obviously places where they'd be more useful now than standing on the hillcrest. Volunteering themselves into the carnage below would take a great deal of moral as well as physical courage, though, and they were hesitating.

The sun was a flattened orange ball on the eastern horizon. The artillery continued to shoot, but the missiles were aimed at the second wave of hellplants just arrived from the sea. At least a hundred plants had been reduced to smoldering corpses on their march to the hills, but twice that number were now too close for the catapults and ballistas to strike.

The plants that'd spent the night in the fields, all those that'd survived the rain of quicklime, had reached the human fortifications. Spears, billhooks, and torches on pike shafts stabbed over the earthworks—and still they came on.

Double, standing at the east end of the screen, roused from his trance. He gave Tenoctris a thick-lipped smile, then pointed his athame toward the nearest pile of plate: a large serving dish and a pair of goblets set with tourmalines.

"Eulamon," Double chanted. "*Restoutus restouta zerosi!*"

The air about the dishes went rosy with a fog of wizardlight. The silver blurred.

"*Benchuch bachuch chuch . . . ,*" Double called. His voice was thin but so piercing that Sharina had the feeling that everyone around Calf's Head Bay could hear the words. "*Ousiri agi ousiri!*"

The haze thickened. A thin shimmering sheet spread above it, orange with the reflected light of the sunrise.

"Eulamon," Double chanted, shifting his black wooden dagger so that it pointed at the next pile of silver. The salver and cups of the initial pile had vanished; the tourmalines lay on the ground. "*Restoutus restouta zerosi!*"

At a dozen places in the trenches dug in front of the line of breastworks, soldiers threw torches to ignite the piles of brush prepared for the purpose. There hadn't been enough fuel to fill the entire frontage, but where the fires rose to full life, the plants trapped in them struggled and died. Green bodies ruptured, pouring saltwater onto the flames, which then gushed out white steam.

The flames damped temporarily, but the fires were too hot for a few barrelfuls of water to put them out. They blazed again, shrinking still further the blackened remains of the dead hellplants.

"They don't back away or try to escape," Sharina said. What she'd just seen made her queasy. "They throw themselves into the fires."

"They're seaweed, dear," Tenoctris said quietly. She continued to watch Double, chanting as he formed the final piles of silver into a gleaming wall in front of the canvas screen. "They have no minds of their own. The wizard who controls them cares no more about their feelings than you do about those of a leaf of lettuce."

More plants came on, moving with the slow certainty of clouds drifting across the summer sky. The thickening mist had turned them to dark lumps; they began to lap upward to cover the earthworks on the higher ground.

Where there weren't prepared firesets, the hellplants swayed down into the trenches and wallowed there for a moment. Picked soldiers, generally light infantry who ordinarily fought with javelins and didn't wear armor, stood on the breastworks and hurled bags of quicklime into the open reservoirs in the plants' bodies.

Sharina had heard Liane discuss the plan with Lord Waldron and his aides, but she'd doubted whether the soldiers would throw their small missiles accurately in the stress of the attack. In general, they did: the bags splashed into the water and exploded in fire-shot steam.

But the plants came on, bubbling and sizzling. They drew themselves out of the trenches with their tentacles, then reached for the human de-fenders. Ignoring the fire inside them, they snatched the spears and bill-hooks being driven into their green flesh.

Supported by the plants behind them, the leaders half climbed, half tore down the breastworks. Light ballistas slashed at them as artillerymen risked hitting their own comrades in the hope of stopping the monsters which the infantry alone couldn't. Bolts which punched their charge through a hellplant's body walls usually tore the creature apart even though the same amount of quicklime thrown into the reservoir from above wasn't effective.

Some of the soldiers ducked low and thrust their swords into the tendrils on which the plants crawled. For the most part the men died in vain, seized by tentacles and either torn apart or flung to their deaths in the plain below. One plant toppled and couldn't rise again, though its massive body crushed the man who'd crippled it.

Sharina licked her lips. While her mind was elsewhere, her hand had reached unnoticed for the horn hilt of the Pewle knife she wore under her cloak. She wouldn't need the weapon today—the Blood Eagles would see to that—but soon, perhaps. . . .

"Tenoctris," she said. "I think they're going to break through shortly. At the very worst I can outrun any plant so I'm going to stay with the army, but you'd better—"

"Wait," said Tenoctris. She raised her left hand without taking her eyes from Double. "Hush please, dear."

"*Kato katoi . . . ,*" Double said, pointing his athame at the center of the long film of silver shimmering in the air beside him. "*Kataoikouse neoi. . . .*"

The silver film rippled and seemed to stiffen. Tenoctris gripped Sharina's wrist and walked with quick determination to the right. *Toward Double,* Sharina thought, but that was only incidentally true. Tenoctris was leading her to the side where they wouldn't be standing between the mirror and the battle at midslope.

"*Abriao iao!*" Double shouted.

The silver twitched, changing in smooth lines that Sharina couldn't have described though she watched it happen. Because the film formed a perfect mirror, Sharina saw not the thing itself but a subtly distorted image of the battlefield below.

The mirror caught the rising sun and threw it back as a point of white fury at nearly right angles to its position in the sky. The beam sawed across the hellplants climbing the breastworks at the northern edge of the half-bowl. Double continued to chant.

A plant exploded in steam, then a second, and after a slight delay a third. The point of light touched also the head of a soldier lunging forward behind his spear. He had time to scream as his helmet melted in spatters of bronze; then he fell backward. The plant in which his spear wobbled collapsed inward and sank down into the trench from which it'd heaved itself.

"Sound recall!" Sharina shouted. "Captain Ascor, sound recall! Now! Get the men out of the way of this wizard's work!"

She'd drawn the big knife and stepped toward Double when she saw the soldier die at the mirror's focus . . . but the wizard was doing no more than the ballista crews had done, risking their fellows for the chance of saving the kingdom. She would pray to the Lady for that man and for all the brave men who'd died today, but first she must survive the day.

Ascor looked from her to the battlefield, then barked an order to the cornicene standing beside him. The signaler put his curved horn to his lips and blew the five-note recall signal: a long, three short, and a final long.

Sharina'd thought Ascor might protest: Princess Sharina was acting ruler of the Isles, but she had no authority on the battlefield except to issue commands to Lord Waldron himself. Ascor obeyed her anyway, perhaps because the bodyguard regiment considered itself separate from—and above—the army as a whole, but also because here on the hillcrest it was obvious that getting the troops out of the way immediately was the best way to save their lives.

That wasn't obvious from Lord Waldron's position in the center of the fortifications farther down the slope. A courier left the Waldron's entourage, obviously heading for the signaler blowing the unauthorized call. The man slipped and stumbled on the hillside; he'd lost at least his helmet in the fighting.

Sharina took off her cloak and waved it toward Lord Waldron. He wouldn't understand what she meant, but it might be enough to convince him that there was a good reason for what probably had seemed to him mutiny.

The cornicene continued the call; other signalers took it up, horns and trumpets both. From where she stood Sharina could see troops abandoning their positions and streaming up the slopes. The men who'd survived this long probably thought the recall was the hand of providence, saving their lives at a time when they were sure they were doomed.

Many troops *hadn't* survived; Sharina could see that too. Close combat with the hellplants was a sentence of death, particularly now that most of the fuel had been burned.

The soldiers close to where the mirror's deadly beam struck were already retreating. They were fleeing, more accurately, throwing down weapons and equipment, but it was wizardry that'd panicked them rather than the enemy—even this unnatural enemy.

The silver bowed and shivered under Double's chanted commands; its point of focus cut like a fiery razor everywhere it touched. The hellplants' sodden flesh burst and blackened, leaving behind only masses of stinking compost as the light moved on.

Twice Sharina saw a fleeing man step into the directed blaze. Neither was at the focus, but they were close enough to it that one died screaming and the other's steaming flesh oozed through the segments of his armor as his body toppled backward.

Lady, cover them with the cloak of Your protection. Lady, may their spirits dwell with You.

The mirror shifted, drawing its light along hellplants bunched at the line of the fortifications. Even when the troops had abandoned their positions, the works delayed the massive, sluggish attackers. The mere touch of the light did as much sudden damage as the heaviest jars of quicklime hurled by the artillery.

Waldron must finally have seen what was happening. He and the knot of cavalrymen around him, his personal retainers, backed out of their redoubt with their faces toward the plants; his four signalers joined the general chorus of Recall. The courier, halfway between the command group and Sharina on the northern crest, stopped in puzzlement and looked back toward the army commander.

Sharina had expected cheering; there was none. The troops who'd been fighting the hellplants were too exhausted for enthusiasm even at a miracle that'd saved their lives for the time being.

The mirror continued to warp and shimmer. It'd initially faced nearly due south, catching the sun in the southeast. As the sun rose higher and the mirror's focused light grew even more devastating, Double drew it around the whole smooth curve of the bay. There was no escaping its beam, but the plants didn't bother trying. They continued to waddle up the slope, oblivious of the shrunken, smoldering carcasses of their fellows.

The line of fortifications was clear of living plants. Where there was motion, it was a wisp of steam lifted by the breeze or a numbed soldier crawling out of the pile of corpses which had concealed him.

Double moved his ravening light onto the squadron of hellplants which had come out of the sea since sunrise. The dank miasma that'd half-hidden the plain now burned away in swirls. Wet fields steamed, the stubble burning and the soggy furrows crumbling into arid dust as the light swept over them.

Calf's Head Bay was again free of the monsters which had swarmed over it. The tide washed in, bringing only the normal wrack of foam and flotsam.

"Mekisthi!" shouted Double. The film of silver, sunstruck and brilliant, vanished like the dew. A shining track on the rocky soil marked where it'd fallen when the spell suspending it had ceased.

Sharina looked at her shadow in amazement; it slanted sharply eastward. The battle had gone on from daybreak to well after noon, when she would've guessed that less than an hour had passed.

The stench of burned flesh and rotted vegetable matter had risen even to the hillcrest; a score of fires were burning on the plain. Nothing now moved but the smoke.

"I am Cervoran!" Double screamed triumphantly; and, screaming, fell backward, drained by the exertion spent in his art.

"A *very* powerful wizard," Tenoctris repeated quietly.

Chapter

12

"THESE LOOK LIKE grapes," said Ilna doubtfully, using her left thumb and forefinger to pluck one of a bunch of purple fruit. It hung from the large-leafed vine which wound about the Osage orange forming a stretch of the hedge on their right side.

"They *are* grapes, Ilna," Merota said in surprise.

"Indeed, dear heart," said Chalcus. "What else is it that they would be?"

"Oh," said Ilna, squeezing the fruit against the roof of her mouth with her tongue. "I thought grapes grew one by one; the ones I've seen in the borough. These are in bunches."

"Oh, muscadines," said Merota dismissively. "These are much better!"

And perhaps they were. At any rate, the skin wasn't as thick as what Ilna was used to and the juicy pulp was even sweeter than she'd expected. She'd have willingly accepted a tart mouthful to've avoided being embarrassed by not knowing something that "everybody knew." Everybody knew but Ilna os-Kenset, the peasant from Haft.

"Wild grapes are tasty things, to be sure," said Chalcus, twisting off a small bunch with his left hand alone. "These are the kind they grow for wine in great plantations, good as well. And it's no surprise that they'd be the planted sort here rather than the wild, not so?"

"We drank beer in Barca's Hamlet," Ilna said, her voice expressionless. "Bitter beer at that, since we brewed it with germander instead of hops."

If she'd never left home, she wouldn't have been constantly embarrassed by her own ignorance. She'd—

The anger swirling in her mind—but only her mind—subsided. If she'd never left home, she wouldn't have met Chalcus and Merota. It was hard to remember how life had felt before they'd come into it, because the only details in that gray expanse were the frequent flashes of blazing, frustrated fury.

"We've got our pick of fruits and nuts, surely," Ilna said aloud. "Perhaps if we continue searching we'll find a field of barley? I'd say 'wheat,' but as you know, I'm not an optimist."

"Or we could see what roast chimaera tastes like," said Chalcus. "Assuming we can build a fire, as I trust we could manage."

Ilna smiled faintly. The sailor was probably joking as she'd been joking—more or less—but the question of food did concern her. She didn't need meat—she'd almost never eaten it as a child—but bread or at least porridge would be good. Exploring the entire maze on their own would take months or years if it was even possible. The little folk who lived here should know its ins and outs. . . .

While her companions ate grapes and talked with the ease of long acquaintance, Ilna's fingers worked. She could feel eyes on her, though she knew from experience that if she snapped her head around she'd see only a blur before the watchers vanished. One of the little folk was staring at her from the holly to her left at this very moment.

Ilna turned slightly to the right. "Chalcus?" she said in a calm, pleasant tone. "Merota; I want you both to close your eyes now."

"Why—" Merota said. The child must've seen the cold anger on Chalcus' face—not at her, but at what she'd done—because she instantly screwed her eyes shut.

Ilna used both hands to spread her knotted pattern toward the holly. There was a tiny squeal and a thrashing within the hard leaves.

"All right," she said to her companions, hiding the fabric in her sleeve without taking the time to unpick it. She stepped quickly to the hedge. "You can look now."

She paused for a moment, then reached through the tangled branches with her left hand and pulled out the little man whom her pattern had paralyzed. He was as wiry as a squirrel; even Chalcus, the most tightly muscular man Ilna had ever seen, carried more fat under his skin.

The little man—Ilna refused to call them the Prey, though she didn't doubt that was their place in the garden's society—was as wide-eyed as a hooked bass; he'd been caught with his mouth half open. Ilna laid him on the ground and quickly trussed his arms behind his back with her noose.

She gave the free end of the silken rope to Chalcus. "I'm going to wake him up now," she explained. She brought the fabric out of her sleeve and undid several knots in a precise sequence. "He may try to run."

"There's never been such a wizard as you, dear heart," the sailor said; half-jesting, but only half.

"It's no more wizardry than what I've seen you do with your sword," Ilna said sharply. She didn't like talking about her skills, in part because talk reminded her that she'd gained them in Hell. It would've been closer to the truth to call her a demon than a wizard. . . .

She spread the revised pattern before the little man's staring eyes. He gave a convulsive leap before he even blinked. In midair, halfway to the holly, the rope snapped tight and jerked him down to the grass with a thump.

"Sister take him!" Chalcus shouted, quickly wrapping the silk around his left hand. He'd been holding it with his fingers alone. If he'd been even slightly less quick or less strong, the little man would've jerked free and escaped into the hedge with the rope.

The little man jumped again, this time in the opposite direction. Chalcus threw his right arm in front of his face, expecting the captive to go for his eyes or throat. His sword winked in the unchanging sunlight, point upward where it wouldn't spit the little fellow by accident. Instead he sailed over Chalcus' shoulder, trying to escape to the Osage orange.

Again the noose snubbed him up. When he hit the ground this time he curled into a ball and lay there. His breath hissed, and small bubbles of foam formed between his lips.

"I had him, dear one," Chalcus said with a hint of reproach. "You needn't have done that."

"I did nothing!" Ilna snapped, unreasonably angry at the situation. "Did he hit himself too hard on the ground?"

Merota knelt by the little man and stroked his cheek. "He's afraid, Ilna," she said. "He's shivering here! Feel him."

The little man's eyes were open but there was no more mind within them than in a pair of oysters. "We aren't going to hurt you," Ilna said, more harshly than she'd intended. "We just want to ask you some questions."

The little man didn't speak or even move, unless you counted his violent trembling as movement. Voices chittered in the hedges on both sides.

"*Please,*" Merota said. "He's really frightened. Can't we let him go, please?"

"Yes, of course," said Ilna, bending over the little form. Standing he wouldn't come up to more than her waist. She was furious—at the little man, at herself, and at life.

Mostly at herself, of course; as usual. She'd used her skills to throw a harmless creature into numb terror for no benefit to herself. That was the kind of monster that *she* was.

When Ilna'd loosed the bonds she straightened and looped the rope back around her waist. The little man stayed where he was, still trembling.

"You can go now, sir," Merota said in a tone of stilted formality. He trembled.

Ilna's cheeks were stiff with disgust and rage. The part of her that'd grown up with normal people wanted to damn the little man to the Underworld for making her feel this way—

And the other part of her was sick, knowing that by trapping him that way she *had* sent him to a Hell which'd consumed him as completely as the place a misstep had taken Ilna os-Kenset. She hadn't meant to do that to him any more than she'd meant to do it to herself; but she had, and the consequences were her responsibility.

Ilna picked up the little man in both hands and carried him back to the hedge from which she'd taken him. This time the holly jabbed her because she wasn't trying to avoid the sharp leaves. She *needed* to be punished.

"There," she said, turning to her companions. "Let's get on from here, shall we?"

She'd left her former captive in a crotch among the scaly branches, his head higher than his feet. He'd come around in his own time or he wouldn't; she'd done what he could.

There was a scrabbling in the hedge; Ilna looked back. The holly twitched and the little man was gone.

If I could believe in the Great Gods, I would thank them now.

"Aye, there's nothing here to hold us," Chalcus said easily. "Is there a direction in particular—"

"They let Dee go," peeped a tiny voice. Then, in a chorus like frogs in springtime, *"They let Dee go!"*

Little faces were staring from the hedges on both sides. There were more than Ilna could count on both hands.

Chalcus lowered the point of his sword to the ground. Merota put her right hand in Ilna's left and edged closer.

"Princes?" said the little woman peering from the place in the holly where Ilna had snatched her captive. "I am Auta. Have you come to save us?"

"Get the firewood up here!" Donria shouted. "We're going to burn down the gates!"

"I don't think we'll need that, lad," said the ghost in Garric's mind. *"The gate leaves don't close so tightly. You can get your axe through and lift the bar if they were in too big a hurry to pin it."*

And what's the chance of that? Garric thought, but that was just a gasp of exhausted despair. Nothing seemed very practical at the moment, but that wasn't going to keep him from trying. He knew—he *remembered*—that Carus had won a good number of his battles by pressing in just this fashion, for the opportunity that the enemy shouldn't have given him—but had regardless, because people make mistakes and frightened people make even more mistakes.

"Come on," he muttered to Metz. Duzi! but his right shoulder hurt, hurt like fire! There was nothing better for the wound than using it, though, and there wasn't any choice besides.

Garric stepped into the bog. He sank to his knees as expected but slogged on. It wasn't but ten feet—two double paces—to the gate, though he'd often run a mile with less effort than this took him.

"What are we doing?" Metz asked, wheezing between the words. He was at Garric's side, moving a little more easily than Garric did since he was more used to this accursed swamp.

"We're going to open the gate," Garric said. Then he added, "The ground's solid inside but we've got to get there."

Metz's uncles had followed also. One'd been badly bloodied on the right side of the head and his ear was in tatters, apparently from a Corl's teeth. He saw the surprise in Garric's expression and grinned broadly. "That was before I broke his back!" he said proudly.

They were supposed to be watching the rear, Garric remembered.

"Don't worry about what's behind you," Carus said with a grin full of murderous delight. *"If Torag knew how to fight a battle, you wouldn't have gotten this far."*

The ghost laughed and added, *"Says the man who lost his life and his fleet because he underestimated his enemy. But not this time, lad. Not this time."*

Garric reached the gate. Each leaf was a mat of wickerwork, folded vertically to double it. The interwoven fibers would've been harder to cut through than boards of the same thickness even if he'd had a steel axe, but Carus had correctly seen that the crossbar was the weak point.

Garric reversed his axe, stuck the butt end into the crack between the gate leaves, and shoved upward with all his strength. *Duzi it hurts!*

The bar didn't move. A warrior thrust his spear through the gap; Garric ducked away, warned by the shadow moving inside. Metz grabbed the shaft just below the delicate flint head and jerked the weapon out, though his uncle Abay's return thrust was vain also.

A troupe of eight women including Donria were half-carrying, half-pushing a raft of brushwood. It was already burning. Somebody—

"Donria or I'm a priest!" said Carus. *"By the Lady, what I could've done with her beside me!"*

—had realized that it'd be much easier to get the fire going on the relatively firm matting than in the mire at the base of the wall. The women shoved the mass hard against the stockade at the right edge of the gate and staggered away. Already the hard, oily stems were crackling and stretching their flames higher.

Metz put a hand on Garric's left arm. "Not so close," he said, tugging gently. "When a house burns in the village it'll sometimes light the

next one just by heat, without even sparks touching. This wall if it gets
going. . . ."

"Right, back to the mat," Garric mumbled. He was suddenly so
tired he could barely get the words out. If the Coerli sallied now . . .

"If they sally now, we'll deal with them," said Carus, smiling like a tor-
turer. *"But they won't, lad. Their world's turned upside down, and they're not
the folk to roll back onto the top of it."*

Light glittered in the clouds overhead. Lightning, Garric thought,
but the flash was a vivid red: wizardlight. The gray mass of sky, paler this
morning than generally in Garric's experience of this sodden land, began to swirl widdershins. As it turned, it thickened like butter forming in
cream.

A raindrop smacked Garric; it was the size of his thumbnail. More
drops slammed down, sending up high spouts from the bog. The fire
which'd been roaring toward full life began to splutter gouts of black ash.

Garric paused, looking from the struggling fire toward the sky. Sirawhil, of course. Torag and his warriors had lost their heads in the disaster, but she had not. If she could keep the humans from winning by
daylight, darkness and the pause to regroup would give the battle to the
Coerli.

Give the humans over to slaughter by the Coerli.

". . . semimenaeus damasilam laikam. . . ."

Sirawhil chanting—but it couldn't be, it was from *behind.*

Garric turned swiftly. Marzan sat on firm ground a short distance
from the mat which bridged the bog. He wore his headdress of black
feathers and held a separate feather, longer than the others, as a wand. He
chanted over the topaz, *"Iesen nalle nallelam. . . ."*

A wind was rising; cat's-paws fluttered puddles and chilled the sweat
on Garric's shoulders. Somewhere in the mid sky a much greater force
awoke with a low howl.

"Malthabeth eomal allasan . . . ," chanted Marzan. The young girl
who'd been helping him walk now stood behind him with a fire-
hardened stake. She glared fiercely, turning her head to watch everything
around them. It seemed to Garric that she was more concerned that another villager would bump the wizard than that the Coerli would attack.

Marzan's face showed the strain of his art, but Garric recognized also
a hint of smug triumph in the wizard's expression. Carus and he hadn't
considered Sirawhil's powers when they planned the attack, but neither
had they remembered that Marzan was on their side.

And Marzan had the topaz. Within the jewel was an azure spark around which whirled the cloudy flaws.

The rain built to a thunderous downpour; to Garric it seemed more like standing at the base of a waterfall than being caught in an ordinary storm. The blaze that'd started to devour the stockade slumped back into steam and angry spittings.

A fist of wind shrieked out of the sky and whirled a hollow dome above the fire. In it glittered azure wizardlight; the rain splashed and runneled away as though from a rock. The fire quickly regained its enthusiasm, carving into the fabric of the wall. Rain quenched the curtains of sparks swirling up beyond the shield of wind, but within its heart the blaze swelled into an inferno.

Garric turned his face away, watching through the corners of his eyes. The heat was too fierce for his cheeks to bear.

The flames roared so loudly that Garric couldn't hear Marzan's chanting, but the wizard's feather continued to tap to the rhythm of his moving lips. The rain lashed him and his helper just as it did the other gathered humans, but Garric noticed that the drops falling toward the topaz disintegrated in blue flashes a finger's breadth above it.

The upper gate hinge, a flat wicker rope, burned through. The lower hinge held for a moment, but when the leaf tilted inward it tore also. The gate fell open with a gush of sparks. Several Coerli sprang away from the ruin with despairing wails. The rain noticeably slackened, then stopped.

"Fellow humans!" Garric shouted. Carus had been right—of course: Garric was ready to fight now, and he'd have *been* ready if Torag had led another sally. "We'll go in as soon as the fire's burned back enough from the gap. Remember, we're deciding today whether this world belongs to men or cat beasts!"

"There's only one rule here," said Carus, watching through Garric's eyes but seeing more than Garric would ever see in a battle. *"Don't stop, don't slow down; don't quit while there's one of them standing. Never quit!"*

"Come along, Leto!" Donria said. "Mirza, you're next, and where's Keles?"

A woman carrying a bundle of brush that hadn't gone into the fire now threw her load off the end of the matting. It sank slightly in the bog, but buoyancy and the way its weight was spread kept it high. It didn't submerge even when another woman stepped onto it to drop her similar load a full stride closer to the stockade.

A third woman was struggling forward with what was more of a tangle than a bundle. The withies that'd bound the brush together had come untied at some point in the march or the recent fighting, so sticks kept dropping out.

The fire was burning in both directions from where Donria's raft had kindled it. It advanced through the stockade at the speed a man could walk. The wicker had been rained on daily for as long as it'd been up, but the core of the withies was dry and sapless. Heat sufficient to sear through the surface layer brought a return of many times greater flames, though these burned down quickly to white ash.

Garric looked at the gap, then at the waiting villagers. Some were apprehensive, but to his surprise more of them watched the destruction of this symbol of Coerli dominance with awed delight. The fight wasn't over yet, but that was a better mind-set than fear.

Garric grinned. Though fear was certainly justified.

The third bundle of brushwood went into the bog; two other women had helped the bearer tie it back together. Where the stockade gate had been was now a hole you could drive a team of oxen through if you could convince them to step in hot ashes. Garric couldn't see any cat men.

"Nets ready!" Garric shouted. He raised his axe; he didn't have a minnow net anymore himself. "Come on, fellow humans! The world for Mankind!"

With Metz at his side and behind them Abay and Horst, Garric charged the opening. Smoke stung his eyes, but he noticed with pleased surprise that the pain of his wound had subsided to a dull ache. "The world for Mankind!"

The last bundle of cut brush rotated slightly as Garric jumped from it. He landed short, on firm ground but tilted forward and about to fall on his face. He dabbed his left hand down and bellowed; he'd put his weight on a live coal hidden under the ashes. His callused feet might not have minded it, but his palm certainly did.

"It's on fire!" Metz shouted. "It's burning!"

Of course it's burning, we started the fire ourselves! Garric thought, but the snarl—really over his blistered hand, not anything Metz had said—didn't make it to his lips. Fortunately, because otherwise he'd have had to apologize.

The slave barracks was ablaze. The damp thatch gushed a pall of choking white smoke. The slave women—the cattle, as they'd been—

had opened the gate in the cross wall. They were pouring into the Coerli portion of the compound, each bearing a torch and generally a weapon as well: a stake, a club, even a bag with enough wet dirt in the end of it to knock a man silly.

To knock a cat man silly. Garric saw Donria's rawboned deputy Newla, but she seemed to be leading rather than commanding the revolt. The slaves' only future had been to become cold dinners for the Coerli, later if not sooner. All they'd have needed to riot was an opportunity. But where had they gotten the fire?

"When you and Donria fled . . . ," said a voice in Garric's head. It was the first time since the attack began that the Bird had spoken to him directly. "Soma concealed the block and firebow I'd brought you. She lit a fire when the attack began. By the time the Coerli realized what was happening, she'd begun distributing torches among the other women."

"*Soma* did?" Garric said in amazement. The only Coerli he saw was one who'd been wounded in the fighting outside the stockade and had apparently died from the gaping hole in his chest while crawling toward Torag's longhouse, and a dead warrior close to the gate from the slave quarters.

"Yes," said the Bird. "She led the attack on Sirawhil here in the courtyard. She killed the warrior guarding the wizard by thrusting a torch into his mouth. Not before he disemboweled her, of course."

"Half a dozen of you pick up that burning hut!" King Carus shouted, taking control of Garric's tongue while Garric was too stunned by what he'd just heard to be fully aware of his surroundings. "We're going to throw it into the longhouse. That's where the cat beasts have laired up!"

One of the half-dozen beehives that housed the warriors in groups of two or three was burning with the same sluggish determination as the slave barracks. The blanket of white smoke it spewed out hovered at waist height, drifting slowly westward now that Marzan's whirlwind no longer ripped through the compound. Though the fire didn't look enthusiastic, it'd devoured about a quarter of the thatch dome.

"Right!" said Garric, puzzling nearby villagers who thought he was talking to himself. "Come on, five of you! Metz, you and your uncles guard us. Come on, grab a post!"

Garric deliberately put himself closest to Torag's longhouse, at the edge of the pall of smoke. He gripped one of the hooped poles support-

ing the frame and tried to lift it with his left hand only. The pole was
sunk too deep for him to pull it out of the ground that way.

He dropped the axe and shoved both hands through the thatch to
seize the pole, then straightened his knees. His vision blurred. Duzi it
hurt!

"Put your man in it!" old Cobb used to say when he'd hired Garric
at fourteen to grub a drainage trench through a boulder-studded field.
"Put your—"

Garric came up with the pole in his hands. The hut shuddered,
spewing sparks and rising all along its circumference as villagers lifted
their poles also when Garric had broken the weight free to begin with.

"Let's go!" Garric bawled, barely able to see for the tears and pain.
He staggered forward, in the direction memory told him the longhouse
ought to be. If the cat men made a sally, he'd be dead before he knew it.
This wasn't strategy or even tactics, it was a buzzing determination of a
horsefly which is willing to die so long as she can drink blood first.
"Let's go!"

"It's the way to win battles," growled the king in his mind. "Never
flinch, never quit."

"Torches!" Donria screamed. "Throw your torches! Throw them,
Newla!"

Garric more felt than saw the brands whickering past in smoky arcs,
bouncing from the roof and on the porch boards. A Corl, perhaps Torag
himself from the volume, shrieked in maddened fury. If they'd been
preparing to rush, the rain of torches made them hesitate.

Garric's foot stubbed against the porch. "Now!" he cried. "Throw
the—"

He lifted and heaved, twisting his body out of the way. The burning
hut slid past him under the grunting effort of the villagers still pushing
the load.

Garric landed on his side and arm; the left arm, thank the Shepherd,
but it wouldn't have mattered. It wouldn't have mattered if he'd torn his
whole arm off because he'd succeeded. They'd beaten the Coerli.

The hut, fanned to brighter flames when they moved it, crunched
into the porch of the longhouse. Smoldering bits of thatch broke off, but
a considerable quantity must've gone through the central door. Almost at
once white smoke curled from the windows at either end.

Metz helped Garric up and slapped the butt of his stone axe into his hand. Garric's fingers closed over the weapon thankfully, ready to meet the rush of Coerli warriors that he knew now would never happen. The fire had beaten them; and more than fire, the shock of facing men who understood war and who carried the fight to their enemies.

Metz pulled him back. The walls of the longhouse crackled more fiercely than damp thatch as the flames mounted. "Is there another way out?" Garric asked hoarsely.

"I sent my uncles around the building with nets to cover any doors they found," Metz said. "The cords'll burn, but they'll hold till the fire finishes the business."

"There are no other doors," said the Bird with crisp authority. It landed on Garric's left shoulder, a gossamer weight and a comforting presence. "Besides, the Coerli would not run."

"Then they'll die," said Garric, lifting the axe slightly. His arm felt as though it belonged to somebody else, not so much painful as a vividly described pain.

He remembered watching the Coerli kill and devour a woman with slavering gusto. "Either way they were going to die," he added.

The ridgepole broke; the roof of the longhouse collapsed on the interior in a shower of sparks. A handful of thatch lifted in a spiral, then fell apart twenty feet in the air. It dribbled back as scattered smoke trails. Garric thought he heard a cry of agony, but it might've been steam squealing from a burning log.

"I have brought the hero who freed us from the Coerli!" quavered a voice.

Garric turned, feeling the heat of the burning longhouse on his back. Marzan stood where the gate of the stockade had been. His right arm was over the shoulders of the girl aiding him, but his left held the topaz out before him.

"I have conquered!" the wizard cried. "I am Marzan the Great!"

"You know, lad?" said King Carus. *"I think I'd have to agree with him. But he sure picked the right sword for his fight."*

Around them the flames hissed, and a plume of smoke climbed into the gray skies.

CASHEL ROCKED A little as he felt coarse soil under his feet. He and Protas didn't move—it was more like the world moved under them—but each time it happened Cashel *felt* like he ought to be falling on his face.

It was night. The moon in its first quarter hung low in the west and the stars were bright but unfamiliar. One constellation looked a little like the Widow's Donkey, but just a little. Something wailed dismally at the back of the cold, dry wind.

"Umm," said Cashel, pulling the slippers out from under his belt where he'd stuck them. "Here, Protas. They're still wet and muddy, but you'll probably be better with them on."

The boy stood on one leg to pull a slipper on the opposite foot. When he started to topple he caught Cashel's arm.

"Best sit down," Cashel said, disengaging himself without being too harsh about it. Protas thumped to the ground, and Cashel resumed looking all around them.

A new guide ought to be picking them up, and there might be other things looking for them besides the guide. It was hard to tell what was howling in the distance, and there was no way at all to know how big it was.

He and Protas were on a mound of dirt dried to crumbly stone. Around them were more mounds, bigger or smaller, their sides carved by the rain that must fall occasionally. Not any time recently, though. Spiky bushes and clumps of grass were scattered widely. Each stood on the pedestal which its roots protected from the scouring wind.

"Hello?" called a voice. "Hello, are you there?"

"Sir?" said Cashel, turning the direction the sound came from. The bigger mounds were clearly banded, though he couldn't tell colors in the faint moonlight. Here and there what looked like big bones were weathering out of the dirt. "Lord Protas and me're this way, sir!"

He wasn't completely sure it was a man calling, the voice was that thin and squeaky. Well, if it was a woman, he'd apologize.

"What's that?" the voice said. A yellow light bobbed around a pinnacle as tall as a man but not much wider than the quarterstaff was long. "All right, I see you now. Don't move!"

"Move where, Cashel?" Protas said in a low voice. The boy was looking at the landscape too, though there wasn't much to see. That wasn't the worst thing they could've found, of course.

"I think he's just talking," Cashel said. "But in case the ground's going to swallow us whole if we step off this little hill, we'll stay right where we are."

"Oh!" said Protas with more enthusiasm than Cashel's comment warranted. He'd probably read books the way Garric and Sharina did, all full of wonderful things that hadn't really happened or didn't happen much.

Sometimes they did happen, though, so Cashel was staying where he was. A shepherd learns to be careful. There's nothing so unlikely that some ewe, some day, won't manage to get herself in trouble doing it.

"Yes!" said the man with the lantern. He was as tall as Cashel but thin as a rail. "There's two of you, then. Well, come along, we mustn't waste time outside. It's quite dangerous, even this close to my dwelling. And we can't possibly try to go on at night, that would be hopeless, completely hopeless! I don't know why you came here at this time of day!"

"Who are you, sirrah?" Protas said sharply, making his voice seem to come out of his nose in that way he had. "I am Protas, son of Cervoran, and my companion is Master Cashel, the great wizard. We are not men to be ordered about by some nameless flunky!"

"What?" said the guide, drawing himself up full-height and holding the lantern closer to Protas' face. It was just a candle, likely tallow, behind horn lenses and didn't do much to aid the low moon. "I'm Antesiodorus, that's who I am. A scholar and a man who deserves respect even from ill-mannered boys."

"I don't mind standing here," said Cashel. "But if you've got water in your place, Master Antesiodorus, I'd appreciate a drink."

Cashel was smiling, more on the inside than with his lips. He'd been ordered around by no end of angry little people who thought they were more important than the world thought. He didn't make a fuss about it; he didn't fuss about much of anything. If Protas wanted to bring somebody up short for being impolite, though, that was all right with him. The boy was being a lot nicer about it than Ilna would've been, that was for sure.

Protas raised his left hand and touched the topaz crown.

"I'm not afraid," said Antesiodorus, this time with a kind of stiff dignity. "I have my duty and I'll do it. If you'll come with me, sirs, I'll provide such hospitality as I have available."

Cashel heard rustlings around them as they traced a winding path between the cutaway mounds, but it didn't seem there was anything big or anything particularly interested in them, either one. What he thought at first was a bird swooped close, but it flew more like a bat as he watched it flutter away.

A low house was built between a couple of miniature buttes ahead of them. Light, probably from a single candle, winked through chinks in the walls.

"Are those logs?" Protas asked. "Where did you find trees so big here, sir?"

"They are not logs, they are bones," said the guide. "I didn't find them, they were found by those persons who built the dwelling I am forced to occupy. And while I can only conjecture, it seems reasonable that they dug the bones out of the hills. Similar ones are weathering out even now."

The house was long and rambling. Instead of going through the doorway covered with fabric pinned to the transom, Cashel walked to the southwest corner to look at the place in the moonlight. They were bones all right, thighs mostly but with big shoulder blades slid in sideways between layers and chinked with mud. The roof trusses were ribs, covered with sod. Well, dirt anyway, and Antesiodorus must keep it wetted down because coarse grass grew all over it instead of just tuffets here and there like the landscape in general.

"Sir?" Cashel said. He tapped a bone with his knuckle; it made a *clock*ing sound like well-cured oak. "What did these come from? Giants? Because there's never been an ox so big."

"They came from mastodons," Antesiodorus said, pausing with the door curtain lifted. He looked sour, but Cashel guessed he was the sort of fellow who looked sour more times than he didn't. "Are you any the wiser, Master Wizard? They're animals and they're obviously bigger than oxen; or they were, because so far as I know they've been dead for more ages than there've been men. At any rate, all I've seen around here are bones."

"Thank you," said Cashel quietly. "And I'm not really a wizard, sir."

Antesiodorus cleared his throat in embarrassment. "Now, if you're quite done out here," he said, "would you care to come in? The bones look much the same from this side, and the things that might decide to eat you can't get through the walls."

"Sorry," Cashel said, straightening. "I've never seen a house built like this."

He nodded Protas inside and followed the boy; Antesiodorus pulled the curtain across the door behind them. The walls were solid enough to keep out wolves or whatever it was the guide worried about, but just a cloth hanging in the doorway didn't seem like much.

It was a cloak of black velvet, covered in symbols embroidered in silver thread. Cashel felt the hairs on the back of his hand tremble when he touched it.

Antesiodorus was looking hard at him. The lantern in his hand and the yellow-brown tallow candle on the table lighted the long room surprisingly well.

"You recognize it, then?" Antesiodorus said in a challenging tone. "The Cape of Holla?"

"No sir," Cashel said. "But I see why you don't worry about things coming through the door to get you when it's hanging here. My sister could probably tell you more, but I see that much."

"Then you *are* a wizard," Antesiodorus said, putting just a hair of emphasis on "are." He sounded puzzled.

"Not like people mean," Cashel said, embarrassed to talk about what he didn't understand. He looked around for a place to sit and didn't see a good one. "Ah?" he added. "If I could have a mug of water—or beer if you have it—I'd find it welcome."

"I don't have beer and the water's alkaline," said Antesiodorus, shuffling to the corner that seemed to be his pantry. He was barefoot and his clothing, a tunic and a short cape, was of some coarse vegetable fiber that wasn't much better than sacking. "It suffices for me, and I'm afraid it'll have to suffice for you."

Cashel didn't answer. Antesiodorus wasn't the old man he'd thought him when they were outside. Oh, sure, he must be forty—but Lord Attaper was forty, and he could give a fight to most men half his age. The guide *acted* old, though, and very tired. That was what was in his words, age and tiredness this time rather than anger.

Protas was stepping briskly around the room, looking first at this thing and then at that. The only real furniture was the table, a slab of yellow limestone that might've been local supported on either end by a tusked skull with huge eyesockets. The top was piled high with books and scrolls, some of them open.

The bone walls of the house wouldn't keep out a driving rain, but here in the center of the long room was probably safe. The roof wouldn't leak; or anyway, wouldn't leak quickly. Cashel knew storms in this climate could be fierce, but he didn't imagine that they'd last long.

Protas glanced at the books, but mostly he was looking at the things along the walls. They'd been put on trays made by sticking bones from smaller animals end-on into the cracks between the mastodon thighs. There were boxes of shell and alabaster, and one little casket was made of some purple metal like Cashel had never dreamed of. There was a rusty iron helmet that looked like scrap to be turned into horseshoes, and a dagger with a moonstone the size of a baby's fist in the pommel. The boy was fascinated.

"Here," said Antesiodorus, offering Cashel a cup. "I have flat bread and goat cheese if you're hungry."

Instead of being terra cotta or a simple wooden masar, the sort of thing people who dressed like Antesiodorus generally drank out of, this was glass clearer than the water that filled it. Gold-filled engraving on the inside showed hounds chasing an antelope, a nice picture and very well drawn—except that the antelope had six horns, not two.

"I only have one cup," Antesiodorus said. "I've never had visitors."

Then, angrily, "I *shouldn't* have visitors! I should be left to my studies! I don't ask for much, do I?"

Cashel drank instead of answering. He wouldn't have spoken anyway, since their guide wasn't asking a real question. The water was all right, though it had an aftertaste that seemed to coat Cashel's tongue and the back of his throat. He'd drunk worse, but it made him miss the days when he could walk down to Pattern Creek and fill his wooden bottle from the cold, clear current just above the stones of the bottom.

The thought made him smile, and smiling made him think of Sharina; he smiled wider. He handed back the cup.

"Thank you, Master Antesiodorus," he said. "I'd like some of the bread and cheese you offered, if you would. And if you've got a few scallions, that'd be better still."

"Yes, of course," said their guide, stepping back to the pantry. "And more water? It's simple fare, but I believe it cleanses my body and helps me think."

"Water, please," Cashel said. With a grin in his voice he added, "I don't know how much this sort of food helps me think, but it's what I've eaten pretty much all my life."

"Master Antesiodorus," said Protas, holding what looked like a sand painting that'd been glued onto its backing. "Where did you get this? Where did you get any of these things?"

The boy gestured at the wall he'd been walking along. From the bone core of a bison's horn hung an amber necklace; one of the pieces was near as big as the topaz, and it had something inside. Beside the necklace was a wax tablet, and beside *that* was a set of doctor's tools with gold handles and blades of bright sharp steel. There were more things than there'd been sheep in the largest flock Cashel had ever watched.

"Would you like food also, Lord Protas?" Antesiodorus said, coming back with cheese and bread wafers on a silver tray.

"My father had things like this," Protas said, challenging and talking through his nose again. "Only not so many or so fine. You're a wizard, aren't you?"

"I'm a scholar!" Antesiodorus said. "That's all I ever wanted to be. Can't we leave it at that?"

"Only if you're so great a wizard," Protas went on, back to sounding like a nervous boy, "why is it you live this way, sir? We . . . we have to depend on you guiding us, you see."

Cashel broke a piece from the wafer and a piece from the hard, flat cheese, then munched them together. It seemed to him that the boy had a point, though it wasn't one that he'd have thought of himself. There wasn't anything unusual about the way Antesiodorus lived—by the standards of a poor boy from Barca's Hamlet.

"I choose to live like this," Antesiodorus said. Cashel couldn't read the emotion behind his expression, but it was a strong one. "I made a mistake. That's all it was, just a mistake. I didn't mean the other things to happen!"

He lifted his hands in a broad gesture. "I've agreed to help someone in exchange for being allowed to live quietly," he went on. "I find things for him. I'm a scholar, I can use the books and manuscripts I gather in ways that others could not. And he provides . . ."

Antesiodorus gestured again. "I don't need much, I don't want much!" he said. "Just to be left alone with enough food to live and water drawn from the well I dug myself. Why can't they let me have that and leave me alone?"

"It's good cheese," said Cashel. "Thank you. Where is it that the goats are at, sir?"

If Antesiodorus kept animals, Cashel would've smelled them. Besides, he didn't see the scholar making any better of a goatherd than Tenoctris would. Talking to the wizard's servant might tell them things that Antesiodorus himself wouldn't.

Antesiodorus looked at him. "Yes, of course," he said pettishly. "Why would you care about my troubles? The food is delivered to me. Sometimes the items I've located in my research are taken—I won't say in exchange, just at the time the food arrives. Sometimes they're not taken at all, as you see."

"I'm sorry for your troubles, master," Cashel said. "But I don't know how you came to be here or what it was you did. I couldn't say much without knowing more."

He looked Antesiodorus in the eye and smiled again, not quite the same expression as before. Cashel didn't look for people to fight, but he'd had plenty fights in his life and he guessed he'd have more.

"What I *can* say," he went on, "is that it's good cheese and I appreciate you sharing it with me."

Antesiodorus swallowed and seemed to sink into himself, hunching and looking even thinner than he'd been. He picked up a little silver pin on a shelf beside him and looked at it hard; a fish, it seemed to Cashel, but mostly it was just a glitter in the candlelight.

"I didn't mean for the other things to happen," he muttered. "I was young and it was just a mistake."

"Master Antesiodorus?" Protas said. The boy stood stiffly, formally, but he wasn't putting on airs like he did when he was angry. "Are you here to work off a debt, or are you serving a sentence?"

"Is there a difference, milord?" Antesiodorus said, smiling faintly. He held the pin against his chest, his fingers covering it completely. "If a debt, then it's one I'll never be able to pay; and if a sentence, it's a life sentence. That was how I made the mistake, you see. I thought it was important to save my life."

He shrugged. "Have you both finished eating?" he said. "Then we'd best get some sleep. We'll need to set out as soon as the sun comes up in the morning. I have some wall hangings that'll have to do for bedding, though I'm afraid there's nothing but the floor to sleep on."

Antesiodorus looked up. "Or my couch," he added sharply. "But that's stone."

"The floor will be fine," said Cashel. "Won't it, Protas?"

But the boy was holding the topaz in his left hand, and his eyes were far away.

"YOUR HIGHNESS," SAID Lord Tadai forcefully to Sharina, "you have no business being here. You should be in Mona where you can have proper control of the government."

The troops in the fortifications around Calf's Head Bay were standing to arms. Reinforcements who'd been billeted on the north end of
the island had arrived during the night, clanking and muttering. They'd
cursed the mud and the darkness, called for the liaison officers who were
supposed to guide them to their new positions, and argued among themselves over location and rations and who had precedence on the paths.
Blood Eagles guarding Princess Sharina had prevented tired soldiers
from stumbling over the guy ropes and bringing her tent down on top
of her, but they couldn't make the night quiet.

That was all right; she'd seen what the troops had faced the day before. A disturbed night's sleep was little enough to suffer by comparison.

"Milord," Sharina said, "I'm exactly where I need to be. Initially I
thought as you did, that I'd be in the way. I'm not in the way. Messengers
can reach me here, and I can sign documents just as easily as I could back
in the palace."

"It's a very inefficient way to rule, Your Highness!" said Tadai. "The
clerks—"

"The clerks will cope," Sharina said. "You will cope. Because the
soldiers out there—"

She gestured to the south wall of the tent. Beyond the canvas wall
was the slope to the battlefield and then to the sea from which they
could expect more hellplants at sunrise.

"—are coping with something much more difficult than a seven-
mile journey over a bad road. So long as they're here fighting, I'll be here
too. Just as my brother would've been. As you know well."

"You can't *do* anything, Your Highness," Tadai said, but his protests
had lost their fierce edge. He didn't agree with her, but he knew by now
that she wasn't going to budge.

"I can be seen, Tadai," Sharina said. She smiled; it wasn't something
a man like Lord Tadai could understand. "The troops can see me watching them as they fight to save the kingdom."

Though salvation was in Double's hands, at least for now. If the wizard failed, the army would at best delay the attacking plants.

More wood, brush and heavier timbers as well, had been brought up
during the night; it filled the trenches in front of the breastworks. That
would hold for a time, and the soldiers' swords would hold for a further
time. The phalanx had marched across the island; perhaps its twenty-foot
pikes would prove more useful than the shorter spears of the regular infantry.

But after that, human resources were exhausted. Without Double, it was simply a matter of how fast the hellplants could walk and how many more would come out of the sea. Not that there was any reason to fear failure after the wizard's triumph the previous day. . . .

"If you'll excuse me, milord," Sharina said, stepping out of the tent past the nobleman. "It'll be dawn shortly, and I want to talk to Tenoctris beforehand."

She and Tadai had discussed everything there was to say about her location. In truth she didn't have any important business with Tenoctris either, but the old wizard was a friend in a fashion that Lord Tadai—smart and skilled and completely loyal though he was—could never be to someone who never forgot she'd been raised as a peasant.

Tenoctris was a noble also, but all she'd ever cared about was her studies. She'd spent much of her life in garrets and the dusty basements of libraries, oblivious of her surroundings and completely untouched by notions of birth and family. Tadai was plumply sleek and studiedly cultured. Like Waldron, a noble of a very different sort, Tadai was brave and hard working—but neither man could look at another person without first determining where that person ranked in the social order.

Friends are equals. Sharina was no more comfortable with Tadai's deference than she'd have been with with him ignoring her if she were waiting tables in her father's inn.

The tent didn't have a charcoal brazier, but the dozen candles for lighting and the watchful Blood Eagles—present by Attaper's order no matter who was talking to Sharina—must've warmed the interior more than she'd realized. The dank sea wind was stronger than she'd expected. She hugged herself and started back inside for a wrap.

"Here you go, Princess," said Trooper Lires, one of the guard detail. He swung the cape he must've brought from the wardrobe in the tent's curtained anteroom. "I figured you'd want this, so I grabbed it."

"In the Lady's name, my man!" Tadai protested. "Show some respect for your ruler."

"He's keeping me warm, which is better," Sharina said, letting the soldier help her on with the garment. Blood Eagle officers were noblemen, but even they weren't courtiers. It hadn't occurred to Lires that it wasn't more important to give Sharina the cloak than to do so in a properly subservient way—

And Sharina agreed.

It was a formal garment, black velvet with a lining of crimson silk.

That didn't prevent it from blocking the chill breeze as well as cruder, cheaper fabric could've done. Sharina walked to where Tenoctris sat cross-legged on the ground.

One of the wizard's guards had spread his half-cape beneath her, though Sharina was sure Tenoctris hadn't thought to ask for it. She'd drawn a figure in the dirt; in this light Sharina couldn't describe its shape, let alone the words of power drawn around it. The older woman looked up as Sharina approached.

"Have you learned anything?" Sharina asked, squatting beside her friend.

"I feel like a mouse between a pair of granite mountains," Tenoctris said with her usual cheerful humility. "I can see the—"

She gestured with the bamboo split in her hand.

"—structures, call them, which Cervoran and the Green Woman are preparing, but until they act I have no way of judging their intent."

She grinned. "Except that it's unlikely that the Green Woman plans anything that will benefit humanity," she added. "And I'm more than a little doubtful about Cervoran as well."

Sharina looked to where Double stood with his head down at one end of where he'd raised the mirror. The post-and-canvas form remained, shuddering in the wind, though the silver had vanished into the ground.

"Has he moved since the battle yesterday?" Sharina asked quietly. Then she added, "I haven't seen him eat."

"No," said Tenoctris without being specific as to which comment she was replying to. "He'll be rousing soon. It's almost dawn, and I can—"

She looked at the sky, faintly gray though the brightest stars were still visible.

"—*feel* the balances shifting. I wish I could really describe what I see, Sharina, but I suppose it doesn't matter since I don't know what it means myself."

"Here they come!" a soldier bellowed. Horns and trumpets blew Stand-To in shrilly. So far as Sharina could tell the whole army was already in position behind the earthworks. She hugged her friend again and stood up.

The tide was coming in and with it dark ugly lumps. More hellplants bobbed farther out to sea. They stretched so far into the distance that

Sharina couldn't tell the shapes from those of the waves. Spume flew inland, driven by the sea breeze.

Double shook himself like a dog coming out of a high wind. He gave Sharina a fat-lipped grin, then pointed his athame at the ground.

"*Eulamon,*" he said. "*Restoutus restouta zerosi!*"

As the words of power sounded, blue wizardlight twinkled coldly along the ground before him. The wind, already strong, picked up. It drove dust and leaves and mist.

"*Benchuch bachuch chuch . . . ,*" Double chanted, the same words as on the day before. He lifted the point of his athame; silver rose from the soil into which it'd sunk at the end of the previous day's battle. The sun, just above the horizon, flared red on the film of metal. "*Ousiri agi ousiri!*"

Some of the soldiers began cheering. The sound was scattered, but there was no mistaking what it was.

Tenoctris looked down the slope. The sun spread the shadows of the oncoming hellplants in long blurred masses.

"I think that's the first time I've heard laymen cheer a wizard," she said in a musing tone.

"It's only the troops who were here yesterday," Sharina said. "The ones who survived the battle."

"Yes, well . . . ," Tenoctris said. She gave Sharina a wry smile and shrugged. "I started to say that I hope there'll be even more cheering tomorrow, but I think instead I'll just hope for the best result."

Sharina opened her mouth to ask what that would be. "Ah," she said instead, nodding. If Tenoctris had known what the best result was, she'd have stated it. Looking at Double, his face waxen and grinning like a badly molded doll's, she understood why Tenoctris would be unwilling to hope outright for that creature's victory.

The mirror was complete, a silver shimmer as precise as the edge of a sword. Even as low as the sun still was, the metal waked a dot of light that tracked the plant on the southernmost end of the attacking line. The creature began to smoke, but the fog was thickening.

Something swirled past Sharina on the breeze. *Spider silk,* she thought; *gossamer;* one of thousands of strands drifting from the sea. She'd seen its like often in springtime: egg sacks hatched and tiny spiderlets sailed across the meadows, lifted on long threads of silk. But this—

A strand, many strands draped themselves on Sharina's arms and hair. They were blowing up the slope in numbers beyond any hatching in her memory. They didn't support spiders, and they seemed to be of coarser vegetable material rather than silk. The breeze carried them onto the mirror where they clung, squirming across the metal and linking as though the wind were weaving them.

The silver film deformed as the threads squeezed wrinkles into the surface. The dot of light searing the distant hellplant blurred into a vague brightness quivering harmlessly through the fog.

The initial line of monsters squelched closer. A second battalion was already marching up from the sea.

"*Olar akra!*" Double shouted, suddenly agitated. "*Zagra orea!*"

The mirror shook violently and smoothed itself, bursting vegetable fibers and flinging them aside. For a moment the dot of light steadied again on a hellplant, but more threads wriggled through the air and took the place of those which'd been broken.

Though Double continued to chant, the fibers poured up on the wind in ever-increasing quantities. First like chaff on a threshing floor, then thicker yet and knotting into a mat which covered the silver. Only when the fabric was opaque did it begin to squeeze again, this time inexorably.

"*Audusta!*" Double snarled. The mirror collapsed, though the vegetable mass continued to twitch and tremble where it'd been. Double turned away and clumped back toward his ancient oak work chest.

On the plains below the mist grew thicker, and the plants marched on.

"IT'S A PLEASURE to meet you, Mistress Auta," said Chalcus with a sweeping bow. "Who is it that you're to be saved from, if I may ask?"

The sailor's gestures were always excessive by anybody else's standards, but somehow he carried off what would've made a courtier look absurd. *If I made the world,* Ilna thought, *gray and brown would be all the colors needed, and people would behave as if they too were gray and brown. There'd be no Chalcus in that world . . . and very little for me, despite that's what I think I'd want.*

"Why, from the Princes!" said another little man. He'd edged into plain sight, sitting cross-legged on a holly branch near where Ilna'd caught and released his fellow. There *were* differences among the little folk: this one's hair rose in a pronounced widow's peak, for example. Because they were so small and quick, distinguishing marks were hard to catch.

"From the other Princes!" Auta said instantly, shooting the man a fierce glance. "Prince Ilna, did the One bring you here to rid the garden from those who have preyed on us from time out of mind?"

"We're here because someone wanted us out of his way," Ilna said. "I doubt he intended to help you or anybody besides himself. He may not even know that you exist."

She hadn't snarled, but she'd probably frowned as she considered the situation. She hadn't meant anything by it; she generally frowned when she considered the world and the things that happened in it. Auta'd taken the expression personally, though, so she'd shrunk back toward the hedge.

"Our main concern's to get out of this place and back to the world of our friends, that's so, little lady," said Chalcus. "We're glad to meet you, but no one sent us to be saviors."

Ilna walked to a birch tree growing out of the Osage orange, taking out her paring knife. She hadn't seen the little people use tools, but there were rocks in the soil of the hedges. Even without skill the little people could hammer stones together till they chipped an edge on one.

"Is Dee all right?" Merota asked, squatting on the grass. "Really, we weren't going to hurt him."

Two of the little people, a man and a woman, dropped to the ground instead of watching from the hedges. Their heads were just on a level with the kneeling child's.

Ilna pulled down a branch and nicked it. She peeled away the papery outer covering—it was of no use to her—and stripped off four strands of the fibrous brown inner bark.

"Dee, come show yourself!" Auta called commandingly. "Our Princes think they've hurt you. Come out!"

Ilna could understand the little people's language, but besides having very high-pitched voices because they were small, they had an accent that reminded her of the clipped way people spoke on Cordin. She wondered who'd woven the tapestry and how long ago that had been. Perhaps when she got back to the room where it hung in Mona, she'd have time to examine it properly.

The couple who'd left the hedge minced over to Merota. The woman reached out with one hand, holding her male companion's wrist with the other. More of the little people stepped onto the grass.

"Go ahead," Merota said soothingly. "You can touch me, little person."

Ilna wiped the blade of her knife and slid it again into its bone case. She returned to the gathering, now crowded around Merota like doves feeding on grain beneath their cote. The woman who'd first come forward was running her fingers through the child's fine hair while the others watched admiringly.

"Prince Merota," Auta said, though Ilna noticed that her eyes were really on Chalcus. "Can you not help us, great Prince? The Princes, the other Princes, take us one at a time or several together. We who escape hear screams and then the bones of our friends breaking. We are helpless, but you are strong and can save us."

"You can save yourselves," Ilna said sharply, moving to Merota's side. The little people skittered away, again like doves; their behavior made her angry. Unreasonably angry, she knew, but she felt the flush regardless. She held out the four ribbons of bark. "Watch what I do with these."

As Ilna spoke, she began to knot the strips into a grid. She forced herself to let her fingers move slowly and deliberately so that the little people could see exactly what she was doing. When she'd completed the demonstration, she had a neatly woven net no bigger than the palm of her hand.

Ilna held it out to Auta; after a moment, the tiny woman took it and bent close to puzzle over the joinings. They were simple reef knots, easy for even the untutored to make.

"But what is this, Prince Ilna?" said the man sitting on the holly branch.

"It's a net," Ilna said. "A very small one, of course, but there's trees enough in this garden to make a net any size you please. Now, how many of your folk are there? All of you together."

Auta looked at the circle of her folk in consternation. "Great Prince," said the seated man, "we are simple folk. We couldn't answer such a question."

"Many and many," said Auta. "The Princes prey on us every day, but still we remain."

"So I thought," said Ilna with a crisp toss of her head. "Well, it's time for you to prey on Princes. I've seen you crawl through the hedges like fish swimming. You can hang nets before and behind these so-called Princes, then drop another net on top of them. Catch them one at a time."

"Oh-h-h!" said the crowd, gasping as a single tiny person.

"There's rocks here," Ilna continued, grim-faced. "You can kill the creatures with rocks."

"Aye," said Chalcus with grinning animation. "And as a hint, tying a thong the length of your arm onto a rock for a handle'll give enough speed to your blow that you'll break bones instead of just bruising the devils when you hit them."

"Oh, we could never do that, great Princes!" said Auta. She dropped the net and backed as if it was soaked in filth. "You're so brave and strong, but we are small."

"You'll save us, Prince Merota," cooed the woman stroking the child's hair. "You're great and strong. It would be nothing to you to save us from the other Princes. You'll save us, won't you, great one?"

"So many of us are gone," said a little man, his head bowed low. "A pounce and a crunch and then gone, nothing but a splotch of blood on the grass."

Merota looked at the sailor. "Chalcus?" she said. "We could, couldn't we? You and Ilna could, I mean?"

Chalcus laughed, but Ilna saw the veil go up behind his eyes. Talk of killing brought not only wariness to his expression but also a degree of professional calculation: Chalcus had always been a sailor, but for part of life he'd been one of the Lataaene pirates. He had a great deal of experience with killing, and from the scars on his body he'd repeatedly come close to learning about being killed as well.

"We're not here for hunting, dear lady," he said with his tongue and his lips; not with his eyes, though, not so that Ilna couldn't tell the truth. "We're here only till we leave; and the sooner we leave, the better for ourselves and our friends back home. Though perhaps if Mistress Auta can tell us where the way out of the garden may be, we could do her and her friends a favor or two before we left, eh?"

Chalcus grinned broadly. "And who knows?" he added. "Would Garric like a chimaera pelt to stuff for a throne cushion? That'd be a fine thing for the King of the Isles to sit on, would it not?"

"There's no way out of the Garden, Prince Chalcus," said a little man.

"No way at all," said another. "Except . . ."

He looked around, frightened to have spoken—though he *hadn't* really spoken.

"Except?" repeated Ilna, her voice harshly insistent. Hearing people talking around a problem, refusing to face it baldly, angered her more than a personal attack would. "*What* is the way out?"

"Prince Ilna?" Auta said. The little woman laced her hands together, then held her arms out from her body and wriggled the fingers while looking down. The shadow of her hands hirpled on the grass as Ilna remembered another shadow—the Shadow—doing while one of the little folk screamed and vanished.

Auta clenched her fists when she saw that Ilna'd understood the gesture. "That way only, Prince Ilna," she said in a small voice. "No way except for that: death or worse than death."

The man in the holly hopped down and gripped Merota's knees. "Mighty Prince Merota," he cried, "please! Of your goodness save us, for we cannot save ourselves."

"Chalcus?" the child said, her voice a mixture of pleading eagerness. "We could, couldn't we? It wouldn't take so very long. And we're here anyway, you know."

Chalcus drew out his dagger, probably without thinking about it. The little people gave a collective gasp, but they didn't flee.

Chalcus spun the dagger up in the air and caught it by the hilt when it dropped, without ever looking at the bright steel. His eyes were on Merota and the little people; and at last on Ilna.

"So," he said. "What is it that you think, heart of my heart? There's something to what the child says, don't you think? We *are* here for the time being, and it wouldn't hurt me to do a bit of hunting in a good cause."

"They will save us," Auta whispered. Her assembled fellows sighed a wordless prayer of thanks.

"We will not save you," said Ilna. She bent and picked up the miniature net she'd knotted as an example. "You can save yourselves. *Look* at this!"

"Oh, no!" said Auta. Around her echoed *no-no-no-no* in piping whispers.

"We cannot do that, Prince Ilna," said the man still bowed before Merota. "*You* will save us. Great Merota, tell your—"

"No!" said Ilna in a fury. The little people scattered back from her like children frightened when a banked fire suddenly flares. "People who won't try to save themselves don't deserve to be saved. The world isn't meant to be safe for those who don't care!"

Chalcus sheathed his dagger with a motion as smooth as the sun on still water. "Aye," he said. "I take your point, dear one."

He made a sweeping gesture. "Since our little friends here don't know the way out," he went on, "and we've no other business with them, we'll take our leave. My sincere best wishes, Mistress Auta, to you and your fellows."

The little people vanished, leaving the three of them alone in the clearing. Ilna smoothed the net between her palms, then set it on the grass in case someone, some day, came back to look at it. People can learn; sometimes at least. Ilna os-Kenset had learned certain things, about people and about herself, in the course of her life.

They weren't always things she was happier to know, but that couldn't be helped.

"It seems to me," said Chalcus as he sauntered toward the next turning of the maze, "that though the little people don't know the way out of this place, those who prey on them may. At least if we put the question to them the right way."

"Yes," said Ilna. Her face was rigid and her mind was a pit of burning rock. "I wouldn't mind convincing some of these Princes to tell us things they prefer to hide."

Chapter

13

GARRIC SNEEZED. THE ruins of Torag's compound smoldered in a dozen places. Though the smoke hadn't affected him while the battle was going on, it did now.

Besides the sullen haze, there was the stench of bodies. The blackened corpses of the Coerli looked more human than the creatures had in life, but their wet fur smoldered with a unique pungency.

Soma lay on her back just inside the cross-wall. A warrior's barbed spear had entered below her navel and ripped upward, dragging her intestines with it. Her face was suffused with rage. Garric remembered what the Bird had said: that she'd thrust her torch through the mouth of the Corl who'd killed her.

"Shall we leave her here or throw her into a bog?" Metz asked. "Donria's told me how she tried to kill you."

"I'd like you to have her buried properly, or however you treat your dead here," Garric said. "The woman the Coerli killed was a valued ally to me and to all of us."

Metz shrugged. "I never had much use for her," he said. "But if you say so, Lord Garric."

"Lord Garric," said a woman's voice behind them. "Let me see your wound."

Garric turned; the movement made his shoulder flame as if somebody'd just run a hot plow coulter through it. It hurt so much that his vision blurred and his knees wobbled.

"Stand still," said the woman—the girl who'd been helping Marzan. The wizard sat nearby, his back against the side of a beehive hut that'd housed some of the warriors.

The girl was chewing a cud of something; green juice dribbled from a corner of her mouth. She gripped Garric by the biceps and the top of his shoulder, bringing her face close to the puckered entrance hole. She spat a wad of fibrous paste onto the wound, then worked it into the hole with a prod of her thumb.

"Duzi!" Garric screamed. He tried to jump back, but the girl kept her hold on his forearm. She was un*godl*y strong.

"Stand still!" the girl repeated. She popped what looked like a piece of root into her mouth and began chewing it with enthusiasm. It'd been about the size of the last joint of her thumb.

"Lila's a good healer," Metz said approvingly. "People from other villages came to her mother for healing."

His uncle Abay, the one with the lacerated face, grinned horribly. "Marzan should've married her instead of Soma when his first wife died," he said. "Guess he figures that way too, eh Lila?"

The girl didn't reply, but juice squirted around the edges of her smile. "Turn around, Lord Garric," she said in a mushy voice.

Garric obeyed, steeling himself for another piercing jolt. Lila spat. This time the pressure of her thumb felt more like a hammer blow than a blade. A pleasant warmth was already spreading from the wad of paste she'd packed into the entrance wound.

"Are you ready to return to your own time, Garric?" asked the Bird.

Garric looked up in surprise. The Bird was perched on the cross-wall of the stockade. Though he was within twenty feet of Garric, smoke and the omnipresent mist blurred his glittering shape.

"Yes," Garric said. He wondered if the villagers had heard the Bird's question. "Of course I am."

"Are you going to leave us, Garric?" Metz asked. The hunter was trying to keep his face blank, but an expression of blind terror flickered on and off it. *That answers the question of whether the villagers could hear. . . .*

"I have duties in my own time," Garric said. The day before he'd wanted nothing so much as to leave this miserable gray bog; now he felt pangs of guilt at abandoning people who trusted him. "I have to get back, Metz."

"But what will we do, master?" said Horst, rubbing his heavy chin in concern. "We could never have beat the Coerli without you."

Garric felt his face harden as his mind shuffled through options. He wasn't angry, but he'd been a king long enough to understand the sort of decisions a king had to make if he and his people were to survive.

"You've had me," he said. "You've seen what I did, what you did yourselves when I showed you. You can do it again."

"But Lord Garric," said a woman Garric didn't recognize. She'd been one of the captives, he thought. "There are so many Coerli and we are few. This was only one keep."

"There's other keeps, sure," Garric said, "but there's many more human villages. Metz, uniting your neighbors is as important as attacking the Coerli. You *can* unite and the cat men never will. This—"

He gestured at the smoking ruins of the keep.

"—was a real fight for your village alone, but if there'd been three or four villages together Torag wouldn't have had a prayer. You've got booty for trade, Coerli tools and fabrics—"

"And excess women," Carus added. *"There's many a chief whose opinion could change if you offered him the sort of young, healthy woman that the cat beasts picked for their own uses."*

That was true, but it wasn't something Garric was going to say or even allow himself to think. He continued aloud, "—that'll help you convince other villages that this isn't a wild risk. And you've got Coerli weapons. They'll impress neighbors who aren't completely willing. It's the *world's* safety at stake."

He took a deep breath. He felt oddly euphoric; the root that Lila'd pushed into his wound must have more than a simple healing effect.

"You've got to do it yourselves, Metz, all of you," he said, "but you can. And you should, because it's your world you're saving, not mine."

"Lord Garric?" said the woman who'd spoken before. "If you could stay with us for just a little while, then we'd be able to take over ourselves when you left. There's so much we don't understand!"

Carus watched through Garric's eyes with grim humor, his knuckles on his hips and his arms akimbo. "Just a little longer" was the most common plea a king heard. . . .

"There'll always be things you don't understand," Garric said, speaking to Metz but pitching his voice so that all the villagers could hear. "There'll always be things that're new to me too. This is *your* world. You're better off running it than I'd be—and if you're not, then you'll be leaving it for the Coerli. I hope and pray that's not what happens, but the choice is yours to make."

Donria whispered something in Metz's ear. The former hunter, now chief, straightened and said, "Garric? You've helped us. What can we do to help you?"

"By the Lady!" Carus said in delight. *"That Donria'll be the making of this world. This* kingdom *before long, I shouldn't wonder!"*

"Bird, what must I do to get home?" Garric asked. His conscience still troubled him, but he knew what he'd said was the truth: there'd never be a time that he couldn't be of some benefit to the Grass People, but he really had given them sufficient tools to save themselves.

"We must go to the cave in the abyss from which the Coerli enter this time," the Bird said. "I am not a wizard, but I can analyze potentials and adjust them. We will be able to do what you wish and what I need. We will go alone."

"But Garric?" Metz said, frowning in consternation. "That place is full of monsters. And the cat people as well, going to and from. *We* never went near it, even before the cat people came to the Land. Things live there that live nowhere else, terrible things."

Garric held the axe he'd taken from the Corl he'd killed when escaping. He turned to get a little room, then swung it back and forth in a wide arc. His shoulder felt like glass was breaking in it, but the weapon moved smoothly nonetheless.

He looked down, expecting to see blood start from the entrance wound; it didn't. Lila was back at Marzan's side; she gave him a smirk of satisfaction.

"When I have to," Garric said, "I can be pretty terrible myself. If the Coerli can pass that way, so can I."

The Bird jumped/flew/fell onto Garric's left shoulder. "Then let us go now," it said. "You're tired, but time is critical."

"Yes," said Garric. "Metz, fellow humans—my heart will be with you as you reclaim your world from monsters."

"And I suspect it's time and past time to do the same for the Kingdom of the Isles," said Carus. *"Because I don't believe the wizardry that brought you here didn't have more effect than that!"*

Captain ascor cleared his throat and said, "Your Highness, it's best you and Lady Tenoctris start back for Mona now. Things are apt to get—"

He paused to look down to the fog-wrapped plain.

"—pretty busy here soon."

Sharina smiled despite herself. Those weren't the words Ascor would've used if he'd been talking to another soldier.

She drew the big knife from beneath her outer tunic. "Ascor," she said, "provide a detail—a section, I think—to escort Lady Tenoctris to Mona. I'm going to remain here with the army."

"Your Highness, it's not safe!" the captain snapped.

"I know it's not safe," said Sharina, an edge in her voice as well. "That's why it's my duty to stay. With respect, Captain—precisely what do you think I could save by running away? Except my life, that is, which of course would be worthless if I were a leader who abandoned her troops."

"Oh, I'm not leaving, dear," Tenoctris said. "Apart from anything else, Cervoran hasn't been defeated yet. That was just a skirmish, another skirmish."

Sharina's eyes and the Blood Eagle's too shifted to Double, who'd arranged on the ground several objects he'd taken from his case. One was crinkled and amber. At first Sharina took it for a tortoise shell, but closer attention convinced her it was the husk of a cicada of remarkable size; her spread hand wouldn't have covered the thing.

Double bent and scribed a hexagram in the soil with his athame. He made the strokes separately instead of angling each side into the next in a combined motion as most people would've done. The amulet containing the lock of Ilna's hair wobbled on a silver neck chain.

One of the small ballistas released with a loud *crack*, sending out a caustic-headed quarrel. It struck at the base of a hellplant's torso, just above the squirming legs. All down the line of catapults and ballistas, men with long wrenches were tightening the springs of their weapons. The artillery couldn't be left at full tension for very long without warping the frames and weakening the coiled sinews. This morning the crews hadn't started cocking the weapons until they realized Double's wizardry wasn't going to save them.

"*Huese semi iaoi . . . ,*" Double chanted, dipping his athame to a different angle of his hexagram with each syllable. "*Baubo eeaei.*"

The *cracks* of more artillery—including a heavy catapult which must've had a picked crew—echoed around the bowl of the hills. Several plants ruptured and collapsed, already beginning to decay into the sodden ground. Another staggered in a wide curve to the right, gushing steam from its wounded side.

"*Sope . . . ,*" said Double. "*San kanthare ao!*"

The ground seemed to bubble. Tiny sharpnesses jabbed Sharina's feet between the sandal straps and up her ankles; she shouted in surprise. A guard jerked off his cape and began slapping it at his feet as though he were beating out a fire.

Locusts, some of them the length of a man's middle finger, were hatching out of the ground. That's all it was—locusts; but thousands upon crawling thousands of them.

"It's all right," Tenoctris called. Sharina doubted whether any of the soldiers heard her or if they'd have paid attention if they had. "This is Cervoran's doing. He's helping us!"

Crawling, fluttering, flying in slow, clumsy arcs, the locusts converged where the linked threads had crushed Double's mirror. The air was full of them and the ground for as far as Sharina could see shivered as still more insects dug up through it.

"*Eulamon,*" Double chanted. "*Restoutus restouta zerosi!*"

Sharina held the Pewle knife in her right hand and clung to Tenoctris with her left. She knew she was reassuring herself instead of supporting the old wizard; though perhaps she was supporting Tenoctris as well.

The hump of smothering vegetable matter vanished under the insects' jaws, individually tiny but working in uncountable numbers. The hellplants had slowed their advance, but fresh threads swept up on a rising breeze. Locusts curved to intercept them, snatching the strands from the air like falcons stooping on doves.

"*Benchuch bachuch chuch . . . ,*" chanted Double. His puffy, waxen face showed strain, but a look of triumph suffused it as well. "*Ousiri agi ousiri!*"

The film of silver lifted again to catch the risen sun. For a moment the swarming locusts distorted it, but they hopped and flew out of the obstructing pile that had devoured the linked threads. White light glared on a hellplant, ripping it instantly apart. The claw of light shifted and destroyed the next plant in line.

Lord Waldron spoke to his signalers; horns and trumpets blew Retreat. Troops began thankfully leaving the earthworks even before their own unit signalers passed on the command. When Double's wizardry was ascendant, all humans could do was to get in the way.

"Lady, thank you for Your support," Sharina whispered. "Lady, I will build a temple here for the salvation You have worked for the kingdom and for Mankind."

The wind died, dropping the threads which it'd lifted from the sea. The locusts continued to circle in swirls and clusters.

The sea's surface danced with foam. Birds rose from it, sweeping toward the ridge of the hills.

Not birds, fish! Fish flying!

They curled out of the water and flew low over the fields, leaving faint ruby trails in the dense fog. At the base of the hills they swooped upward, silvery bodies writhing and pectoral fins stretched out like sword blades. Their slender bodies reminded Sharina of mackerel, but their heads were things out of nightmare or the deep abysses: the eyes bulged, and the jaws hinged down into open throat sacs like those of pelicans.

When Sharina was a child, an earthquake had shaken the Inner Sea. Barca's Hamlet was protected by a granite seawall built during the Old Kingdom. The shock had slammed great waves into it, kicking spume a hundred feet in the air. The next day the tide brought in fish with heads like these, their bodies burst when they were sucked up to the surface.

A fish dived toward Sharina, its open mouth fringed with ragged teeth. Sharina stepped in front of Tenoctris and brought her knife around in a quick stroke. The fish wasn't attacking. Rather, it'd swept through the cloud of locusts, gulping down a mass of them and then cocking up its rigid fins to bank away.

Sharina's blade sheared off half the right fin and the tail besides. The fish tumbled out of the air and slapped the hard soil, its body trembling as its mouth opened and shut. Wizardlight dusted the air around it scarlet, then vanished as the creature died.

Fish slashed and curvetted through the mirror. The silver film reformed after each impact like water pelted by raindrops, but the ripples robbed its surface of the perfect focus which alone could concentrate the light into a sword. The hellplants resumed their march.

"*Tacharchen!*" Double shouted, pointing his athame toward the sea; his film of silver collapsed again into the soil. Double turned and stalked back to his case of paraphernalia.

"Oh, my goodness . . . ," Tenoctris said. Sharina glanced at her; the old wizard was staring raptly at what seemed empty sky.

Tenoctris was aware of—perhaps "saw" wasn't the correct word—the play of forces with which all wizards worked. Sharina suspected from past experience that Tenoctris actually understood those forces better than did wizards who had greater ability to affect them.

"What's—" Sharina said, but she fell silent because her coming question—what's going on, what do you see?—was idle curiosity and Tenoctris was clearly busy with important things.

Using Sharina's arm as a brace, the old wizard seated herself on the ground and pulled out a bamboo split. She quickly drew a pentagram in the thin soil. As she concentrated, she muttered, "Don't let anyone disturb me, if you please."

"Captain Ascor!" Sharina ordered, much more sharply than she'd intended. "Put a ring of men around Lady Tenoctris. Don't let anyone or anything close to her, *any*one!"

A squad of Blood Eagles shuffled about the old wizard, facing outward and lifting their shields as much by instinct as for cause. Sharina, glancing between the men's legs, saw Tenoctris scoop a shallow depression in the center of her pentagram. She filled it with what seemed to be water from an agate bottle with a stopper of cork.

Double took a spray of black feathers from his case. He crossed them on the ground into a six-pointed star, then began chanting. Sharina couldn't hear the high-pitched words over the whistle the fish made as their fins cut the air.

Tenoctris bent toward her image, mumbling words of power. If the guards heard her chanting, they kept that awareness out of their stolid faces.

Fish swooped and sailed, gulping down locusts but paying no attention to the assembled troops. Some soldiers batted at them with swords or spear shafts. They were harder to hit than they seemed, banking and curving more easily than such stiff-bodied creatures should've been capable of.

When a fish was knocked down, it flopped brokenly for a few moments, then died in a haze of escaping wizardlight. It didn't matter: there were thousands more flying, and a roiling sea from which any number could lift if the Green Woman found it necessary.

"*Anoch anoch . . . ,*" Double shouted, raising his athame like the staff of a banner. "*Katembreimo!*"

Though fog thick as a storm cloud darkened the basin of the hills, the sky overhead was blue and promised a hot day when the sun rose higher. Flecks speckled it suddenly: growing, diving; screeching like steel on stone. Each speck was a bird with a feathered serpent tail and its toothed beak open. They screamed as they tore into the fish. The birds had come from a clear sky and they continued to come, as many as raindrops in a summer storm.

The birds struck their prey with beaks, talons, and sometimes the hooked claws projecting from the angle of their stubby wings. They knocked the fish down with gaping wounds and flew on to kill more, never pausing to devour past victims. Sometimes locusts, freed from the torn bellies of falling fish, fluttered off dazedly.

Double was chanting again, his words barely audible through the chorus of his terrible birds. Familiarity made the spell ring in Sharina's mind, though: "*. . . benchuch bachuch chuch. . . .*"

The mirror rose, catching the full sun and sending its blazing radiance onto the plain again. Light carved through the mist, spinning pale whorls to either side and striking a plant that was mounting the abandoned breastworks. It fell apart.

The birds dived and screamed and killed. Friends—allies, at least—though the creatures were, Sharina kept her knife ready in case one flew too close. Seemingly the birds avoided humans in their circuits, but they fouled the air with the stench of a snake den.

The sea was silent, almost glassy smooth, while the mirror licked another hellplant and the next. The plants moved sluggishly, lacking the inexorable certainty with which they'd begun their assault.

Double was chanting. The skin over his white forehead was tight but his lips were twisted in a grin and he stood as firm as a tree with deep-driven roots. Sharina knew how physically demanding wizardry was. She had no trust or affection for Double, but as Tenoctris had said from the beginning: his strength was remarkable.

The thought made Sharina glance at Tenoctris, who continued to mouth words of power. Though her bamboo wand tapped out the syllables, no flicker of wizardlight brightened the air above her figure. The water in her bowl shivered.

The ground trembled faintly but unmistakably. Sharina felt as though she were standing on the back of an ox, feeling the beat of its great heart through the soles of her feet. She turned to Tenoctris, but the old wizard's concentration was so fierce that Sharina didn't even start to ask the frightened question that instinct had brought to the tip of her tongue.

The fog over the plains below cleared. Everything within the bowl of hills was as clear as the facets of a jewel. The wind and the birds were silent, and the hair on the back of Sharina's neck rose.

The hills softened and slumped the way dunes collapse when the surge undermines them. Men shouted, losing their footing and dancing in desperate attempts to keep from sinking into what had been rock or firm soil. The violent shuddering sifted the breastworks back into the trenches from which they'd been dug and shook the emplaced artillery. A large catapult toppled onto its side, and several ballistas pointed skyward.

Double kept his feet, but the frame of posts and canvas twisted in tatters as the ground gave way beneath it. The silver film smeared the surface instead of sinking into the subsoil as it'd done in the past. Looking to the west, Sharina saw flat marshes for as far as her eye could travel. The ridge had vanished utterly, leaving mule-drawn wagons mired where there'd been rocky switchbacks up the hills.

The hellplants were advancing with renewed vigor. On soil this wet, they could move as fast as a man. Their tentacles writhed, ready to grip and rend.

ILNA STEPPED AROUND an oak growing at a corner of the maze. The hedge down the aisle now before her was holly to the left and quickset to the right. Crouching in the middle was a three-headed dog as big as an ox.

She raised the pattern she'd knotted in anticipation of this meeting or one like it. She hadn't anticipated three heads, though: the great dog lunged toward her before stumbling and crashing onto its shoulder with a double yelp.

Chalcus shouted and drove past her with his sword and dagger out. He'd wanted to lead—but then, he'd wanted to guard the rear and also to fly over Ilna and the child so that nobody could approach from above. Ilna'd insisted on leading because she could capture rather than merely killing or chasing away whichever Prince they next met. That logic still held.

"Get out of the way!" Ilna said, making a quick change to the pattern—gathering a bight in the middle of the fabric because there wasn't time to do the job properly with an additional length of yarn. She was furious: with herself for not being better prepared and with Chalcus for assuming—well, acting as if—she wouldn't be able to recover from her error in time.

Mostly with herself. As usual.

Chalcus jumped aside as quickly as he'd come. The dog was already backing with the heads on either side turned away. The middle head was frozen in a look of slavering fury, like a trophy stuffed and nailed to the wall. The beast's right foreleg dragged and there was a hitch in the movements of the left hind leg as well.

"This is my territory!" snarled the left head.

"You have no right to—" began the right head.

Ilna spread her fabric. The dog took the new pattern through the open eyes of its middle head. It dropped where it stood.

"Now," said Ilna crisply. "You're going to answer the questions we ask or my friend Chalcus will cut pieces off you. I'm going to change my pattern enough to allow you to speak. If you choose not to help, we'll ask one of your fellow Princes, but we won't do that so long as you're alive."

The dog's breath stank of rotten meat. Knowing that the meat had been human wouldn't change Ilna's behavior, but neither did it dispose her to like the creature better. Instead of adjusting a knot of the pattern, she simply put the tip of her little finger over one corner.

The dog's left head jerked around to glare at them. "This is an outrage!" it snarled. "You—"

Chalcus stepped forward and flicked out his sword. One ear of the head that'd spoken spun into the quickset hedge. The dog yelped much louder than before; the head thrashed violently but the creature couldn't get away.

Merota gasped and clapped her hands to her mouth. Then she looked up with a distressed expression and said, "I'm sorry, Chalcus. He deserves it!"

"Ah, child," Chalcus said. He grinned broadly. "This one deserves far worse, I'm sure; and if he's stubborn I'll take pleasure in giving worse to him, that I will."

"We want to leave this tapestry," Ilna said, "this garden if you prefer. What is the way out?"

"I don't know—" said the dog. It jerked its head with a howl as Chalcus shifted minusculely.

"No!" said Ilna. "Not till I decide it's not answering. Dog, where do you *think* the exit is? You Princes talk to each other, don't you? You must talk about that!"

"We don't know," the dog said, speaking very carefully. Its tongue licked out of the narrow muzzle, trying to reach the blood slowly creeping from the severed ear. "No one has ever left the Garden. But some think . . ."

It licked again, this time swiping into the blood. The fur above where the tongue reached was matted and glistening.

"Some think, I say . . . ," the dog continued, "that perhaps the One built the temple in the center of the Garden to Himself. And perhaps when He finished the building, He took leave from the Garden at that place."

"I saw the temple!" Merota said. "I was looking at it when I fell into the maze!"

"Aye," said Chalcus. He'd sheathed his dagger so that he could very deliberately wipe the tip of his sword clean with a folded oak leaf. "And I too. What does it look like inside, this temple, good beast?"

The dog's chest rose and fell as it breathed; Ilna had been careful to paralyze only the creature's conscious control of its muscles. It would be very easy to freeze *all* movements, though, and to watch the dog slowly smother. How many little people had gone down those three gullets over countless years?

"I've never been there," the dog said, its eyes rolling desperately. Perhaps it'd understood Ilna's expression. "None of us have! It's, well, we don't know, of course, but some think, some *imagine*, that the other lives in the temple when it's not hunting somewhere. None of us know, nobody knows, but if the other *has* a particular place, it could be there."

"The other," Ilna said. "The Shadow, you mean."

She'd spoken with deliberate cruelty, so furiously angry at her prisoner that she risked summoning the Shadow just to make the dog howl in terror. As it did, voiding a flood of foul-smelling urine on the ground and its own hindquarters. Like breathing, that was an unconscious reaction. Merota squeezed her hands together and stared at Ilna.

"Gently, Ilna, dear heart," said Chalcus, a look of concern in his glance. "If you want him killed, I'll do that thing without regret; but if it's answers we're after, then he's giving us those."

"Yes, all right," said Ilna coldly. "The other, then. What makes you think it lairs in the temple? Have you seen it there?"

"We don't see it anywhere else, that's the thing!" said the dog. "Except when it strikes. We've none of us been to the temple, I *told* you that! But there's nowhere else it could be, is there?"

Ilna sucked her lower lip between her teeth and bit it. She knew what to do—what *she* would do—and she'd almost stated her wish as an order. She had to remember that hers was only one opinion among three, now.

"Master Chalcus, what would you that we do?" she asked formally.

"The longer we stay here," said the sailor, "the likelier it is that we'll meet something we'd sooner leave to itself. If the way out's through this temple, then I'll gladly go to the temple whatever it may be that lives there. I'd sooner we met it at home at a time of our choosing than from behind at a time of its."

"Merota?" Ilna said. She *could* give orders to her companions and force them to agree as surely as she'd bound this three-headed dog to her will. She'd been that person once, in the days just after she'd come back to the waking world having journeyed to Hell.

Never again. No matter what.

"I want to leave, Ilna," Merota said in a small voice. "I'm not afraid. When I'm with you and Chalcus, I'm not afraid."

Ilna sniffed. "Aren't you?" she said. "Well, I'm certainly afraid."

But not for myself. If I was sure that I alone would die, I'd smile and go on.

"All right, then," she said. "We'll find the temple and then do as seems best."

Chalcus flicked his sword so that the tip brushed the dog's curling eyelashes before it could twitch its head away. "And this one?" he asked. "Shall we have him guide us, then?"

"I don't need a guide to find a pattern, Master Sailor," Ilna said in a tight, dry voice; her lip curled as if she'd swallowed vinegar. "There's nothing about this beast that'll please me as much as his absence. Stand back—and you, Merota."

Her companions edged aside. Chalcus was trying to keep Ilna, Merota, and the great dog all in view at the same time—and to watch lest something come up behind them.

"I'm going to release you now," Ilna said to the panting dog. "I don't want to see you again. If I do, I'll kill you. Depending on how I'm feeling at the time, I may or may not kill you quickly. I hope you understand."

She folded the fabric between her hands and stepped back. The dog gave a spastic convulsion, its legs finishing the motions they'd started before Ilna's pattern cut them adrift. The big animal lurched to its feet and blundered sideways into the quickset hedge. Spiked branches crackled, but despite the beast's weight and strength the hedge held.

The dog got control of itself and backed away. "You belong with the other!" its middle head snarled. "The other has no honor and no courtesy. It's a monster that kills. You belong with it, monster!"

Ilna started to raise her hands, spreading the pattern again. The dog turned and bolted out of sight, its great paws slamming back divots of sod.

Ilna shrugged, trying to shake off memory of the dog and its stinking breath. "To the left here," she said, nodding to the junction of paths ahead of them. She sighed and began picking out knots to have the yarn ready for use the next time. "And to the left again at the next turning. Come! I have no wish to stay here."

Merota put her little hand on Ilna's arm as they strode off. "You're not a monster, Ilna," she said quietly.

"You're wrong there, I'm afraid," said Ilna. "But I'm your monster, child; and in this place, you need one."

Cashel heard the scholar get up, so he rose from his bedclothes also. It was still before dawn but light gleamed through the eastern wall where adobe hadn't perfectly sealed the chinks between mastodon bones.

He reached over and tousled the boy's short hair. "Wake up, Protas," he said quietly. "We're going off shortly."

"I'm tired!" the boy said, screwing his eyes tightly shut, but a moment later he threw off the tapestry covering him and sat up. He kept his face bent down, until he'd scrabbled under the covers and come out with the topaz crown. When he'd set it firmly on his head, he grinned shyly at Cashel and stood.

Antesiodorus was placing objects from his collection on a rectangle of densely woven cloth—a saddlecloth, Cashel guessed. It was figured in geometric patterns of black and white on a wine-colored ground. The scholar had already packed several books and scrolls; now he was choosing among the phials and caskets scattered along the sidewall.

"I can carry that for you if you like, sir," Cashel said. The bindle would be pretty heavy over any distance at all, and Antesiodorus looked like a high wind'd blow him over.

"I would not like," the scholar snapped. "You have your duties, I'm sure. You can leave me to mine."

Cashel nodded and walked to the pottery water jar. It'd been glazed red over a black background; winged demons with female heads were tormenting a man tied to the mast of his ship.

"I'm sorry, Master Cashel," Antesiodorus said to his back. "I'm upset because of what I'm being required to do, but that's not your fault."

"It's all right," Cashel said, smiling deep within himself. "Prince Protas and me know we're strangers. We appreciate your help."

He refilled the cup and gave it to the boy, who gurgled the water down greedily. This air was dry as could be.

Antesiodorus paused, then took a wand with a tentacled head from its shelf. Cashel thought first it was a plant, then realized it must be a sea lily like the ones that weathered out of a limestone bluff on the road from Barca's Hamlet to Carcosa. Those were all turned to rock, though. The lily Antesiodorus slipped under his sash was dry, but it was fresh enough that Cashel could smell salty decay clinging to the hollow shell.

"Do you need something to eat?" Antesiodorus said, taking the cup from Protas and edging past Cashel to dip it full again. "It's not far. That is . . ."

The scholar drank, paused, and finished the water. He looked doubtfully at the jar, then set the mug down.

"We'll be there in at most two hours," Antesiodorus said, looking squarely at Cashel. "If we can reach it at all. I assume that since you've been sent to me, there may be those who wish to prevent your journey?"

He raised an eyebrow in question.

Cashel shrugged. "I don't know," he said truthfully. "I'm here to help Protas, but nobody told us what was going to happen."

With a broad grin he added, "I'm used to people not telling me things. I wish it didn't happen that way, but it does."

"Well, I don't suppose it matters," Antesiodorus said with an angry scrunch of his face that made the words a lie. "We'd best be going. The sun's up. That will keep the worst in their dens, but the more quickly we get the business over, the better off we are."

He gestured them through the doorway and followed. Outside the scholar fingered the cape over the opening. He frowned and straightened, turning his back on the long dwelling.

"We're going eastward," Antesiodorus said. "I know it's difficult to hold direction in these eroded gullies, but there's a white peak on the horizon. You can orient yourself by it."

Cashel grinned, thinking of what his sister would've said to a comment like that. "Yes, and I can breathe air, you city-bred fool," or perhaps something more insulting.

But that was Ilna. Cashel being Cashel, he said instead, "I thought you might wear the cape this morning, sir. Instead of leaving it over the door."

"Did you?" snapped Antesiodorus. He set off at a brisk pace among the rotting hills. Cashel could keep up, though he usually traveled at the rate a ewe ambled. Protas, walking ahead of him, wasn't having trouble either. Occasionally he touched the crown, but it was firmly seated.

After a moment, the scholar said in an apologetic tone, "The cloak would only protect one of us. Better that it stay where it is so that if I don't return, those who investigate can see that I was faithful to my trust."

He looked over his shoulder at Cashel. "Do you understand that?" he said.

Cashel nodded. "I guess I do," he said mildly.

The stretch of mounds and gullies gave way to short prairie. The grass was yellow-brown, but its roots were healthy enough to hold the soil. A small herd of browsers saw the three humans and fled northward in a gangling canter.

"Were those deer?" Cashel said. "They looked different from the deer I've seen before."

"They were camels," Antesiodorus said, "if it matters. You can be thankful if you see nothing worse."

"Are the birds dangerous?" Protas said. He was looking up at the sky where three dots circled slowly upward on the morning breezes.

"Not unless you're dead," Antesiodorus said. "Or until you're dead, perhaps I should say."

"They're buzzards, Protas," Cashel explained quietly. "Though I've never seen buzzards so big. If I'm right about the size, they'd weigh as much as a man."

The scholar had no need to snap at the boy that way, but he was obviously keyed up. People did that sort of thing.

"They'd weigh more than I do, at any rate," said Antesiodorus. He looked back at the boy and then Cashel. "But they don't kill prey themselves. There's plenty of others to do that, but perhaps we'll avoid them."

A mixed herd was grazing on the southern horizon. There were horses for sure but the other things could be . . . well, could be a lot of things, none of them familiar.

"Those deer have six horns, Cashel," Protas said.

"They're antelope," Antesiodorus said, correcting him.

The land to the north sloped down slightly. In the middle distance was the bed of a stream, probably dry in this weather. Bushy cottonwoods fringed both banks, and deeper in the gully grew alders. The trees pulled water from the currents flowing under the ground.

"There's a deer in the gully," Cashel said. "Three of them, I think. See, Protas? Under the cottonwood that still has some of its leaves?"

He didn't point; shepherds mostly didn't. If you pointed at a ewe, she was likely to run off in a blind panic. That hurt the meat and made her give less milk both, and that was if she didn't manage to tumble down a ravine and break her fool neck.

"Stand very still!" Antesiodorus ordered.

Cashel froze. "What—" said Protas, turning to Cashel in worried surprise. Cashel didn't move or even scowl, but the boy took the hint from his perfectly blank expression.

"I never wanted to be a wizard," Antesiodorus said softly, his face turned toward the watercourse. "I'm a scholar. I found things, that's all. Found them in space and even in time, but only to study them."

The three deer-headed humans stepped up from the gully to stand beside the big cottonwood. Two were men and one a woman. Like reindeer, she as well as the males had antlers. They were browsing the alders, plucking leaves off with their narrow muzzles.

"There were twelve of us in our sodality," Antesiodorus continued. "Our brotherhood, I suppose I should say if I want you to understand."

"I know what a sodality is," Protas protested in an injured tone.

Cashel frowned. He *hadn't* known, but could generally figure out what people meant from the way they said it. Anyhow, when their guide was telling them things they might need to know, they shouldn't interrupt.

The trio of deer-men stopped eating and stared intently in the direction of Cashel and his companions. After a moment they vanished into the gully so suddenly that there didn't seem to have been movement: they were on the bank and then they were gone.

Antesiodorus breathed out. "All right," he said, "we can go on now."

"Were they dangerous, sir?" Cashel asked, falling in behind Protas as he had in the past.

"No," said Antesiodorus. "But when something's hunting them, they're in the habit of leading the hunter across the trail of prey that can't run as fast as they do. And then running away."

"What a cowardly act!" said Protas.

"What do you know about it, boy?" Antesiodorus snarled. "Do you know what it's like to be hunted? *Really* hunted!"

"*I've* been hunted, Master Antesiodorus," Cashel said. He didn't raise his voice or let any emotion into it, but his tone made it clear that he was stepping in front of the boy now. Protas had put a foot wrong, which was a pity, but it wasn't a thing he'd meant to do.

Their guide looked over his shoulder; his lean face was anguished. "Yes," he said, "I suppose you have. But you always knew you could fight, didn't you, Master Cashel?"

"Yes sir," said Cashel. "But I haven't known that I'd win every time. I just knew I'd rather die than live knowing that I'd handed my bad luck off to somebody else."

Antesiodorus faced front and shifted a little to the left of the line he'd been following; a faint buzzing and a glitter of wings in the air showed that they'd been about to walk over a yellow-jacket hole. He said, "Yes, that's the problem, isn't it? Being able to live with the person you find behind your eyes when you wake up in the darkness. But you haven't had that problem, have you?"

"No sir," Cashel said quietly.

There was a herd of big animals to the northeast, grazing in close company. There were more than Cashel could count on both hands. They acted like cows, but they were bigger and they had dark wool over their forequarters and horned heads. One of them watched the humans for a moment, then went back to its food.

"I knew so *much*," Antesiodorus said. "So very much. And that's all I cared about. I never used the objects I found except to find more. I let my brothers use them, but that was their choice. I never wanted to do wizardry. It's not fair now that I should be forced to!"

"Who's forcing you, then?" said Protas. That was an honest question, but the boy asked it in a way that showed he'd been bothered more than a little by the scholar snapping at him.

Cashel kept watching the wooly cattle. A couple of them raised their heads; they were looking due north. One of the big beasts gave a snort;

the whole herd jerked its heads up. After a moment they started moving southward slowly while a big bull stood braced and looking the other direction.

"I found things and gave them to my brothers," the scholar said. "I never used them, *never,* except to find more . . . things. *They* gained by my actions, not me. You see that, don't you?"

"You did what you wanted to do," Cashel said. He glanced in other directions too, especially straight behind them, but mostly he kept his eyes on where the bull was looking. "You and your friends both got what you wanted."

"I found a spell," Antesiodorus said as though he hadn't heard the comment. "No one else could've done what I did—no one, I'm sure. It was carved on a plate of gray jade as thin as parchment. It'd been broken into six pieces, every piece as necessary as the next for the spell to work, and I found all six. I alone!"

"What did the spell do, then?" asked Protas. He'd lost his testiness and become a curious little boy again.

Cashel saw movement on the other side of the cattle. The ground rolled and whatever it was kept down in the grass besides, but things were watching him and his companions.

"The spell?" repeated Antesiodorus. "It permitted the user to control a demon. I'd never have done such a thing myself, of course. Never!"

He cleared his throat. "I found the sixth piece," he continued. "It was no use alone, none. Only with the other five did it have meaning, and only I could have searched out the entire plaque. But the one who'd possessed the piece heard me take it and followed."

"The owner," Protas said. "The owner caught you."

"How can someone own a thing that was old before men and which had no value to the possessor?" Antesiodorus said, his voice cracking. "It wasn't his, it was just a thing he had! And he didn't catch me, no."

He looked back at Cashel, not Protas, and said, "He didn't catch me then, because I left the piece with my brethren, the members of my sodality, and fled while they examined the plaque. They were delighted, you see; they couldn't praise me enough. We were sworn to support one another in all ways, and they all spoke of what a valued brother I was. They didn't know."

"You saved yourself by setting a demon on your friends," Protas said. There was nothing at all in the boy's tone, just the words. It was as though all the feeling had been shocked out of him.

"No!" Antesiodorus said. He laughed brokenly. "Or perhaps yes, if you look only at the surface. It wasn't a demon, it was much worse than that. And they weren't my friends; they were brothers of my oath, but not friends."

"And you didn't escape," said Cashel. "It caught you anyway, and you serve it now."

"You think you're so smart!" the guide shouted.

"No," said Cashel. "I don't. I'm not."

"I think perhaps you're wrong, my simple friend," Antesiodorus said in a broken voice. "You're too smart to find yourself in my situation, at any rate. Now that I've had time to think about it, I believe the way the jade was broken and scattered was a trap for . . . someone like me. Someone who liked to find things. I've had a great deal of time to think about it, as you'll appreciate."

"Sir?" said Cashel formally. "Look to the north, please. On the little ridge there. They've been looking at us ever since the cattle started to move."

The things watching them had risen into sight. They looked like dogs but they were the size of horses, and they had the huge crinkled ears of bats. There were five of them, one for each finger on a single hand.

"Oh," said Antesiodorus. He kept walking but he stumbled on a tussock of grass and almost fell, slight though it was. "Oh. Oh."

He took a deep breath. "One moment, please," he said, kneeling on the prairie and opening out his bindle before him. "I'd thought that by going by daylight we'd avoid at least them, but it seems that I was wrong. Wrong again."

The bat-eared dogs were ambling down the hill, spreading out slightly as they advanced. They were a pale color like mushrooms that grow in a cave; what Cashel'd thought when he first saw them were stripes seemed now to be wrinkles on their bare skin.

Antesiodorus rose, clutching his bindle under his left arm. He had a book open in that hand with his thumb marking a place. "Come along!" he said. "Don't run, but keep moving steadily."

Cashel began to spin his quarterstaff as he walked. It worked his torso muscles and, well, it made him feel more comfortable.

He wasn't afraid of a fight, but the dogs were big and there were five of them. It would be hard to keep Protas safe, and that was what he was along to do.

Cashel smiled a little. If things went the way he expected them to, he wouldn't be around for anybody to complain to. Still, he'd give the dogs a good fight.

As the beasts walked on, a little faster now, their mouths dropped open into clown smiles. They had long, pointy teeth like snakes did, and their lolling tongues were forked.

"Go on ahead of me now," said Antesiodorus, drawing the sea lily from his sash; he must use it for a wand. He focused on the book in his hand, then called *"Dode akrouro akete!"* and slashed the sea lily down.

Scarlet wizardlight danced and crackled across the prairie. Nettles and thistles rose, spread, and interlocked, growing into a hedge as dense and high as a range of mountains. The ground shook and there was a roar like cliffs falling into the sea.

Antesiodorus staggered backward, dropping the book and the bindle but continuing to grip his wand. "Come along," he whispered. Then, more strongly, "Come!"

He bent to pick up the bindle. Cashel took it and the book instead and handed them to Protas to carry.

"Yes, all right," said the scholar. "But come."

They set off at a shambling trot. Cashel would've offered to carry Antesiodorus if he hadn't thought it was better that he keep both hands on his quarterstaff. The scholar did all right, though, after the first few strides where he wobbled like a drunk on an icy road.

Cashel glanced over his shoulder. The high thorn hedge ran from horizon to horizon without a break. Antesiodorus'd said he was a scholar who wasn't interested in wizardry. Cashel'd thought that meant he was like Tenoctris: somebody smart and who knew a lot of things, but who wasn't strong enough to do much.

The fellow who'd raised that hedge with a stroke and a short spell was a powerful wizard, no mistake. That meant whoever had Antesiodorus by the short hairs was more powerful still.

A mixed herd of animals was running southward. Cashel could see horses and deer and more of the funny long-necked camels, but there were other things besides. It was like the way a grass fire drives animals.

Cashel grinned as he jogged. He'd met plenty of people who'd rather face a fire than wizardry. Even if neither one was aimed at you, they were likely uncomfortable to be around.

They were moving toward the tall white peak on the horizon. Cashel knew enough about distances under a sky like this to be sure that the mountain was days away and maybe weeks. Antesiodorus had said it'd only take a couple hours to get to where they were going. If they made it at all, that was.

Cashel looked back again. To his surprise he saw two of the dogs already on their trail again; the other three were squirming the final bit of the way through the thorns. They'd done it by brute strength, not wizardry: the leading dog had scratches on its bunched shoulders and it'd torn the lobe of its right ear to tatters, but it loped along easily. It had a tail like a pig's, short and curled and pointed toward the sky.

"They're coming again," Cashel said. He wasn't talking because he was afraid: he just wanted to let Antesiodorus know what was going on.

Protas looked over his shoulder. His mouth fell open and he stumbled, but he just turned around again and kept on running. He was really a good boy.

"It's not far," Antesiodorus said. He was gasping; Cashel thought he'd have shouted if he'd had enough breath. "Not far."

"Sir, neither's the dogs!" Cashel said. In another few strides—a couple double handfuls at the most—he was going to turn and see what he could do with the quarterstaff. He'd be willing to give himself even odds against the first dog, but the second wasn't but a few lengths behind it. If the other three caught up—and they would, no doubt about that—it was just a question of whether they worried his body for a while or killed him quick and went on to finish the others.

"Why me!" Antesiodorus said. This time he did manage to shout. He added in a gasp, "Pass me my equipment, boy. And in a moment we'll stop."

Protas trotted up alongside the scholar, holding the bindle out in both hands. Cashel for his part dropped back a little, moving to the side so that he could have both his companions and the dogs at the edge of his vision.

The lead dog ran a funny way, its hindquarters not quite tracking its forequarters so its body was slightly skewed. It seemed comfortable like that, and it didn't have to stretch to gain on its human prey. Its eyes were small and glittered like an angry shoat's.

"We're stopping!" the scholar wheezed.

Cashel slowed and turned. He'd planned to put himself well in front and squarely between the nearest dog and his companions, but that animal angled to its left while the one behind it was slanting right. They'd done this before. . . .

Of *course* they'd done it before. They hadn't gotten that big sucking at their mother's dugs.

Cashel backed so he was close enough to touch his companions, bad for a fight but his only chance to maybe keep one of the beasts from slipping behind to gobble up Protas and the scholar while the other was keeping Cashel busy.

And then there were three more.

Antesiodorus scattered the contents of a little alabaster box in a broad arc toward the dogs. It looked like sand, but it might've been tiny jewels for all Cashel knew. Even if it was sand, it wouldn't have been just sand. He pointed the sea lily at it and shouted, *"Io gegegegen!"*

This time the flash of wizardlight was as blue as a sapphire in bright sun. The roar and shudder threw Cashel off his feet though he'd thought he was ready to ride it out. Dust rose in a great pall, curling backward blindingly.

Cashel stood, his eyes slitted. He put his left arm over his face so that he could breathe through the sleeve.

For a moment he couldn't tell what was happening on the other side of the dust cloud, but at least there wasn't a dog bigger'n a horse lumbering through with its mouth open. He risked a glance back. Antesiodorus was slumped in a sitting position with Protas bracing him so he didn't fall flat.

The dust cleared a little, enough for Cashel to see that what'd been rolling plain between them and their pursuers was now a gaping chasm. Two of the dogs had reached the edge on their side. One hunched like it was getting ready to jump.

Cashel walked a few paces along his side of the gap to put himself where the dog would land if it made the leap. That didn't seem likely, though he wasn't taking any chances. The sudden gully was wider than he could toss a stone across; wider, he thought, than an archer could shoot and expect to hit a particular target, though he didn't doubt an arrow could fly to the other side if you didn't have anything in mind but sticking it somewhere in the ground there.

The dog must've had the same thought; it relaxed for a moment. The rest of the pack joined the two leaders. All together they went over the lip of the chasm, each scraping out a trail of dirt and pebbles in a high rooster tail behind it. The wall was steep but not quite sheer, and the dogs didn't seem to be having any trouble with the slide.

Coming back up the other side would be a lot harder, but Cashel didn't figure they'd have started down if they didn't think they could make it up too. Given how big they were the dogs didn't have much of a turn of speed, but nobody could teach them anything about determination.

Antesiodorus had staggered to his feet; the boy did everything his little body could to help. The scholar muttered something; somehow he was still hanging onto the sea lily.

Protas turned to Cashel and called desperately, "He says to come on! It's close, he says!"

Cashel scooped Antesiodorus up in the crook of his left arm. "Bring the bindle!" he said. It'd take some time for the dogs to make it up the near side of the chasm; from the look of the scholar it'd be longer yet before he was able to walk on his own legs, let alone run.

Cashel didn't have a direction except the general one, toward the distant mountain, so he followed that. He held the staff out to his right side so it'd balance the scholar's weight. He didn't like to run and he wasn't good at it, but he could lumber along the way an ox did when unyoked after a long day and scenting water.

It was there in front of them, a square slab of granite flush with the ground. You had to be right on top of the stone to see it, and even then it was because there wasn't grass growing on it. A figure with more angles than a hand had fingers was carved onto the surface.

"Get on the heptagram!" Antesiodorus said. His breath was whooping in and out. "Please. Please, quickly."

Cashel placed himself in the figure and hugged Protas close; it was a tight fit for the two of them to stay inside the lines, which he figured they'd better do. But—

"Master Antesiodorus?" he called. "What about you?"

The scholar pointed his wand at the stone slab. "*Choi . . . ,*" he said. "*Chooi chareamon. . . .*"

Blue light glittered briefly among the knotted arms of the sea lily. Protas had dropped the bindle before he stepped onto the marked stone, but Antesiodorus ignored it. The roll'd opened when it hit the ground, spilling a zebrawood baton and a pair of scrolls tied with red ribbon.

"*Iao iboea . . . ,*" Antesiodorus said. Again wizardlight, this time scarlet, danced on his wand. He was speaking the words of power from memory instead of reading them from one of the books he'd brought. His face was set in an expression of utter determination.

The head of one of the great dogs lifted above the rim of the chasm.

It slipped back in a fresh cloud of dust and gravel kicked out by the beast's scrabbling claws, but two more dogs got their forepaws over the edge and bunched their shoulders to leap onto the plain.

"Sir!" Cashel shouted. "The dogs!"

"*Ithuao!*" Antesiodorus shouted. The dogs lurched up, got their hind legs under them, and galloped forward. Their slavering jaws were open.

Light, blue and red and then merging to purple, flared on the many-pointed symbol. Cashel felt the stone give way beneath him in a fashion that'd become familiar.

"I kept my oath!" Antesiodorus called as the dogs lunged.

The curtain of purple light thickened, blocking sight of the world Cashel was leaving with the boy. He heard the scholar's voice crying, "This time I kept my—"

The words ended in a scream, or perhaps that was only the howl of the cosmos as it whipped Cashel away in a descending spiral.

Chapter

14

Lᴏʀᴅ ᴀᴛᴛᴀᴘᴇʀ ꜱʟᴏꜱʜᴇᴅ toward Sharina. The Blood Eagles who'd been with him—all those but the section with Sharina and Tenoctris—followed in a ragged wave.

"Ascor, you idiot!" he shouted in a voice loud enough to be audible over the general tumult. "Get Her Highness out of here! What are you standing around for?"

Attaper'd compromised between his duty and the desire of a warrior to be part of the battle instead of standing out of it as an observer: he'd placed the hundred or so men of the bodyguard regiment in the earthworks directly between the ridge where Princess Sharina stood and the direction of the hellplants' attack. At the time, of course, he'd assumed that Her Highness would be able to flee if the struggle went badly. . . .

"No!" Sharina said—to Ascor, but then turning to Attaper she cried, "Milord, we have to defend Lady Tenoctris! She's our only hope!"

The guard commander probably couldn't hear her, but Ascor did. He hesitated. His orders came from Attaper, not from a princess who, though exalted, wasn't in his chain of command.

Sharina wasn't sure what Ascor would've decided if he'd made up his own mind, but Trooper Lires chuckled and said, "Don't you worry, Princess. The captain remembers how you'n Lady Tenoctris saved things back in Valles. He got promoted that time, and I guess maybe they'll make him deputy commander this time, hey Cap'n?"

"That's if we survive, Lires," Ascor said in a taut voice. With a smile almost as sharp as his words he added, "Which I doubt we'll do, but you're right—I doubted it in Valles too."

Double had fallen with everyone else when the hills flattened. He got up slowly, as though he had to consider each separate movement, then staggered to his box of equipment. It lay on its side, half sunken in the mud.

The two trumpeters with Lord Waldron blew the quick, ringing notes of Stand To, halting the retreat. The cornicenes took it up, then signalers throughout the army. The soldiers Sharina could see—she didn't have the vantage point of the ridge to look down from—slowed and looked behind them, milling in indecision.

Lires chuckled. "Look at 'em," he said. "It's a bloody good thing that it's all gone to muck underfoot, ain't it, Cap'n?"

Sharina looked from the trooper to Ascor in surprise. She'd heard all the words, but they didn't mean anything to her.

"Your Highness," Ascor said, looking out at the advancing hellplants. "If the ground was firm, well . . ."

He shrugged. "Nothing against the line regiments, Your Highness," he continued, "but once troops start to run, it's next to impossible to turn them. Even good troops."

Lires stamped. His boot slurped ankle-deep in mud. "They couldn't get to running in this, you see?" he said. "Nothing to do but stand the way the trumpets tell 'em to do."

Attaper was within ten yards, slogging on in silent fury. He'd widened the gap between himself and the soldiers who'd been with him, even though most of them were younger than he was. In the morning, if Attaper lived that long, he'd be in agony with pulled muscles in his thighs, but he didn't allow pain or the mud to stop him now.

Thinking of what she was going to tell the commander made Sha-

rina look back at Tenoctris. The old wizard continued to chant within
the fence of soldiers' legs. *How long will it take to—*

With a sudden convulsive movement, Tenoctris stabbed her bamboo
split into the center of the scooped basin in front of her. She cried,
"Sabaoth!"

The air sparkled faintly blue. The water in the basin froze.

Ice spread outward in jagged curves from the basin, crackling and
forming a white rind over the marsh. The soldiers guarding Tenoctris
were taken by surprise. They leaped up and stamped, breaking their
boots free of frozen mud.

Sharina saw the ice sweeping toward her. She tried to jump over the
oncoming change, but she hadn't allowed for her fatigue. She stumbled
forward and felt the mud congeal about her feet as the broad swath slid
past her and on. It left the rime behind it gleaming like a slug's track.

She tried to pull free, twisting against the soil's cold grip. Lires drove
the butt of his spear into the ground beside her left foot, smashing the
thick crust and allowing her to lift her feet out of it.

All around Sharina soldiers shouted in fear and amazement. As
Tenoctris' spell spread outward, its effect speeded up. The soil froze to
the edge of the bay, turning windblown foam into a coating of rime.

Men hopped up and down, freeing themselves, but the hellplants
stopped where they were as if suddenly rooted to the ground. Their tentacles moved sluggishly, no faster than the blooms of the heliotrope following the circuit of the sun. Plants don't like cold any better than they
like darkness. . . .

"Lord Attaper!" Sharina said as the guard commander struggled to
her side. "Now's the time to attack, while we can move and the plants
cannot. Can you give the signal?"

Attaper looked first shocked, then puzzled. Then the meaning behind the words dragged his mind out of the set, angry rut in which it'd
been running and he saw that she was right.

"You, cornicene!" he shouted to the signaler from a line regiment
standing a few yards away. "Sound Charge!"

He turned. "Blood Eagles, follow me!" he bellowed. "Sharina and
the Isles."

Sharina waved her Pewle knife in the air. "The Isles forever! Attack,
attack, attack!"

The Blood Eagles turned around. Nobody else was paying attention to Princess Sharina; indeed, the Blood Eagles probably weren't either, but they saw their commander slant his sword toward the enemy. That was enough for them.

Sharina could've stayed where she was; *should've* stayed where she was, she knew, because there were ten thousand male swordsmen in the regiments assembled here. Every one of them was better for the purpose than a woman with a knife, even a healthy young woman with a *big* knife.

She advanced on the hellplants anyway, with Lord Attaper at her left and Lires on her right. The trooper had loosened his shield strap so that he could hold it out in front of the princess if he needed to.

Lires wasn't a great thinker, but he knew battle and he knew his job. He had the ability many smarter men lacked, the knack of connecting his experience with the situation he'd be facing in the immediate future. Thus the shield strap.

The ground had occasional patches of greasy slickness, but the soil had been gritty enough that even frozen it gripped the soles of Sharina's sandals well enough. The soldiers' hobnails dug in; the texture of the ground was like that of the first hard freeze of winter, not the surface of a glacier.

Tenoctris had collapsed over her symbol and basin. One of the guards had lifted her head off the ground and was placing his rolled cloak under it; the rest of the squad stood around her as they'd been ordered to do, looking unhappy.

Seeing them allowed Sharina to relax slightly. If they hadn't been there, she'd have had to go back and stay with her friend; but then, if they hadn't stayed where they'd been ordered to, Attaper would've dismissed them from the Blood Eagles and very possibly had the squad leader executed. A princess has the right to determine for herself where duty lies. A soldier does not.

Lord Waldron was trying to reorganize his forces after the multiple disruptions caused by wizardry; his subordinate commanders had even more basic objectives, to halt men on the verge of panic and to get them to listen to commands again. Nobody had time for or interest in a single signaler sounding Charge on the horn wrapped around his body.

They noticed the bodyguard regiment, though—a hundred and some big men in black armor, advancing toward the enemy in a reasonably compact mass. Sharina's bright blond hair hadn't regrown to the splendor it'd been before she'd had to shave it a few months earlier, but it still stood out like a banner in a sea of soldiers.

And even troops who couldn't see the princess among her guards were drawn by the attack. Often it's easier to move toward danger than it is to wait patiently for imminent danger to come to you.

Once men looked in the direction the Blood Eagles were advancing, they saw that the terrible enemies they'd feared as even brave men fear were frozen and motionless. They were no more dangerous now than so many cabbages.

The hellplants were ripe for revenge.

Sharina jogged and skidded over ground that was more solid than the week before when it'd been plowed fields. It was better footing this way too, since the furrows had slumped closed when the farm'd turned to marshland. It was tricky to run across furrows and almost impossible to run along them without stumbling in a soft spot or where a clod turned underfoot; Sharina knew. . . .

Tenoctris *couldn't* have done this! To undo the work of the Green Woman would've required a wizard of equal power, and only Double—

Sharina looked over her shoulder. The whole army was returning sluggishly to the attack; that was gratifying. But Double was where Sharina'd last seen him, standing beside his case of paraphernalia and wearing a look of blank incomprehension. She didn't think his legs had moved since the spell took effect; was he frozen to the ground?

Tenoctris had done *something*. Perhaps she'd summoned Cervoran? But she'd claimed that Double *was* Cervoran!

A hellplant had advanced a few yards ahead of its fellows; perhaps it'd crossed the earthworks at a place where the rampart had slumped. Three Blood Eagles and a line soldier fell on it just ahead of Sharina. One guard had come from a cavalry regiment and still carried his long sword; he thrust it deep into the hellplant's barrel and twisted as it jerked it back.

A crinkle of ice followed the steel; the reservoir in the creatures' bodies had frozen along with the fields. No wonder the plants had stopped advancing!

Four men hacking at one object, even an object as large as a hellplant, were enough. More blades without careful coordination meant the attackers would cut one another, and Sharina had seen too many battles by now to imagine that "careful coordination" was possible in the midst of one.

She ran to the next plant. Attaper and Lires flanked her as before. She half-expected Attaper to object, but instead he saved his breath for better uses.

The score of tentacles fringing the top of the hellplant's barrel were blackening from the cold already. One moved feebly toward Sharina; she sheared it with a side stroke, then bent. As the soldiers slashed at the plant's vast body, she began methodically to chop off the white, worm-like tendrils on which the creature walked.

Each blow crunched the blade through into the ground beneath. She'd have to sharpen it after the battle, but there was no time for finesse. Nonnus would've understood that.

Lady, bless the soul of my friend and protector. Lady, make me worthy of the life he sacrificed for me.

"Back, Your Highness!" Attaper said. Before he had the last syllable out, he'd grabbed Sharina by the shoulder and dragged her away. *There's no time for finesse.*

The plant slumped like a mass of snow sliding off roof slates, a quiver building to a rush until it crashed into the hard ground. The green body burst at every point a blade had cut it. A slush of half-frozen seawater oozed out, smelling of iodine.

A javelin stood up from the mass, then fell free as the remains rotted with the usual suddenness. The spear hadn't been there when Sharina and the guards attacked the creature: one of the soldiers behind them had thrown it while they fought, missing the humans by the Lady's grace and doing no significant harm to the plant, as any *idiot* should've known by now!

Sharina started to laugh. She took two steps toward the next hellplant, but there was already a squad of men around every one of the creatures in the immediate vicinity. She stopped, her laughter building hysterically. She knelt and set the Pewle knife flat on the ground; she was afraid she'd cut herself as she laughed uncontrollably.

"Your Highness?" Attaper said. "Your Highness!"

"I've read the Old Kingdom epics, Attaper!" Sharina said. Concentrating to speak helped her to regain self-control. "They've all got battles in them. Sometimes they're mostly battles."

"Your Highness?" Attaper said, this time in confusion instead of building concern.

"Not once in an epic, milord," Sharina said. "Not *once*. Is the king killed when one of his own men accidentally sticks a spear through him from behind. I'm beginning to think the poets aren't trustworthy guides to the reality of battle!"

She dissolved into laughter again, resting her palms on the hard ground. Around her rang the triumphant cries of her men as they cleared Calf's Head Bay of living hellplants.

GARRIC PAUSED AT the lip of the abyss. He'd been expecting a narrow canyon—for no particular reason, he realized. It was just an assumption he'd made.

A foolish assumption, he saw now: the abyss was more or less circular as best he could tell through the mist. The walls were steep, crumbled back slightly around the rim but close to vertical in many places farther down as Garric's eye tracked it. He heard water roaring over the cliff somewhere though he couldn't see the falls themselves. They were probably the reason that the depths of the abyss were even foggier than the general landscape.

"Is it a sinkhole?" Garric asked the Bird on his shoulder. He bent and rubbed the rock exposed on the track leading downward. "It can't be! This is hard, basalt I think. Sinkholes are in limestone that the water's eaten away."

"There was a bubble in the flow of a great volcano," the Bird explained. "The top wore away. That took longer than you can imagine—longer than this world has known life. But it happened."

It clucked audibly, then added, "There's an hour left of daylight. We should start down. It'll be more dangerous after sunset."

"All right," said Garric. "Ah—I won't be able to see any farther than my hand outstretched when we get any ways down in that, even now."

He wasn't complaining, just making sure the Bird understood the situation.

"A little farther than that," the Bird said. "But yes, I'll guide you. We'll keep to the trail as long as we can, but if we meet a party of Coerli we'll have to move to the side. The other creatures have generally learned to avoid the trail themselves, but even that isn't safe."

Garric chuckled as he started down. It was too narrow for a pack animal, even an unusually sure-footed donkey, but it was only moderately steep.

"Safe was when I was tending sheep back in the borough," he said quietly. He thought of the afternoon the pack of sea wolves had squirmed out of the surf, great marine lizards. "And even that had its moments," he added.

The dense basalt was slick with spray condensed on its surfaces. Though the path wasn't particularly regular—the footing humped and sagged, and at some points the track was undercut so that the side of the cliff bellied out above it—it certainly wasn't natural.

And it showed considerable wear. That would've taken a long time in rock so hard.

"Did men cut this, Bird?" Garric asked. Part of him felt silly to vocalize the question when he knew the Bird heard his thoughts, but he found it more comfortable to pretend this was a normal conversation. "It's too worn for the Coerli to've done it if they just arrived here a few years ago."

"A normal conversation with a crystal bird," Carus said, grinning. *"In a land of swamps and shadows, with one really deep hole."*

"Others than men built the path, Garric," the Bird said. He'd taken to flying ahead and perching on an outcrop or a tree just at the edge of Garric's vision; a dozen feet or so away. "The cave in which my people lived has drawn visitors since before there was intelligent life in this land, though those who made the path were intelligent."

Garric thought of asking more, then decided not to. The Bird had shown itself a friend. If it didn't volunteer information, there was probably a reason for its reticence.

"I am not your friend, Garric," the Bird said in a tone of dry disapproval. "Our purposes happen to coincide, that is all. But I will not harm you or yours by my own choice."

I wish I could be sure that was true for all the people who say they are *my friends,* Garric thought. *And particularly those who say they're friends of Prince Garric.* He grinned but he didn't speak aloud.

The walls of the cliff were covered with ferns and air plants, some of which draped broad gray-green streamers like tapestries far down over the rocks. When Garric saw treetops jetting out from a central stem, he thought he must be nearing the bottom of the gorge. By the time he'd clambered down far enough to be among them, he saw that he'd been wrong: the trunks were dim pillars vanishing far below.

"The trees at this level are three hundred feet high," the Bird said. "It will be some time before we reach the floor. Unless you slip."

"Was that a joke, Bird?" Garric asked.

"No," said the Bird. Then it clicked two body parts together—not its beak—and said, "Stop. I hear something. A band of Coerli has started up the path."

As Garric climbed and slid down the cliff path, he'd heard occasional noises over the background thrum of the falls: a booming croak, a bell-like chiming, and once a shriek like a child being torn limb from limb. He'd left his axe and knife in his sash because he needed both hands free to move safely; even so he'd twitched toward the weapons when he heard the scream.

Now, hunching where a crevice the width of his palm crossed the path, he heard nothing. "What do you recommend?" he asked, moving his lips without letting any sound pass them.

"Get at least twenty feet off the trail and stay very still," the Bird said. Then it added in emotionless apology, "The Coerli have no fixed time to use the portal in the cave. Whether we met a party or did not was purely a matter of chance."

"You didn't tell me it was going to be easy," Garric mouthed as he crept sideways over the edge of the trail.

The slope here was more gradual than in many places, less than one to one, but the rock had a slick covering of hair-fine moss. He found a crack to stick his right big toe into, then settled his weight onto it as he reached down with his left hand. There was nothing better than a hand-ful of moss to grip, short and slippery, but he clung to it as best he could.

"There is a root on your right side," the Bird said, fluttering in the air beside him. "It's narrow, but it will hold you."

Garric swept his hand over the rock and found the root, crawling up the rock from a plant lower down. It was no thicker than a piece of twine, but its suckers held it to the stone like ivy on a brick wall. He pinched the root between his thumb and forefinger, afraid to wrap his whole hand around it lest he pull it away from the cliff.

Garric could hear the Coerli now, the rasping rhythms of their voices. He couldn't tell how many there were, but he doubted he'd be able to handle one healthy warrior in his present condition.

"Though we'd try," cautioned the ghost in his mind; and *of course* he'd try and die trying. But better to avoid the problem.

"There are five warriors and their chief, Grunog," the Bird said. "Grunog has no females, but he hopes to gain enough prestige in this new land to make himself powerful in two years, or perhaps three."

Garric had stuck the axe helve under his sash, but when he squeezed himself to the rock face the blade gouged him over the hipbone. He'd have been all right if he'd shifted the axe before he left the trail, but he hadn't thought of the problem until it jabbed him.

Supporting himself by his hands alone, Garric removed his right foot from the crack and felt below him for another toehold. He was sure the axe was drawing blood. As soon as he got another safe foothold, he'd—

His right arm spasmed in response to the shoulder wound. Garric lost his grip and tore through plants as he crashed down the cliffside. He bounced from rocks to the bottom, fifty feet below, where he'd started. Above him the Coerli were calling excitedly.

My fault! Garric thought. Intellectually he knew it really wasn't anybody's fault: he was pushing himself to the limit, and if that sometimes meant he went over the edge—literally, in this case—that was inevitable.

But he still blamed himself.

"This way!" the Bird said, fluttering around the nearest tall trunk. Garric got to his feet and followed.'

He'd lost the axe but the knife was stuck hilt-deep in the ground beside him. He snatched the weapon, a single piece of polished hardwood, as he ran. He'd probably been lucky not to put it the long way through his thigh.

It didn't strike Garric till he'd started running that he might be badly injured by a fall like that. Duzi, he could've been killed . . . and he'd known that, but he hadn't let himself think about it because that might've made it so. That was superstitious nonsense!

"And the soldier who isn't superstitious has the brains of a sheep!" said Carus. *"No matter who you are, bad luck can kill you. You may pray to the Great Gods or trust your lucky dagger that you wore in your first battle, but there's going to be something."*

Garric could see better than he'd expected. His eyes seemed to be adapting to the greater-than-usual dimness, but mostly it was the phosphorescent fungus coating patches of the trees and ground. The soil was loamy and damp with a thick layer of leaf litter. Many of the fallen fronds had been eaten away into blue, yellow, and vaguely red skeletons that would've been gray if there'd been even a little more ambient light.

Roots spread around the base of each massive trunk, as though the tree had been flung straight down and had splashed. Instead of bark they were covered in scales, though Garric noticed that the patterns varied from slants to curves. One tree—otherwise no different from the others for as high as Garric could see—had flowers growing in the middle of diamonds of lighter scales, set off from the rest of the trunk.

Garric could hear the Coerli calling to one another as they pursued. They must've come down the side of the chasm also, though probably under better control than he'd managed. In the maze of trees he couldn't tell how close his pursuers were or even the exact direction their voices were coming from, but he didn't doubt they'd catch up with him soon.

"Can you swim?" the Bird asked.

"Yes," said Garric.

At least he hoped he could. Though he'd gotten up immediately and begun running, he was feeling the effects of his fall. Nothing was broken, but the bruises on his right ribs and the side of his left knee hurt worse than stab wounds. The chilliness of his right buttock almost certainly meant it was oozing blood that cooled in the air.

Working bruised muscles was the best thing he could do for them, and you don't really lose much blood from a scrape. Besides, if he was going swimming, that'd clean him up.

The Bird swooped in a jangle of light around the biggest tree Garric'd seen in the Abyss yet; at the height of his head above the ground, it must be twenty feet across. On the other side of it was a pond on which pads of fungus floated. There was enough current to keep the center of the broad channel clear of the scum of spores that covered both shorelines, but he couldn't see anything actually moving.

Garric started for the shore, a band of faintly glowing muck. "No!" the Bird said. "Not there—follow!"

It angled to the right and fluttered ten or a dozen yards to what seemed to Garric to be an identical piece of fungus-covered mud. "Here!" the Bird said, flying out over the water. "Cross it as fast as you can."

As I planned to do, Garric thought. In a manner of speaking it wouldn't have made any difference if he'd said the words aloud—the Bird heard him the same either way—but consciously at least he wasn't trying to win stupid verbal games in the middle of a real life-and-death struggle.

He thrust the wooden dagger under his sash and ran into the water. He didn't dive since he didn't know how deep it was. The far shore was about a hundred feet away; the only reason he could see it in this mist was that the pond was black, while rosy phosphorescence dusted the mud of the shore.

Garric splashed two steps in to reach knee height, then threw himself forward and began swimming. The water was warmish and had a cleansing feel, unlike the tidal millpond in Barca's Hamlet where he'd learned to swim.

He felt a flash of white pain when he stretched out his right arm for the first time in a crawl stroke, but then he settled into a rhythm. He supposed he hadn't stuck his arm straight overhead since he'd gotten the shoulder wound.

Stretching's good for it, he thought, his mind grinning though his mouth was too busy sucking in air. *Of course, if I'd fainted and drowned, that wouldn't have been so good; but it might not make a whole lot of difference. Unless maybe the cat men can't swim?*

"They swim better than you do," the Bird said in its dry mental voice. "Get out of the water quickly. Run!"

Stagger rather than run was the word for the way Garric left the pond, but at any rate he got out as quickly as he could. Every muscle hurt and it felt as though his feet were sinking in deeper on this side than they had in the forest on the other side.

Maybe they were; certainly they were cutting ankle-deep through the mud and leaving swirls in the fungus on the surface. Unless the cat men were blind, they'd be able to track him easily.

"Even if they were blind they could follow your scent," the Bird said. It landed in the crotch of a tree that branched like a candelabrum. "Can you climb to here?" it asked, fluttering its wings to call attention to itself. "It will help some if the Coerli manage to cross."

The crotch was only fifteen feet in the air, and the rough trunk provided a good grip. Ordinarily Garric would've been up it with a few quick hunches of his shoulders and kicks of his tight-clamped legs.

In the present circumstances it was much harder, but it was necessary regardless. If the cat men had to climb to get at him, it gave him a chance to kill one or two that he wouldn't have on the ground surrounded by creatures so lethally quick.

Garric made it, throwing himself into the crotch and letting his tensed abdomen hold his weight. He whooped for breath through his open mouth as the Coerli came like lithe ghosts from the trees on the other side of the pond.

The maned leader followed the tracks to the water with his eyes, then up the far bank to the tree where their prey sat wheezing. "There's the animal!" he cried. "The heart and lungs to the warrior who drags him down!"

Instead of depending on his warriors to do the job, Grunog leaped into the pond and started across. He moved as smoothly as an otter despite holding his wooden mace out in front of him. His warriors arrowed into the water to either side of their leader.

To Garric's surprise, he hadn't lost the knife in swimming. The Coerli didn't have bows and didn't throw their spears. They'd use their hooked lines at first, but by keeping close to the trunk he'd be able to keep from being wrapped by them and dragged down.

The hooks would probably pull off chunks of flesh, but pain didn't matter much now. The Coerli were going to kill and eat him before the business was over, after all.

The warrior on the right side of the line disappeared, thrashing all four limbs. The other cat men didn't appear to notice. They'd reached the middle of the slow stream.

"Bird?" Garric began.

Grunog let out a scream like skidding rocks. He twisted and raised his mace to strike. Before he could, he sank straight down. A moment later the mace bobbed to the surface; the wood was dense and floated very low in the water.

"Large salamanders live in the lake," said the Bird. It was clinging to the tree sideways, just above the level of Garric's head. "You crossed at the boundary between the territories of two of the largest. The splashing drew them to investigate, but they're sluggish. You'd reached the shore before they arrived."

Garric didn't ask how much clearance he'd had; it didn't matter, after all. There wasn't any other choice.

The remaining warriors milled uncertainly in the water. Garric stood on the branch, no longer exhausted and perfectly confident. He pointed his dagger at the cat men and shouted, "Begone, interlopers, or I will loose the rest of my minions on you!"

A Corl gave a hacking cry and thrust his stabbing spear beneath him. Blood bubbled to the surface. He called out again and went down. From the roiling water rose a corpse-white creature with an oval head and a tail as fat as the body proper. It rolled under again and disappeared.

The surviving cat men paddled back the way they'd come. When they reached the shore, they scrambled up and vanished into the forest. They hadn't said a word after Garric had called his empty threat.

"I see what you mean about big salamanders," Garric said. He wasn't feeling pain, but his whole body was trembling from reaction. "That was a good six feet long, including the tail."

"That was a small one," said the Bird. "Normally they wouldn't come close to their larger fellows for fear of being eaten themselves, but when they smelled the blood they were too excited to keep away."

"Oh," said Garric. *His* blood. The Coerli themselves had been taken too recently for their blood to have spread far. "Just as well I scraped myself, I suppose."

"Yes," said the Bird. "Now to the cave. It's not far. I hope we won't have any more difficulties before we get there."

Garric lowered himself by hanging from the limb with both hands, then dropped to the ground. His knees flexed but didn't buckle as he'd thought they might, especially the left one.

"Yes," he said. "I hope that too."

" '*N*OW SOME OF *these days and it won't be long,*' " sang Chalcus, his voice soft in the still air. " '*You'll call my name and I gonna be gone.*' "

"I hear water close," said Merota, walking a step behind Ilna with her hands pressed tightly together in front of her. She was obviously very frightened, but she was trying in every way she could to hide the fact. "I hope we're near the lake."

Ilna pursed her lips. The child was talking because she was afraid, not because the words would do any real good at all. It made Ilna angry—

Because Ilna was afraid also, afraid that she wouldn't be able to get Merota and Chalcus out of the trap they were in because of her. Which made her want to snarl at whoever was closest to let out the anger and fear churning inside of her.

With a tiny smile of self-mockery, she said, "It's just the other side of the hedge to our left, I believe, but it may be some way before I find a passage through—"

The aisle kinked to the right. She stepped around it, her back straight and a knotted pattern closed in her hands ready for need. White mist rolled through the gap in the hedge, clean-smelling and the first thing in this garden that had felt cool.

The mist was as thick as a feather pillow. Ilna couldn't see through it.

Chalcus joined her in the opening, keeping Merota between them. He reached over the child's head and stroked Ilna's cheek as lightly as a butterfly's wing.

Merota knelt and thrust a hand down into the mist. "I can feel the water!" she said excitedly. "It's running really fast!"

"Stand up, dear one," Chalcus said. "We're not swimming out into that without being able to see more than I can now. Not unless we have to."

"There'll be a way across," Ilna said. "I just need to follow it through in my mind."

She sounded grim, even to herself, because she was frustrated that she hadn't already found the way to cross. That was the path she'd been following, the one that would take them to the temple. She was sure of it!

" '*I wish I was a rich man's son . . . ,* ' " Chalcus sang, and let his voice trail off. To Merota he said, "I came from honest folk. Honest but poor as the dirt they scrabbled in to earn enough to eat, or almost enough. I swore to myself that I'd never be poor the way my parents were."

Ilna stared at the mist. She couldn't see through it, but there were currents as surely as there were in the stream she heard purling beneath its concealment. She followed a whorl, dense white on dense white but forming a pattern in her mind.

"I haven't always been honest, child," Chalcus said. He tousled Merota's hair, but it seemed to Ilna that he was speaking as much to his own younger self as he was to the girl. "And often enough I haven't had money. But I've never had to beg the straw boss for something to buy a crust for my family. Nor sent my wife to beg him when he wouldn't grant it to me."

Merota put her hand in the sailor's. He squeezed it, then released it and edged aside. He was carefully not looking toward Ilna.

Ilna's fingers were taking apart the pattern she'd knotted for defense—or attack, if you wanted to call it that. Defense to Ilna had never meant riding with the other fellow's blows.

There were probably ways to puff air or wave her arms in the mist to change the way it flowed, but there were other ways too. If she matched the rippling white on white with the right sort of links in the yarn she carried, it would—

She held up the pattern she'd created. There was movement in the mist.

"Ilna, I can see something!" Merota cried. "It's a bridge! I see a bridge!"

"Aye, a bridge," said Chalcus in a quiet, neutral voice. "And where, dearest Ilna, would you say it'd come from, eh? This bridge."

"It was there all the time, Master Chalcus," Ilna said. It was a hump-backed affair with a floor and railings of pink stone on a gray stone frame. The supports were carved with leaves and flowing stems, but the pink slabs which feet or hands might touch were mirror smooth.

"Heart of mine," Chalcus said, not testy but with a hint of restraint in his gentle tone. "The fog is thick, I'll grant you, but Lady Merota pad-dled her little fingers in the place where the abutments now rest, gneiss and granite and each harder than the other."

"It was always here, Master Chalcus," Ilna repeated. "I had to turn it so that we could see and touch it, that's all."

She smiled faintly, wondering if a person who had more words in her tongue could've explained what she'd done. Perhaps, but it might be that a person with more words couldn't have wrapped the mist in just the right way to wring the bridge into sight.

"Ilna?" Merota said. "Who's the lady?"

For a moment Ilna didn't know what the child meant: there was only the bridge arching its back to midstream before falling into the mist in the direction of the central island and the temple. On the railing, though, slouched and then straightening with the grace of a cat waking, was a woman.

Wearing silk, Ilna thought, but it wasn't silk. The woman was dressed in her own flowing hair; her hair and the mist. She looked at them but didn't speak.

"I'll lead, then, shall I, darlings?" Chalcus said. He made the words a question, but he was swaggering up the pink stone before they were out of his mouth. Though his hands were empty, Ilna knew he could have a blade through the woman's throat before she had time to suck in a breath.

Merota started to follow the sailor; Ilna put a hand on the child's shoulder and held her back. Merota sometimes needed guidance, but she never objected when matters were serious.

Everything in this garden was serious, to Merota's mind even more than to her guardians.

While Chalcus was still a double pace away the sinuous woman smiled and said, "Welcome, strangers. Have you come to use my bridge?"

Her voice was musical but pitched a little higher than even a slender woman's normally would be. Her face and mouth were both narrow, but her smile was welcoming.

"Your bridge," Chalcus said easily, letting the words stand without emphasis. "Would there be a toll for that use, milady?"

The woman laughed. "My, so formal?" she said. "A small toll, stranger—a very small one. Few people visit me here and I never leave. If you would tell me a story, any story you choose, that would give me a pleasure I could revisit in the long days when I'm alone. But if you can't or won't—"

She shrugged, a graceful movement that shimmered down her whole covering of hair.

"—then what could I do to block a strong man like you from crossing with your companions? No, a story if you choose to tell a lonely woman a story, and free passage regardless of your courtesy."

The mist was clearing. Ilna saw the wooded island beyond the moat. In the middle of the woods gleamed a temple with a golden roof.

Chalcus glanced back, careful to keep the woman in the corner of his eyes. "Ilna, dearest one . . . ?" he said.

"I'll never be known for courtesy," Ilna said, sounding harsh and angry in her own ears. The woman on the bridge was very beautiful, and her voice was as pure and lovely as a bird's. "Still, I've always paid my debts. Give the lady a story, Master Chalcus, and we'll cross her bridge."

The woman looked at her and smiled sadly. "You don't trust me," she said in a tone of regret. "You've had a life of disappointment. I see that in your eyes."

She gestured up the bridge beyond her and toward the island. "You and the child are free to pass, mistress," she said. Every gesture, every syllable, was a work of art and beauty, though there was nothing studied about her. "All three of you may pass freely, as I said."

"Come along, Merota," Ilna said. She hated herself—well, hated herself more than usual—for her jealousy and lack of trust. "Master Chalcus will tell the lady a story to pay our way."

Ilna walked briskly up the smooth surface. The slope was noticeable, but she didn't slip even though the mist had coated the gneiss.

She could've held onto the handrail, but that would've meant touching stone with her fingers as well as her feet. Ilna *hated* stone. Even if she hadn't, she'd have hated every part of the bridge that this lovely, graceful woman claimed.

"Well then, milady," Chalcus said in a cheerful, lilting voice. "If you'll not think me immodest, I'll tell you of the time in my travels that I found a woman chained to the face of a cliff at the seaside. She was more lovely than any other, saving your own good self and Ilna, my heart's delight."

He nodded to Ilna and Merota as they passed. Ilna nodded back; coldly she supposed, but she couldn't help that. Merota squeezed his hand as she went by.

The girl was grinning happily; to be reaching the center of the maze probably, but Ilna didn't ask. If she spoke to Merota, it'd sound as though she was saying, "What do you have to smile about?" And that's what she *would* probably be saying, so she kept her mouth shut.

"Why are you smiling, Ilna?" Merota asked.

"Am I?" said Ilna in surprise. "Yes, I was. At myself, I guess you'd say. I was thinking that I'm never going to learn to be a nice person, but I'm getting better at not saying what I think."

Ilna stopped at the hump of the bridge, a polite distance from where Chalcus stood speaking to the woman. His voice came to her faintly, ". . . rising out of the sea, an island to look at save for its bulging eyes and its teeth as long as temple pillars. . . ."

"It's hard to hear him, Ilna," Merota said, frowning.

"We have no need to hear him at all, child," Ilna said severely. "He's giving her a good story. When he's finished, he'll join us and we'll go on together."

She deliberately turned her face toward the island. The temple was a simple one: round and domed instead of the usual square floor plan with a peaked roof, but she'd seen round temples occasionally in recent years.

There weren't any temples, round or square, in Barca's Hamlet or in the borough beyond. People had shrines to the Lady and the Shepherd in their houses. There they offered a crumb of bread and a drop of ale at meals; most people did. On the hill overlooking the South Pasture was a stone carved into a shape so rough that only knowing it was an altar let you see that. The shepherds left small gifts on it to Duzi, the pasture's god, at Midsummer and their own birthdays.

Ilna refused to believe in the Great Gods, the Lady who gently gathered the souls of the righteous dead and the Shepherd who protected the righteous living. Ilna believed in Nothing, in oblivion, in the end of all hopes and fears. She'd had few hopes in life and those had been disappointed, every one. Death wouldn't be a burden to her; quite the contrary.

"You're smiling again, Ilna," Merota said.

"I shouldn't be," Ilna replied, "but that doesn't surprise me."

The mist was getting thicker; she could barely see the temple roof. She turned her head and found it moved glacially slow. Something was wrong.

Chalcus continued to talk with animation to the woman on the bridge below. His lips moved but Ilna could no longer hear his voice, even faintly. The mist between her and Chalcus was very thick, smotheringly thick.

Merota screamed, piercing the fog like a sword blade. The heaviness gripping Ilna's muscles released. Merota pointed into the water, suddenly clear where it'd been dark as ink since the bridge appeared. In its depths were bodies of the Little People, the Prey. There were more than Ilna could count, preserved by the cold stream; and they were all male.

Chalcus saw also. "By the sea demon's dick!" he shouted. His sword flicked from its sheath and toward the lounging woman.

Swift as he was, the blade cut air alone. The woman—was she a woman?—slid into the stream like a water snake. For a moment she looked at Chalcus; then she trilled a musical laugh, gamboled for a moment among the drowned bodies, and vanished. Ilna couldn't tell whether she'd gone up or down stream, slipped into a hole in the bank, or passed from sight in some other fashion.

Chalcus joined them. His smile was forced and he dabbed his dry lips with his tongue.

"So, my fine ladies," he said. "Shall we cross the bridge as we planned?"

"Yes," said Ilna. "I'd like to get off it. I don't like stone."

And she hadn't liked the woman, either. She felt herself smile, this time because she'd had a better reason than mere jealousy to dislike and mistrust the creature.

" 'Goodbye, pretty baby, I'll be gone,' " Chalcus sang as he finally sheathed his sword.

Although—

" *'Goodbye, pretty baby, I'll be gone.'* "

Because she was Ilna, she also had to admit that she'd been jealous.

" *'You're gonna miss me when I'm gone.'* "

CASHEL FELT PROTAS grip him harder, then release as a new world formed around them. It felt as if the void had frozen into the shape of a mountain pass opening down into a circular valley.

A woman with wings and a round, ugly face waited for them. Her hair was a mass of snakes. They twisted sluggishly, the way snakes do when they crawl out of the burrow where they've wintered and wait for sunlight to warm life into their scaly bodies. They were harmless sorts, snakes that eat grasshoppers and frogs and maybe a mouse if they're lucky; anyway, Cashel didn't expect to come close enough for one to bite him.

"I am your guide," said the woman. Her thick lips smiled. The only thing she wore was a belt of boars' teeth; her skin was the color of buttermilk, thin with a hint of blue under the paleness.

"Who are you?" Protas said. He had both hands on the crown; not, Cashel thought, to keep it on but because he felt better touching it. The way Cashel felt better for having the quarterstaff in his hands.

The woman laughed. Her voice was much older than her body looked, but she couldn't have been more ugly if she'd studied to do it for a long lifetime.

"You can't give me orders, boy," she said, "but that doesn't matter: a greater one than you commands me. I'm Phorcides, and I'm to take you to where you choose to go."

She laughed again and added, "Since you're fools."

Cashel grinned. He'd been told that many times before and it wasn't a judgment he argued with. But he knew too that the people, and not always people, who said that to him generally didn't have much to brag about in the way they ran their own lives.

Aloud he said, "Then let's be going, Mistress Phorcides. Unless there's reason we should wait?"

Phorcides looked Cashel over carefully. He met her eyes and even smiled; she wasn't challenging him, just showing curiosity for the first time since they'd met.

"My name's Cashel," he said. "And this is Prince Protas. In case you hadn't been told."

"Do you know what you're getting into?" the woman said carefully. The snakes squirmed slowly on her forehead; doing a dance of some sort, it seemed.

"No ma'am, I don't," Cashel said. He looked at Protas, but if the boy had different ideas he was keeping them to himself.

"But you think that you'll be able to bull through anything you meet," Phorcides said. "Is that it?"

"I think I'll try, mistress," Cashel said. "Now, should we be going?"

"We'll go now, which is what you mean," Phorcides said. Her belt of curved yellow tusks rattled softly as she turned toward the valley. "As for whether we should—I have no idea. Perhaps you'll come back and tell me after you've gotten where you're going."

She started down the slope into the valley. Her wings were large and covered with real feathers, but Cashel didn't see how they could possibly support a full-sized woman flying.

There were real birds circling in the updrafts from the valley walls, though. They were high—higher than Cashel could even guess—but he could make out wings and bodies instead of them being just dots against the blue sky.

The sides of the valley were pretty much raw rock with splotches of lichen, but there were a few real plants growing in cracks where wind-blown dirt had collected. Cashel didn't recognize the most common sort, pretty little star-shaped flowers, but there were bellflowers too.

On a distant crag, well above the pass the woman'd brought them in by, three goats with curved horns were staring at them intently. It made Cashel homesick for a moment, though "home" wasn't so much Barca's Hamlet as the life he'd led there. He and Ilna stayed in their half of the mill; he'd tended sheep and picked up a little extra by doing whatever work required a strong man. There'd been nobody stronger than Cashel or-Kenset, in the borough or among the folk from distant places who came in the fall for the Sheep Fair.

Protas picked his way carefully, his face set. Cashel frowned but he couldn't help. The path wasn't bad but it was rocky; not so much a path at all as a way to get down the slope through a carpet of low plants. The boy had only slippers meant for carpeted palace floors on his feet.

Cashel was barefoot, of course, but he was used to that. Even now that he wasn't a shepherd anymore, his soles were near as tough as a soldier's boots.

When Cashel lived in Barca's Hamlet—when he was home—

Sharina was the daughter of the innkeeper, educated and wealthy as people thought of things in the borough. She'd been far beyond the hopes of a poor orphan boy who couldn't so much as read his own name.

Cashel smiled, embarrassed even to have that thought in the privacy of his own mind. The present where Sharina loved him was better than anything he'd ever dreamed of at home.

They'd gotten down to where the rock was covered with grass and many little flowers—primrose, gentians, and buttercups. They made a nice mix of pink, blue, and yellow in the green. There was hellebore too, though it was past blooming. Cashel wondered if Ilna would like the pattern the flowers made on the ground. She might, though she didn't use colors much in her own work. This'd be a fine pasture, but there didn't seem much in it to eat the foliage.

A gray-backed viper sunned itself on an outcrop, turning its wedge-shaped head to follow their progress. Cashel started toward it from reflex, readying his staff to crush the snake's head; but then relaxed.

The viper wasn't close enough to hurt them, and Cashel didn't have a flock of sheep he needed to keep safe. He'd kill in a heartbeat if he needed to, a snake or a man either one; but killing wasn't a thing he did for fun.

The valley floor was flat and broad, wide enough that an arrow wouldn't carry to either side from where they walked in the middle of it. The walls were steep and gray; near as steep as the walls of the mill-house. At their base was a scree of rock that'd broken off the cliffs.

"Why aren't those sheep moving?" said Protas, nodding toward a lone pine under which three gray shapes clustered. "They haven't moved even their heads since I saw them."

"They haven't moved because they're stone," said Mistress Phorcides. "And anyway, they were ibexes, not sheep. Wild goats."

The boy opened his mouth to ask another question but glanced at Cashel before he did. Cashel shook his head slightly. Protas forced a smile, swallowed, and walked on without speaking further.

There were plenty of things Cashel wondered about, but he didn't think talking to the winged woman was a good way to get answers. The less contact they had with her, the better he'd like it.

He didn't doubt she'd take them to where they next were to go like the other guides had, but if they gave her the least opening there'd be something bad happening. Cashel trusted her the way he'd trust a weasel: you know exactly what a weasel'll do if you give it the chance.

Phorcides led them toward a rock face. Cashel thought the stand of beech trees concealed a cave or maybe even a bend in the canyon, but they came around the grove and found a sheer cliff. The rock layers were on end. A plate of mica that Cashel couldn't've spanned with his outstretched staff gleamed in the solid wall.

Phorcides turned and smiled again. Cashel didn't like the smile, but that made it a piece with most other things about their guide.

"I've brought you here," she said. "I can't take you any farther."

"Do we go through the rock, then?" Protas asked. He was using his adult tone and holding the crown in front of him with both hands.

There was a man—the statue of a man—looking toward them around the trunk of a beech. Another—statue—was half-hidden in the stunted rhododendrons a stone's throw away, and a third crouched behind a juniper. Cashel didn't know if Protas had seen them. If the boy had, he was pretending he hadn't.

"Go through it?" Phorcides said. "That's up to you. I can't take you."

Her fat, pale lips spread even wider in a grin. "If I could," she said, "I would have gone myself."

Protas turned toward the mica and raised the topaz crown slightly. Cashel shifted sideways so that he could keep an eye on the boy and the woman both at the same time.

Phorcides opened her lifted hands toward Cashel like she was making an offering. The snakes on her brow were twining faster.

"I've carried out my duty," she said. "Now, Master Cashel—free me."

"I can't free you," Cashel said. His voice was harsh, surprising him. "I didn't bind you, mistress, so I'm not the one to free you."

"*Cheun . . . ,*" chanted Protas. It wasn't his voice. All ten fingers gripped the topaz, but bright lights glittered deep inside it. "*Cheaunxin aoabaoth momao.*"

"Free me!" Phorcides said. Her grin changed to an expression Cashel couldn't describe. "Say that I am free, only that!"

"*Nethmomao . . . ,*" said whatever was speaking through the boy's lips. "*Souarmi.*"

"Leave us," said Cashel in a growl. He lifted his staff. "Leave us now!"

The snakes in Phorcides' hair rose. She had a third eye in the middle of her forehead. It was closed, but the lid fluttered.

"*Marmaraoth!*" the boy's lips shouted. The cloudy mica was melting into the wall of a mirrored chamber that swelled to enclose Protas and Cashel too. There was a figure in the room already.

Cashel stepped so that he stood between Phorcides and the boy, holding his staff vertical before him. She gave a shriek of baffled rage and whirled away, her middle eye still closed.

The mirrored room closed about Cashel and the boy. In the entrance, the only opening, stood a creature the size of a man but with a cat's long face. It gave a cry like a hunting panther and leaped, its stone-bladed spear aimed at Cashel's throat.

Chapter

15

SHARINA WALKED SLOWLY back to where Tenoctris waited in her hedge of Blood Eagles. The old wizard was sitting up. A guard had found a shield for her to sit on, though her green silk robes were already probably beyond salvation from when she'd seated herself in the muck to work her incantation. She smiled to see Sharina and tried to rise.

"Don't," called Sharina. "Just make room beside you."

She meant it as a joke, but she really was bone-tired. She'd sheathed the Pewle knife, though she'd had trouble getting the tip into the mouth of the sheath. The muscles of her right arm were spasming so badly in reaction to her repeated chopping blows that she wouldn't have been able to keep the heavy knife in her hand.

The guards stepped aside to pass Sharina, then began chatting with the men who'd accompanied her in attacking the hellplants. She sat with an unexpected thump; her legs'd given way when she was halfway down.

"Are you all right?" Tenoctris said with concern. "Your sleeve—"

Sharina looked down in surprise. "Oh!" she said, remembering it. "I used the sleeve to wipe my knife. I couldn't use the plants' bodies."

She grinned. "That would be the traditional way to clean the blade, you see."

She leaned back and twisted so that she could see Double. He lay on his back in front of the ruins of his mirror. He didn't move at all though his eyes were open; Sharina wasn't sure whether or not he was conscious.

"Tenoctris?" she said. "Did you make the swamp freeze?"

The old wizard smiled in what Sharina decided was a look of shy triumph. "I made it possible for it to happen," she said. "Yes, I suppose I did it. In a manner of speaking."

The sun was at zenith; the struggle with the hellplants had taken longer than Sharina'd thought while it was going on. The sheer scale of the business was staggering.

The haze had burned off; the mud had thawed and now was drying. The hellplants had been reduced to stinking lumps, but the smell wasn't any worse than Barca's Hamlet when the first rains of springtime released the varied sourness frozen during winter. Besides, a strong sea breeze was cleansing the air, blowing inland without the arc of hills to constrain it.

"*How*, Tenoctris?" Sharina asked. "Double there—"

She nodded.

"—is a great wizard, you said so yourself. How could you defeat the Green Woman where he couldn't?"

"Cervoran and the Green Woman are amazingly powerful," Tenoctris said. "But they're equals in strength. One might gain an advantage for the moment, but only for a moment. You saw how the struggle between them went. Saw what a layman could see, at any rate."

"Yes," agreed Sharina. "Although it seemed to me that the Green Woman was winning until you . . ."

She didn't know how to describe what'd happened, the sudden freezing and the clearing of the sky. She spun her index finger in a circle and said, "You did what you did."

"That was only a setback," Tenoctris explained. "As the others had been. Cervoran—"

She nodded toward the fallen wizard, now beginning to stir. She never called him Double.

"—was gathering strength. And that was the key, you see. I'm almost powerless compared to either of those wizards, but I could see what they were doing. Possibly—"

Tenoctris smiled, again in muted pride.

"—better than either of them could see. And as they acted, I . . . linked their actions, I suppose you could call it. So that they neutralized one another instantly instead of stroke for stroke as they'd been doing. Everything stopped, all the wizardry. Leaving it a matter for men. And one woman."

Sharina hugged her older friend. "Leaving it to Mankind," she said.

Waldron was reorganizing his troops with Stand To signals and a tempest of swearing from officers of all ranks. A number of injured men were being carried to the rear by their fellows or walking while clutching their wounds. That surprised Sharina—the deep-chilled plants had been as sluggish as one *expected* plants to be—but only for a moment. No, the plants hadn't been a danger, but the troops had cut themselves and their fellows in the wild slashing melee that'd swept the bay clear of the Green Woman's minions.

Double got to his feet with the jerky movements of a marionette. He looked around with a slack expression. *He doesn't know what happened,* Sharina realized. She hugged Tenoctris again.

Tenoctris looked puzzled. "Dear," she said. She took a fresh bamboo split from the packet at her feet, but she didn't attempt another spell for the moment. "Something is building."

Sharina looked southward, to where the Fortress of Glass gleamed on the distant horizon. "The Green Woman is attacking?" she asked.

Double bent and picked up the athame he'd dropped when he fell. His face was no longer vacant, but he didn't appear to be ready to resume the difficult business of wizardry.

"I don't know," Tenoctris said. "I don't think so, but I don't know."

With sudden decision she went on, "Help me up, please, Sharina. I think I would rather be standing for whatever's about to happen."

A RECENTLY FALLEN tree lay across the path. Its trunk was thicker than Garric was tall. He eyed it. He'd climb over if he were sure of his right arm, but . . .

"The band of Coerli we escaped went around the root end," the Bird said. "That's to your left."

Garric took the implied direction; he could see the clawed footprints. "Will they clear the path?" he asked. The detour added at least fifty yards to the trip.

"No," said the Bird. "Stone tools aren't satisfactory for cutting anything so large, and no band has more than twenty or so males to do the work. The trees are giant horsetails, and they don't live long anyway. The Coerli find it easier to go around fallen trees than to maintain a straight route."

"An uncle of mine was a great hunter of wolves," said the ghost in Garric's mind. *"There were wolves on Haft in my time. He covered his banquet hall with wolfskins instead of using tapestries. He'd have liked these cat beasts even better for sport."*

Then he added, the musing humor gone from his voice, *"I wouldn't mind that either. We'd see how long it took to convince them that eating human children had been a bad idea."*

Rain had washed the upturned roots clean of leaf mold. There wasn't a taproot and the mat didn't seem sufficient to support the massive trunk.

"There is no wind here," the Bird said. "The abyss was a very peaceful place when my people lived; and even now, compared to much of the world."

Garric didn't reply. He tried to imagine how he would feel if everyone he cared about—if every human being—were suddenly killed, but he survived. He couldn't begin to understand such a terrible thing. Even toying with that as a possibility made him very uncomfortable.

"Do not be concerned, Garric," the Bird said. "Grief is as alien to me as love would be. Besides, it will be over soon."

The cave was a smooth oval punched in the coarse black walls of the chasm. Garric paused when he saw the shadowed curve, staying close to the fallen horsetail so that the fan of roots would break up his outline to anyone watching from inside.

"There are no Coerli in the cave," the Bird said. "There is no one, Garric. Except in my memory."

"All right," said Garric, uneasy again. Holding the wooden dagger in an underhand grip, he walked briskly to the cave through the undergrowth of knee-high mushrooms.

For a moment he was in darkness. The Bird fluttered ahead with its usual jerking motion. Points of light appeared in the ceiling, floor, and walls, then spread into a glow that suffused all the surfaces. Garric's foot trembled—not quite pausing, but almost—then came down. He walked the rest of the way into the inner chamber without hesitation.

It was a half-sphere, covered entirely with mica. Apart from the oval entrance passage there was no distinguishing aspect to the interior. The muted light seemed to come from deep within the surrounding rock.

Garric turned slowly. No matter where he looked, he caught reflections of himself in the corners of his eyes; it made him edgy. King Carus, watching through the same eyes with the reflexes of a warrior who'd lived his whole adult life by his quickness and his sword, became much *more* edgy.

The Bird hovered in the middle of the inner chamber; the exact center, Garric guessed, though he couldn't be objectively sure because of the wall's curve and mirrored reflections. He looked toward the entrance passage, then back to the Bird. Its wings were still, but it hung in the air regardless. Lights glittered in sequence within its crystalline body.

"Bird, what should I do?" Garric asked. He spoke to hear a voice in the charged stillness.

"Wait," said the Bird. "I will accompany you to your world. I must arrange the forces in a fashion that will serve your purpose and mine as well, that is all."

Garric turned away from his guide. The play of light in the Bird's body disturbed him in fashions he couldn't put words to. The rhythm was like the low vibration that heralded an earthquake. He thought he saw figures moving within the mirrored walls, but he couldn't be sure.

"Are you a wizard?" he asked. Speaking to hear a voice, but he *had* to hear a voice in this inhuman, lifeless place! "Are you, Bird?"

The Bird's cluck of laughter broke Garric's tension. "I am a mathematician, Garric," it said. "I move points on a scale and adjust potentials. There is no mystery to what I do, and no art."

There *were* figures in the walls, but they weren't identifiable; they weren't necessarily even human. Some were superimposed on others the way a painted canvas may show ghosts of earlier pictures beneath the present surface.

"How is what you do different from what Marzan does?" Garric asked. "Or Sirawhil?"

"Marzan can achieve effects that I cannot," the Bird said. He clucked again. "But then, I know what is really happening, and he does not."

Black spots appeared in the walls and floor. Garric thought they were where the points of light had first glittered. Beams of red and blue wizardlight, thin as spiderweb but of densely saturated color, spread to weave the spots together.

Lines pierced Garric's chest and left forearm. Moving put him in the path of other lines. He couldn't feel any contact; if he closed his eyes, he wouldn't have known they were there.

He transferred the dagger to his left hand for a moment and wiped his right palm on his tunic. The coarse cloth was sodden, but the touch helped somewhat. He flexed his right hand several times, then took the dagger in it again.

"Prepare yourself, Garric," the Bird said. "We will accomplish your purposes, and then I will accomplish mine."

The hair stood up all over Garric's body; the web of wizardlight burned even brighter. The Bird clucked, louder than before.

The mica walls vanished, plunging Garric into a plane of interweaving figures.

ILNA FOLLOWED CHALCUS and Merota off the cold, polished stone of the bridge. The grass between her toes felt good by contrast.

The round temple was in front of them, brightly sunlit in a grove of pines. The roof was gilded—or simply gold? she didn't suppose it mattered—and had a circular window in the middle. There were tall columns around the outside and half as many thinner columns in an inner ring. Both numbers were too large for Ilna to count without a tally, but she was instinctively sure of the proportion.

Merota looked back at Ilna but her eyes then drifted past. "Oh," she said. "It's gone."

Ilna glanced over her shoulder. The bridge, a solid mass of pink and gray, had vanished into the wall of curling white. Only here and there could Ilna see above the mist the top of a tree growing from the maze beyond.

"There's nothing in the hedges that we wanted, child," said Chalcus, giving their surroundings a different sort of look from the ones he'd been shooting about him from before he stepped off the bridge. Instead of looking for dangers, he was now considering the island as a place where a young girl and her companions might want to be. "The sun's clearer here. And should we wish to go back, why, our Ilna would have us there in a flick of her fingers. Would you not, dear love?"

"I don't think that will be necessary," Ilna said austerely. She walked toward the temple, letting her mind drink in not only the shape but the reasons behind the shape of the building in every detail. She'd laid lengths of yarn parallel in her left palm and clamped them with her thumb, but she didn't start tying them yet.

The island had plenty of vegetation—the pines surrounding the temple and the flowers and grasses covering the ground. It was all pretty enough, if you liked that sort of thing, and Cashel would doubtless tell her it'd make a fine pasture.

There was nothing here for human beings to eat, though. Well, Ilna had no intention of staying on the island longer than it took to find their way back to their own world. She had business there with Double.

She walked up to the temple. It stood on a platform of three low steps. The floor within was a mosaic of tiny stones in a pattern as delicate as the interlocking fibers of a bird's feathers. From any distance the floor would've looked gray; in reality it was black and white, always one or the other. Only the eye of the viewer mixed the colors.

Chalcus was taking Merota around the structure, keeping himself and the child out of Ilna's way. It wouldn't have mattered: when she focused on a difficult pattern, nothing intruded on her concentration.

And this was a *very* difficult pattern. This was every leaf and rootlet of the tapestry garden, and it was more.

Ilna began to knot her bits of yarn, using them to work herself through the greater pattern in the stone. She stepped into the sanctum proper and concentrated on a tiny segment: a piece small enough to cover with the palm of her hand.

She looked up at the roof opening. It was the eye of the building, not only part of the pattern but the garden's window onto the wider cosmos. The grating over it was woven from gold wire so fine that it blurred in sunlight like the sheen of oil on water. There could be stories in an oil slick, too, and the soul of the garden was in this golden eye.

The beasts who called themselves Princes had spoken of the One who created the garden. If the One existed, he'd left his mark in this eye; but increasingly Ilna believed that the garden, the tapestry, had woven itself while the cosmos congealed out of chaos.

There was danger here.

Merota screamed. Ilna looked out from the light-shot complexity of her mind. Merota *was screaming,* probably had been screaming, but Ilna hadn't noticed until the pattern she was visualizing warned her of what was going on in her immediate surroundings.

Chalcus stood beside the building, in the curved shadow of the roof. His sword and dagger slashed in bright arcs—through nothing, dark shadowed nothing that formed about him. The Shadow was separate from what lay on the ground in normal fashion. His face was set and his lips were closed in a taut line.

Ilna acted by instinct, sweeping off her outer tunic and spinning it to a part of the mosaic floor that no one—not even her with her eyes and intellect—could have told from any other part of the interwoven design. The soft wool fabric settled silently, blocking the pattern in stone from the pattern in the light streaming through the grille over the temple's upturned eye.

The Shadow vanished. Chalcus tumbled free. Only now did he shout: wordlessly, mindlessly—the bellow of a great beast loosed from a trap. His blades danced again, rippling the empty air and plowing razor-fine furrows in the soil. Grass and a dozen buttercups fell, yellow victims of the flickering steel.

Chalcus looked at Ilna, his eyes wide and full of horror. "Dear one?" he said.

"It's all right," said Ilna. "It's a—"

She nodded to her tunic. She'd woven the cloth herself, a simple fabric as fine and soft as the best silk.

"I disrupted the pattern," she said. "The Shadow's a part of this temple, really. Part of the tapestry, a necessary part, I see. I can deal with it."

Ilna looked at the knotted pattern in her left hand. She hadn't dropped it when she took off her tunic. She had no recollection of how she'd moved, just that she had. Her . . . her soul, she supposed. Her soul had known what to do and her body had done it, without her mind being involved.

"While your tunic's there, the thing's trapped? Is that what you're telling me, dear one?" Chalcus said. He jerked his head in a nod toward the garment she'd flung with deceptive ease to the pavement. "Is it then, we're safe?"

Merota stood silent, biting on the knuckles of her left hand and staring at Chalcus. She twisted her eyes for an instant to Ilna, then returned them to the sailor.

"We're safe, yes, I told you," Ilna snapped. She walked to the tunic, picked it up, and shrugged into it with more trouble than she'd had taking it off. "Not because of this—"

She tapped the pavement with her big toe. She disliked stone but she could use it. She could use the thing that laired in this pattern, too, though it was as cold and heartless as the tiny chips that gave it life. Gave it existence, at any rate.

"—but because I see it whole. It won't dare to bother us again." Ilna started to smile but swallowed the expression; that would have been boasting. She went on quietly, "Another time I might have to cover another part of the pattern here in the pavement; but I could. It won't be back."

"Then, dearest . . . ," Chalcus said. "Dear one, dear heart—let us go out of this place now, may we not?"

"I want to leave," Merota whispered. "Please. Please."

"If you'll be quiet," said Ilna sharply, "we'll be able to leave that much sooner. The exit's in the eye overhead. It shouldn't take me very long to find a way to open it for us."

"I'm not afraid to die, dear heart," Chalcus said. He smiled, but his face showed as much sadness as Ilna had ever seen him express. "The place that thing was taking me, though . . . If there's a hell, my love, that's where it was taking me."

"There's Hell," said Ilna, remembering infinite grayness and the voice that had whispered to her. She looked at Chalcus, then down to the yarn in her hand. She began to pick out the knots and rejoin the strands into a different pattern.

"Master Chalcus," she said, eyeing the interwoven mosaic as her fingers worked, "I think before I open the door for us, I'll leash the Shadow. That way it won't come back while I'm occupied with getting us out of this place."

"That would be . . . ," Chalcus said. His face spread into a rollicking smile. His curved sword and dagger slid into their sheaths over his left and right hips with the same liquid ease that Ilna showed while weaving. He stepped toward her, swept her into his arms, and kissed her hard.

Ilna frowned in amazement when the sailor backed away, still smiling. "Master Chalcus," she said, "this is scarcely the place for such."

"And what better place could there be, my dearest?" Chalcus said. "It's where you are and I am, and both of us living. Life's a chancy business, love; and what a fool I'd feel should I die in the next moment without having kissed the love of my life once more when I could have. Not so?"

Ilna sniffed, but she didn't snap back at his foolishness. He'd put it as a joke, but in her heart she recognized the simple truth of what he'd just said.

She stepped to Merota, hugged her, and then held an arm out to Chalcus as well. The three of them stood tightly together for a moment; then Ilna backed away.

"Now," she said, "don't disturb me. I can do this thing—"

"You said you could, Ilna," said Merota. "Of course you can!"

"I can do this thing," Ilna repeated, "but I can't start and not finish." She allowed herself a slight smile.

"If that happens, the Shadow will finish me and I suppose all of us, because it will be very angry. Do you understand?"

Chalcus nodded and grinned. Merota opened her mouth to speak—to agree, almost certainly—but Chalcus touched a finger to the girl's lips before a sound came out. He moved with the grace of falling water and the speed of light itself. . . .

Ilna looked at the golden grating over the eye. That was where the key was, not in the floor itself but in what the grating's shadow threw onto the mosaic. She began to knot her cords, making herself a part of the pattern.

She could feel the Shadow's strength. It was aware of what she was doing, but she had it now. There was no way it could escape unless she let it escape, and she would die before she did that.

Ilna's lips were tight with concentration but she smiled in her mind: she would certainly die very shortly after the Shadow escaped, should that happen. From what Chalcus said—and more from what she'd seen in his eyes as he said it—that would be a very bad way to die.

Chalcus and Merota had gone outside the temple. The child was picking flowers. The sailor watched her pick flowers and watched Ilna knot yarn and watched every other thing around them that might become an enemy or hide one.

She was very close to completion; a few more knots and the fabric—yes, she was not only binding the Shadow but bending it to her absolute will. The tapestry was even more marvelously complex than she'd realized before she wove herself into it. Only a master could have created the Garden, and Ilna os-Kenset was that One's equal to be able to reweave what He/She/It had—

The domed roof of the temple shone and became unnaturally clear. The eye and the grating still existed, but not in the universe that was forming itself over the temple. Ilna continued to weave, her fingers carrying out the understanding of her mind.

Merota cried out; Chalcus had drawn his blades. Cashel, Protas, and the dead-alive Cervoran were standing beside Ilna in the center of the temple.

Cashel had his quarterstaff raised to strike. Rushing toward them were cats the size of men, snarling in fury with their weapons raised.

Ilna wove.

CASHEL COULDN'T MOVE as quickly as his leaping opponent, but reflex honed in many fights jerked him back at the same time as the quarterstaff rose in his hand. He didn't so much hit the cat man as lift the iron-bound hickory into a place the cat man leaped through. Leaped *into,* at any rate, because Cashel was arm's length back from where the creature'd thought he'd be when it lunged.

Air and blood *whuff*ed from the creature's mouth as the staff smashed its ribs. It flew upward into the mirrored ceiling, hitting hard enough to flatten its skull. It'd already been dead.

Another cat man was bounding down the entrance passage toward Cashel. There was no other way in or out of the domed room. Cashel stepped forward, again confounding his attacker.

This cat man carried a spear whose springy double point was barbed on the inside to grip and hold. A fishing spear Cashel would've said, but bigger and stouter; this was meant to catch men. He couldn't dodge the spear-thrust so he stepped into it, knowing that a head like that wouldn't stick him too badly.

The twin cane points burned like hot coals as they gouged Cashel's chest, but that didn't slow him. The cat man easily avoided the straight thrust of the quarterstaff, but it wasn't expecting the side stroke that crushed it against the wall of the passage. The lithe body slipped to the gleaming floor, flat as a discarded rag.

Cashel backed, breathing through his open mouth. Additional cat men filled the passage, more than he could count. They stayed two double paces back, warned by what'd happened to their fellows.

Cashel had room to move, while the attacking cat men were bound by the passage. Soon one would get past him, though, and it'd all be over. They moved like light glinting from silver, too quick for thought.

The mirrored walls let Cashel see Protas standing with the topaz crown in both hands. The boy's face was set in a death mask. This would be a good time for wizardry. . . .

To Cashel's surprise, Protas hurled the crown against the floor. The great yellow jewel shattered—not the way a stone breaks, but rather like a soap bubble vanishing. Where it struck, the wizard Cervoran stood—

wearing the same garments and the same sneer as he had when Cashel last saw him in his room in Mona. He pointed his bone athame toward the cat men and chanted, *"Nain nestherga!"*

A cat man with a short-hafted stone hammer in one hand and a wooden dagger in the other sprinted toward Cashel, ducked low, and sprang. It easily avoided Cashel's lifted staff, but it hadn't expected him to kick upward with his left foot.

Cashel's soles were hard as a horse's hooves, and he'd put as much muscle in the blow as an angry mule could've. The cat man's cry became a startled bleat. It hit the passage ceiling, then the floor, and was thrashing in its death throes as it bounced back toward its fellows.

The remaining cat men paused. There were many of them, too many.

"Drue," Cervoran said. *"Nephisis."*

Protas was staring at his father, not paying any attention to Cashel. That was all right, since there wasn't a lot the boy could do regardless.

A cat man twice the size of any other bulled his way to the front of the group filling the passage. He was snarling at them, just noise to Cashel but words to the other cat men, that was sure. The big leader sorted them out, mostly by growling but once with a slap with the hand that didn't hold a wooden mace; his fingers had real nails and drew streaks of blood across a smaller cat man's scalp.

Three of the creatures poised. Their big leader was right behind them, his mace lifted as much as it could be in the passage. It was easy enough to figure how things would go: one springing high, one low, and one straight up the middle.

Experience and strength had saved Cashel this far, but he knew he'd had good luck besides. His luck was bound to run out and anyway, he couldn't stop three of the creatures coming at him all at once; especially not with the big one following to finish the business with his mace while one or two of the little fellows chewed on Cashel's throat.

"Stherga!" Cervoran shouted. Cashel lunged forward, trying to catch the cat men off balance. They were too quick, launching themselves at him like so many arrows.

The chamber and passage vanished. For an eyeblink, Cashel was in a circle of pine trees. Ilna was there, grim-faced as her fingers tied bits of yarn that went on forever at the corners of Cashel's eyes. The cat men were coming at him and—

Cashel was alone in a flash of red wizardlight. He was blind, but he could feel each of his bones and muscles.

The light vanished. Cashel was back in the domed chamber with Protas and Cervoran.

Cervoran continued to chant, his face a mask of puffy triumph. The circle of trees and the cat men, living and dead, were gone. Figures formed in the mirrored walls.

Chapter

16

CHALCUS MOVED LIKE a wraith, facing the cat men. His sword licked out. A leaping cat man somehow managed to get its spear up in time, but the slender wooden shaft couldn't block the steel: the edge sheared through the spear and throat both.

Two others were springing toward Chalcus at the same time. He kicked at one. The cat man dodged in the air like a hawk striking but the thrust of its stone-pointed spear missed also.

The third had leaped high. The sailor's dagger blocked the swing of the cat's stone hammer, but the wooden poniard in its other hand plunged home. It was withdrawing from Chalcus' chest when his return stroke swiped a bloody smile the width of its furry throat.

Ilna was gathering the threads of this garden, of this small universe, into her mind; the knots of her pattern fastened them. Everything was connected: every stone, every flower, every life. To stop now would be to fail; to loose the Shadow on herself, which didn't concern her, and to loose it on her friends, which she would not do.

She'd never doubted that she would die one day. She wouldn't willingly die because she'd failed, though.

The cat men ringed Chalcus and Merota. The big one, the leader, ducked past the curved sword like water curling around a bridge piling, but Chalcus caught the creature's mace on his dagger and kicked it in the groin. Two cat men speared the sailor in the back as his sword beheaded their maned leader.

Merota screamed and grappled with one of the cat men as Chalcus turned. Another crushed her skull with a stone hammer. Chalcus stabbed the killer through the heart, put his dagger point through the temple of the creature which the child continued to hold as she convulsed in death, and then thrust behind him to kill the cat man clinging to the spear whose thin flint point poked through the front of the sailor's tunic.

I never imagined they would die, Ilna thought. *I would die, but not them.* She finished the task she'd set herself; too late, of course, but that couldn't be helped now.

Chalcus opened his mouth to speak. Blood came out but no words. He smiled, though, before the light went out of his eyes and he fell over Merota's small corpse.

There were still as many cat men as Ilna could count on the fingers of both hands. They'd paused, perhaps doubting that Chalcus was really dead, but now they eyed Ilna.

You should have killed me first, she thought, and she opened a knot of her pattern.

Darkness formed around the cat men. They looked startled, then began to howl. They must've been trying to move, but their limbs wouldn't obey them. It was like watching them dissolve in acid, flesh melting from the bones and then the bones themselves dissolving.

Ilna retied the last knot and put the fabric in her sleeve. She was smiling. *Odd. I didn't think I'd ever smile again.*

Chalcus and Merota lay where they'd fallen. The dead cat men remained also, but the Shadow had taken its prey out of this universe.

Ilna carried the bodies of her family into the temple and placed them under the golden screen. Chalcus weighed more than she did, but it wasn't a difficult task. She was quite strong. People in Barca's Hamlet had commented on that, how strong the little orphan girl Ilna was.

She knelt beside her family and thumbed their eyelids closed. After kissing them for the last time, she rose.

Chalcus' blood was on her lips. She licked it carefully away and took out more yarn.

Looking upward to the eye of the temple, Ilna began to tie another pattern. Everything was clear to her, now. Everything except for the question of why she was still alive.

$\mathcal{T}$HE CAT MEN were gone, even the musky smell of them. Cashel turned his head slightly so that he wasn't trusting the reflection in the walls to tell him what was happening behind in the chamber.

Protas was staring at Cervoran, who chanted *"Iao iboea ithua"* with strokes of his bone athame. Ruby light flooded the world at the final syllable. Cashel felt himself squeezed—not in his body or his mind either one, but some third way that he couldn't explain.

The pressure released. He wasn't in the domed chamber anymore; neither were his companions. Protas and Cervoran shimmered in the mica walls, gray and as dim as if Cashel was seeing them through morning mists. Ilna was in the mirror also, and Garric with something on his shoulder that looked like a bird made of quartz.

"Sal salala salobre . . . ," piped Cervoran's voice, though his lips didn't move. His body was as stiff as a painting on the shining wall, but he and Cashel and the others in the mirror spun around a dimly glimpsed dirt field where the center of the chamber had been.

Sharina stood there beside Tenoctris. A shield lay on the ground nearby. *Sharina's there!* The women looked up, frowning like they saw something nearby and couldn't be sure what it was.

"Sharina!" Cashel called, but his lips didn't move; he couldn't even feel his heart beating. Though the cry sounded only in his mind, he thought he saw Sharina smile in dawning understanding.

"Rakokmeph!" Cervoran shrilled, though his image in the mirror was as frozen as Cashel's own.

Red wizardlight, searingly cold, divided Cashel's body into atoms and re-formed him on mud thawing under a bright sun. He staggered, paused to be sure of his balance, and took a single step forward to enfold Sharina in his arms. He held his staff clear so that it didn't rap her on the back of the head.

"Cashel," she murmured against his chest. "Cashel, thank the Lady you've come back!"

They were on a flat wasteland. Garric was holding Liane, both of them talking. Garric looked like he'd been between the millstones, but Cashel guessed whoever'd been making trouble for him looked worse. The bird on his shoulder was alive, turning its head quickly like a wren hunting dinner.

Soldiers, maybe the whole army, stood in noisy formations across the plain; the air stank of salty mud and rotting vegetation. There was Ilna, a knotted fabric in her hands and her face as thin and hard as an axe blade.

Cervoran looked around with dazed incomprehension. "Where . . . ?" he said. "Why am I here?"

The double Cervoran'd made before he went off with Cashel and Protas stumped toward them. Both wizards held athames, but Double's was of old oak instead of a rib bone.

Tenoctris stood with an expression Cashel couldn't read, wary and reserved. She was looking out to sea. On the horizon, glittering brighter than it should've been even in this sunlight, was the Fortress of Glass. As Cashel followed the old wizard's eyes, he saw blue wizardlight flash from the crystal mass.

SHARINA FELT HERSELF relaxing for the first time in days, safe within the circuit of Cashel's muscular arms. His presence made her feel as if she stood in a stone-walled castle. It wasn't just protection—though Cashel with his quarterstaff was protection enough—but also a feeling of solidity, of permanence.

Lords Waldron, Attaper, and Zettin—the admiral of the fleet—were talking simultaneously to Garric; their aides stood in a ring about the commanders, looking eager but keeping silence in the presence of their superiors. If Lord Tadai hadn't been back in Mona, he and his clerks would be part of the scrum pressing Garric too. . . .

Sharina squeezed Cashel's hand and stepped back from him. Aloud she said, "I felt sorry for my brother when I saw the way he was pestered before. Now that I've been regent myself, I pity him with the benefit of experience."

"I should be inside the Fortress!" said Cervoran, facing Double and glaring with his bulbous eyes. Double glared back, a mirror image on a slightly smaller scale. "Did you drag me here, you fool?"

Cervoran pointed his athame toward Ilna. "Come here, you!" he snarled. "I will teach this puny simulacrum what it means to thwart my plans. I will crush it! I am Cervoran!"

"I am Cervoran!" piped Double, tone and diction identical to those of the wizard who'd made him. "You cannot rule me now. No one can rule me!"

"No, by Duzi!" Garric said, blasting the words out like thunderclaps. "This will *wait!*"

He pointed to a junior officer, one of Admiral Zettin's aides. "Lord Dalmas, I'll take your sword if I may," he snapped. "If I may" was a polite form but the tone was an order. "Until I can get my own back. This—"

He held out what Sharina first thought was a tent peg, then recognized as a wooden knife of some sort.

"—was well enough when there was nothing better to be had, but I'll feel less naked with the weight of steel on my hip again."

Sharina touched Cashel again. Garric was her brother, but he was no longer the child of a rural innkeeper—and neither was she. Perhaps that was one of the reasons she so needed Cashel's presence: he *hadn't* changed from the solid, imperturbable youth she'd grown up with.

Dalmas and three other soldiers started to unbuckle their sword belts. Garric gestured curtly to the others, then took the gear—waist belt, shoulder strap, sword, and dagger sheathed on the other side for balance—from the named aide and put it on with remarkable ease. Moments like this reminded Sharina that Carus, the warrior-king, shared her brother's mind.

The commanders had moved back slightly. "A man's at a disadvantage without his clothes on," Cashel murmured to her. "And the clothes this lot cares about is a sword. Garric's really smart."

Sharina glanced at him. *Yes, my love,* she thought. *And in this way and so many ways, so are you. You don't miss the things that go on between any kind of animals, people included.*

Cervoran and his Double stood arm's length from one another, no longer speaking verbally but from the look of it communicating in some other way. Their expressions reminded Sharina of dead carp glaring at one another.

In the bustle and excitement of Garric's reappearance, Ilna continued to stand alone. Sharina stepped over to her friend and hugged her. Ilna was never demonstrative, but today Sharina felt as if she were embracing a marble statue. Something was badly wrong. . . .

"Haven't you been able to find Chalcus and Merota yet?" Sharina said.

"I found them," said Ilna. Her voice was clear and precise, as always; and there was anger underneath it for a friend to recognize, again as always: this was Ilna os-Kenset.

But Sharina had never heard anger as cold and consuming as what was in these clipped, simple words.

"I wasn't quick enough," Ilna said. "They were both killed by things that looked like cats the size of men, on their hind legs. I wasn't good enough to save them."

"I—" said Sharina. She fell silent with her mouth still open, backing a step away. She felt as if she'd been drenched in ice water.

"The cat men attacked you?" Garric said, breaking away from the officers to stride over Ilna and Sharina. "The Coerli, they're called. Were you in the Land too, swamps and rain all the time?"

Sharina stared in horror: Garric was a prince, a leader, but this wasn't the time—

Garric's hard expression melted. He put his arms around Ilna and held her. For a moment she remained the same block of frozen anger that Sharina had held; then her arms went around Garric and she clung like a drowning woman to a float. Her face didn't change, except that she closed her eyes for just a moment.

Liane had followed Garric. She held a wax tablet and a writing stylus; a soldier walking behind carried her traveling desk. She looked at Sharina and mouthed the word "Killed?"

Sharina nodded. She sucked her lower lip between her teeth and bit it hard.

Liane turned and started to walk away. The soldier with the collapsible desk couldn't get out of the way in time; Liane bumped into him. She hurled her writing instruments at the ground, put her hands over her face, and began sobbing. Ilna watched her dry-eyed.

Cashel stiffened. He shifted his hands on his quarterstaff, spreading them as they'd be at the start of a fight.

"Master Cervoran?" he said. His voice trembled. Cervoran and Double remained where they were, locked in a silent staring match.

Garric glanced at Liane but he continued to hold Ilna. His eyes were anguished, but his lips were in a tight line.

"*Cervoran!*" Cashel shouted. "Look at me or I'll tear your head off!"
Cashel doesn't shout. Cashel doesn't threaten.

Garric put Ilna behind him and turned, facing the wizards but keeping Cashel in the corner of his eye. He flexed his arms. He had a wound all the way through the muscle of his right shoulder, but you'd never guess that by the way his sword arm swung.

Nearby soldiers were bracing themselves. Some of them touched their weapons but took their hands quickly away lest they precipitate what they felt in the air.

Cervoran and Double both looked at Cashel. Their heads turned slowly, as though they were swimming in honey.

"There were cat people where we were," Cashel said. He wasn't shouting now, but it was hard to tell the words because of the way they slurred out through his stiff lips. "Then I saw Ilna and they were gone. Where did you send those cats, Cervoran?"

"This body must live," said Double.

"Nothing else matters," said Cervoran.

"I am Cervoran!" said both wizards together.

"Cervoran died a week ago," said the bird on Garric's shoulder. "The creatures you see before you are one of a pair of wizards from a place and time too distant to imagine. They fell here. This one animated the corpse of Cervoran."

Everyone stared at the bird. Its beak didn't move, but Sharina was as certain as she was of the sun that the words in her mind came from the shining creature.

"Its former partner fell into the sea," continued the bird. "Having taken for itself alone the treasure the two had stolen together—the bodies of my race, all but me."

"Look," said the mirrored wizards together. They pointed toward the sea.

The Fortress of Glass had risen higher from the sea on three crystalline legs. It took a step toward the land with the deliberation of a stalking mantis.

"The Green Woman is coming," said the wizards. "But I will crush her!"

𝔊ARRIC'S SHOULDER HAD been throbbing as though a mule'd kicked him there. Now he didn't notice it.

"It's always like that in a fight, lad," said Carus, his eyes focused on something far away in time. "There's time enough to hurt afterward; or there isn't, and it doesn't matter either way."

"Master Cashel," said the Bird. As usual, every mental syllable seemed to have been cut from hard steel. "Did you think the one called Cervoran took you with him for protection?"

"Yes sir," Cashel said, polite to a stranger—even an inhuman stranger—

even now that he was as close to blind rage as Garric had ever seen him. "I was to protect him and Prince Protas, I thought. Wasn't that it?"

"Not in the way you think, Master Cashel," the Bird said. "That one needed a twin present so that he could through his art shift danger from himself to the other twin. To your sister and her companions, that is."

"It was necessary," the wizards said. "Any price you humans pay to preserve me is cheap. Look!"

They pointed again to the Fortress of Glass pacing toward land. Garric knew the water that far offshore was at least a thousand feet deep. The glittering mass was larger than he'd realized, far larger than the cave the Bird and its people had occupied.

"What you see is thin as a soap bubble," the Bird said with its usual dispassion. "But it exists in many universes at once, so nothing in this world alone can harm it."

"Only I can defeat the Green Woman," the wizards said. Their paired voices were slightly apart in timbre, creating a shrill dissonance more unpleasant even than those voices separately. "The two humans who died do not matter. No number of dead humans matter. I—"

Garric drew the borrowed sword, a long horseman's weapon like the one Carus had carried in life and Prince Garric had learned to use under the tutelage of his ancient ancestor. It came out of the scabbard smoothly, despite the blinding jab of pain when the blade came clear and Garric's right arm rose above the shoulder.

Cashel was already moving, the staff out like a battering ram. His left hand led and the whole strength of his massive body was behind the blow. The iron ferrule was within a hand's breadth of Cervoran's swollen, smiling face when it stopped.

Cashel froze as though turned to stone; his shout of effort ended with a smothered grunt. Ruby light dusted the air.

Garric brought his sword around in a whistling arc. His body tingled as it had an instant before lightning blasted a tree nearby when a summer storm had swept the pasture while he watched the flock. The blade stopped above Double's head; he couldn't make the blade move any farther. Garric felt as though he'd been buried in hot sand, the grains individually yielding but together a weight beyond the ability of even his strong young body to force through.

"—will crush the Green Woman!" the wizards said. "I will be God!"

They turned to face the oncoming Fortress, raising their athames. "I alone matter!" they shrilled. "I will be God!"

Chapter

17

ILNA WATCHED THE Fortress of Glass walking toward them. It was easily the most complex—and therefore lovely—pattern she'd encountered in the waking world, though when she entered her reveries she glimpsed the threads of the cosmos itself. Occasionally Ilna had even followed those threads far enough to imagine the existence of the Weaver through Her work.

Considering herself as a thread in another's pattern, Ilna felt her lips twist in a wry smile. To her surprise, quite a number of things now struck her as amusing. That in itself amused her.

Everyone was talking but almost nobody seemed to be listening. Because Ilna was silent, no one paid attention to her. She was used to that, and indeed it was the state that she preferred.

The wizards who'd been responsible for the deaths of her family had set a fallen brazier upright on its tripod legs and lighted the charcoal with a spark of wizardlight. They were chanting, ignoring the humans about them.

Ilna looked at their dead, puffy features. Only the bodies were dead, of course. The inhuman spark within them used the flesh merely for transportation, no more a part of the real being than a sailor is part of his ship.

A sailor. . . . Well, Chalcus had never doubted that he'd die someday. Merota would've said the same thing if she'd been asked, though she was probably too young to understand just what that meant. Perhaps not, though: she'd been a clever child, and she'd stood beside Ilna and Chalcus in places where death was a more likely outcome than life for all of them.

As Cervoran chanted with his Double, Ilna remembered the feel of the cold, waxen flesh as she'd dragged the wizard off the pyre which would otherwise have consumed him. What would've happened if she'd let the fire have its way? Certainly that flesh, that form, wouldn't have loosed the Coerli on Ilna and her family; but would that have changed the result? As the thing of crystal marched toward them from the sea, it was easy to imagine a being of fire facing it and the whole island beneath a blackened waste.

The pattern was beyond Ilna's comprehension. What she knew, with a clarity that none of her friends could imagine, was that a pattern existed.

Sharina gripped Cashel's left wrist in both hands and tried to move it. He remained frozen, as motionless as the sun at its peak in the pale sky. Sharina turned, caught Ilna's eye, and cried, "Ilna? Can you do something? Tenoctris says she can't."

Tenoctris stood with a quiet expression. She held one of her slender bamboo wands, but she appeared to have forgotten it as she looked at the bird. It turned its head, unaffected by his paralysis, but it'd stopped talking.

"I can't grasp the pattern, Sharina," Ilna said, speaking in a normal voice. She was picking out the knots of the fabric she'd made to return herself from the tapestry garden. "It's far too complex for me. Even for me."

"Then there's nothing," Sharina said, despair giving way to resignation. "Nothing any of us can do. If those two—"

She nodded unhappily toward Cervoran and his Double, dabbing their athames toward the brazier as they chanted.

"—can't stop the Green Woman, then we're doomed."

"I didn't say there's nothing I could do," said Ilna sharply. The only emotion she'd brought out of the garden was anger. She was back to where she'd been for the first eighteen years of her life, before she'd met Chalcus and Merota. "I said I couldn't see where any action I took fitted into the whole fabric, but I've decided that doesn't matter. I'll deal with the part of the pattern that's before me, and somebody else can worry about the rest."

"I don't understand?" said Sharina. She glanced from Ilna to the fortress, approaching with ponderous inexorability. It didn't move fast, but it didn't need to. She drew the Pewle knife from its belt sheath.

"The Green Woman hasn't harmed me, Sharina," Ilna said calmly as she drew the other knotted pattern from her sleeve. "I'm not fool enough to believe that makes her my friend, but I know very well who my enemies are."

Ilna nodded toward Cervoran and Double. Smiling, she loosed a knot of the second pattern.

The short noon shadows beneath the wizards and their brazier broadened and deepened. For an instant, no one else noticed. Cervoran screamed, and a heartbeat later his Double screamed in near unison.

The Shadow swelled over them. They turned their heads to stare at Ilna. None of the other victims had been able to move even that much after the Shadow had gripped them.

Ilna smiled. Good. They must feel every hair-fine detail of what was happening to them.

They screamed. The flesh melted and the bones as well, but still the screams hung in the air as unseen portions of the wizards continued to dissolve; and Ilna smiled.

The Shadow dimmed and vanished. Cashel and Garric broke out of their trance, looking around with the startled expressions of men who'd taken a step that wasn't there while climbing stairs.

"It was your choice, Mistress Ilna," said the silent voice of the bird on Garric's shoulder. "But if you hadn't acted, I would have. They did to me what they did to you."

"I'm sorry," Ilna said. "I'm very sorry to hear that."

She stepped over to the brazier and threw the fabric into it. The yarn shrank, blackened, and finally burst into flame. The pungency of burning wool struggled with the general vegetable stench of this soggy wasteland.

"You are destroying the garden?" the Bird said. "You know that most of the denizens will die when they're freed back into their own worlds, do you not?"

Ilna shrugged. In the palace in Mona the ancient tapestry was smoldering to ash just as this fragment of her own making did.

"Everything dies eventually, Bird," Ilna said. "Even you. Somebody cruel made a menagerie, and I've ended it. That's all."

"Even I will die," said the Bird. "But not you, Mistress Ilna. Not for longer than you can now imagine."

"No?" said Ilna. "Well, I've had other disappointments."

She looked at the creature sharply and added, "Are you a wizard, Bird?"

"No, mistress," said the Bird. "I am a mathematician. Usually I would say that means I understand things that wizards do not, but in this case I do not think that is true. Still, I believe I understand enough."

All about them people were running, talking; praying, many of them. And to the south, the Fortress of Glass rose higher with every stride as the sea bottom shelved toward the bar closing Calf's Head Bay. Its steps thundered, and waves came rolling in.

S HARINA RESTED HER left hand on Cashel's shoulder; just for the stability, not for anything he could do or she even wanted him to do. Just because he was Cashel. The ground shook each time the fortress's shining legs paced forward.

Horns and trumpets were calling the army to Stand To. Soldiers who'd scattered during the chaos of the past hour were now forming back behind the standards of their units. Most of them had only swords: their spears, useless against the hellplants, were stacked far to the rear with their baggage.

Spears wouldn't be any use against the Fortress of Glass either. Nor would swords, of course.

Garric turned toward her and said, "Sharina? You've been regent while I was gone? Can you think of anything I should do? Because I've just fallen into this."

Liane hovered at Garric's side, face set but her eyes dry again. Had she been able to explain anything to him in the few minutes since he returned from wherever he'd been?

"No," Sharina said. "It's all—"

Suddenly the frustration gave way and she was again a girl talking to the brother she trusted completely. "Garric, it's been like falling off a cliff. Liane and I—"

She looked at Tenoctris, standing nearby with a cheerful, intent expression.

"—and Tenoctris, of course, and everybody, we've been trying to do something, but mostly it was Cervoran and the Green Woman, and now there's just her. It."

At the corner of her eye, she caught Ilna standing alone with a faint smile. Her fingers were weaving yarn into a pattern that only she could understand. Garric had been in a place where there were marshes and rain—and murderous cat men. . . .

Sharina's fingers tightened on Cashel's arm. *Cashel is here. He'll always be here. He won't die and leave me.*

"That's what I guessed," Garric said. "I'll join Waldron, then. May the Shepherd protect you, sis. And you too, Cashel."

"But Garric . . . ," Sharina said. She didn't know how to go on. Her brother wore nothing but a sword belt and a ragged tunic that seemed to have been made from sacking. He was bruised and scraped, and his shoulder wound should've been disabling; perhaps it would be as soon as he stopped moving and his body got a chance to remind him of its presence.

She coughed. "I don't think the army will be able to do much," she said. "Do you?"

"All the more reason for the prince to stand with his troops, don't you think?" Garric said, giving her a lopsided smile. He turned, gave Liane a quick hug with his left arm, and set off toward the royal standard. As he walked, he drew the borrowed sword again. Liane followed at his side, a half-pace back.

The crystal bird hung in the air before Sharina. It was exactly where it'd been when Garric was talking to her. Its wings were motionless, but the play of light over and within the creature seemed to be more than merely sunlight on uncountable facets.

"Guess I'll get limbered up," Cashel said with a shy smile. He moved a few paces in front of her and began spinning his quarterstaff. As it rotated in slow circles, wizardlight trailed the ferrules in blue sparkles.

Sharina licked her lower lip; she'd drawn blood when she bit it. "Tenoctris?" she asked. "Will he be able to . . . ?"

She nodded toward Cashel's back. About anyone else that would've been a joke or a madman's question, but Cashel's powers went well beyond the strength of his great muscles.

"No, dear," Tenoctris said. "The thing that you see—"

She nodded toward the oncoming fortress. Though it walked on its tripod of legs, rising increasingly high above the sea's surface, it didn't strike Sharina as a living thing. Watching it was like standing in the path of a vast landslide, swift-moving and terrible but not alive.

"—is only a surface. The real Fortress of Glass exists in many times. Nothing that happens to it in this world alone can affect any significant portion of the whole."

The old wizard looked at the hovering crystal bird and said, "Isn't that so, milord?"

"I am Bird, not a lord," said the glittering creature. "I was one of many equals, and now I am one. But you are correct about the fortress, Tenoctris."

It made a clucking, clicking sound with its body, then resumed in its mental voice, "Nothing I saw in the ages I lived with the Grass People suggested that I would meet humans who understood the equations that are my life."

Tenoctris lifted her chin in the direction of the Fortress of Glass. Each step now sent the sea rolling onto the shore with a snarl.

"Those are the bones of your race, Master Bird," she said. "Will you leave them in the hands of their slayer, to kill more beings as innocent as your people were?"

"I told Garric that I would return him to his world for his purposes and for mine," said the Bird's silent voice. "I will complete my purposes here. But Tenoctris—you know what that will mean for your world and your people?"

"I know," said Tenoctris, nodding. "Forces must balance. But it must be done."

"The sides of the equation must be equal," said the Bird. "But I regret the cost to you and yours, for some human beings have treated me as one of their own."

"Go," said Tenoctris, pointing her bamboo wand toward the fortress towering against the clear sky. "There's very little time."

"There is enough time," said the Bird. It rose into the air and headed seaward with jerky, fluttering motions of its wings. Faintly, as though from an unimaginable distance, the mental voice added, "There is all eternity."

CASHEL SPUN HIS quarterstaff in a simple circle before him, varying the movement with an occasional figure-8 to make sure he was working all his muscles. The rhythm was simple and soothing; his body could keep it up all day, leaving his mind free to watch the dance of universes on the surface of the Fortress of Glass.

He couldn't follow the pattern, not really, but it was a delight to watch something more wondrously formed than anything in this world or any single world. Cashel's eyes saw shimmering light, but his mind showed him the connections stretching through time in all directions. Ages rose and rolled and tumbled again into the depths, not of *this* universe but of the cosmos that was all universes. The Fortress of Glass was perfect, and because it was perfect there could be nothing more beautiful.

It was going to crush Cashel and everyone he loved. It was his duty to stop it. That was impossible but of course he'd try. Of *course* he'd try.

"Cashel," said Sharina behind him. "Stop spinning your staff and hold me. It's all right. Hold me!"

Something flickered into Cashel's line of vision. Because he was focused—eyes and mind both—on the fortress, for a moment it was just that: a flicker. Then—

Cashel saw the Bird that'd been on Garric's shoulder. It was flying toward the Fortress of Glass, and like the fortress the Bird's shimmer held all worlds and all times.

"Cashel, it's all right," Sharina repeated. "Please—hold me. Something's going to happen."

This time Cashel brought his staff to a halt and held it upright. He stepped backward, putting himself beside Sharina and holding her in his free arm. He didn't take his eyes off the fortress and the crystalline glitter that flew toward it.

The Fortress of Glass had a cold, perfect beauty, but Cashel or-Kenset was human and of one world. In Cashel's world, Sharina was as close to perfection as there could be. He smiled shyly, his eyes on the looming fortress and the bird mounting so high in the air that it now looked like a mote wheeling in the sunlight.

Tenoctris said, "The fortress is bigger than it seems. I suppose you and your sister know that, Cashel?"

"Yes ma'am," said Cashel. He was speaking for Ilna, but he didn't have any doubt about it. It was all so clear that he sort of couldn't imagine that it wasn't clear to everybody. He knew it wasn't his eyes that were seeing the fortress as it was, though.

Sharina nestled close to him. It was so wonderful. . . .

"Whatever happens to the fortress," Tenoctris continued, "happens in all the times that the fortress is part of. If the fortress vanishes, something will take its place. I think the times themselves will merge to balance what's being taken away."

"I don't understand," said Sharina.

Cashel didn't understand either, but it wasn't the sort of question he cared about. He couldn't change whatever it was that Tenoctris was expecting, so he might as well wait to learn. He'd deal with whatever it meant when it'd happened, just like he always had in the past.

He smiled. Sharina didn't think that way, or Garric or most people. The kingdom needed shepherds as sure as it did princes.

"Things will move in time rather than space," Tenoctris said. "I can't guess how great an area will be affected, but the fortress is very large. *Very* large."

One leg of the Fortress of Glass settled onto the bar at the mouth of Calf's Head Bay; the earth shook itself like a wet dog. The crystalline mass of cliffs and peaks was so nearly overhead that it seemed a fiery cloud, and the legs that'd looked slender when the fortress started walking were each thicker than the gate towers in Valles. The legs shifted the way sand pours through a timekeeping glass rather than by bending like snakes.

"There," Sharina said. She pointed upward. "The Bird flew into the other. Did you see it, Tenoctris?"

"I trust your young eyes, dear," the older woman said. "And that's what he would do, of course. Return to his people."

The next step the fortress took would put a huge foot onto the mainland. Cashel didn't know how much the Green Woman saw from wherever she was inside the crystal, but he figured she saw enough to make sure the foot landed where it'd do the most good. If the legs shortened and brought the body down onto the ground, it'd easily cover the whole muddy plain and all the people standing on it.

Cashel held Sharina a little tighter instead of bringing his staff around again. That was what she'd said she wanted, and he wasn't about to refuse Sharina anything in these last moments.

The back leg of the fortress rose and started to swing forward. It stopped as suddenly as iron hardens as it flows from the smelting pot. A flash of—

Cashel couldn't describe it. It wasn't light, it was *not*-light, penetrating blackness.

—flooded the world. For an instant the Fortress of Glass wasn't visible. The sky was empty, but inside it there was an infinite blackness.

The crystal mass reappeared, shifting from the shape the Green Woman had formed it into. "The Bird!" Sharina cried, and it *was* the Bird, now the size of the fortress it replaced.

A voice screamed the way Cervoran and his Double had screamed in Ilna's net of shadow. Cashel's fingers tightened on the hickory staff, then relaxed. Ilna hadn't needed help to pay back the ones who'd taken Chalcus and Merota from her; the Bird didn't need help either.

The glittering wings fluttered, but there was no sign of the violent wind they should've fanned across the bay. The Bird lifted, but not into the air or not *only* into the air. The Bird shrank as it moved away from the world of men.

There was a rumble too deep and loud to be sound. Everything flowed, earth and sea and air. Cashel held Sharina tight.

Nothing else mattered. Nothing else in the cosmos mattered.

Garric clung to Liane, watching realities tumble around and through him. Lord Waldron stood as stiffly as if he'd been tied to a post as an archery target, but many of the troops in his personal regiment had knelt with their hands flat before them in an attitude of prayer.

"It's not an earthquake!" Liane said. "The ground isn't shaking!"

Rock and earth and sea and once the trunk of a gigantic tree wavered before Garric and were replaced. He could breathe normally and his feet remained firmly set as Liane had said, but a fog of other worlds half-concealed *his* world and blurred the figures of the people about him.

The enveloping sound was like the whisper of leaves as wind rustles a forest ahead of a violent storm. It was so loud that Garric could hear Liane's words only because she shouted, and even then he was reading much of the meaning from the shape of her lips.

Near Cashel and Sharina was Tenoctris, looking about with her usual bright curiosity. Liane followed Garric's gaze and said, "Does she know what's happening? She seems to, don't you think?"

No, Garric thought. *She's Tenoctris and she'd show the same interest in runes on the blade of an axe brought to behead her.*

But he'd heard the carefully controlled hope in Liane's voice. He didn't think she was afraid, exactly; but Liane defined herself by the things she knew. What was happening now was beyond her understanding. Probably beyond human understanding, but if anybody knew, Tenoctris would.

"We'll ask," Garric said, and with Liane clinging to him started toward his sister and friends. It was like walking across the flats when the tide is in, pulled and twisted at the whim of forces whose full strength would've been beyond human imagination.

King Carus was a silent presence in his mind. Carus had drowned a thousand years before when a wizard had split the seabottom with his art and sucked the royal fleet into it. If this was a similar disaster, the result would be worse than the centuries of chaos which had followed Carus' death. The Isles hadn't really recovered from the fall of the Old Kingdom; a second collapse would end civilization forever.

Garric's skin tingled. Patches of air cleared momentarily, but once Garric saw clearly a two-legged creature which held a jeweled athame and stared back at him through faceted insect eyes.

"Tenoctris!" Garric said. He had to shout to be heard, but tension would've raised his voice anyway unless he'd fought the tendency very hard. "Do you know what's going on?"

Tenoctris turned her head and smiled to acknowledge their presence, but she didn't respond to the question; either she didn't have an answer or she simply couldn't hear him. Garric grinned: probably both, since if Tenoctris had heard she'd have shaken her head out of natural politeness.

The sound ceased so gradually that even after it was gone Garric heard echoes in memory. Around him reality shifted, flowed, and at last stiffened like grain shaking down in a measure.

He looked southward, blinked, and looked again: the Inner Sea was gone. In its place was a forest of unfamiliar trees. On the horizon lifted mountains, purple and misty with distance.

Liane bent and plucked a bell-shaped purple flower. There were scores of them, growing among the knee-high grass covering what had been a mudflat when the Fortress of Glass marched toward them.

Men shouted. A Corl warrior bounded from a grove of straight-stemmed shrubs with feathery leaves. The only weapon he carried was a flint dagger with a bone hilt, but his leather harness was beaded in a complex design.

"Watch him!" Garric shouted. He still held his naked sword, but he had no illusions about being able to outfence a Corl in open country. "They're quicker than you can believe!"

The warrior bounded straight toward Garric, but it wasn't attacking. Its eyes were wide and desperate. It wailed, "Who are they? So many!"

I understand him! thought Garric as the Corl changed direction at the last instant—and flew headlong as Ilna's noose, spun out in perfect anticipation, tightened about his right ankle. The Corl gave a despairing shriek and slammed the ground. Before Garric could get to him, Cashel had rapped the cat man behind the ear with his quarterstaff.

"Is he still alive?" Garric said, sheathing his sword. "Good, tie him and mind his teeth if he comes around. I need to question him. Apparently I can still understand Coerli speech even though the Bird's gone."

He glanced toward the empty sky to the south. *Was* the Bird gone? He didn't see the crystalline creature or hear its voice, but it might have left a legacy of its presence. The Bird had been more than a helper: it had been a friend.

Tenoctris watched as Garric tied the Corl's wrists behind its back with his sword belt. He looked back and asked her, "Do you know where we are?"

"Garric, nobody knows this place," the old woman said quietly. "This is a land that's never been before. It's many times, mixed together. It has no history; *none*."

Garric thought of the dream figure he'd met when Marzan summoned him to help the Grass People. "The Kingdom of the Isles?" that one had said. "The Isles have been gone for a thousand years. . . ."

"We'll give it a history," Garric said. "It'll have the history that we make now."

Ilna had retrieved her noose. She knelt beside the trussed Corl and twisted his harness up.

"Careful," said Garric. "They're fast and they're really dangerous."

"This one won't be," Ilna said calmly as she slid the warrior's dagger from its sheath. The flint blade was so thin that light wavered through it within a finger's breadth of both edges.

"Wait!" said Garric. "We need—"

Ilna gripped the Corl by the topknot and slit his throat with a quick, firm stroke. Blood spurted an arm's length, a hand's breadth, and finally the width of a finger as the cat man died thrashing.

Ilna straightened, leaving the dagger on the ground. She wiped the back of her right hand on the Corl's harness; she'd managed to avoid most of the spraying blood with her usual foresight.

"Ilna," Garric said, trying to understand what'd just happened. "We needed the prisoner. There must be more Coerli here, and he didn't look like those I saw hunting the Grass People. This may be the Coerli *home,* or part of it. There may be thousands of them!"

"Good," said Ilna in a voice that rustled like a snake's scales. "Then there's a reason for me to live after all. I'm going to kill all the Coerli."

"Ilna," said Liane. "Please. You can't do that."

"No?" said Ilna. She shrugged. "Perhaps you're right."

Something huge and hungry bellowed from the depths of the great forest. The sound echoed, bringing swords to the hands of the soldiers who didn't already carry their steel bare.

"But I can try," Ilna said, and her smile chilled Garric in a fashion that the monster's cry had not.

An unfamiliar bird wheeled high in the heavens. In Garric's mind the ghost of Carus repeated, "*. . . the history that we make now. . . .*"